I moved to stand back from the door, inside my room, then drew sword and dagger. The door was flung open and a man burst through. I allowed him to pass me then struck him down just as his comrade entered. My blow had been true so that the thief died without cry. I think the one who followed believed the small sound of a blade cleaving flesh was made by his friend as he slew me.

He grunted approval, then spoke low-voiced. "Is he dead?"

I closed with him. My dagger went home even as my other hand choked back his cry. His dagger snapped on my mail. He thrashed after that as he died.

The third thief must have been bewildered by the dark. He blundered into me, seized my arm, and muttered angrily, "You make too much noise about it, you fool. You'll have the innkeeper up here."

"A good thought," I agreed. I lifted my dagger, striking him hard across the side of the head with the pommel before he understood my words. I caught him as he sagged, then lifted my voice in a bellow, "Ho, innkeeper, aid here? Aid to your guests beset by thieves."

"Although the basic setting is familiar after more than 40 years' worth of Witch World stories, the book's quite convincing picture of a land without rulers or laws in the wake of disaster is more than a little timely."   —*Booklist*

TOR Books by Andre Norton

The Crystal Gryphon
Dare to Go A-Hunting
Flight in Yiktor
Forerunner
Forerunner: The Second Venture
Here Abide Monsters
Moon Called
Moon Mirror
The Prince Commands
Ralestone Luck
Stand and Deliver
Wheel of Stars
Wizards' Worlds
Wraiths of Time

Grandmasters' Choice (Editor)
The Jekyll Legacy
    (with Robert Bloch)
Gryphon's Eyrie
    (with A. C. Crispin)
Songsmith (with A. C. Crispin)
Caroline (with Enid Cushing)
Firehand (with P. M. Griffin)
Redline the Stars
    (with P. M. Griffin)
Sneeze on Sunday
    (with Grace Allen Hogarth)
House of Shadows
    (with Phyllis Miller)
Empire of the Eagle
    (with Susan Shwartz)
Imperial Lady
    (with Susan Shwartz)

WITCH WORLD NOVELS
    (with Lyn McConchie)
Duke's Ballad
Silver May Tarnish

CAROLUS REX
    (with Rosemary Edghill)
The Shadow of Albion
Leopard in Exile

BEAST MASTER
    (with Lyn McConchie)
Beast Master's Ark
Beast Master's Quest
Beast Master's Circus

THE GATES TO WITCH WORLD
    (omnibus)
    Including:

Witch World
Web of the Witch World
Year of the Unicorn

LOST LANDS OF WITCH WORLD
    (omnibus)
    Including:
Three Against the Witch World
Warlock of the Witch World
Sorceress of the Witch World

THE WITCH WORLD (Editor)
Four from the Witch World
Tales from the Witch World 1
Tales from the Witch World 2
Tales from the Witch World 3

WITCH WORLD: THE TURNING
I. Storms of Victory
    (with P. M. Griffin)
II. Flight of Vengeance
    (with P. M. Griffin & Mary
    Schaub)
III. On Wings of Magic
    (with Patricia Mathews & Sasha
    Miller)

MAGIC IN ITHKAR
    (Editor, with Robert Adams)
Magic in Ithkar 1
Magic in Ithkar 2
Magic in Ithkar 3
Magic in Ithkar 4

THE SOLAR QUEEN
    (with Sherwood Smith)
Derelict for Trade
A Mind for Trade

THE TIME TRADERS
    (with Sherwood Smith)
Echoes in Time
Atlantis Endgame

**THE OAK, YEW, ASH, AND ROWAN
CYCLE** (with Sasha Miller)
To the King a Daughter
Knight or Knave
A Crown Disowned

THE HALFBLOOD CHRONICLES
    (with Mercedes Lackey)
The Elvenbane
Elvenblood
Elvenborn

SILVER MAY TARNISH

ANDRE NORTON AND LYN McCONCHIE

TOR®
fantasy

A TOM DOHERTY ASSOCIATES BOOK
NEW YORK

This is a work of fiction. All the characters and events portrayed in this novel are either fictitious or are used fictitiously.

SILVER MAY TARNISH

Edited by James Frenkel

A Tor Book
Published by Tom Doherty Associates, LLC
175 Fifth Avenue
New York, NY 10010

www.tor.com

Tor® is a registered trademark of Tom Doherty Associates, LLC.

ISBN-13: 978-0-765-34553-0
ISBN-10: 0-765-34553-6

First Edition: December 2005
First Mass Market Edition: November 2006

Printed in the United States of America

0 9 8 7 6 5 4 3 2 1

ACKNOWLEDGMENTS

To Andre Norton first and foremost. Her books gave me great joy for most of my life, and to be let into two of her worlds to write in them in my later years was kindness beyond measure. She was a lady of wit and generosity, and I shall miss her phone calls, her letters, and the occasional time I could spend with her in person, for many years to come.

This book came about in part because of Andre. Several years ago I was possessed of a short story and I sat down to write. To my bewilderment, after a week I found I had written some 12,000 words. What could I do with that? There is little market for a story of that length, and I feared I could find no suitable market for a story of 12,000 words. Because it was set in the Witch World, I sent the story to Andre to ask her advice. She rang to say that I was wrong.

She told me the work was not a short story, but three chapters of a Witch World fantasy novel and that I should sit down at once and write the book. I looked again and saw that, yes, she was right. Out of her instruction came *Silver May Tarnish*, with the original story forming—in revised version—chapters four, five, and six. Andre read the finished book and loved it, and so was born a new chapter in the Witch World, and a cluster of new dales. To Andre then, *ave atque vale*.

To Jim Frenkel, who edited this book, and to the copy-editor; next time there'll be fewer mistakes, I swear. But I appreciate the time given and the care taken this time.

—L. McC.

SILVER MAY TARNISH—a sword song

Silver may tarnish, gold may be taken,
Years may flow by like—wind on the grass.
Nought is eternal, nothing else lingers,
Only the land, the land does not pass.

Silver may tarnish, gold may be taken,
Blood wash away in—the wind and the rain.
When all else is gone this—still is a true word,
The land has not vanished, the land still remains.

Silver may tarnish, gold may be taken,
All life may vanish, and why none can say.
Memories die and—blood is forgotten,
Only the green land, your own land will stay.

Silver may tarnish, gold may be taken,
Life, love, and joy may—all pass one by;
Only worth keeping, only worth holding,
Is your own green land under blue sky.

Silver may tarnish, gold may be wasted,
Friends may betray you, clan-kin may lie.
What does it matter, so long as you hold yet
All of your keep lands under fair skies?

SILVER MAY
TARNISH

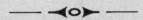

Lorcan

I

I was born in Erondale in the Year of the Pard. It was not a large dale, yet it was prosperous. My father was of the House of Paltendale and of that House men whispered. As well they might. My older brothers told me tales of some of our bloodline who had done monstrous things. But I was a child. Tales such as these were ancient stories told around the fire and their truth could not be easily measured.

When I was old enough to understand, I was told that our wise woman had foretold for me at my birth, and the fate she had given me was strange. She had studied my tiny hands before peering deep into wine in the bottom of a cup. Then she had spoken.

"Three sorrows shall come upon him in this place before he goes from it. Nor shall grief be done with him." At which point I am told my mother cried out and my father rose to say "enough."

"For all men there is sorrow," he said.

"That is the truth, Lord Joros. Yet for this one there shall be more sorrow than comes to many. He shall wander and in that wandering he shall find treasure unlooked for. Gold shall it be, and flowing, heart to his heart. Then shall he cease to wander."

After which saying she sat silent, and when they saw she would say no more my father gave her a silver coin and the parting cup. I think he believed much of her fore-telling as folly since everyone knew Ayneta was more herb woman than woman of Power. But my mother was com-forted by the promise I should do well once sorrow had passed.

I knew that my father was a good man, ordering our keep well. He was also a patient man, slow to anger and a good teacher. By the time I was seven summers, my brothers, both some years older than I, were already training to be warriors as was the custom for lads of noble birth. There had been two babes between us but both had died when the coughing sickness came in the Year of the Pronghorn. It was a sweet and peaceful life, but nothing lasts forever, and at the start of the year I would turn eight the bad times began.

"Lorcan, do not be daydreaming. Father says he will take you hunting with us this time." My brother Anla called up the stairs to where my mother brushed my hair. I squirmed free.

"I must go."

"At least take a cloak. It will be cold in the hills."

I caught up a well-worn short-cloak descended to me from Anla. "I'll bring you back flowers, Mother."

She laughed. "Bring back meat as well. Although," her face was wistful, "I would like the scent of hill-roses. Win-ter was over-long this year." I smiled at her.

"I'll bring both." She was ungainly in late pregnancy and women at such times crave strange things, so my father said. I would bring her hill-roses. The wise woman from the village said that this time the child would be a daughter. That pleased me. I would like to have a small sister. I slipped out to join my father and Anla.

"Slow-poke," Anla greeted me. "You'll catch nothing standing about. Let us ride." Devol brought my pony. I thanked him and he winked as he boosted me to the saddle. I liked Devol. He had always some amusing tale and he made me laugh. He had wandered in from another dale and stayed to work since he did well with horses.

My pony was small but swift on his hooves, fast to turn and twist. I grinned up at my brother. "Beat you to the thicket by the hill path." Before he could reply I was gone. Drustan laid his hooves down in a soft thunder as we flew up the narrow winding track. It was not until we were almost at the thicket that Anla had room to pass us. He did so in a burst of speed before reining in, laughing at me affectionately.

"A forfeit. I claim forfeit." His voice was gently teasing.

I nodded. It was fair and besides, he was complimenting me by treating me as a man in this and not as a child. "I'll unsaddle for you, and lay out your bedding if we stay in the hills tonight," I promised. Anla reached over to pat my shoulder.

"Good lad. You are growing." He turned back to my father, who had joined us quietly on his big gray. "Where do we ride, Sir?"

"To the valley where Merrion killed the pronghorn last Summer." Merrion was my other brother but just now he was at Paltendale learning from the arms-master there.

We nodded and fell in behind him as he rode. Presently he began to talk politics with Anla. I listened, keeping my tongue between my teeth. It was man's talk and if I interrupted they might change the subject. Anla was speaking.

"The last time he was home Merrion said that the men of Alizon are causing trouble again."

My father sighed. "I heard. It is always so. If it is not one who makes trouble it is another. But I think this will come to nothing. Even so, I will have you lads well-trained in war. A man must hold what he has. He must rule himself before he rules others. Next year you go to Paltendale; Lorcan, too, once he is twelve."

I forgot my resolutions of silence and squealed in excitement. "To Paltendale, to learn the sword?"

My father smiled down. "The sword, and many other

things besides. There is more to a keep ruler than the sword. He must be able to tell quality in goods, beasts, and men—he must be able to rule men. To command and be obeyed. He must know tactics in war or skirmish and be able to do all that is needful so he may know if his men do well and aright."

I made a face. "Why must Lord Hogar teach me such things? You are my father."

His eyes grew serious. "I am indeed. But already you have learned some of what I can teach, and in the bearing of arms a boy learns better from one who is not of his close family. That is why we foster each others' sons, as we did Hogeth for three seasons."

I fell silent. I had not liked Hogeth. He was a third son even as I was, though he was more than twice my age. He had left our home only the previous Fall and I had been glad to see him go. He was a bully. One who was always just that much too rough—though he called it play. Horses and hounds tended to move away when he was near. My father saw this, I knew, but he said nothing. Hogeth was son to Paltendale. Erondale was a cadet branch and we owed fealty to the older, larger dale.

We rode on at a steady pace for much of the day. I was weary when at last we made camp but I paid my forfeit honorably. The next day we hunted. It was a good hunt. Two pronghorns fell to my father and Anla. I had only a sling, but when a pheasant rose whirring I cast my stone and the bird fell. I took up another stone and waited. A rabbit, disturbed by the horses' hooves, hopped to one side and again my stone struck squarely. After that I missed my shot at another rabbit. Still, my father was pleased as we took up our game.

"It is well. A barren hind and a spiker buck. The rabbit we shall eat for breakfast. We shall have grilled deer's liver tonight and the pheasant shall be roasted once we are back." I licked my lips. Roast pheasant as our cook prepared it would be a treat at the high table. My mother would be pleased. I must remember to gather hill-roses for her before we were down from the hills.

The camp that night was joyful. My father laughed and told old tales, Anla carved a whistle from a twig and played. I sang the song which went with it, a Dales march called "Pick up Your Feet." It was sweet that evening. I slept well and rose early to build up the fire so that we might eat my rabbit before we rode home. I rode ahead after a while and found a patch of the hill-roses. They were starting to bloom so that the pink and white petals scented the air. I picked buds just beginning to open, bedding them in damp grass before placing them in my saddle-bag. They would do well enough until I could give them to my mother.

We returned to a bustle in the stables as the deer were carried away. I carried the pheasant myself. It was my quarry and none should bear it but me. Cook received it from me in true appreciation.

"Good lad. A fine bird, and it will make a good meal. I'll roast it as you like."

"With glazing of honey and pork fat?" I licked my lips as he nodded. "Mother likes it that way, too."

"True, now, here's a slice of fresh bread. Take yourself out of the kitchen. We'll be busy from now on."

I accepted the bread, sprinkled lightly with honey crystals, and departed. I ate it on the way to my mother's solar. There I opened the saddle-bag and presented the roses. Mother caught them to her with a cry of pleasure.

"Oh, Lorcan. They smell so sweet. Talsa, a vase." Her elderly maid brought it and my mother busied herself arranging the roses. "There, place them on the shelf by the window." I was pleased to see her joy in them and bethought me of my pheasant.

"I brought you something else."

"And what was that, I see nothing more you carry. Is it hidden? Do you have it under your cloak?" She pretended to look for it, tickling me so that I squirmed and giggled.

"A pheasant, it's a pheasant. I brought it down with my

sling. Cook has it. He's roasting it the way we like." I spluttered out the information through laughter as I dodged her tickling hands.

My mother sat back. "So, that was a good hunt. I shall eat roast pheasant and praise the hunter." I felt pride in her words. We talked a while longer before I left. The food that night was good. The pheasant was all I could have wished and cook had made a pastry case around a haunch of venison stewed in its own gravy. I ate heartily of both and slept so soundly I was late rising.

All was pleasant for two days, then I came inside to find a commotion. Mother's maid was speaking earnestly to my father as he stood looking worried. He waved me away angrily when I would have stopped to listen. Yet I caught a little of their words.

"I fear . . . not well."

My father nodded. "Call Ayneta." He stared around before his eyes fell on me again. "Lorcan. Go to Ayneta and say she is needed here."

"Who's ill?"

"I have no time to answer questions. Get Ayneta, hurry."

I always obeyed my father, but this time there was something in his voice which made me run desperately, almost panicked by that tone. It could not have been fear. My father was a brave man. But I felt my own heart pounding as I bolted for the wise woman's cottage. Once there I pounded on the door calling her name. She opened it and recognized me in an instant.

"Lorcan?"

"Come quickly. Father says you must come."

She asked no questions but turned on her heel, snatched up a padded carrysack, and ran heavily towards the keep. I pelted alongside. Once at the keep Ayneta swept up the stairs to my mother's rooms. I would have followed but Anla held me back.

"Come and help me in the stables." I'd seen the look my father gave him. I was afraid.

"It's Mother, what's wrong with her?"

In his own way my brother did his best. "She's just bearing. It takes time. Come and help me school the new horse. I need someone light to back him." I hesitated, torn. I loved my mother, but if it was just a baby there was no need to worry. She'd had five safely. In the end, the delight of helping Anla at his own request outweighed my anxiety. But when we returned to the keep my worry rose again. My father was not in his seat. There was no sign of my mother, her maid, or Ayneta either.

I asked questions which were ignored. I would have gone to my mother but the way was barred by a shut door. Those inside would not open to me. At last Anla was able to pull me away and get me to bed. I slept uneasily, fearing I knew not what. I woke early and crept out towards the stairs. Slowly I ascended them to the tower where my parents had their own private rooms. Then I sat on the steps and waited. Sooner or later the door would open. I was hungry but I remained.

Towards mid-morning it did open. Talsa came out bearing a small wailing bundle. She saw me and stopped.

"Lorcan, how long have you been here?"

"I woke at dawn."

"Well, this is your new sister, Meera." I moved up a step to gaze on a small pink face. Huge unfocused blue eyes gazed up. I had a sister. The door was open behind Talsa and I looked past her. My mother lay white-faced upon the bed. Her eyes were shadowed and her face was drawn, the skin tight upon the bones. Her eyes met mine and she spoke, but so weakly I could not hear. My father appeared and beckoned me. I walked past, trying to keep myself from showing my fear for her; I could smell blood, and within me I knew what I would not allow myself to believe.

"Mother?"

"Lorcan, listen to me. I love you, my son. Look after your sister. Obey your father. Remember me." Her voice failed and Father took me by the shoulders.

"Where is Anla?"

"Working with the new horse again, I think."

"Bring him, quickly, Lorcan."

I ran again, trying to outrun my own fear. I burst into the yard, frightening the horse so that Anla dodged plunging hooves and swore.

"*Lorcan*! What do you think you are doing."

"It's Mother. Father says to come at once." He stared at me so that I blurted out what I feared. "Anla, I think she's dying."

He said nothing, but loosed the horse and bolted. I followed him, knowing nowhere else to go. I heard his boots clatter ahead on the stairs. I walked more slowly then, step by step, until I was at the door again. Inside, Anla was speaking in a small choked voice. I entered in silence, watching as he held my mother's hand. Her voice was soft, gentle, and full of love as always. My throat closed until I could hardly breathe.

She beckoned me to her, then. I came to take her other hand and hold it. She smiled at me, a tiny, weary smile.

"Lorcan, I did love the roses." My father stood then, from the seat nearby. He took us by the shoulders and led us out of the room. Talsa followed, leaving our sister in a cradle by the bed.

"Talsa, take the boys down to eat. Stay until I come for them."

We went with dragging steps. It was no time to beg or argue. Behind us we heard the door shut, then strange faint sounds like a man weeping. Not the crying a boy might make, but the harsh tearing groans wrenched from a strong man who feels agony and can no longer keep silent.

My mother died before sunset. In her room the hill-roses I had brought her four days ago still filled the air with their sweet smell. They lived, but my mother did not. My first sorrow had come to Erondale.

After that things did not change greatly in outward appearance. My father still ruled kindly, still spent time with us all, but it was as if a light had gone out behind his eyes. My brothers and I knew the story. His had been no match made by bargaining parents. He'd met my mother when he rode to a nearby fair. One look, as they had both told us, and they had known. After that, parents became involved as they must, yet to the two in love such matters had no place in their hearts.

My father, Joros, had been twenty, oldest son of Erondale. Ashera, my mother, was fifteen, with a fair dowry, and well educated by the Dames. They were a good match from a financial point of view and their parents had no objections. They wedded a year later. For more than twenty years the only nights they spent apart were when my father hunted. In early days my mother had often ridden with him on those excursions. Together, too, they had ridden amongst men-at-arms to visit Paltendale, or the Spring fairs. Now my father rode alone.

We laid my mother to rest in the family cemetery, and after the rites were completed I took my pony and rode out alone. Deep in the hills I found a small bush of the hillroses and brought it back. My father found me planting it at the head of the narrow turned-earth strip. I think at first he was angry that I had gone riding without leaving word—until he saw what I was doing. Then he helped me to plant the thorny bush. When we were done he touched a bloom lightly.

"She loved them. It was well done. Come now and eat. Remember my words, Lorcan. Even in fear, sorrow, or danger a man must eat and stay strong." In a time to come it would be this simple battle-wisdom he said to me that I would remember and which would aid me to survive.

A year passed slowly. Anla was fourteen that Spring, and once the deep snow had cleared from the mountain passes he rode to Paltendale to begin his training. Merrion came home in exchange, seventeen and a man. He took after our father, being tall and broad, whereas I took more after our mother. At eight I was strong enough, but it was a wiry strength, I would be of medium height, so Talsa said. But my reactions were very fast. It had amused Berond, our master-at-arms, to begin teaching me the previous Spring. I think he began it as a way of occupying my mind, of diverting my grief for my mother. But then he became interested.

"You may never have the muscle for an ax or mace, lad. But a sword, one of the lighter kind with point and edge, with that in time you may do very well. Look now." He hailed one of the guards, Harkon, who used an ax, and demonstrated. "See you. I parry his weapon with little power. His own strike takes him off-balance."

I saw. After that, and for the next two years after my mother's death, I practiced. Nothing too onerous, mainly exercises to strengthen my arm and the basics of sword-drill. But I practiced hard, since it did indeed take my mind from grief. I learned well, so Berond's measured praises were no empty words. My small sister Meera grew, toddling about the keep. I was her beloved brother; she followed where I went, a joy to me and a pleasure.

Some time around then, Devol left Erondale while I was away hunting for two days with Anla. No one would talk of it on our return. I missed his humor and jests but something took him from my mind soon thereafter, for my second sorrow came to Erondale. That third Winter in her life, Meera took a chill. In less than twenty-four hours her life went out as a candle blown in a breeze and dark closed in. We buried her beside our mother and I did not think it unmanly to weep.

After her death, though, I needed no distraction. Word was of war and our father rode out often. Sometimes to Paltendale, or other dales, sometimes to the coast to talk with the Sulcar and learn what they might have heard. Oft he took me with him, teaching me the ways of a riding warrior: how to ride hard yet make the journey lighter on my mount; how to scout, to make smokeless fires or a cold camp. I was ten that year and believed myself almost a man.

There was unease amongst the lords in the dales at this time. There had been word of spies during the past year. There were strangers riding the dales asking questions, and more disturbingly, some appeared to be studying keep defenses. Such a man came to Erondale claiming the hospitality due a man of good birth. My father feasted him with Ayneta at the high table, but before the meal was over the man's head was in his plate. He snored mightily as my father and the wise woman smiled knowingly at each other. When the stranger rode on next morning he had a sour look. I think that his head ached and he had found out little.

We harvested hard that Fall. My father had a store of food and weapons in a small cave high on the trail over the hills. An alternate way to Paltendale, it could be used only by those on foot or riding experienced horses or the hill ponies, sure of foot and slow to panic.

Merrion returned to share Winter with us at Erondale. The Year of the Moss Wife ended. And the time of the third sorrow came upon us. Rishdale lay near to our own small dale. The keep lord was a grim man, impatient and hard. He had wed again recently and the gossip was that his new wife was only a girl, spoiled and lazy, and they did not do well together.

But because both dales were smaller than many, the invaders split their forces. One machine of the kind the invaders used came to each; the one that would attack our dale appeared towards dusk as we were that much further from Rishdale. I was in the keep stables with Anla and Berond talking of my new pony. He was only five and of good blood. I had named him Drustan also, after my older mount, now relegated to bearing game when we hunted. Suddenly the keep shuddered, and I heard cries of alarm all about me. I could hear stones fall, as the shuddering came again. My father came running.

"There is no hope. The machine they have will batter down the walls and have us out as a sea-dog takes a hermit crab from its shell. Berond, gather the guard. We will use the old escape tunnel. Let Harkon and one of his choosing go first. Then the women. The guard last."

Berond looked grave. "The tunnel is too small to let war-horses pass."

"I know. Take ponies. Let the larger horses flee through the postern gate once most of my people are gone. The beasts are valuable and may distract the invaders if they seek to capture them. It is close to dusk. If we have an hour or two we may escape notice in the hills and win safe to Paltendale."

Up the stairs I could hear old Talsa organizing the women. I wondered what had become of the village. Had Ayneta warned them? Faint cries came from outside the keep walls. I would be able to see from my mother's tower room.

I slipped away and climbed the stairs. The tower was to one side, while it was at the main gates the invaders labored to break through. In the last light I could see below. Great swathes of the land were blackened, the village burned. Directly below me a knot of the invaders swirled about a pale figure upon the ground. Flames shot up and I saw her face: Lisia, the weaver's daughter, two years older than me and pretty. At first I did not understand what it was the invaders did. Then I heard her screams. I staggered back from the window. Blackness swirled around me as my father came running, bow in hand.

"Come on, boy. We must hurry. They'll be through the gate in a moment more." I could only point. He looked, swore bitterly, snatched out an arrow and shot once. "The best I can do for the poor lass." I had a final glimpse of the invaders turning away in anger. Behind them a small white body lay still, the arrow shaft jutting from her breast.

Much of that night is still a blur to me. The invaders did not lose us as we had hoped. They had strange lights which shone out in the dark. With these they followed. My father dropped back with the guard time and time again to hold the enemy back. But always they come on our trail again. Each time they did so more of those I had known all my life fell, and the bodies had to be left behind. At some time during the running battle my father fell. Merrion, trying to save him, died also. So beset were we that their bodies were left behind as they lay. An hour, two, past moonhigh, then towards dawn, Anla died in the next attack and we rode on, praying to lose those who followed like winter-starved wolves.

They found us again. We were a small band now: only Talsa, Harkon of the ax, Berond, and myself. Most of us were mounted on work ponies, though the beast I bestrode was my new Drustan. I knew not what had happened to some few of those who had fled with us. Of many I knew all too well. I had seen them die: my family, guards who had been my friends, maids who had served my mother. I blinked back tears and rode. I was keep lord now. I must be strong. Behind us I heard shouting. Berond slowed, despair in his voice.

"They're devils. They've found the trail again."

Harkon was dour. "Aye. So we fight again."

Talsa shook her head. "I'm old and tired. I can ride no further. I'll stay back. If they find me it may be they'll delay enough for the rest of you to get to safety." I remembered Lisia.

"I forbid it." My voice trembled but I forced it to a steady tone. "I am keep lord. We throw no friend to the wolves."

How it would have been settled, I do not know. I am thankful I never had to find out for it was then that a handful of the invaders came howling at us out of the dark. Talsa fell to a sword as Harkon fought. One of the invaders fell, too, but four remained. Then three. In my mind's eye I can still see Hakon's ax carving arcs in the moonlight, steel gleaming dully as he kept them back. But one must have been cannier than his fellows. He had a bow and used it.

The first arrow took me in the shoulder, so that I yelped in pain and surprise. Berond spurred to my side. With one hand he snapped the shaft at my clothing. With his sword-hand he struck a deadly blow at the man who rode up alongside. The invader fell and our ponies trampled him. A third arrow glanced off Berond's mail. He wasted no more time. In a leap he was behind me in the saddle and, with his own pony running at our knees, he held me upright as he raced our mount for the sheltering dark.

I was near fainting, but as we fled I heard Harkon giving tongue to the hunting call, the notes with which one wishes good hunting to those who go forth. Then it broke off and I knew where the next arrow had gone. I mustered strength to ask.

"Will they pursue?"

Berond was letting the over-burdened pony slow. "I think not. One is wounded." I must have made a sound, "You saw not? Old Talsa. He slew her, but she fleshed her dagger in his thigh as she fell, and she'd know where to strike. He's like to bleed out before he can be got back. I think the archer will not follow. He never closed with us hand to hand." I thought the man a coward but was grateful if it was so.

Perhaps the archer was too busy getting his comrade back, or perhaps he was indeed less eager to fight with steel against steel. For whatever reason it was, none followed. Berond was able to remove the shaft in a cold camp later that day. The point had come through my clothing at the front and he had only to draw it out. After that, he tied me down and poured grain-spirit from a flask through the wound. I screamed, fighting my bonds before I fainted. Once I came around again, he gave me a few mouthfuls of the spirit. That was the soldier's way.

We made for Paltendale. I had kin-right and they would take us in. It took several weeks to reach them, since the hills were filled with bands of the invader who shot at anything they saw. I was young and healthy and thanks to the grain spirit the wound did not fester. It even healed a little as I rode. Each night I worked on sword drill with Berond until I was exhausted enough to sleep. Many nights I

dreamed: of how some in the village must have died. At
least my father had given Lisia a clean death. I dreamed of
Talsa and Harkon. Of my father and brothers, and when I
woke to remember they were no more I wept silently into
my bedding.

But at length we came to sanctuary and they opened the
keep gates to us. I was now the Keep Lord of Erondale in title, ten years of age, but everything I cared about was gone.
I came as a beggar to Paltendale, riding in bitter sorrow.

II

Yes, they took us in. Berond, because he was a seasoned and canny warrior. Me, they took reluctantly, yet I was kin, and Lord Hogar's pride would not allow him to turn me from the door. I ate the bitter bread of charity there for the next few years. Perhaps in recompense to my pride, I worked with all my will at learning the sword. At first with Berond still. Then, when he left to ride scout, Faslane, Lord Hogar's own master-at-arms took me in hand. He had not noticed me until that time and I think he was surprised.

"Come at me, boy." I obeyed, using all I had been taught, and because he was not wary of a child I almost managed to pass his guard. His eyebrows went up.

"Ho, someone has taught you well, it seems. Who was your master?"

"Berond," I said proudly. "Master-at-Arms of the House of Erondale."

"Berond." He nodded thoughtfully. "A good fighter. A good teacher as well, it would appear. "What other weapons can you use?"

I hesitated. I was expert with the sling but I had only

used it at small game. Did that count? I had a child's bow but it had been lost in our flight. I had used none since, though I'd done well enough with it. Faslane saw that I was uncertain. He turned to more direct questions then, and discovered soon enough that I could use both bow and sling. He vanished to return with a child's bow and quiver of arrows.

"Show me, boy." I satisfied him that I knew the use of a bow and had a good eye, though as yet my muscles would not drive a shaft any great distance. Faslane dropped a stone in the sling, giving it to me then pointing at a target. "See if you can hit that." Boy-like, I grinned. It was well within my capabilities and I hit home. Faslane nodded approval. Silently he pointed out another target and another. I hit them all. He took back the sling and his eyes on me were kind.

"Walk with me, boy, and listen." I obeyed, wondering what he would say. I did not expect his words but Faslane was ever a man who saw well.

"You chafe at being here." It was a statement and I made no reply. "You think it charity which takes you in. Yet a man must care for his kin, else when the cold winds blow who shall come to his aid? It is not charity but a trade, though men do not name it as such. And you could earn your place. I think this war will not end quickly."

I nodded. I had heard enough talk around the keep to believe this was likely. Then his words caught my understanding. I was yet a child. I would not always be so, and if the war continued trained fighters would still be needed. I looked at Faslane.

"You would train me?"

"I would. If you will always do your best, I will teach you. But there is something else you can do, boy." I waited attentively. "The larger game around Paltendale is killed or driven away since so many people came to shelter here." I knew that for truth. A number of masterless fighters or fleeing kin and their retinues had come to safety behind the walls of Paltendale.

"Meat is scarce and becomes scarcer. Many fighters are not hunters. Others disdain to take smaller game, thinking it beneath them." He did not say so but I knew he thought of Lord Hogar and his sons. "Yet still a fighter must eat, nor does a hungry man disdain a plump pheasant or perhaps a well-roasted rabbit or hare. You could help there. You came with a good pony. Take him, go beyond the wall, and hunt. Let the meat you provide pay for the food you eat while you learn to be a warrior."

I felt joy at the thought. None would remark my going. I was just another boy Lord Hogar had no time to train. I would feel less beholden. I could be free with my thoughts to roam outside Paltendale's walls. Free to remember, and if while I was alone my eyes filled, there were none to see and make mock of me. I looked up at Faslane.

"I will do so. When will you teach me?" If I were to learn from Faslane I must know, else I might leave to hunt when he would have looked for me.

"I have my own work. Yet you yourself may learn. Each night find some quiet place. Drill with your sword, teach your muscles to move smoothly and without tiring. Do this even when you are weary. A fighter must not let his body rule him. He must rule his body." I knew that. It was something my father and Berond had often said.

"I will see you here in the exercise yard at this time every fifth day unless there is other work I must be doing. Between-times, let you hunt and practice what I shall show you. Hunt well, boy." He looked down thoughtfully, his eyes assessing me.

"Your father was a good fighter. Your brother Merrion looked likely to be so as well. But you have the fighter's eye and greater speed. I think you have it in you to best them both." Before I could reply he had walked away, leaving with me the weapons he had brought me to try. I gathered them up. They were good arms, the sling well made. The bow and arrows and the sword I believed likely to have belonged to one of the lord's sons when they were younger. I would use them well, as Faslane had said.

Use them I did. At first I stayed close enough to Hold walls until I knew the land. Then I roamed out further afield. At first I brought back rabbits, the occasional hillhare, and a few times I brought back fine plump birds. The cook became my friend, always eager to see with what prey I had returned.

Faslane had been right. The game I found helped feed us all but some there were who laughed, saying it was fit work for a child. Hogeth was not the slowest of those who mocked my hunting. Once, when I was lucky in the hunt, I returned with three pheasants. The cook made of them a fantasy, setting them at the high table as if they crouched in cover from a dog, the undergrowth being made from pastry and the pheasants roasted with their feathers carefully replaced. The dog was pastry also and colored to look like a hound.

It was at a time when meat was scarce and we had visitors on behalf of two of the other Keep lords. I think the cook had feared lest his master's table look poor before them. So he did his best with what he had, but was mightily happy when I returned from my hunting bearing the birds in triumph. It may be that his master, too, had feared a poor table, since Lord Hogar came later to the kitchens to speak to the cook while I was there.

"That was well done, Leerin. But whence came the birds, I knew not any were left nearby?"

The cook bowed. "Lord, this lad brings much game to the kitchens, saying it is his kin-duty to do as he can, being not yet old enough to ride as a fighter. Instead often he rides deep into the hills and it is rare for him to return to my kitchen empty-handed." He spoke thus as a friend and wishing his Lord know I did my duty.

"Who are you, boy?" I stood forward at that and spoke clearly.

"Lorcan of Erondale, Lord Hogar. Keep's Heir, son of Joros, and kin of that branch of your House."

From the lord's side where he lounged I heard Hogeth snort. "A cock crows loud on his own dunghill, let him crow quieter on another's. Erondale is gone." Lord Hogar was a hard man, as I knew, but that day he showed also that he was fair, for he turned to look at Hogeth and his face was grim.

"The boy is kin and does his duty as custom demands. I see nothing in that at which a man might sneer. Let you be silent, my son, until your lord bids you speak." Aye, he was fair was Lord Hogar, but I saw Hogeth's eyes on me and knew he had made me an enemy.

Now and again Berond was at the keep. The war had slowed. Men had found swiftly enough that the invader machines were not indestructible. But the invaders poured in from the coast and those defenders who could fight were hard-pressed.

Berond was often leading one of the Paltendale scouting parties in the hills near the coast. Sometimes it was many weeks before he returned to call for me. Each time I listened eagerly to all he could tell. He had struck up a friendship with Faslane, too, so that I think he went first there to hear of how I did. Near three years after we had ridden to Paltendale, Berond sought me out, meeting me in private in my room with a small leather bag, which he handed me as soon as he had barred the door.

"Berond, it's good to see you. Where have you been this time and what's this?" As I spoke I was opening the bag. I upended it upon my bedding and a small trickle of wealth showered down. I gaped at the small gold disks and the sprinkling of uncut gems. "Berond? Have you taken up gambling or have you been robbing the invaders?"

He smiled. "Neither, lad. Keep it hid and tell none what

you have." He gathered the contents up again in one large hand, pouring them back into the bag and handing that to me. "Keep it safe. Time enough for spending. When that time comes you'll know it."

"But Berond, where did this wealth come from?"

"Erondale." The word struck me like a blow so that I could only sit and gape at him. He nodded. "Listen, lad. I had business for Lord Hogar over by the ruins of Rishdale. I had time owing to me and he granted me leave thinking only that I wished to look again upon what had once been my home. Therefore I rode there alone. Erondale fell, yes. But it had secrets the invaders never found. The land is ruined. They came with fire and destroyed it, all the village, the lower pastures. I think it will be many years before that land will bloom again. Maybe generations to come, for the land is poisoned." He saw me wince.

"Aye. Erondale is gone. But once this war is done many dales will lie dead. In some it will be the land which is ruined, in others the people who are gone or dead. And thus may things match. No war lasts forever. In time to come it will end and you, if you live, will be keep lord without keep or dale. It is then that you must seek out another place. You do not wish to live here on Lord Hogar's kin-charity forever?"

I shook my head violently. I'd had too long of kin-charity, and while I repaid to some extent, it was a sickness in my heart knowing how it was begrudged me, by Hogeth at least.

"Good lad. Well, this is earnest that you still have some inheritance. Your father trusted me. We were boys together and I knew all the secrets of his keep. This is one. I would keep secret the others longer but," he sighed, "the invaders press us hard. We are falling back slowly towards Paltendale and I fear. Twice have I taken minor wounds. The next may be lethal and if I die without sharing my knowledge you lose what I know."

I was not surprised that my father had trusted Berond.

They'd fought together as warriors when my grandfather
Joran held the keep as lord. I'd heard my father say once
that he owed his life to Berond, since a skirmish with bandits when they were both lads. If anyone knew the secrets of
Erondale it would be Berond. He was glancing at the door.

"We have been here together behind a barred door long
enough. There are those who will wonder why if we remain so longer. Let us ride out hunting and camp the night.
There I will tell you the rest of what I know."

I agreed with that. In my time at Paltendale I had learned
to keep my business to myself. We rode far out and hunted
well. With saddle-bags bulging we made camp at dusk.
Over food and drink Berond began.

"What do you know of the beginning of Erondale?"

I shrugged. It was a common tale, a younger son with a
wish to hold his own land. Paril of Paltendale, who had
wiped out a large group of bandits and found their hoard,
used that to seek out a suitable dale and settle there. Once
settled he had wed the daughter of a wealthy ship-owner of
the Sulcar. With her dowry he had cleared the land—
extending, too, the keep—which in turn made Erondale a
more desirable place with which to wed daughters. I said
much of this but quickly.

"The dales were open and half-empty," Berond agreed.
"A man could make his own way and Paril did. He kept the
badge of Paltendale, being a son of the House. Four generations ago Erondale gave shelter to one who came riding
bearing that same badge." Some half-remembered tale
sprang up in my mind so that I exclaimed.

"Pletten the Wicked!"

Berond looked at me sharply. "Yes, indeed. Pletten of
Paltendale. A man who knew no law save his own ap-
petites. Far to the South-west, deep in the hills which skirt
the Waste, Erondale rode to a wedding with Pletten at his
side. And at that far keep evil was done so that Erondale
rode home kin-shamed. Yet Pletten remained. He was kin
and to thrust him forth might bring feud down upon the

keep. Nor could he say aught, since Pletten was son to the
main line of the House and thus above him.

"But that was forgotten when the Lord of Erondale
found Pletten seeking to abuse a lass in the hills. She was
not of our race or kind, but she was young, like to a child,
and in his rage and disgust he struck. Pletten the wicked
died, his victim unharmed, for her rescuer had come in
time. But Erondale's Lord sank to the ground and cursed
that wicked man with all his heart. For under kin-law he
must ride now and admit his crime to Paltendale."

"Was Pletten the oldest son?"

"No, and in that lay hope. For it was possible, if he could
raise a great enough payment, Paltendale might accept it
and absolve him. Were he not kin there would be no question, Paltendale would cry feud, but he was lord of a cadet
House and blood payment would be acceptable were it
large enough. But the amount would surely be great and
Erondale, though prosperous in other things, had little
coin. So the lord sank down, seeing that the girl he had
freed had fled, and gave himself over to worry."

I broke in. "He must have done something. We don't have
a feud with Paltendale or they wouldn't have taken us in."

"He did nothing. Two days later as he rode in the high
hills still trying to think of a remedy, the girl returned. In
her hands she bore a bowl filled to the rim with riches. This
she gave him speaking formally. 'For a life you gave, for a
life you took. For payment to be made.' From her hands he
accepted it with gratitude saying that if less was needed,
then that which remained should be returned to her."

"What happened?"

"Payment was accepted by Paltendale. You have seen
the second curtain wall?" I nodded. "It was that which was
built with Erondale's coin. But there was still much wealth
left over. Many men would have kept it, counting it as payment for the danger of feud. But not the Lord of Erondale.
Once all was agreed, he rode home, and taking the riches

unused he went to the hills seeking the one who had given them."

I was listening intently. I'd heard a garbled part of this tale from Anla many years ago. But much of it was still new to me.

"Two nights the Lord of Erondale searched the hills with four of his men. On the third night one came to him. Not the girl, but it could be seen she was kin to he who came. The Lord of Erondale and the one who came to him went aside and spoke for a part of the night, and none know for certain what was said between them. Only this is known—that as the dawn neared, the other arose. He accepted the coin offered, but as he did so he said this openly before those present:

" 'Honor was more to you than blood. So shall your keep be Blessed as long as the grass grows upon your pastures.' " I recalled Berond's description of Erondale now, and wondered if it had been the invaders' machine which had broken that blessing. " 'Your Hold of Erondale may fall, but your House shall rise again. Never so long as the Power holds, shall it die. That which you could have kept is given back to you. In a time when it is required let it be used. The gratitude of my House be upon you and yours and your heirs. We live long and do not quickly forget.' " Berond broke off and I stared at him.

"What has this to do with the coin you brought me? Is it from—them?"

Berond nodded, saw my awed look, and grinned. "Aye, lad. While the Lord of the Hills accepted the offer of the unneeded coin, he returned it as I have said. Erondale made hiding-places in the keep into which they placed portions of the wealth. Over the years they changed much of it to ordinary silver where and as they could. There is a goodly amount of it remaining which lies hidden. This bag was held aside should it ever be that one fleeing should have need of an amount they could carry easily and hide well."

I closed my fingers about the bag, from where I had placed it on a thong about my neck, weighing it in my hand. The coins were gold, the gems good quality. In my single hand in that bag I held wealth enough to buy a war-horse, a pack pony, full mail, a fine sword, and have coin enough to live fat for many months. I hefted the bag. I was not quite thirteen. As yet I had no need of such wealth. Best I let the bag's contents lie. I said as much to Berond and he agreed.

"Aye, spend it at a whim and it shall not be there when there is great need." He glanced at the dark hills around and lowered his voice. "Then, too, there is more where that came from. It is weighty, being mainly silver, but there is enough to re-build a keep should the one who spends waste none of it. In times to come the dales will be poor, and coin such as that will be a great prize when this war is done. See that none guess what you have about your neck, nor that there is more where it came from." I heeded well that wisdom as I had listened to my father's words in the past.

Berond was gone for three months after that, but when he returned we went hunting again and I asked him a question which weighed on me. This was, should I give a share of the gold to Paltendale, which had taken us in? Berond shook his head.

"I think not. The lord may be fair most times, but he is a hard man. He will say that you are only a boy and that you are kin-bound to his House, therefore what you have is his to take; and take it he will. He would not see that as wrong or unjust. Nor has he done so badly by opening his gates to the two of us. I have fought well for him these past years. Faslane tells me you have hunted and brought in to the kitchen many times more than you would have eaten. No, we have repaid. Let be. If there comes a time when you should share what you have, I think that you will know it."

So I took his advice and kept silent upon the matter. I wore the bag on the long thong so it lay on my breast within my clothing and none saw. Moreover, I was cunning. I made an apparent charm bag using a scrap of cloth to cover the bag Berond had given me. That empty bag I had blessed by the Hold's wise woman, and into it I later tipped again the gold coins and gems in the privacy of my room. Any seeing the bag would know it for a charm and few would wish to meddle with one of those. It pleased me to have thought of this, and I hugged my secret to me because I had little else that was mine.

Six months later sorrow fell on me once more, so that I grieved deeply in secret—not wishing to appear unmanly before the keep's fighters—for a long time. It seemed as if everyone I had ever cared for was taken from me and I was always left alone. I wondered, as I mourned, if Berond had given me the gold and told me all he knew because he had forseen his death? He was slain in a battle unlooked for, but now that I am older I think that it was the wisdom of an experienced warrior. Berond was no young man and he must have known that his muscles stiffened, his speed in battle slowed.

So it was that, as he battled one enemy fighter, a second came against him and Berond fell. The enemy having been drawn off later, Berond's men were able to return with the body, so that Erondale's master-at-arms was not left to the birds of the hills but buried in honor in a grave that was deeply dug, and marked with a wooden headstone that I carved myself. I mourned Berond deeply. He had been the only one left from my old life; now he was gone there were none and I walked alone.

But life goes on. I reached fourteen and Faslane spoke that I should join Paltendale's fighters. I did so, and had a year of it until the invaders struck deeper into the dales and Paltendale fell. I was fortunate in that I was gone with a small group which had been sent to carry a message to a nearby dale. Faslane and some of his men broke free at the last with the Lord of Paltendale and his son, Hogeth.

There, where I was polishing my sword in my tent, Faslane found me to break the news that I was homeless once more.

"It went ill, lad. My lord would have it that the invaders could not break through the walls. Thus he took few precautions." He sighed. "He was wrong and it was others who paid. Soon he rides with his men to join with Lord Imgry. What will you do?"

"I do not know. Your advice has ever been good, Faslane. Do you give it to me now."

"Since you ask, lad. Let you leave and seek another lord to follow. You'll get nothing from Paltendale and less from the keep-heir."

"Hogeth," I said, lowering my voice to a whisper none would hear who were not inside my tent. Faslane, too, spoke in a whisper as he replied.

"Aye. Hogeth." I saw the shadow grow in his eyes until at last the words seemed forced from him. "I cannot swear. It may be I am wrong and do very ill to speak of it. But all know how he resented being third son. Paltendale has lost keep and kin. But the Hold could be repaired, the fertile land remains, and I daresay my lord may find coin enough to rebuild somewhat when the war is done. Hogeth will inherit. There will be desperate maids aplenty also, and he will take one of good blood, perhaps with some dowry but no kin to stand for her. That will please him well."

He paused and I saw he would change the subject, yet I must know. If I should not ride with Hogeth I had to know what manner of man was he that Faslane, who owed sword-duty to his House, would caution me.

"Faslane," I spoke quietly. "Always you have been kind to me. I am kin to Paltendale, and Berond, who was our master-at-arms, was your friend. Tell me what shadows you. What did you see when the keep fell?"

He took in a great breath. "I cannot swear. His older brother fell honestly fighting two men at once. But Halin was fighting only one. Another came at him from behind and Hogeth leaped in. Halin fell and Hogeth slew the man.

Later I looked at Halin's body. He died from a dagger-thrust in the back when none save Hogeth had been behind him and, Lorcan, there was no dagger nor dagger-sheath on the enemy." He fell silent again and I, too, held my tongue while thinking on what he had said.

"Perhaps the dagger was snatched up by another fighter?" I said at last.

"Perhaps. But there was no sheath. The battle still raged and I had little time to be sure. But from Halin's wound it was no small blade that struck him. None would have paused in the midst of such a fight to unstrap a sheath of that size; they are usually double-strapped."

"Hogeth wears a long-bladed dagger in such a sheath. He had it from that enemy scout he slew and he wears it always."

"That was in my mind," was all Faslane said.

I leaned back against my saddle. "I owe Hogar kin-duty but you are right. When his son rules there will be no place for me nor would I wish it. I can take up a blank-shield and choose another lord to follow."

Faslane looked at me narrowly. "Can you so, lad? Remember, if you leave Paltendale you must repay him for all he has given you. Walk away and aye, that is exactly what he will have you do. Walk. Without mount, weapons, or mail of your own."

I smiled. "Do not fear for me. Berond had a little coin which he gave me against such need. You forget that my pony is mine, not one of Paltendale's mounts. I came riding him with his gear, I shall go the same way." Faslane nodded and said no more.

The next day I went hunting alone to think over my next move. Just a few weeks earlier I had turned fifteen and under Dales Law I was a man. Moreover, though I had no dale to rule, legally I was Lord of Erondale and a free man. Did I wish to depart from my kinsman's service, I was no child nor oath-bound man to be held.

The day after that I rode with Faslane to join the Lord of

Paltendale's small group. I kept silence as we rode to join Lord Imgry. It would be foolish to stand before Lord Hogar now and demand freedom, out here in the hills where there was neither market nor hirer. But my eyes and ears were the busier. By the time we were close to Imgry's camp, I knew who had a good sword they would sell. I would take Drustan; he was no longer young as horses go, but I could ride him at first until I found a younger horse to buy, then Drustan could carry a pack. None in our group had spare mail, but in Imgry's camp it was likely there would be smiths to make, or merchants to sell, what I would need.

I sought out Lord Hogar the night before we should reach Imgry. The main camp was only a few hours ride down the road and I had a plan for that at need. Faslane showed me into the tent and I bowed low to the lord of my House. He was abrupt, perhaps fearing that I would ask coin from him.

"Lorcan of Erondale. What seek you from me?"

"My freedom, Lord. Your son once spoke rightly. Erondale is gone. I have nothing and must make my own way. I would ride as a fighter, earn what I am worth, and if I do well I may come to a place where I am able to regain a portion of what was lost to me." I saw at once that what I said did not please him.

"Fight then for me. You are young and green but I have not sent you away from amongst my men." I knew he had few men to bring to swell Imgry's ranks and I thought that he did not wish to lose even one, young and green as I might be.

"That is so." I told him, holding in my temper at the contempt on his face. "But I would be free, owing nothing to anyone."

Faslane was right. Lord Hogar stood and his face reddened in sudden fury, while his words were scathing, his tone contemptuous. "You ungrateful whelp. If you go from my service as you demand, you go naked and afoot. There is nothing you have that you did not take from my hands." I was young, as he kept saying, and his tones cut into my pride like a knife, nor had I yet learned that too much pride can sometimes cost a man too dear.

"What expense have I been to you, Lord, that I have not repaid with my hunting and my work?"

Hogar's eyes dismissed me like a poor servant. "Well then, boy. Keep your clothes. I'm a fair man, I would not have one who *claims* my blood go naked from my tent, and I daresay you have not even the few coppers they are worth." I felt a pang of fury at the insinuation in that, as if I was not truly of his blood and we both knew it, but covered it over for the sake of the family name. He insulted my honor with his hints.

Hogar turned to his man. "He leaves everything else behind, Faslane. His mount and gear, his mail and weapons. See to it!"

I found my voice harshly. "Lord. I ride when I leave. The beast is mine and his gear. I came riding him from Erondale. As for the clothes you leave me, I, too, am a fair man. The House of Erondale does not take where it cannot pay." I had several silver coins and one gold in the secondary coin-pouch at my belt, I would give him a silver coin, that would pay anything I owed. My hand was shaking so hard I could feel nothing as I fumbled the coin out without looking at it. I stepped forward and dropped it at Hogar's feet. I was almost done speaking before my eyes focused on the coin and I saw what I had done. I felt horror and shame slide up my spine at that sight. Gods, but I was a fool, I had let my anger betray me into flinging gold in Hogar's face.

"I will leave my mail and weapons with Faslane as you demand. Let that coin repay you for my bed and board. I leave owing nothing. If I come to another keep as lord it shall not be the badge of Paltendale I raise."

I had only time to see the stunned look on his face, as he recognized the worth of the coin, before I all but fled. Faslane came with me, his face glum, saying nothing. He stood by as I dropped my chain hauberk, coif, and weapons at his feet.

"There, take that to Hogar and tell him he's not been cheated."

"I know you're no cheat, lad. But you've done ill. Didn't Berond teach you to keep tight purse-strings and tighter lips? Well, what's done is done. But I'd be out of here as fast as you can." His mouth turned down as I would have apologized, explained my error, and offered him information as to my plans.

"Nay, no time for explanations, and don't tell me where you will ride. That way if I'm asked I can answer truly that I know nothing." He took my hand. "Do no deeds in days to come which your father or lady mother would have scorned. Go with my blessing since you have no father."

He gripped my hand briefly, stepping back to allow me passage. It was clear I would do well to be gone now and not wait in Hogar's camp to haggle for the sword or chainmail I'd hoped to buy. Nor should I waste time explaining that the coin I had flung down had been meant to be silver. As Faslane said, what was done was done. I swung onto Drustan's back, nudged him into a fast walk, and when I looked back at the camp edge Faslane was still standing looking after me. The gear Hogar had demanded he take back was piled at my friend's feet.

III

◄○►

I looked back once as I topped a small ridge. I lifted my hand, paused long enough to see a hand raised in return, then the camp was out of sight. I had chosen my time carefully. It would be dark in another hour, but if I rode steadily I would be well down the main road in that time. Two hours on the road by moonlight and I'd be at Imgry's camp. I was young, but I knew about such camps. Where there were a number of lords and very many soldiers there would be supplies, stables, at least one inn, and aught else a man might need or desire.

I reached the camp as I had planned and drew rein at the fringes. Torches flared about the perimeter. In their light I could see avenues between rows of tents and crude huts. Stalls lined the widest avenue. I sucked in a breath of satisfaction. Then I dismounted, and leading my weary Drustan I walked forward. There were guards, but I was clearly a man of the dales, and none halted me. I slid into the clamor and lights and was gone from the view of any who might have followed me.

I must work as swiftly as I could. By the time Hogar and his son came riding in with the men of Paltendale, I wished to be unnoticeable in case they inquired for me. I stopped at a stall selling used clothing. There was a stack of cloaks to one side. Good warm riding cloaks which would wrap a man from head to boot heels when he was riding. I fingered a gaudy cloak.

"How much?"

The stall-owner looked me up and down. "To you, lad, nine coppers."

I nodded. "And to anyone else, three."

"Nay, I'd not cheat you. See how warm it would be. And the embroidery; you would look fine in such a cloak." He might speak truth there, but I preferred a less obvious cloak and one which would be warmer, if less elaborate.

I shrugged. "I'll look at other stalls first."

I moved on, disregarding his scowl. I needed to find a money-changer. Showing gold here would be as dangerous as bearding a pard in his den. I took the opportunity to cast my eyes over other stalls, and next to find a stable for Drustan. I did not wish any to identify me by him. Leaving Drustan munching happily in his hired stable, I went on. I found the stall I sought at one end of the street. It was, as always, two tents. One in which a man might ask his questions, the other inner tent in which he might make the transactions. Both were well guarded. I approached openly and I saw the guard's eyes go to my weaponless side.

"Mistaken your way?"

"I would change coin."

A small wizened man stepped past him. "Then you are in the right place. What would you wish of me?"

"I have coin I would change for silver and coppers." He nodded, seemingly unsurprised that such a young soldier would have gold or foreign coins.

"Come to the inner tent then, and I will weigh what you have." I followed him in. I was not wholly unarmed. I had a dagger given to me by Berond, a good blade taken from an enemy. And between Berond and Faslane I had been well-taught in the tricks of dealing, even unweaponed, with surprise attack.

As for haggling in the market and assessing the quality of goods, I was well taught—first by my father, who believed that any lord should understand the quality of most usual goods and how to bargain for them lest he be cheated as a fool, and then by Berond, since after our arrival in Paltendale we had few coins to spend and certainly none to waste. Berond had seen that our poverty was likely to last for some time, so he stood over me when he could, teaching me to know good weapons and gear when I saw them and what to say to stall-holders in a marketplace.

"Now, what coins are they which you would change?" I had thought on this. I needed enough silver and copper to pay my way. The gold coins had clearly been changed at some time in the past. They were no uncommon sort for the dales. That was not the danger. I produced five.

"I would have the value of four and one half in silver, the value of the last half in coppers." I was eyed sharply.

"If I asked whence these came . . ."

"They were honestly come by in war. As for further answer, are you Lord Imgry's steward to ask of me?"

He gave a quick bark of amusement. "Nay. Well enough then. I think you speak the truth and it's no concern of mine." He worked carefully, checking that the coins were indeed gold and honest weight. Then he counted out the twenty-two silver, the half silver bit, and the remaining copper. He threw in a belt-pouch and bowed me out. I did not see him make any sign to his guards but, nonetheless, I turned on my heel and slid between tents, ran a few steps, and circled. I came back into the street the way I had come, watching my back. There was no sign of pursuers.

I made my way to the stall-holder with the cloaks, bargained, and purchased the one he had first shown me. It was gaudy but rather thin quality. I turned it inside out and went to another stall. There I found the cloak I really wished for. I took it up casually.

"Ten coppers." The stall-holder here was a motherly-looking woman.

I looked shocked. "Ten. For this?"

"Well, seeing as you're only a lad, I'll say nine."

I shook my head sadly. "Three, and that's over-pricing it."

She threw up her hands. "If I sell at such a price I'll go hungry. Eight." I shook my head again. "Seven then, and my final price."

"Five—and mine." We shook hands at six.

I paid her, took up the cloak, and dodged quietly behind a tent. There I rolled the gaudy cloak embroidered-side within and donned the other. It had been a good purchase. It was worn, but nowhere near threadbare, dark wool lined with rabbit fur, high collar, and a hood with drawstrings which could be buttoned on outside the collar. It was a cloak for a plain man who rode in all weathers: warm, unobtrusive, and well made.

I stepped out into the bustle again and found me a carrysack such as any soldier needs for his gear. I set about filling it quietly—a blanket here, a fire-striker there—until I had all that I required. I took the carrysack back to the stable and reclaimed Drustan. I paid the reckoning and walked him away to where I had earlier scouted an inn.

"How much for three days? Myself and two mounts, all found."

"A room which can be secured, two meals a day, stabling for two beasts, fodder and care for them. A half silver would pay all. I'll throw in a bath each night an you wish."

"Done. I'll pay now." He bowed at that. It was no unusual arrangement in a camp such as this. A man might be drawn into gambling and lose all he had. Or be robbed of the same if he were careless. I paid, and left again once I had secured my gear in the room and seen the pony settled. I wore the dark cloak away. In the market I found the other items I required and came at last to the weapons stalls. There I chose a sword. It was too plain but the blade was good and the hilt fit comfortably into my hand.

"Aught else, Sir? I have good bows, horse bows. Long bows? Daggers?"

I chose a horse bow, a strong well-made weapon with a full quiver as well. I studied the daggers. There was one— small, but with a razor-sharp blade and a sheath made to lie against a man's forearm. I turned over others and found a second. I bought both. As I walked away I slid my arms within the cloak, as unobtrusively I fastened the first weapon into place along my forearm. Slipping between tents I knelt warily and fastened the second at the back of my calf. One of Faslane's tricks. Berond's gift I wore openly upon my swordbelt. Let men see it and think that it was all I had.

From where I was I could hear the horse-lines. I moved in that direction and found myself by a pen filled with sleepy beasts who drowsed three-legged. I had required little formal training to know a good horse when I saw one. A keep lord's family is born into owning horses, they ride before they walk, and from childhood we are are constantly grooming, riding, breaking, or handling the beasts.

I made no move, but studied the nearest tethered animals one by one before moving on. None of them there were worth my coin. They were thin, dispirited animals and I thought all of them were old. I wanted a good hill-horse, one like my cloak, made for hard use, serviceable, and not drawing the eye. I found him at the end of the lines.

"Ah, you seek a mount. A fine beast this one. Young, spirited, fit for a lord." If the lord wished a horse that kicked everything in sight that was true, I thought. I knew those laid-back ears and hunched hindquarters.

"What about this one?"

"A wise choice. Now this horse is young and will carry you day and night. He is . . ." I'd looked into the beast's

mouth before he finished. The vendor saw that I knew how
to read a horse's teeth and without even a blush for his lies
waved forward another beast. "This one then. A fine strong
animal, young, as you can see." It was also clumsy as I
could tell by the marks at the back of the fetlocks. I needed
no over-reacher, forever going lame.

At last he worked his way to the horse which stood at the
back of the pen. It watched him warily. He drew it forward
by the rope halter and posed it as best as he could. I hid a
smile. It was no beauty and it was clear the dealer was
wondering what points he could praise which would please
a young man. I went over the animal carefully. It was about
seven. The legs were a little less than fine but they were
strong and unmarked. The nose was the opposite of an
aristocratic dish and the color was a dusty clay with some
black mottling. It was a gelding, that I approved. A gelding
is not apt to cause trouble with mares or stallions and the
color would be unobtrusive while I was scouting.

"I'll throw in gear if you buy, sir. Bridle, halter, saddle.
He's just been shod again." The man was beginning to be
hopeful of a sale.

I continued to check. Then I looked up with an unenthu-
siastic glance. "A good enough animal, I suppose. I might
offer a half-silver."

The dealer gaped at me. "Lad, lad. In an army camp any
mount is worth gold. Good beasts are in short supply. True,
he has no great looks, but he's sound, not old, and he's sensible. I couldn't let this horse go for less than a silver and a
half." I beat him down copper by copper, but in the end I
led my new horse away.

I went at once to the next stall I had marked down. They
had mail, mostly used, but it had all been well-repaired and
I had already seen a hauberk which would fit me. At fifteen, I would still grow, but not so greatly the chain could
not be added to and let out a while. I bargained so well a
chain coif was thrown into the deal.

Weaponed, chain-mail clad, and with my new mount I returned to my inn. I stabled the horse by Drustan, took food and ale to my room, secured the door, ate, then fell asleep almost at once. Those at the inn had seen me only briefly and by night. Before they saw me again I would look a little different. I took up the basins of hot and cold water they brought come morning, picked out rags I had purchased, and with them packets from my carrysack.

Using one of my small daggers I trimmed my hair short. Then I rinsed it twice with water and the contents of one packet. My hair was a dark honey color, but as I gazed into the small steel mirror I saw I had done well. It had become a brownish shade, neither dark nor light but in-between and hard to describe. I washed in the hot water, rubbing onto my skin with another rag the contents of the second packet. Then I looked again into the mirror. I smiled slowly at my reflection.

My skin appeared darker, more weathered. I looked older. More importantly, I looked not at all like Lorcan of Erondale. The dye would last months before it wore off slowly, by which time I should have tanned more heavily. If not, I could procure more dye. My hair's shade would last through several washings and, again, I could purchase more of the tint. I was satisfied none were like to recognize me, save Faslane perhaps. I tinted my eyebrows carefully. My lashes would have to remain pale, but if anyone even noticed that they would probably assume it was some family trait.

I ate heartily of the food which the servant brought and went out once I was done. None remarked me as I walked confidently about the crowded camp. At noon I ate at another inn, listening to soldiers gossip while lingering over my single jack of ale. I must find someone who would hire me as a blank-shield; I wanted a man who was well thought of by his men. I also thought of a story and a new name for myself. I could hardly hide my appearance then give out my true name like a veritable farm-boy.

"A game of dice, lad?"

I laughed. "I have few coppers and—no offense—but my father taught me never to dice with those I do not know." The man grinned back at me.

"A wise father breeds a wise son." He quoted. "How else am I to win your money then?" I liked what I saw. I'd lived among soldiers long enough to sum up this one. He'd lend a friend money as quickly as he'd expect them to lend it to him, did they have it to spare. He'd steal, lie, but not to a friend. And he'd know all the byways of any camp within hours of his arrival.

"How long have you been here?" I placed a copper on the table. He flicked it into his sleeve.

"Ten days. I came in with my Lord Salden."

I bowed my head in casual greeting. "I am Farris of Eldale."

He eyed me. "I have not heard of that place."

"Likely. Few have. It's a dungheap dale to the Northwest. The invaders struck there recently. 'Tis a place hard to find, and I'm sure they came upon it by accident only. I alone escaped, being away on my master's business. I returned to find keep and village still smoldering and all dead." For a moment I remembered Erondale and Lisia. I shook the memories from me and continued.

"The swine had not even bothered to loot so I took all I could find and rode to take arms against them. I seek employment. A lord who has fewer men but treats them with honor. I am young but I have my own mount, pack-beast, weapons, and gear. I have had some swords-teaching as well. Where would I find such a man who might hire a blank-shield?" I placed five coppers on the table.

My companion nodded. "A wise son indeed. Well then. Were I such a man I would seek out Lord Altan of Berendale. He uses the Inn of The Silver Ship. If he will not employ you, return here. It is possible my own lord might hire you if I spoke to him." He grinned hardily. "Of course, I would require to be paid again for an introduction."

I nodded. "If I returned here, who should I ask for?"

"Aran of Tildale. Good fortune to you."

I returned his wish and departed in search of Lord Altan. I was unfortunate in that I found the man and he was one such as I had described. But he could not hire me—or would not. I was unsure. But at length I returned to the inn and inquired for Aran. He took me to his lord after relieving me of five more coppers. Thus I was hired as a blank shield by Lord Salden of Tildale and Aran became my friend.

I say my friend and so he was, but I kept a shut mouth on what else was in my charm bag apart from herbs. I wore openly the belt pouch given by the money-changer. From that I dispensed coin as I must and frugally. I loaned Aran coppers when he asked and always he returned them faithfully. We rode mostly as scouts against the invaders, and I learned to kill from ambush, to cut a man's throat silently when needs be, and to judge the best land into which to draw the invaders for a more major attack against them. In another year I was lean and battle-hardened as only a man can be who is constantly riding or fighting on a sparse diet.

I had ridden with my friend for well over a year and was briefly relaxing in our camp, sitting cross-legged while I repaired Drustan's bridle, when Aran came seeking me.

"Listen, Farris, there's talk among the lords." I could read his suppressed excitement. Some momentous foray must be planned.

"Well, what talk? Are we to storm the invaders last coast-camp? Put all to the sword? Or is it some daring trip across the waste?"

"No." His face became sober. " 'Tis the last battle, I

daresay. Word is that the were-riders have gathered once more."

"They have been fighting beside us near three years," I said slowly. "What changes now?"

"I heard that they have the invaders pushed into a corner. Some of us ride to stop bolt-holes. The remainder ride to the final battle."

I never knew whence Aran had the word, but it was good. My Lord Salden rode out next day taking all in his train with him, with Aran and I riding ahead as scouts. Paltendale rode at the same time, though not quite in our direction. I saw Hogar, Hogeth at his side, with Faslane leading the men. I would that I could have spoken to him but I dared not. I had been fortunate in that never in the many months I had been with Salden had we been paired with Paltendale to ride or scout. Many times I had seen Faslane in the distance and always I had gone some other way. I wished to put no strain on his loyalties.

It was nigh the end of the Year of the Hornet. The enemy had been thrust back and back since the Riders joined hands with our cause. Lord Imgry himself had spoken to the men before we departed, saying that the invaders were cast down. Now was the time for a final repaying of our debt, yet it would not be easy. The invaders were isolated, maddened, and desperate. I wondered then as I rode, if Aran was right and this was to be the last battle.

I was just seventeen, Lord of ruined Erondale. What of me if the fighting ceased? Where would I go, whose dale was ash and rubble? Hidden there in that same rubble was wealth, yet how would I use it? Where should I raise my banner now? Well, I would let the questions bide until after the battle. If I lived I could seek answers. And of my survival I was none too certain.

Near day's end Lord Salden gathered us and spoke as was his wont, quiet and straightforward words to men he knew and trusted.

"A day's ride from here is Hagar Pass. Lord Imgry believes that if his army break the enemy in this battle, some will seek escape through the pass; near to it to the west lies a second similar pass. Paltendale ride to that one to hold the door tight shut." He paused.

"Both Lord Hogar and I have sworn that should our enemy be slain then those of us who live shall ride to aid the other. Mark that. If I fall I would not be forsworn." I heard their voices lift about me as the men agreed. Salden nodded grim-faced, raising a large parchment to hang on a frame.

"The plan is simple. Here is the pass we are to guard and the country which lies about it. Better we meet them on the far side. Thus if they push us back they must fight uphill, seeking to force an exit which grows ever narrower against them."

Aran spoke up. "My Lord, how many might attempt the pass?" The reply explained Salden's grimness and his talk of oaths given.

"Who can tell? The scouts say it could be five or six score. But of late the invaders have shown less liking for battle. In the place where Imgry will meet them they are like to take this formation." He sketched swiftly with a charcoal stick. Around me men nodded sourly. "Aye. As you see. Those in the rear may break away and flee if they think the battle well lost. There are only two passes they can take if they try for the coast again in hopes of a ship. Also their last camp lies on our line and supplies will doubtless be left there in readiness for them. Paltendale hold one pass and we the other. Imgry is determined to wipe out all of the invaders. Our orders are to hold the passes." He looked around us, his gaze meeting each man's look in turn.

"To hold. There are no further orders." I understood and so, by the faces of those about me, did my comrades. We were to hold until only men of one side were left standing.

I thought ill of Imgry that he did not allow more men for the passes. Then I thought of the main battle and guessed he could spare no more to ride with us. Salden was sketching lines on the map again.

"Aran, you and Farris shall ride on ahead to scout the pass. I would be sure this map is correct. Unless Imgry is brought to battle sooner than he expects, it will be the day after tomorrow when we see the enemy." I made for my horse as he commanded. My pony would be brought along by the pack-horse herder. With Aran at my shoulder, we rode out briskly.

I had named my horse Tas soon after I purchased him. It was the word for one of the hardy scrubs of the Waste. One which lived despite the heat and lack of water. The name was well-chosen—he was as tough and enduring as the plant. I was fond of the beast and he of me, coming when I whistled and nuzzling hopefully for the crusts I saved when I could. We rode until full dark when the pass was before us. Aran's voice to me came out of the night.

"Shall we scout on foot before we make camp?"

I agreed. Things often go wrong once battle is joined and it could be that Imgry had been forced to fight early. If so, the enemy could be upon us before we expected. But there were no signs of them. Even after we had scouted the land before the pass, then climbed high and looked into the darkness. There were no camp fires to be seen, so we descended and made camp in a sheltered spot where their scouts could not spy our fire. In the dawn I scouted yet again while Aran climbed higher on the mountainside. Still we saw nothing until, in the distance, our comrades approached.

I left Aran to report to his lord while I took Tas. I rode at a steady trot far out before the pass, along the trail to where another peak stood proud. This I urged him to climb as far as he might. I halted him when his upward plunges became too labored. I stared across the trail, and in the far distance I saw dust. If that was the enemy they would not be up to the pass until I had been back two candlemarks or more. Still, I wasted no time in descending and putting Tas to a steady hand gallop.

"My Lord, I see dust on the trail beyond the next peak." His reply was a signal to the master-at-arms. Horses were run back beyond the pass and picketed there. Soldiers ran to agreed positions and lay down. Aran and I knew already where we were to be. We went there and waited. I had been unsure if those approaching were the enemy, but so it turned out to be. There were only thirty of us and the odds were almost four to one.

It was a vicious battle. They were desperate men and we were but a little less desperate. All of us had lost friends or family at their hands, so we held as they pushed us into the throat of the Pass and there we stood firm. They could neither force us further back nor drag us down. They came at us again and again and died. Enemy they were, and they had done terrible things in their time, but let none say these were not brave men. They died in their tracks and whatever they may have done at Imgry's battle, here none broke or fled.

At length there were few of us remaining. Aran and I; he with a wounded leg which made it hard for him to stand, I with my left arm roughly bound. Lord Salden was down, and most of our comrades. Only two stood beside us now, both wounded. We faced no enemy, I had slain the last as he ran through the master-at-arms. It was late afternoon and we had fought for several hours. Aran staggered to one side and sat heavily upon a stone.

"What do we do now?"

I looked at the three. "I ride. We gave our oath that we would seek out Paltendale and aid them if there was need." Aran made to stand and I shook my head. "What use will you be to Paltendale if you bleed out in the hills between? You are already almost too weak to stand. Stay and rest with our comrades, eat and sleep. My wound is shallow and the bleeding is stopped. I may be of little use as a fighter but at least I can reach the other pass and bring back word of what happened there. In the morning, if I am not back, gather the beasts and return slowly to the main camp and Lord Imgry. I will catch up if I can."

So I rode alone to the second pass which Paltendale had held. I came upon a scene of death there, though I had guessed it beforehand from the buzzards as they dropped from the skies ahead of me. Lord Hogar lay there, together with Faslane and others from Paltendale whom I had known. They had died with honor, for, as I saw from the lack of tracks, no enemy had succeeded in passing them.

I searched quickly amongst the bodies but found no sign of Hogeth and, something that made me frown when I noticed it, Faslane had died of a dagger wound from behind. I recalled his tale of another man who had died that way and I resolved to discover the truth one day, if I could. I saw, too, that the hoof-marks of a single horse led away from the pass in another direction.

I took nothing from that grim scene. I would tell Imgry of it if Imgry still lived. Let him send his men to scavenge among the dead. I met Aran two days into his return and rode back with him to a camp where men ran mad in drunken celebration. I looked on them and knew such was not for me. I would ride on. We sold the horses we had brought back from our battle, dividing the small amount of money equally—horses were not of so much value with the war over. I stayed one last night to drink with Aran, losing to him a little of the coppers and silver from my belt-pouch. He would have need of it when he returned to his own dale.

Aran would have had me return with him, but his dale was not mine. I would look again on the ruins of Erondale; after that I did not know. I had still most of the contents in my charm-bag about my neck, more coin from the sale of the mounts, and I would not starve. My friend wrung my hands in silence, his eyes brimming over.

"If ever I can aid you, call on me."

I replied with similar words and wished I could have gone with him. But Erondale called, and with morning I saddled Tas and pack-saddled Drustan. With mail under my cloak, sword and dagger at my side, I left as quietly as I had once come to camp. After that I rode slowly for Erondale. I had only vague memories of the night my home fell to the invaders. Perhaps I had been wrong and there had been less damage than I believed. Yet Berond had spoken of "rubble." I dropped from the high hills into Erondale to find both Berond and memory had been right.

I camped two nights in the ruins mourning Berond and my family. There was nothing here of casual loot, the ruins of keep and village had been picked over many times. Yet Berond had told me well. I scouted carefully, and once I was sure none were about I found the secret—and the treasure of my House which lay hid. I left it untouched and rode on.

For nearly a year after that I rode with other soldiers loosely oathed to Lord Imgry. Men whose work it was to scour the land in search of any invaders who might have escaped that final slaughter. It took time until we could be sure none remained. But two days after my eighteenth birthday, at the end of the Year of the Unicorn, I rode South. I rode without plan or map, wishing only to see and learn the lands I did not know. Twice I dropped down into dales which received me with hatred or fear until they were certain I rode alone without men to follow. Already lordless, landless men were banding together, striking like wolf packs as they ravaged dales that had survived the war.

I was far to the South-west now, traveling in a slight curve down the lands. The Waste shimmered hotly to the North, far East lay the sea. Ahead to the South and a little East lay Sorn Fen. I had taken a day to wash my clothing and put on the only clean things I had left. Under my cloak I wore a threadbare tabard with the Paltendale arms. I had meant to throw it away many times but had not done so. It was too small for me and I had let out the strings as far as I could. The day was fine and I galloped Tas, out of my joy in living, Drustan following. I rounded a bend on the trail and men barred my way. I recognized one with a cry of amazement.

"Devol?" It was he, the groom from Erondale I had liked as a child. My friend with his winks and tricks and his jokes which had always made me laugh when I was young. Just when I thought everything of my dale was lost—when I believed everyone from Erondale was long since dead— here was an old friend.

"Devol, well met. What have you been doing through this war, are these your friends?"

He smiled, crowding his horse up to mine. "My friends, yes?" I saw he had not quite recognized me, though the dye was long since washed from my hair and skin. A child changes far more than a grown man in ten or twelve years.

"Devol, it's Lorcan, Lorcan of Erondale." He beamed hugely then.

"Little Lorcan! What do you here, are you alone, what of Erondale and your family?"

I felt a surge of sorrow. "Erondale fell to the invaders early. My father and brothers were killed as we fled. But it is wonderful to see you again and alive."

Devol nodded. "A great occasion. Dismount, eat and drink with us, Lord Lorcan. We have good wine." His band were a ragtag lot and I did not like the look of them, yet this was Devol of Erondale. I dismounted as he asked, sat and ate with them, drank heartily of the wine they offered me, toasting Erondale, Lord Imgry, friends and fallen com-rades and the downfall of the invaders. I felt a strange muzziness come over me as I raised my mug to drink the last toast and as I slumped sideways onto the ground I saw that Devol still smiled. Yet now it seemed like the smile of one who gloats and not the grin of good comradeship. I had barely time to curse my folly before I was drowned in darkness.

Meive

IV

I awoke still hearing the screams, seeing the fires. I had
seen or heard none of it, but the knowledge of how it
must have been lived in my heart, and in my dreaming
mind when I slept. I came shuddering into the here and
now of a still warm night. The peace enwrapped me, sooth-
ing and calming until at last my gasping breaths slowed.
The thundering pulse of my heart ceased to shake me. In
the new silence I could hear a soft drowsy hum from the
hives. I reached out with my mind and found they slept. All
was well. I lay back on my bedding and remembered.

I was a child when the invaders came to the dales. Their
coming meant so little to me or to those of my home that I
am not even sure when it happened. It took time for any
news to arrive at our remote and isolated valley. Officially,
my home was Landale, although in truth we were so small
that to call us "dale" was but a courtesy. Nor were we known
to our neighbors by that name. Instead, a traveler had once
named us Honeycoombe in jest. That name was more true to
ourselves, so it remained the title most often used.

On the maps, however, we were Landale after the first of
our lords, a younger son who came here to take up land
four generations ago. He and his family lived in a state

barely more luxurious than those of us who looked to him, yet that suited both him and his. It suited us also, and there was strong affection and loyalty between his line and the village about his large stone house.

For his estate he had taken a tiny dale, a valley steep-sided, deep in foothills, with a second smaller vale leading from the inner end. We did not make our coin from rich fertile lands and sheep or cattle. No, our wealth, such as it was, came from the uplands beyond our dale. Uplands rocky and steep, but where grew great swathes of the low thick bushes known as beelove covered in massed purple and white flowers.

In Winter our few goats grazed there, nibbling the grass beneath the bushes and nibbling back the tastier portions of the shrubs themselves so that in Spring they flowered ever more profusely. That was our time: Spring, when the bees of our more than twenty hives flew forth to garner nectar and make of it honey. That we gathered with as much care as the winged-ones and traded it and the other bee-products for modest wealth for Honeycoombe.

I lay in my bed remembering that year when I had been ten and eager to learn. We had our own wise woman in Honeycoombe, old Ithia, who spoke to the bees and instructed us in their care. She it was who told us when the hives should be carried down to the valley before Winter. Who told us the right time to return the winged-ones to the Uplands so they might fly forth again in the growing warmth. She was much respected and many girls looked at her in hope. To be titled the Wise-Woman of the Bees was to be blessed—as well as the owner of a cottage and independent. And it was to me that year that she spoke.

"Meive, come with me, child." I went eagerly.

"Take my hand and listen." I stood before the hive to which she had led me and waited. Ithia smiled. "Do not try so hard. Let your body relax. Let your mind hear only the winged-ones humming. Let it carry you where it will." I did as she bade me and it was so. I saw strange and wondrous things. I could not later recall all I had seen, but I knew I had been welcomed. And Ithia knew it, too. When at last I came to myself again she was smiling.

"It is well. The winged-ones accept you."

I was disappointed. Was that all? They accepted everyone in the dale. All but Neeco, and he had left almost two years ago. I said so, diverted by the memory of that angry departure.

Ithia shook her head slowly. "The bees know more than they speak. They rejected Neeco in a way which made me fear for us all. It was for that I spoke to Lord Lanson, and he found a place for the boy beyond our dale."

"He didn't want to leave," I said matter-of-factly.

"No, but it was right. There was that within him which disturbed the winged-ones. If he remained it would not have been well."

My eyes rounded. "Would they have left us?"

"Perhaps." She shook her head in warning. "Bees which have been angered or distressed have less honey to share also. The bond between us and little ones stretches thinner as they remember that we caused their worry. Nothing of that is well."

She shrugged, throwing off our memories of the angry boy shouting threats as he left the dale. Neeco had not wanted to leave home and family. He'd been thirteen, though, old enough to take up a job several dales away. He'd been good with dogs and Lord Lanson had found him a position as assistant kennel-boy in Merrowdale, two days wagon-ride from us. His family had been sad, but resigned to his departure. Neeco, however, had to be taken by force to his new place. He'd screamed at us all as he was dragged away.

"I'll come back. You'll see. I'll come back and make you all sorry." The lord's men had been rougher at that. Neeco had cried out in pain and anger. "You'll pay, all of you. My life on it." The master-at-arms had clapped a hand over Neeco's mouth and we had heard no more. He had gone, and almost had I forgotten him until this day.

"Couldn't he have stayed? He could have kept away from the Uplands."

"The hives return to the bee-barn in Winter," Ithia reminded me. "How would he stay away from his home then? No. It was not kind, but it was necessary. I cannot be oath-certain what ill omen he would have brought to us, but the queens showed me death. They believed he would bring death to us." She laid a gentle hand on my shoulder.

"Now, to return to why you are here. I have said, the winged-ones accept you. Not as they accept others but as they speak to me. Would you like to be my apprentice, child? If so, then I will bespeak your father."

I was eager but doubt held me back. "Would I have to leave my family?"

Ithia smiled gently. "Eventually, yes. But not yet. You are young. I think it best that you stay with them a year or two yet. You shall learn from me during the day and return home to your kin in the evening. Does that please you better?" She saw my joyous face and her smile broadened. "I see it does. Well then, let us go and discuss matters with your parents." Both were greatly pleased that I should be chosen. But my father was puzzled.

"Wise One, I have heard it said that to be a keeper of the bees one must have a gift. Never has there been a trace of this in my line, nor in my wife's. How is it that Meive has the gift?"

I was standing to one side and saw my mother's face. There was some secret there. She smoothed out the look when she caught my eye and nodded to me. I knew she would tell me, but not yet. Ithia nodded at my father.

"That is true, but such a gift may arise from nowhere. How think you it came the first time? Then, too, it may lie in the bloodline many generations before coming forth again. It was so with me. My own gift comes from my many-times-grandmother. It was a story in our line, and when it appeared in me none were surprised. Mayhap in your line the story faded and was forgot. But the blood does not forget, nor do the winged-ones."

My father seemed to relax at that assurance. He spoke formally then. "If it seems well to you, wise Ithia, then I agree. Let Meive, my daughter, be apprenticed to you. Will you speak to the Lord Lanson?"

"I have done so. He said if you agreed, it should be so." I was dancing from foot to foot with excitement.

"Da? Ithia said I don't have to leave yet. I can stay here."

My father looked at the wise woman questioningly.

Ithia laughed. "That is so. I think Meive young yet to leave and live with me. Keep her with you two further Winters. Once she is twelve let her join me in my home, which will one day be hers." She spoke lightly, yet even as she said the last words a shadow seemed to pass across her face. But I was too happy to let that shadow dampen my spirits. I would learn, and in time I would be the Wise Woman of the Bees for Honeycoombe. I would have my own home, standing and respect from even the Lord's family. It was enough for any ten-year-old. How should I have forseen what would be my fate?

For two years I was happy. I worked hard yet it did not seem like work to me. To reach out with heart and mind. To share the life of the hive. All of that was a wonder to me. Most of our hives contained the small stingless bees of our ancient heritage. But a year before Ithia bespoke me, she had gone on a journey. From that she had returned with two new queens. They were larger, blacker, and fierce.

These she had given the two new hives, and when they bred we had different bees within those hives. They were not so large as the queens, but they were dangerous. They could sting well, and far more importantly for Honeycoombe, they worked further into the Fall, began earlier in Spring. I watched them one day and marveled at their industry.

"Ithia, where did the new bees come from?"

The wise woman hesitated, then she answered me. "From a place two days walk from here." She moved away around the hives, looking to see that none were nearby. "Meive, this is a thing of the bees. You may not speak of it to any. Do you understand?"

I was proud to be trusted. "I swear. May the bees hear my oath."

Ithia sat on an out-thrust of rock. "Very well. You know I walk often beyond the dale. I search for better pastures for the winged-ones. For different flowers which will enrich their honey for us. I was traveling for that reason ten years ago. In a secret place I found that something called me to come further. I obeyed."

I listened, my eyes widening as Ithia described her adventure. A place of the Old Ones. Yet linked to Ithia by bonds she could not mistake.

"And you were given the queens?"

"Not given. That which dwells there asked if they were willing. They came at their own desire. They remain at their pleasure. They are their own gift."

"It was a great gift," I said, my eyes glowing at an idea. "Should we not return to tell the one who dwells there of how her children do?"

Ithia smiled. "I have done so each year since you joined me."

"Oh." That, I thought, explained Ithia's absences. I had noticed that in past years after the hives were moved into the hills for Spring, Ithia had been gone some days. "Will you take me there next time?"

"Not yet." Ithia stood and smiled down at me. "But I think it is time that you joined me here in my cottage. How will that please you?"

I beamed. "Very well, Ithia. I can bring my things over now. Da will help. Is there anything special I should bring?"

"Whatever of yours you wish to have in the cottage,

child. Go now and tell your father. He may wish you to spend another night or two."

My father did. I found that was because he and my mother wished to have a special dinner for me. I was set at the head of the table, a toast was drunk to me, and my favorite foods were laid before us. I would be sad to leave my family, but my younger sisters Jenna and Saria were delighted. They would have more room now. My older brother, Welwyn, pretended to be pleased, too. There would be fewer sisters to plague him, he growled. But it was he who pressed a last gift into my hands when he and my father left me with Ithia.

I opened the small parcel and gaped. Ithia studied the gift. "So, your brother has a talent of his own." I could only turn my gift over admiringly and agree with that. From somewhere Welwyn had found a root. I know not how much like to its ending its first shape may have been, but now it was a queen of the winged-ones. Every line was perfect and in her head were set tiny black gems as eyes.

So fine was it that almost I expected her to fly free and join the hives. She perched on a small stump of another wood which spread at the base to stand firm. It was a marvelous piece of work and I would treasure it. I carried it inside to place on the shelf my father had nailed beside my bed. There was just room beside my candlestick. Ithia was brisk.

"It is a wonderful gift, but now we have work to do." Before I could start remembering that I was apart from my family, she swept me into such a frenzy of cleaning and polishing that I went to bed and slept dreamlessly in exhaustion. After that the pattern of my days set slowly. I was happy, and it seemed that Ithia was well pleased with my work for I did indeed learn eagerly.

That year she left for the place of the Old Ones to give thanks. Although I pleaded to come with her I would be remaining behind, but to soothe my disappointment, Ithia made me a map showing the path. I knew the first portion, it led to the furthest bee-pastures where we sometimes shifted the hives at High Summer. In certain years rare flowers grew there which produced honey that had abilities other than food and ordinary healing.

The honey from those years Ithia would distill to an essence which was a reviving cordial. There was so little it was never sold, but kept instead for our own people. It saved more than one, but from prudence none spoke of it. Should such a cordial become widely known Honey-coombe could be a target for greedy men, and of those there were always more than enough since the land was no longer at peace. We knew there had been war in the land, but our home was overlooked since it was small and lay hidden in the vast sweep of the uplands.

We lay to the South of the older, more populous dales; South and West with only the final hills between us and the great Waste. A narrow trail swept out in a loop to pass the gates of ourselves and Merrowdale. Yet, while few passed and fewer stopped, we were content. Ithia's small stone house stood at the far end of the village. The road from Merrowdale ran along the slope above. On it one day, as Spring was almost upon us, I saw people walking.

I peered about for Ithia. I did not like what I saw and she was my refuge, the answerer of my questions. I was too late. She was already striding towards the road and those who came limping along it. I followed. By the time I reached her others of the village were there and gossip ran in a buzz of whispering like the hum of angry bees. Well might there be anger. Those who came were the tattered remnants of Merrowdale, fallen not to the invaders but to a large band of our own. Once some lord's soldiers, now they were half-mad and masterless men. Of prosperous Merrowdale only the dozen or so who stood before us had escaped. I saw the Lord Lanson himself listening in silence at the edge of the crowd.

A tall old woman leaned on her staff, shivering in the chill air. Her face was bitter, her mouth twisted in pain and grief.

"I am Merith Eralsdaughter. They came in the early morning. They laid in wait, and once many within the keep were out and about they began their killing. With the keep doors open they entered and killed all within, then they raged through the village. The master-at-arms survived to rally the men for a little. But those who came killed without sense or mercy as rabid beasts kill."

Her tall figure bent a little, as if cradling pain. "We were weak. Our lord and his sons took all those able-bodied men to the last battle. He and his sons did not return. Only a handful of his men came home and they were each left crippled in some way. Our lord's lady ruled us well, our master-at-arms was her cousin. He and his few men died trying to save her and those in the keep."

Lord Lanson spoke without accusation. "How then came you and those alive from that slaughter?"

She straightened a little. "I was up with a sick ewe. I saw what would come to us and took up supplies in a bag. Then I left. In cover on the hills I waited to aid those who survived—if any did. I know a little of herbs and heal-craft. Better to aid the wounded than add one old fool to the slaughter."

Ithia took her hands then. "Be welcome, sister. What you did was wise. And these?" Her gesture encompassed those tattered figures which slumped on the ground, blood staining their clothing here and there.

"They are from the village. Hann was our baker. He, too, was awake early. The woman is his wife, the girl and the boy here theirs." I judged the girl to be almost fourteen, the boy perhaps a year younger. The woman looked up at Merith's words, her eyes blank. She wailed softly. Merith spoke. "Her oldest daughter was maid to the lady of the keep. Although we waited in hiding, the girl did not win free to join us." Merith resumed the count. "Tral and his sister, Trela, were caring for a sick cow. They escaped un-harmed, also bringing out their mother from the house. The other four are men whom we met on the road. They come from Hastdale. That, too, has fallen, or so they have told us."

About us I saw faces agape in horror. Always the war had seemed so far away. But we knew Merrowdale our neighbor. Hastdale, almost a week's journey to the North, and with which we occasionally traded, had also fallen? Would we be next? Merith was still talking.

"My mother was nurse to Lord Malrion's mother, we were children together and friends. He talked frankly to me of the things he learned. The war is ended. The invaders flee. But many dales were destroyed. Too many soldiers have lost lord and home and hope. They ravage now like hunger-maddened weasels. If they have nothing, not even hope left to them, then that, too, they shall deny to those of us who still possess something."

"What sought these ones in Merrowdale?" That was my father.

"What such men always seek: loot, women, mounts to replace those lost." She bowed her head. "They came in strength to our dale: many less will leave." Her head came up in pride. "Our people fought. They were not taken like rabbits which scream and cower beneath the weasel's fangs. Blood-price they had for their going." She slumped again, staying on her feet with difficulty. Ithia lent her shoulder.

"Come. Best you have food, drink, and a bed." Her eyes sought Lord Lanson. He nodded, leaving these decisions to Ithia.

"The village will take you in. Let any family who can host one of these come forward. Merith, you shall guest with me and my apprentice. I think Lord Lanson will have other work. In the morning you shall speak with him as he wishes." Recalled to himself, our keep lord nodded again to Ithia and hastened away. I joined my teacher and added a younger shoulder to Merith's support.

I was just turned thirteen. We had celebrated my name day barely ten days gone. All my life had been without sorrow. I found the tale more exciting than fearful. Besides, Honeycoombe was apart. Only those who knew where it lay would find it. And none from here had ridden to the war. Lord Lanson had no soldiers. At need the men of the village armed to follow him, but he kept no men permanently under arms save Jerin. I grinned at the thought.

Jerin had been arms-master to both Lord Lanson and his father, the Lord Lanrale. Jerin was a spare upright old man who now taught weapons-work to the lads of our village. But he was *old*. Nonetheless, it was Jerin who came striding to our house soon after dusk. He would have spoken privately with Merith and Ithia, but Ithia insisted I share their discussion.

"She is a child."

"Would you say so if she were male? She is thirteen and sensible. And if the killers come, will they say she is a child, harm her not?" Ithia's voice was tart.

Jerin grunted. "Well enough. Let her listen."

So listen I did. At first I could not believe what he said, but the women nodded and agreed. We were to make up travel bags. A watch would be set on the main road. If those we feared were seen the alarm would be given and all would flee into the hills. My own father was even now taking the three pack-ponies owned by the village into the uplands. They would bide in the hut on Foral Ridge. The killers would not have them and if we must flee we would have the ponies to aid our escape.

Ithia spoke then. "All this is wise. Spring comes swiftly now. I will bespeak the bees. If the weather holds we can move them from the village. The lower uplands hold more than one sheltered place where they will be ready to work.

And if those you fear come, we will have no time to move hives."

"Do as you see fit, Wise One." Jerin gave agreement. He paused at the door then before he left. "Let you all carry knives. If at the last there is no other choice, see that they are keen of point."

I did not know then what he meant, but later Ithia told me. I gaped at her. Slay myself? How? I had never thought to do such a thing. I had no idea where or how to strike. She showed me patiently until I knew the blow. I understood something else then; that this was no longer excitement fit for a child. I think in those moments, as I learned how to kill myself, that I also aged. Ithia eyed me closely.

"I have a great task for you, craft-daughter." I waited. "You shall go with the bees to the uplands when we move them. I have in mind the furthest pastures, where there is a cave. A small stream runs nearby. You know the place?" I nodded. "Good. You shall take a supply of the Winter-syrup. If the weather chills again you can feed the hives." She smiled gently. "Take with you your Queen which Welwyn made you. I shall see you have all else."

That she did, loading one pony with bedding, food, the Winter-syrup, and other small comforts. We left the next day. Behind us trudged the ponies, the other two loaded with the carefully lashed hives, which hummed with anticipation. The hives were light enough so that behind them the two also pulled long, hive-laden sledges. We would return the next day for the remaining hives. We did that and spent the day setting out the hives so that their inhabitants' flight-lines should be free of strife. The cave was small but deep. With Ithia's preparations it would be warm and comfortable for me. I felt buoyed up by a sense of importance.

She left me early the morning after that. Before she did so she took me in her arms and hugged me warmly. Then she tilted my chin up with one hand and stared into my eyes as if impressing what she would say upon my mind. "I trust you with our wing-friends, Meive. You are kin to them. In a time of need they will rise to protect you." She turned to stare out across the swathes of white and purple beelove just beginning to bloom in the early Spring warmth.

"I love you, child. Your family loves you. Remain here, guard the bees as they will guard you. Do not return unless one of us comes to fetch you. Your mother has said she will visit you every three days and bring food. If one day she does not come, you have supplies. Wait another three days before you return and walk with great caution. It may be ill has befallen. It will help no one if you fall into danger with us." She left then, long walking staff swinging in one sun-browned hand.

Now I think that she had some fore-warning. But little of that gift was hers. She saw only that death reached out for Honeycoombe, yet not when or how it should come. When it did not come at once, those of my home were lulled into believing that they could be safe. Thrice my mother made the journey to my cave with food. The third time she arrived before midday and shared my noonday meal. I sat her down with ceremony, offering water from the tiny spring, and honey-cakes made on a fire-heated stone. She gave formal thanks with a smile. Then she sobered.

"I came early this time, Meive. I would tell you of something you should know."

"Why I can bespeak the bees?"

"Yes. Your father does not know. But my grandmother told me before she died." My mother sighed and looked out across the sweet-scented beelove. "Our line lived in Merrowdale at that time. When my grandmother's mother was young she was betrothed to a man she loved and who loved her. The wedding was but a week away. But betrothed, too, was the lord's daughter and many had already arrived for her wedding. Amongst them was one lord's son of a line at which all looked sideways. It was whispered their blood had mingled with those Old Ones still here when the dales were settled." My mother looked at me.

"You are old enough to know of such things. My grandmother's mother was in the high field caring for the sheep when he found her there. He used her as a woman and left her weeping. She fled to her lord's lady and demanded justice. The Lord of Merrowdale was greatly angered by the tale and justice he gave. He could not slay the man for fear of blood-feud. And besides, he rode with other kin who might have fought such a decision. But he stripped him of all that evil man possessed and drove him forth from the dale. Then he gave the plunder to she whom the lad had outraged."

"And her betrothed?"

"He loved her, blaming her not. He held to the bond. But they took what they had and followed their lord's younger son here to Honeycoombe. With what they had been given they purchased the building of a home. His coin and gems purchased them a cow for milk, and other things. And in time my grandmother was born."

"She had the gift?"

"So she told it to me. But she, too, wed a man she loved and laid aside her gift, such an ability being one which can be set aside at will. I had none. But she warned me that often the gift passed by a generation. That my daughter might have some measure of it. In that it seems she was right."

I nodded, thinking. My father loved my mother well. But he feared the Old Ones. Even the tales of them he would not hear. To know that my mother's blood had come through such a thing would have distressed him greatly, even perhaps driven him from her. I met her eyes.

"I understand. To know something is no reason to speak of it. But I would know the name of that man and his dale." My mother whispered it. Then added more. "He was of the line of Paltendale. His father was lord, but the evil one was a younger son. Their arms are shown as a heart pierced by a dagger and a deer with one antler broken short."

After that we spent some hours in simple gossip. I heard

of the small doings of the village. Amongst these I learned that Welwyn was courting Annet, Hann the Baker's daughter. They had come with the refugees. My mother seemed pleased with that and I also. It would be pleasant to have a new kinswoman and I had liked what little I saw of the girl.

My mother left with a parting hug and murmured affection. I watched her pass over the ridge and it was as if of a sudden a chill wind blew through me. I wished to run after her, cling, and swear that I loved her. But I held myself back. This was some Spring breeze and—my mother knew well I loved her.

V

I returned to my cave and tidied it slowly. Then I went to sit with the bees and reach out to touch their minds. I shared their busy lives the remainder of that day, and after I had slept I was myself again. But when the next time for my mother to visit came, she did not. And again that chill wind crawled over my skin. Even sharing hive-life could not distract me. I walked again and again part-way along the path. I climbed higher above my cave and stared far out across the lower hills, straining to see if any approached. None did. To and fro I wandered in an agony of indecision. Ithia had said I was to wait three days. But what if my family needed me?

Yet—the village needed the winged-ones more than any aid I could render. If I deserted the hives and aught happened, how would I face Ithia? I waited the three days and then a fourth. None could say I had not obeyed spirit as well as the letter of my orders. But on the fifth morning I went forth and bespoke the hive queens and their small fierce warriors.

"Wing-kin, I fear danger has overtaken my hive. I must journey to seek out if this be so. Be safe until I may return."

A soft humming arose stretching out to encompass me. I did rightly. One's hive was life. I should learn the fate of mine. But even as I had cared for them and been accepted as hive-kin, so they should care for me. Let me go but return once I knew. Then whatever I did I should have guards of their providing for the path I walked.

I bowed and spoke words of thanks, smiling a little in the midst of my worry. What guards could the bees afford? But I would not have insulted my friends by saying so. I lifted my carrysack, took up the staff I had carved in imitation of the one Ithia carried, and set out upon the path to Honeycoombe. It was less than a half day's brisk tramp but I recalled Ithia's warnings. I circled from the path, taking my rest that night two miles short of the village. I lit no fire but ate cold food and drank chill clear water from a stream.

At dawn I moved unwillingly towards Honeycoombe. I think I already knew death had come there. My nose told me first with the stench of smoke. I lay in the heather looking down upon what had been my home. Two of the cottages had burned. The lord's stone house sent up still a wisp of smoke. Stone will not burn but wooden paneling and furniture burn very well. My eyes turned to my own home. Near the door bundles lay motionless while flies buzzed about them.

I felt sickness rise in my throat and vomited it up. I could recognize the dress one wore; the jacket on another. Below me my parents and brother lay still, abandoned to the feasting flies. I vomited again and again before I forced my gaze to turn elsewhere. Ithia? What of her whom I also loved? It took me the whole day to circle the village, staying from known paths. At last I was sure whoever had done this thing had gone from my dale. At least for now. Then I went down.

My family were dead. Welwyn and my father had died fighting. My sisters lay dead upon their beds, stabbed to the heart. By my mother I think, before she went out to

fight. She, too, was dead, the dagger hilt still with her hand
clasped about it. But by her other hand lay a pitchfork
where it had fallen as she released it to snatch out her dagger. The pitchfork tines were red their whole length. And in
front of her there was a great puddle of dried blood. More
blood before my da and brother showed they, too, had
fought well. I felt a bitter pride. Whoever had come here
had gone away lessened in numbers by the meeting.

There was nothing I could do but give them burial, and
that could wait a little. I started running towards the small
stone cottage up-slope from the other houses. Ithia, could
she have survived? She was wise. Surely, oh surely, Ithia,
of them all . . . I reached the door and spoke her name very
softly. A low croak answered. My heart leaped. She lived!
I entered peering about, seeking her familiar lean figure.
Why did she not come to greet me? The croak came again
and I saw. My body gave me no warning this time. I simply
leaned to one side and spewed up all that was in me. Over
and over until blood taste filled my throat. Then I wiped
my mouth and moved forward numbly.

They had—but no. I will not recall what they had done.
Man of all creatures is the only one which does such things
and I do not wish to remember what was done to Ithia. She
lived only another hour. She had held on to life waiting for
my return. There was no time to tell me how this had happened, nor any need once she said the name of he who had
brought the killers here. Neeco! Thrice cursed, thrice
damned. Kin-slayer, betrayer.

I listened to that weak thread of voice. From here and
there I was to take food and drink. In the lord's house I
should open a certain place in a wall. There I would find
wealth. That, too, I was to take. Those who had come were
gone but for a while only. They hunted the hills but would
return. They must not know any had survived. It was for
that also Ithia had denied my aid. Let them find her dead
where they had left her.

But here in her home she would give me one last gift. I obeyed her directions and stood holding the treasure. A great treasure to be sure, ten small bone phials of the honey-cordial, each laid in a pocket within a small padded bag with a strap for carrying. A treasure for which any dale's lord would give gold. I would have traded them all for Ithia's life. She saw that and gave a tiny broken smile.

"I am not worth so much, craft-daughter. Do as I say, then flee."

"My mother, da?" I could not leave my family unburied.

"Must stay as they are, I have told you what to do. Take what you find and leave. Do not look back." Still I hesitated. Ithia visibly gathered the last of her power and I felt her will bear down on me, blurring my grief and giving me strength.

"Go, my blessing on you all the days of your life. Follow the path but first go back to the winged-ones and tell them of my death. It is fitting they are told by the one who will be their wise woman hereafter. Go, *now*." She fell back and I saw her spirit flicker low like a spent candle. Cordial pack in hand, tears filling my eyes, I fled towards the door.

From Ithia's body I heard a strange soft humming begin, but I did not pause. Her final order and the demand in her eyes held me from turning back. I reached the lord's house and entered, averting my eyes from those who lay within. Portions of some of the walls and a heap of broken furniture had burned, but not all. At the wall behind the High Seat I pressed the carved pattern. Little enough was there of wealth by the standard of the richer dales, but for me it was a fortune. A little gold, more of silver, and a handful of small uncut gems such as are sometimes washed from streams.

I stowed these items within Ithia's cordial bag. Then I moved towards the kitchen. My mother had worked for Lord Lanson whenever he had guests. I knew the kitchen secrets. The cheese press door had no handle and seemed part of the wall. It was opened by a thrust at one side after which it revolved on a center spindle. Within lay rounds of cheese, hard of rind and rich from the goat's milk and added herbs. To one side was a large stack of journey-bread. Hard-crusted disks baked perhaps a day or so before death came hunting. They would last weeks yet. I took all of both I could carry.

The cupboard was not yet emptied and I stood in thought. I was alone now. Ithia had been sure those who had done this would return, but not yet. I would risk a little extra time. I loaded cheese and bread into a bag I made from a discarded shirt. That I carried part-way to cover. I returned to forage. A short sword and dagger laid away in a chest. A warm woolen cloak. A length of cloth with needles and thread. Nothing too bulky or heavy save the food. But I would be more likely to survive with these articles to aid me.

I got the bundles to cover, left them lying under bracken, and returned to my own home. If I was to do naught else I could bid my family farewell. Tell them I loved them one last time. I knelt by the bodies, my throat choked with tears. Oh, my sisters and I had argued now and again. But never in malice. They had rejoiced with me when I had been chosen by the bees. I spoke the words of farewell and kissed their cold cheeks. From each I took an unobtrusive scrap of their clothing. Once I was safe I would sew these into a memory quilt. It would be an heirloom for my house.

I found a wry grin twisting my face. An heirloom for my house? What house? I was alone. But still I added the tatters of cloth to my bag. Then I went down to do the same for da, mother, and Welwyn. I completed the task, weeping again until my eyes were sore and my nose blocked so that I snuffled the last words over them rather than spoke. I rose at last from my knees. There was no more I could do if I was not to bury them. As I left the village I would pass Ithia's house. I had to see her one last time. To speak the words of farewell over my craft-mother also.

I hesitated at the door. I could not see her body in the dimness. Then as my eyes adjusted I saw the outline and something moved. Alive! She was still . . . she could not be. I had seen her die. It must be a rat, some filthy scavenger come to feed. It appeared to be about that size. I sprang forward with a cry of rage, my staff upheld to strike. Then I saw what lay on Ithia's breast. A slow feeling of awe crept over me. My staff lowered as I met great faceted eyes. Love, warm and sweet as honey flowed over me, healing, smoothing out the jagged edges of memory.

Liquid sweet, a voice sounded in my mind. "Craft-daughter. Do as I bade you. Blessed be." I stepped back, permitting the light-haloed queen free passage. Golden wings fanned as she rose. For a moment she hovered, one wing brushing my cheek in a gentle caress. Then she was gone, rising into the fading sunlight, the color of it glinting bright on her wings. I watched as she vanished towards the hills. Quietly, I took up a piece of Ithia's torn clothing. That, too, should go into the quilt I would sew. But I would have no need of it to remember her.

Over the next two days I returned to my cave and the hives. It took time to transport my plunder and that I did not wish to leave behind. I kept a good lookout both before and behind me as I walked but there was no sign as yet of anyone returning. With everything stowed safe I walked to stand in the midst of the hives. With the winged-ones I shared my loss, my sorrow, and the manner of Ithia's going. Both how she had died and what I had seen thereafter. I felt their anger and sorrow merge with mine. The loss of a sister hive grieved them. The loss of their fellow queen, Ithia, still more. But, they assured me, now I was chosen queen in her place. It was for me to begin a new hive.

I protested aloud. "I cannot. I have no one, nothing. I am alone." Events crashed in on me as I knew that for the truth. Everything was gone. My home, my family, Ithia. The comfort she had given me faded as I faced the truth. Sooner or later raiders would find me and I would die.

Slowly and miserably if I could not contrive a quicker
death of my own. I did not wish to die. I sat up slowly from
the earth hummock where I had flung myself to weep.

"I don't want to die. I want to live." My voice deepened
to a hoarse snarl. "I want those who came to Honeycoombe
punished. I want them dead."

The hives hummed agreement. In the sound there was an
anger and savagery to equal mine. A command reached
me. I was to eat, drink, sleep in my place, and wait. I did
not wish to wait. I wanted to act now. What would they do?
The queens' thin honey-sweet voices were a needle boring
into my mind. I was young, with no hive to command as
yet. I should obey. I should wait. I waited as I was bid and
waiting was worth the aggravation it cost me. From the
hives of the two new queens came forth bees the like of
which I had never seen.

Warriors many times the size of a normal bee. They
were completely black and their buzzing was a low dangerous sound which held menace even to me who did not fear
them. Behind they bore stingers over an inch long. One
came to settle on my shoulder. His wings touched my lips
as I turned to study him. I reached up to stroke the black
fur with a fingertip.

"You are strange to me, winged-warrior. But very beautiful." I allowed my mind to hold the same thought so that
the winged-one might understand. In reply the buzzing
came with a pleased note, as the queens hummed approval
from their hives.

Then they pulled me deeper into communion. I swam in
gold, in thoughts of honey and brood cells, of a hive reborn
and what must be done. What could be done. When I came
to myself again I was lying between the hives. The new
warriors came flying to circle me. From them I received
pictures that made me gasp. I saw men, back in Honeycoombe. From the warriors came a rising tide of anger.
These were the killers. The despoilers of the hive. Soon
they would venture in search of me. I must be ready.

"What must I do?" Approval from the queens. It was right and proper that a new young queen should seek wisdom from her elders.

"Wait."

I groaned. "What, again?"

Dark amusement from the warriors and the queens. "Ah, sister queen. *This* waiting will end to your liking. Go. Sleep. Prepare. Be ready to do as we ask when the time comes."

I staggered to my feet and went to my cave. The fire was only coals but I woke it to flames. I ate heartily of the plundered bread and cheese, drank water from my tiny stream, and when exhaustion swept over me, I lay down and slept the night through in dreamless slumber. I woke in the morning, more calm in my mind, and with an idea.

Ithia had bought the new queens from the shrine she visited. If I survived I would go there, taking the hives. Within it the winged-ones would be safe. I would likely be safer there also should such entrance be permitted me. My decision made, I ate and drank again, banked my fire, and determined to spy on the invaders of Honeycoombe. I talked to the queens before I set off. They did not say me nay, but about me when I walked along the trail lined with beelove my warriors flew scout, a full half hundred of them now.

I came to the edge of Landale and lay on my stomach to look quietly through the bushes and dry grass. It was not yet full Spring and the ground struck chill into my body. I remained motionless, watching. I had been cold before, and those whom I loved lay colder still. I saw below through a sudden mist of tears. Then my gaze sharpened. I felt rage flush my face, fury race through my veins. Below Neeco strutted, walking at the right hand of the older man who gave orders to the ravagers of my home.

Neeco, come home to murder those who had sent him forth. I remembered his threats on that day. He had been assistant kennel-boy in Merrowdale. Here he clearly had power and status somehow. Perhaps because he knew many secrets in both Merrowdale and Honeycoombe? Maybe the man at whose side he walked had some special fondness for him? I did not know—or care. Neeco had brought death to all I had loved. He should die in turn. How I should bring home that death to him I did not know. But it should be so. I swore it in my heart, then moved to watch from a better vantage point. Know thine enemy.

The cheeky lad I recalled was gone. In his place a man of eighteen strutted. I could see the arrogance in his manner as he spoke to those with him. I thought they did not like or trust him, but something kept them from him. Whatever that was it would not keep me from my vengeance when the time came.

It took two days before those below were done looting. It had been completed with method and with less destruction than I feared. The leader had sent his men from house to house. Everything portable of value had been placed in a farm wagon. It was the largest wheeled thing ever brought through our narrow entrance, I believe. But they had maneuvered it past the entrance stones and down the steep slope.

Six of the big, slow, powerful farm horses came with it. I watched them covetously. If Honeycoombe had such we could have produced more food. There are some things a small pony cannot do, sturdy and willing as ours were. I wondered if I could set the beasts loose in the night, but the leader had them taken to a barn and guarded. As well he might. Each of them was worth a handful of silver to any lord. A team of six was almost beyond price, though all six were geldings and so could not breed.

I waited, and then it became clear Neeco had seen the bees were gone. He came walking with the Leader not far below where I lay hidden. Their talk floated upwards and I listened fiercely.

"No bees. That means they moved them early to the uplands."

"We've done well enough, dear lad. We have no need of bees." There was a caressing laugh to the leader's voice as the boy leaned into his shoulder. So that was Neeco's protection.

"It isn't the bees."

"Then what?"

"The cordial. I tell you, Garlen, lords paid in gold for one small phial, *when* the old witch would share it."

"The men searched her house. They found nothing."

"Of course not." Neeco's tone was patronizing and I saw sudden annoyance flash across Garlen's face. Neeco should be wary.

"Why, of course not?"

"Because she had an apprentice. The girl will be in the high pastures with the hives. The cordial was probably sent with her for safe-keeping. She'll have the village ponies as well. Three of them, all good hill stock. Maybe other things we can use as well."

"Apart from her, you mean." Their laughter was evil and I shivered. Little enough of mercy would I get if these found me.

"Well, you were saying only last night that the men needed a diversion. These peasants fight more ferociously than they expected."

Garlen chuckled. "So I did say. True enough. In the morning we'll hunt out this girl. She can't know what's happened here. Had she been back she would have buried her kin. Unless she's cleverer than I'd give credit to?"

Neeco snorted in open contempt. "She's daughter to that one who pitch-forked Aylin. No brains in the family, just some gift the old witch wanted to foster."

His leader smiled slowly. "Why then, she'll be easily taken. We have only to go to meet her with the right tale. She'll accept that and we'll have her and all else she may be hiding. As for any gift, that'll go from her as soon as we've had done. Tonight we'll broach a barrel of the ale you found. We'll set out on our hunt in the morning once we've eaten and recovered somewhat." They walked away to rejoin their men, who were still laughing in anticipation.

I sneered after them. About my gift they were wrong, I knew. I was not one of the witches from across the seas. The bee-gift is one which is held so long as the possessor wishes. It can be willed from her but not stolen or destroyed. As for Neeco's other plans, forewarned is forearmed, I thought as I lay there. I might not be such easy prey as they expected. Then despair swept over me. I was untrained in weaponry. I was a girl and only thirteen. How could I fight more than twenty trained men?

One of the winged-warriors sensed my fear and grief. He landed on my shoulder and on the opposite shoulder a queen landed, sending me warmth and comfort, cradling me in thoughts of honey-sweetness and the affection of the hive. But from the warrior flowed a deep hunger. The queens would be my advisers, they were the females who were wise for the hives. The warriors would be my weapons. Let the despoilers of the hive keep their ignorance, soon enough they would learn how dangerous even tiny warriors could be.

I did not know what the wing-friends had in mind, but I believed in their promises of protection and vengeance. I slept that night in a nest of heather and dried grass, woke to eat of the food I had brought with me, then drank from my flask, holding out the cap so my friends might drink in turn. Then I lay down at the edge of the valley again to watch. The fires below had burned high late into the night. I'd heard the sounds of men who became drunk and quarrelsome. That explained their slow rising on a fine clear day.

They came lurching and grumbling to where their leader waited. Neeco stood beside him, smirking triumphantly. No doubt but that today he expected to slay the last in the dale that had exiled him. Why he hated so, I could not see. He had gone to a good home and the Lord of Merrowdale had been well-known as a kind man. Neeco could well have returned to visit his family each Summer once the bees were in the high pastures. Yet that, by his own choosing, he had rejected. Judging from the chaos below it would be an hour or more yet before they set out. I was young, unencumbered, and I knew every inch of the path. I could beat them back to the hives easily. I did so and stood between the two which housed the new queens.

I told the queens all I had seen, sharing in my mind the pictures as I spoke. In return a plan was unfolded, spare and elegant in its simplicity. I nodded slowly as I listened. It might work. If it did not I could always die. My mother had found no difficulty and I had the dagger taken from Lord Lanson's house. I hid that in my bodice and went to do what my queens had shown me. There was ample time before I heard the men approaching. I could even add a few touches of my own.

The raiders found my cave in order but empty. I had banked the fire and left my large cauldron simmering. That was the one Ithia had always used to make bee-syrup in Winter. It was of a very good size, and bronze. A prize in its own right and I had filled it with a savory well-salted stew. On a rock ledge nearby I'd set the last remaining flasks of mead, those I had taken from Ithia's house. *I* had known where to look. In that, Neeco had been correct—those who'd come before me had not.

I lay in the beelove and counted as the outlaws came straggling down the valley track. All twenty-one of them were here. No doubt any feared to stay behind lest their fellows find loot and refuse to share. And my own self would not be the least of that expected plunder. Around the rock outcrop in which lay my cave the breeze always swirled. I lay hidden to one side. The light winds would carry their words to me clearly. I listened and waited.

"Girl's not there, Garlen."

"Make less noise. She's left all tidy. She can't have gone back to the village else we'd have met her on the way here. Neeco, where could she be?"

"Likely she's gone to the uplands. Ithia used to. They look for flowering bushes where they can move the hives in high Summer."

The leader gave a satisfied grunt. "That sounds likely. All right. Look through her cave but throw nothing about outside. Tarro, go to the hill and watch for her."

The man addressed growled. "Why me? Let someone else go. I'll not let my chances of finding something here slip by." His tone turned sly. "Let the boy go. You'll share anything you find with him, won't you, Captain?"

Garlen said no more, but nor did he order Neeco to lookout. It seemed as if the man had some authority over those he led, but not so much they would forego the chance of loot, even at his orders. I smiled to myself. All the better if that was true. I'd left loot for them to find. A cry from my cave signaled that they had done so.

"Garlen! Mead!"

"What's that, lad?"

"Those flasks up there. I've seen them before. They contain mead. Ithia's best."

A deeper older voice cut in. "Ah, do they? Then we'll have a sniff at this." There was a pause and I could imagine him grabbing a flask down, taking a mouthful and savoring the fiery distilled contents. There came a loud gasp.

"Wheeoo, Captain. That's mighty powerful stuff. But by the Gods it goes down so smooth you wouldn't know until it arrives." There came a hubbub as the bandits all clamored to taste. Then the one who had drank first spoke again.

"Look, Captain. There's a fine stew here, mead to drink, and we're where the girl'll not see us when she returns. Let us stay here, use her food and drink . . ."

"And then her," another voice cut in. "Reckon it'd be only right if'n she shares her food 'n drink with us. Then we shares us with her." There was rough laughter and cries of agreement.

I thought from the sound of their voices that Garlen had

little choice. There was a dangerous note to the demand. I heard his voice agreeing.

"That's not a bad idea, Saren. All right, find bowls or use your own. Neeco, share out the stew. And you'll not be drinking." He over-rode the boy's anger. "Saren, wait until everyone has a mug of some sort, then share out the drink. None for the boy, mind."

I listened to the sounds as men gobbled down my stew. They smacked their lips thirstily over the mead and regretted that there was not more of it. I smiled bitterly. The five flasks were all which was left after Winter. But they would find there had been enough and more for them. They were used to drinking beer. The rough ale they usually drank would make a man sick before he became falling-down drunk.

The flasks of Ithia's mead were twice distilled. Even the mug each of them would drink would be enough to send their wits wandering. Ithia's mead was usually drunk from thick-walled thumb-sized glasses in tiny sips that barely wetted the lips. If it was offered in larger glasses then it was watered down by many times the volume. But each man would here drink ten or twelve times the usual tiny amounts. Neeco would not have known, when had *he* ever sat at the high table to see how Ithia's mead was taken?

In an hour those within my cave were finding the mead a heady brew. Their voices rose. Then one staggered from the cave holding his belly. He groaned, sinking to the ground unnoticed. Another joined him. Now the voices rose, but no longer in their rough humor. There was fear in the sound now. I waited in my hiding place. At last no sounds arose save Neeco's cries to them. Those, too, ceased and I guessed he plundered his erstwhile comrades.

I hummed a silent call in my mind. Winged warriors attended me as I went down to meet our betrayer. He walked from the cave, a bulging pack in one hand.

I nodded politely. "Neeco."

I saw his face whiten as he took in my escort. But he was quick enough of wits. How should he know how much I knew?

"Meive. I—I have ill news for you. How long have you been here alone in these hills?"

"I came here more than eighteen days ago," I said truthfully, and saw his mouth curve in a tiny smile of relief.

"Then, you do not know?"

"What should I know, Neeco?"

"The invaders. They found Honeycoombe. All are dead. They came to Merrowdale first. I was out with the dogs and escaped."

"And the dogs?" I thought that part of the tale could be at least half true.

"I followed the invaders with them. I attacked when and as I could. One by one they killed the dogs. Now I am alone. Then these men found me." A sweep of his hand indicated the tumbled bodies. "They were bad men. I have prayed to escape them. Now I have." His eyes fixed on me. "They drank Ithia's mead and died. Why was that, Meive?"

In my mind I touched my warriors. Let them be ready. A humming in my mind assured me that they were. They would strike at my command. At last I could let my hatred show. I smiled.

"Why else, Neeco? Because while it was many days gone since first I came here, I had returned home in that time. I saw what you and your friends did in Honeycoombe. I know you led them here. I came back and poisoned the mead. I knew they would not leave it be." His eyes were turned fearfully now to my warriors as they rose to surround him.

"And me. I didn't drink."

"You should have done so," I told him quietly. "You'd have preferred that death."

He acted as I expected, striking at me. My warriors did not even need my command. They swarmed about him, plunging their stingers into him again and again as he screamed and ran. I had sworn to accomplish his death but I was sickened. It took him time to die. Yet all his pain would not bring back my kin, my friends, or Ithia, my craft-mother, and after a time I could not bear to see and hear his suffering, so in the end I took up my dagger and gave him mercy.

VI

---◆---

So I fetched the ponies and labored for the remainder of the day. I had no need to check the bodies for anything of use. Neeco had already done that for me. I had merely to take his pack. But I hitched a pony to the bodies, one by one, and allowed the pony to drag them to a cliff. I rolled the contorted figures over the edge. Let them lie below, prey to the buzzards which would feast. Neeco's body I sent hurtling downwards last of all. Perhaps his family would have preferred that he lie with them but I could not allow it. By his own actions he was not of us. Let him lie with those friends he had taken.

After that, I returned a while to stay in my dale. There was no need to do anything for Ithia. Her body had crumbled to a fine pollenlike dust by the time I gained my vengeance and returned. I took up a pinch of that and added it to my amulet. The remainder I burned as I wept. Then I used the ponies to aid me as, one by one, I laid the bodies of my kin and friends to rest. It was exhausting and brutal work and I think I was a little mad. I hummed to my bees as I worked, talked to them and discussed what I should do next.

When I was done, I shut up the cottages and the keep as best I could. If I ever returned they should not be ruined with the damp or infested with vermin. Lastly I dealt with the horses. The bandits had their own thin abused beasts. And then there was the team of great-horses. I rounded up all of them, tying them into a pack-train. Taking up the reins of the first of them I led the string down our dale and into the inner valley. The entrance to that was narrow. I left the beasts to feed and blocked their gateway. They could live out their lives in safety there, even if I never returned.

At last I straddled a pony and returned to the hives. I would take my winged-ones back to the place where Ithia had found the new queens. They should be safe even if I died or must leave. I used the sledges and the ponies, moving the hives in two journeys. Each time I halted just short of my goal. When all were there and I could delay no longer, I called the warriors, who surrounded me. With them came the two stranger queens, one alighting on each of my shoulders. In one hand I carried Welwyn's queen.

I reached the shrine and stared about. It was plain, but there was a simple beauty in the curves of stone and the shades of the pavement about the shrine. The small open center building was set in the midst of a five-pointed star. This was outlined with strips of a lighter stone, a warm pale honey. The inner portions ranged from a darker honey to a gentle honey-brown. Somehow the very colors soothed me.

The queens flew ahead, alighting on the edge of a small basin by the building's doorway. They reached out to call me and I obeyed. Even as they, I drank some of what the basin contained. Then I lifted my head and gasped. It was mead—of a sort. But such a sort as any wise woman of the bees would have given her right arm to brew. I could feel strength and healing pulse through me. Still stronger grew the link between my winged-ones and I.

I turned to face the building's entrance. "To the giver of the feast, fair thanks." That was well enough said, but the rest did not seem right. I improvised. "Bright sun and a great hosting of flowers on the morrow. May your wings ever bear you safely and may you have always clean water for your hive." That seemed right. I bowed again and waited.

From the shadowed entrance there came a soft sweet humming. It shifted key and became a voice.

"Enter and be welcome, daughter of my hive."

I moved forward slowly, allowing the voice time to deny me yet, or to give other commands. Nothing came as I passed under the door-frame. A golden light pervaded the room. And in it I saw.

So small a building it had seemed from the outside. But within, it appeared to shimmer, stretching far out before me. At the end of that distance one sat on a great chair, carved in a wood like molten honey. Many would have feared the figure she made. But I saw only the outstretched hand and the kindness in the many-faceted eyes. I stumbled forward, her arms closed about me, and on her shoulder I wept out all my sorrow and loss.

At last she stood, putting me gently from her. "You have wrought well, daughter of my hive. In turn it shall be well-wrought for you. Time shall pass. For that time you shall remain here in safety."

"How long?"

She smiled. "I do not count time here. The wheel turns and when it has come full circle your time will come with it. Be patient and at peace." Her hand lifted to trace a sign. Then—she was gone, but now within the building I had entered I could see a small plain room open to one side. Within was a bed, a washbasin, and such other things as I might need. A table to one side held food. Nectar bread and honey, with an ewer of water, the chill beading the sides.

And so I took up my abode. Welwyn's queen I placed on a ledge where I could see it when I rose each morning. My lady of the shrine spoke truly. Time seemed to slip away so fast it was as if the seasons blurred. Summer rushed past. The bright leaves of the coming Winter appeared, then the first snows. I had feared I would be cold when that came, but some spell about the shrine held back the chill from those within. I was grateful for the care given, yet I did not wish to lose all touch with my own lands. I found bark, melted wax, and made tablets on which to scratch notes of time as it passed and things which I learned.

My lady was kind enough to talk with me now and then, to teach me what I asked, and I learned hungrily as I had learned from Ithia. Of my craft-mother I asked, but of her the lady would say nothing. In that timeless place I could feel my gifts flex and strengthen. Summer came—for the third time I believed. If I was right, then I was now sixteen. My lady summoned me.

"Time has turned for you, daughter, and it is your time. Go from my shrine and seek."

I bowed my head, then looked up. "Lady, what do I seek?"

Her smile was kind. "What all desire. A hive of one's own. Pastures wherein to gather nectar. New daughter-queens to follow you."

I considered that. I thought I was being told that I should go and find a home, a mate, and children. Or at least an apprentice. Into my mind there came warm laughter.

"Even so. Listen well, daughter of my hive. Beyond my place evil has come to walk. Yet from it shall come good if you face it valiantly. One there shall be whose kin-name you know. Remember, the wheel turns. Do not reject good honey though bees from that hive have stung in the past." She lifted a hand and pointed. "Go, and remember what you have learned here." A golden rune flamed in the air and my warriors came to cluster about me. I bowed and turned.

My lady's advice and teaching had always been good before. I would believe that it was so again. I went to my room and changed clothes, donning trews and a tunic. If evil walked outside the shrine there might be need for me to run. That would be easier without long skirts. About my waist I girded the dagger and sword I had taken from Lord Lanson's home. Welwyn's queen caught my eye. If I failed in this quest I might not return. Once I had thought to gift it to my lady. I had not done so then; now I should.

Picking up the figure, I carried it to the place where the wall would draw aside. It did so and I paced forward into the inner room where lay an altar. I laid the queen thereon and spoke softly.

"I go to battle evil and who knows the roads I may take or if I shall return. I offer this as a guest-gift. It is a poor thing compared to those gifts you have given me. Yet is it the best gift I can give and it is given with love."

I felt power surge in the room. Before my eyes Welwyn's queen shivered. It turned bright eyes to study me before rising on powerful wings to perch on my shoulder. For a moment wings caressed my cheek. My gift was accepted but returned to me for a little. I walked in Light and the strength of the Hive supported me. I went from the shrine, tears still wet on my cheeks.

About me flew a hundred warriors and two queens. On my shoulder I bore another. I left the star pavement and felt the warm air about me. If evil walked here I saw no signs of it. Perhaps I would find it beyond the shrine's valley. I hitched up my pack and strode out. In an hour I was near the valley's mouth and I became more cautious in my movements. It was as well.

I dropped into cover and swallowed the desire to spit like a cat. I had hoped that beyond the shrine the land healed. Mayhap it did, but there were still predators who hunted. I spied now on a group like Garlen's band. There were fewer of them and they looked both more hungry and more desperate. More evil also. Their leader was a burly middle-aged man wearing the remnants of what may have once been a uniform.

But soldier or not, he had no more control over his men than Garlen had owned over his band. From where I crouched I could hear the grumbling.

" 'S a waste 'a time. Who's gonna ransom this one? I say we finish him then make fer the coast. Mebbe we could wave down some Sulcar ship."

There was a guffaw from the leader. "Take a ship from the Sulcar? You're crazy, Malen. No. There'll be a ransom for this one. We have only to wait a bit longer." His grin broadened. "If he's bin lying to us then you can do what you will. But until then he stays in one piece, understand. We can take a toy to play with anytime. One who's worth gold is far rarer." There was a growl of agreement from those about him as the men settled back to dicing.

I craned to see as they moved a little. I looked for the face but it was the tabbard I saw first. On it I saw the signs of noble rank. I stared, sitting back on my heels, mouth agape. Into my hands, oh Lords of Vengeance, was the enemy of my house delivered. The sigils were those of the House whose son had ravished my gifts into my great-grandmother's line. My anger burned as I studied the figure of the deer with only one branch of his antlers remaining. That was supposed to show that the House held to peace but would fight at need.

Truer was the other sign, a dagger thrust into a heart. I sneered, then felt Welwyn's queen shift, her wing brushing my cheek as if to remind me of something. I remembered my Lady's words and looked again at the prisoner himself where he huddled.

With my eyes clearer, I saw one who was barely yet a man. Why, he could not be more than two years older than myself. And when he turned his face from his captors I saw the fear he hid from them. I could understand fear, but not the terror he showed me. Why would he fear so greatly unless—unless he had held them off with tales of a ransom which would not come. If that was so then well might he fear.

He was wiry rather than heavy-set. His hair was a fall of dark honey, a little too long, but I supposed as a bandit's prisoner he had little chance to cut it. He had hazel eyes set in an oval face and cheekbones which etched his face into strong lines beneath the wings of hair. There was no evil in that face. No viciousness in the eyes. None of the wet lips in lustful pout I had seen in Garlen's band, and that I saw in the faces of those about this boy. I saw no evil in him and again my lady's words came into my mind.

"Do not reject good honey though bees from that hive have stung in the past," she had said. Well then. I would not. All that day I watched and listened. Evening came chill. It was early Spring and in the South that could yet be freezing at night. I was warm enough in my heavy cloak but I saw how the boy shivered. The leader came to stand over him, wearing a cloak of his own.

"Aye, shiver, Lorcan. If your ransom is not here by morning you'll have better cause to shiver then. We've waited long enough and I owe your noble father an ill deed or two. He had me whipped for stealing and I do not forget."

"Would you waste the gold my kin will pay?" I liked this Lorcan's voice. It was quiet but there was a man's note in it. Nor did he grovel or whine for mercy. I listened to the bandit's reply with interest.

"What gold? My men have been gone for months. I think your kin may have taken them. Maybe you are not required. Two older brothers, wasn't it? Nay. I think you are now a waste of our time. If Belo and Todon are not back by the morrow you shall be ours. My men grow restless, and a good leader knows when to deal with that." He walked back towards the camp-fire after casually kicking the bound boy.

Lorcan turned his face away and I saw in his eyes a black despair. His lips moved in what I was sure were prayers. I slid back silently. I was sure now I was right. Perhaps his cadet branch of the House of Paltendale was impoverished, or gone in the war with all his kin dead. I believed there would be no ransom for the boy, as their leader had half-guessed. What would come to Lorcan in the dawn would not be pleasant. I found I had made up my mind. Enemy of my House or not, I would save this boy if I could.

As I decided, I felt in the back of my mind a sweet approval. It was right I do this. On my shoulders the three queens hummed. I consulted them. Myself, I could think of no better plan than to do to this group of evil men as we had once done to Garlen's band. They were no greater in numbers. But I considered. The boy, Lorcan. I knew this kind of bandit now. If any survived our first attack they would blame the boy and try to slay him before he could be saved. I must see if I could free him first.

"Why not both plans together, daughter of my Hive?" came my lady's voice through Welwyn's Queen. "Do not forget the warriors about you."

My thoughts leaped to catch that. I recalled how Neeco had died. Then, too, there was Lorcan. He must be warrior-trained, and in these days it was likely he was well blooded. That he was desperate I knew. He was not likely to throw away any chance given him. I had the sword I'd taken from Lord Lanson's house. True, it seemed to have been made for a boy, but it was of fine forging. And the lighter weight should only make it easier for Lorcan to use. After being tied so long he would find it hard to move.

I studied the clearing. There would be no way I could get poison into their cooking pot or wine. But my warriors were deadly. I laid careful plans with the queens. Hopefully, they would hatch into a lethal outcome. Then I waited and watched. It was almost dawn by the time I was ready. But what wolfshead rises with the sun? In the clearing the outlaws slept soundly; their single guard was dozing. My warriors moved at my signal, flowing in a small black cloud towards the guard. I followed silently. They struck.

The guard's struggle was as silent as my steps had been.

Men stung in the throat by such a poison as my warriors brewed cannot cry out. In seconds I had reached him and my dagger went home. Although with so many stings I think it went to the hilt in a man already dead. I leaned him against the tree. There was a branch there and over it I hooked his belt, leaning his upper body back in balance against the trunk. It looked as if he merely drowsed. Hopefully, if any woke before I was done, they would not see any reason to give an alarm. Then I circled the camp.

Lorcan's eyes opened as I hissed softly from the nearest bush. He stared, his gaze focusing on me. I held up my dagger and mimed sawing free his bonds. He nodded, his eyes checking the guard before he looked back to me. Then, very slowly, he began to move, wriggling across the hard ground. At last he was able to thrust his hands backwards to where I could reach them without being seen by any who might wake. I cut hastily and the leather strips fell away.

My voice was a thread of sound only he could hear. "Can you walk?"

His voice was no louder. "Not yet. They've had me tied too long."

"Tell me when you can move again, then." I sat in my concealment. My warriors were ready but I did not wish to waste their lives. Better to hold off until we could run rather than fight if needs must be. Lorcan had rolled back a little way and lay with his back to his captors. I saw the tiny movements as he massaged his hands and ankles, his face twisted in pain. Overhead the sky was brighter as the sun rose. We must act very soon.

"Lorcan? Can you walk yet?"

"How did you know—never mind. I think maybe so." I slid the sword with belt and scabbard across the beaten earth.

"Then you can use this?"

His voice was no louder than mine but the exultant note rang clear. "Indeed I can, Lady. Live or die I shall not for-

get that you gave me freedom and a means to die fighting."
I choked back my retort that if he died he'd remember
nothing. Now was not the time to discuss warrior honor.

"Then do not move until you must. Better to live and see
them die." I could see by the sudden snarl that twisted his
mouth he was in full agreement with the comment. I
moved to where I could see over the whole camp. The sun
was almost up but still none stirred. Best I make my move.
If I delayed too long some would surely wake, if only to re-
lieve themselves. In my mind I gathered the minds of all
those winged-ones who waited the command. Then—

Now, brothers! My order was an arrow released from
the bow. During the time we waited, my warriors had
moved in twos and threes, crawling unnoticed within the
clothing of the sleeping outlaws. One warrior to each side
of the throat of any man where they could gain access.
Some could not, but they had all found bare flesh. A man
fell swiftly to the stings of more than a dozen. The stings
of two or three would not kill immediately but they slowed
movement and reactions. They would probably kill in the
end, it would merely take longer.

With their strike delivered, my warriors freed themselves from the clothing. Some failed and died; I mourned
each death. But this was war. And in war deaths are in-
evitable. It does not take two to make death in war. If one
side chooses to lie down in surrender then it is they who
die. But there is still death. I did not so choose and nor did
the bees who were valiant fighters for their hive and queen.

Across the clearing the leader had struggled to his feet.
About him his men staggered, crying out in panic and pain.
The leader, too, had been stung but only once and I think
the pain maddened him. He could have had no idea what
had happened but he blamed his captive. He charged towards the boy and then I saw what mettle I had aided.

Lorcan made no attempt to escape. Instead he seemed to
settle, planting his feet and balancing to meet the attack.
The larger, heavier man would already be suffering the ef-

fects of the sting. But he was still a formidable fighter. Yet it was as if he fought one of the wing-friends.

Lorcan sword-danced. The blows aimed at him were deflected or parried with cool skill. In the camp clearing, men would have come to their leader's aid, perhaps, but my warriors hovered. If any man moved that way he found himself faced with angrily buzzing bees. Outlaws they might have been, but not fools. My warriors were ten times the size of the normal dales bees and the men stayed back.

They saw swiftly enough that their leader was doomed. The poison in their own veins would be working. Already they would feel weakness stealing over them. They may have feared that whatever had freed their captive and attacked them could move further against them at any time. They began to catch up their belongings and slide away to saddle their mounts. I let them go.

These men were not the band that had murdered my dale, yet I guessed from some of the plunder I had seen in their camp that they had murdered others. My heart cried for vengeance upon these bandits on behalf of other innocents dead at their hands. I had seen women's jewelry on their wrists and about their necks. Their leader had worn a woman's fur-lined cloak against the chill of the previous evening.

I turned back to the fight in time to see the final actions. With a burst of rage the leader had swung a mighty blow. His blade, neatly deflected, after so great an effort dragged his body to one side. Lorcan made a long low lunge with his own blade crossing the other's steel, sliding in and up. He stepped back as the older man crumpled. My queens lifted into the air as I approached him. They buzzed in anger, demanding the other members of the band be pursued, but I was weary of death. Sickness rose in my throat as I looked at the leader's body. I refused the queens' demand, but warriors rose at their orders despite my decision. I was a hiveless queen, I could not command warriors.

Lorcan stood panting, his sword pointing downward, his

gaze meeting mine. I had seen too many deaths of late, but he had fought well, so I flung up one hand in the fighter's acknowledgement of a fair win.

His blade lifted in salute. "Lady!" he smiled and lost the hard dangerous look with which he had fought. "How shall I name my rescuer?"

"I am Meive. Meive of—" I would not use the common name. It was not fitting here and now. "Landale," I said. "Save that Landale is no more." I glanced at the body by our feet. "One such as this led men there. I was away and I alone survived."

"What of those who slew your dale?"

I felt my mouth pull into a smile such as I do not think was good to see. "They also did not survive—long."

"Mistress of Power." His sword was offered across one arm. "Take back the weapon you lent me."

I shook my head. "I cannot use it. Let it remain with one who can." He nodded. I met his gaze and spoke. "And you? I watched and I think your tales to them of a ransom were—" I paused and he finished my question.

"Lies? Yes, lady. My House was overrun early while the invaders from the land of Alizon still had their machines. They used them to lay waste to Erondale; it is gone. I was only a child. My father, and those of us who could, withdrew. They pursued. In the fighting my father fell together with both my brothers. I was injured. Our master-at-arms escaped with me before him on his horse. We went to my kin at Paltendale, where I was trained to the sword, but later that dale also fell. I liked not my kin so I left them, taking sword-service with a man I trusted."

I felt pleasure at his words. So, from what he said, his had been a cadet House. Not truly of my enemy. And—he had not liked his kin of Paltendale. Lorcan was still speaking.

"I fought at the battle of Hagar Pass where died the lord I had chosen to serve. After that I fought for a year as one in the patrols which cleaned the land of the few remnants remaining of the invaders. Once that was done I rode away alone. I had no direction, but I found the South pulled me and I answered that call."

"So you have no home, no kin left?" His face was suddenly older, bitter with grief, as he spoke softly.

"Lady, I have no one and nothing." He seemed to drag his mood back from remembering that loss. His face lightened. "Yet you have given me my freedom and a sword. How shall I say I have nothing? May I aid you in your own plans if you have them?"

I had seen him fight. Young though he was, he was a fine swordsman and one whom men would follow. But how had he come into the hands of the outlaws, I asked.

"Through my own folly. I knew Devol as one who had once been of our dale. I was a child then. I did not know he had been cast out as a thief. I remembered only a familiar face whom I rejoiced to see. It was wonderful that someone of my dale was still living. I drank with him, drugged wine, although I did not know that until I woke captive in his hands. I swore my kin would pay high for my return undamaged. I hoped to escape before Devol's men returned with word that both Paltendale and my House were no more. I failed. Had it not been for you—" He shivered.

"And if you had freed yourself? What plans had you?"

Lorcan looked out across the land. "After all that has happened there are many dales left without a lord. I planned to find one such and build a new House to shelter my line. I might have to convince those already there that I was a proper lord, but that I could do, I believe. After that, I would find a lady. With so many men dead there are many girls without living kin to make marriage contracts for them and few have a dowry to give."

"And now?"

He turned those quiet hazel eyes upon me. "Now, Lady? I have taken my life and a sword from your hands. I am your liege-man. Your plans are mine. What do you wish us to do? Though," he gazed about, "if we take what horses and gear we can from here it is in my mind we could find men to use them. There are good soldiers who wish no more than to follow one who gives sensible orders."

He considered that, adding, "I think that there will be husbandless and fatherless women and children, too, who would follow us if we can offer them land and refuge." His gaze was warmer than any man who merely swore to sword-liege. And I had noted that word: not "you" but "us."

I smiled. Honey blended is the sweetest. I would take his plans and blend them with Honeycoombe. He should have a dowry of me. My dale and everything within it. Once we had taken back my home he should go forth. Beyond Honeycoombe there were many without home or hope. They should return with him to find both. My queens flew about us and I could feel their delight. The hive would prosper again, it was well. And faintly in the back of my head I heard the Bee-Goddess's voice through Welwyn's queen on my shoulder.

"Do not forget me, daughter of my Hive, as you have remembered my words."

I grinned, cheerfully watching as Welwyn's queen lifted to return to the shrine. My brother's spirit could be proud. He had wrought better than he knew. I would sew a memory quilt as soon as I had leisure. I had taken cloth from the bodies of all I had buried. I would hang the finished quilt upon the walls of the house, behind the High Seats which Lorcan and I would fill. Once my great-grandmother had been stung by Lorcan's hive. But I suspected the honey I was offered would still be very sweet.

Nor would I forget the shrine. In the years to come I would teach apprentices to remember. Each Spring I would return to walk and talk with she who dwelled there, as Ithia had done. And when at last my time was come, like Ithia, I, too, should fly free, perhaps to stay with my lady forever. I turned to Lorcan. One day I should tell him of my lineage. That he was not completely kinless. For now it would be enough that we were liege-man and lady.

"We shall find those outlaws who fell to the bees and plunder them in turn." I said slowly. "After that, let you follow me, I have an empty dale for which we might find settlers." My tone became warning. "Yet it is mine. I am willing to share, but not to lose what I hold." The bees rose to fly in circles about us.

His hand took mine and lifted it to a kiss. "Lady, lead on. For I think that where you go I shall always be ready to follow. So long as," he added wryly looking up at those who circled about us, "your friends do not object to my company."

Our laughter rang out as we moved to see if any of the outlaws had fallen to the queens' warriors; if so, the bandit's mounts and belongings would be our fair plunder. In the midst of strife we had found peace. So might it always be, yet, if it was not to be more than a temporary peace, still I had good friends and one who might be more to me perhaps in the days to come. I was Meive of Landale, also called Honeycoombe—and I was going home.

Lorcan

VII

*I*t was many hours later when I awoke. My head ached from the wine I had drunk with Devol, I needed to make water, and everything was dark. I shifted, trying to stand. It was puzzling, I couldn't move and my head was so bad I was unable to remember any reason why that should be so. At my side a voice spoke.

"Need to go, do you? Alright then. But don't do anything stupid." Bonds of which I'd been unaware were loosened and I was helped to my feet. I staggered around a tree, did what was necessary, and found myself led back to lie down again. I obeyed dully. I must have been scouting and been taken prisoner. I would wait until I felt better. Then I could escape.

I slept again and woke at dawn clear-headed. Keeping both facts to myself, I scanned the camp through slitted eyes. I could see twelve men asleep. Brush rustled and I guessed at a guard. Thirteen then? Several of the group had soldier's gear. From that and other things I suspected they'd fled as a group. Devol had appeared to lead them yesterday, and he wore the remnants of a uniform. I saw him rise and walk towards me.

"Awake yet, boy?" His boot nudged me in the ribs. Instinctively, I allowed my body to stay limp, my eyes shut. If he was awake, others would be soon, and I might learn from their talk. Devol kicked me again. I stifled a groan and remained apparently unaware. He desisted then and moved to rake up the fire, placing water to heat. The guard came into camp, nodding to Devol.

"Nothing out there. Reckon the boy was telling the truth. He's alone."

Devol grunted. "Mebbe. But just because he's alone don't mean there's no one out there. Wake Malen 'n have him get up that rock spire. I want someone on guard all the time. Boy's a prize."

I felt the guard's eyes on me. "Don't look like no prize."

"Leave thinking to one who can. Wake Malen 'n tell him to git up that rock 'n keep a sharp look-out."

"All right, all right. Don't get no bee in your britches." The man I assumed to be Malen came grumblingly awake and wandered off to guard. The first man returned to the subject as he took himself a cup of something to drink from the pot on the fire.

"Why d'ya say the brat's a prize? Lookit him. A few coppers in his pouch, his gear's hardly better'n ours, and that horse 'a his. Lowser kicked me. Temper like a mule and no looks. It ain't even well-bred. What kind'a horse's that fer a lord?" I smothered a grin. So Tas had taken toll. Good for him. I hoped he hadn't been beaten for it. I strained to hear Devol's reply. I was as interested to know my fate as was the unknown man who asked the questions.

Devol sounded irritated. "I have to do all your thinking for you, Laesen? Sure he doesn't look like he's got anything. You just don't know his breed. Even when they're poor they've got something tucked away."

"He says his dale's gone," Laesen objected.

"That's where knowing what's what comes in." Devol's tone was patronizing. "I lived in his dale for years. Came in when I was in m'late twenties and running after a bit of a scuffle where I'd been. I lived in Erondale a good five years

before the lord drove me out. *An'* I learned stuff. I didn't
just sit on my backside, see."

   "So what'ja learn?"

   "All of these lords stick together. Sure his dale may have
gone. An' that's if'n he was telling the truth about it. But
his father was kin to th' lord o' a big dale to the South of
Erondale. It's a big rich dale and last time I heard it was
still surviving." I thought his news must be well out of date.
It had been several years since Paltendale had fallen. Although, in some ways, he was still right. It was a large and
fertile dale and even with the keep damaged it would be rebuilt now that peace was come. I must be wary of what I
said to these men. It seemed they had been bandits longer
than I could have guessed.

   Laesen was eager. "How rich, and how do we get money
out'a them for the brat?"

   "Wait until he's woken. He'll tell us who to go to and
what message to give them."

   "What if this dale has gone?" Laesen sounded doubtful.
"'S a long way back. Who goes?"

   Devol's reply chilled me to the very bones. "If there isn't
a ransom, then the men can have him. Pretty boy like that
they'll be happy enough. We can sell his horses and gear.
But you remember good, Laesen. No one lays a hand on
him until I say. I know these lords. They don't forget that
kind of injury. If we done that then he got ransomed he'd
come back with an army. I want the money he'll bring us
and no trouble." From the sounds he was getting himself
another drink.

   "As fer who goes. I reckon Belo and Todon. Likely
they'll send three or four guards back with them to watch
the ransom coin." His voice sounded confident. He'd probably done this before, but he badly misjudged the Paltendale that had been. If his creatures had come asking a
ransom for me before Paltendale fell, Faslane would have
seen to it that they were wrung dry. I'd have been freed, the
bandits given a quick rope and no coin wasted on them.

I judged it wise to show signs of returning life now, before they wondered why I slept so long. I groaned softly, stirring as I opened my eyes to stare about. Devol tramped over to me.

"Awake are you, my Lord? Want your lordly breakfast, I daresay. Laesen, fetch his lordship something to drink." Laesen fetched a brimming cup and flung it in my face, guffawing as he did so. The other men, waking to see the jest, bellowed with laughter and called out various comments. I shook the water from my eyes and looked up.

"Paltendale won't pay gold for a man dead of thirst or for a man crippled by over-tight ropes." I heard the soft hissing whisper of that word go around them. Bandits like these would see a lot of coppers, some silver. But gold was a word to fire even such meager imaginations as they had. Devol was quick to take it up.

"Aye, gold. He's a lord and kin to Paltendale. Which of you fools would have known that? No, you'd have killed him and wasted the chance. That's why you listen to me." He stared around, establishing dominance like some old tomcat in his barn.

"So you don't touch the boy, but you guard him, see. Lords are tricky. You don't ever take risks with him or you won't never see any of the gold. But you don't lay hands on him neither. You hear me?" His gaze traveled from face to face until all had bowed to the order. Devol relaxed and I saw that he was uncertain of his complete authority.

I knew enough about bandits to see why. These were evil men, all used to doing as they wished. They could only be led by one more evil or far stronger, and Devol was neither. Somewhere along his life he'd been better taught. They were slightly in awe of his speech, which lacked most of the country slur. But it was possible his position had been growing insecure as they started to resent his assumption of leadership.

I was his chance to prove they did best by following

him. His reaction, if he discovered that Paltendale had been impoverished or, in any case, there was no ransom forthcoming, would be terrible. He would blame me for his loss of power. I knew what bandits could do to those in their hands. I'd seen the results often enough when I rode with those who hunted down the last of the invaders after the final battle. I had to play for time to escape. If Devol needed my ransom so badly, that wasn't going to be easily accomplished.

Nor was it. Two men returned, from tending to the horses, by what they said. Devol spoke loud enough for me to hear some of what he ordered.

"Go first to Erondale. Boy says it was ruined by the invaders. I want to be sure he don't lie. If it's truth then go on to Paltendale." I stared under an arm at the two who might hold my life in their hands. Todon, I thought to have been an ordinary farmer once. There was no look of evil about him. The other, a tall shabby man with missing front teeth and furtive eyes, whined about the journey.

"'S gonna take forever."

"No, it isn't," Devol snapped. "You take two horses each. You don't sleep in and you hustle. Belo, the boy says you talk to . . ." They moved away and I heard no more.

Belo and Todon set off an hour later. They knew where lay Erondale and Paltendale and it was possible they could fall into the hands of some daleslord. If so they would babble about me in an attempt to survive his justice. If the lord owed any debt to Paltendale I might look for rescue still. But best I find my own escape if I could. I watched for days and found no way. The band moved. I supposed their men would know where to find them on their return. Each time they shifted I looked for a way to flee and was thwarted.

Devol used the word I myself had given him to see no one became slack in their guard of my person. After a week of seeing no way of escape I was worried, after three weeks I was terrified. The band had shifted further and further to the South-east and were almost into territory where no established dales lay. Even if I could get away I would be hunted, and here, where there were few dales, I would have little chance of finding one and asking help from any daleslord.

If there was no other choice, I would seek the final gate and die before they used me as Devol had suggested. I would die afterwards anyway. Better to die early—and a clean death. There was yet no sign of Belo and Todon, and it had been almost five weeks, so that increasingly the bandits cast dark looks at me and muttered amongst themselves. Devol kept a cheerful face, talking of gold and what a man could do with it, but I knew he, too, feared lest I was not the prize he had claimed. Once he believed that, he would toss me to his men as a sop to keep their loyalty, what loyalty such men ever had.

I lay bound, late one evening, on the outer edge of the camp, a day over six weeks since I had first fallen into Devol's hands, and for almost an hour I had been conscious that someone stalked the camp. I could hear the faint rustle of brush. That was all, but I knew eyes watched us. The sounds were never great but they circled, pausing as now and again the stalker listened to what was said in the camp. It could not be other bandits, I thought. Whoever stalked us was too good for that. These were the steps of one at home in the land.

My heart leaped. Could it be that Belo and Todon *had* been taken by some daleslord? Could it be a scout who watched and waited? If so, I must be ready. All Devol had allowed me had been my oldest shirt and trews and the over-small threadbare tabard. The wind still struck cold after dusk despite the time of year. I shivered as I saw Devol coming towards me in the firelight, and he laughed threateningly.

"Aye, shiver, Lorcan. If your ransom comes not with morning you'll have better cause to shiver then. We've waited long enough, and I owe your noble father an ill deed or two. He had me whipped for stealing and I do not forget." He kicked me viciously before walking back again towards the campfire.

So that had been the reason Devol had gone from Erondale. Whatever he did, it could not have been theft alone. My father hated to whip a man and would not have done so easily. It had to have been more, something besides theft, so bad it was not spoken of to me when I asked.

I despaired then, turning my face away so none at the fire should see my fear. I would die here and none would know how the last heir to Erondale had died. That I would die I accepted. But I was determined it would not be at the filthy hands of Devol's bandits. I must win a weapon and slay myself, quickly.

I lay awake all that night planning, considering, turning over in my mind how I might accomplish my death. At dawn I heard movement again and allowed myself to appear asleep. The one who had stalked the camp was closing in. Yet I might be worse off in his hands. I would give no alarm but would wait to see what manner of man he was.

I was astounded in what I saw. This figure was no scout, no man. Something, which moved too swiftly in the dawn light for me to see, seemed to have attacked Laesen, who was on guard. He grasped silently at his throat, choked, and seemed to gasp for breath. From the brush darted a slight figure. It reached him, struck home with well-honed dagger, then propped him against the tree so that he seemed to be only drowsing.

Then it vanished into the brush again and I could hear it circling. I watched through half-closed eyelids. It moved up behind me in cover and hissed. I rolled over quietly, opened my eyes, and studied the face which showed between branches. I knew I must be gaping like a yokel at a fair magician. The stalker was a girl some two years short of my own age, I would guess. Her long plaits glinted honey and fire in the growing light. Her eyes were a green-ish tint and her face a soft oval. She was not pretty, but there was strength and character in the bones, pride and courage in the wide eyes that calmly met mine.

She held up her dagger and mimed sawing through my bonds. I nodded, beginning to wriggle cautiously towards her. I knew not how she had slain Laesen so silently, but if we roused the camp I doubted she could slay Devol and his men. Finally, I could thrust my hands within her reach, and felt the blade slide against my skin.

Her voice was a thread of sound. "Can you walk?" I knew I could not. Each night I was well tied and each morn it took some time before I could rise once Devol allowed that. I kept my voice low.

"Not yet. They've had me tied too long."

"Say me when" was all she replied, settling in the brush to wait that time. I flexed my hands and feet frantically. At least she had given me a chance. If I could be fit enough to run before the camp woke I might yet live. I massaged my ankles and prayed fervently to Cup and Flame that I might live and escape. The girl hissed a question, using my name.

"Lorcan? Can you walk yet?"

"How—never mind. I think maybe so." How had she known my name I would have asked before the answer came to me. Of course. She had heard it used by Devol. Nor was there time to sit about asking foolish questions. How she knew didn't matter, getting free of this camp did. Something came sliding across the earth to me and I gripped it eagerly.

"Then you can use this?" came her whisper.

I gripped the sword hilt and swore beneath my breath. Oh Gods. A sword. Good clean steel. Live or die, I could go down fighting. I heard the wild note in my voice as I answered her.

"Indeed I can, Lady. Live or die, I shall not forget you gave me freedom and a way to die fighting."

She said nothing, so I believed she did not understand

how great my danger had been. Instead, she bade me remain still until it was time. Better live and see them die, she
said, and I agreed with that thought. We waited. Minute by
minute I could feel strength flow back into my hands and
feet. I examined the sword carefully. It was a fair weapon,
made for a boy, perhaps, since it was not of great length or
weight. Yet the blade was fine steel and the hilt was good
quality. Made for a lord's son, I guessed, then outgrown.
Whence could the girl have obtained it? Was she a lord's
daughter cast adrift by the loss of her dale and kin?

I saw her rise suddenly, on her face an intent look. I rose
to my feet quickly and stared at the camp. From men who
lay nearby there came thrashing movements and an occasional gasp or cry. Some lay still after a convulsive shudder
or two as others staggered to their feet. By the Flames, the
girl must be a woman of Power. But this was no time to
stand in awe. From the bedding where he slept Devol rose
roaring in pain and fury. He saw me standing and charged,
sword already reaching for me. He snarled as he came.

"Bastard brat. I knew I should have tossed you to the
men earlier. Cursed lordlings, hell be upon all of you. Let
your family rot while I send you to join them."

He would have done better to save his breath. Berond
and Faslane had taught me never to fight in anger. In silence, I settled my feet firmly. Then I began. Devol had
never been the fighter I was now, even with a shorter,
lighter blade, with hands and feet still slightly numb from
my bonds.

When he brought me down before, I had been taken by
surprise, by my own folly. This time I was not mazed with
drugged wine. From the corners of my eyes I could see that
several of the men had escaped whatever doom the witch
had cast, but they did not come to their leader's aid. Something kept them back, but I was too busy to see what that
might be. It seemed they, too, feared the outcome. I saw
them seize saddlebags and flee for the place where the
horses grazed.

Devol saw, too, and gave a bellow of fury. Then he came at me, his sword lashing out with all his strength. I slipped the blow, deflecting his blade to one side. It left him open to mine. I felt my sword go home, twisted automatically, then drew it free. Devol reeled. His eyes, still hating me, went slowly blank as he crumpled. I stepped back and glanced about. The girl was coming towards us, lifting her hand in the way of a fighter acknowledging a clean strike.

I lifted my blade in salute. I owed her my life and honor, I must acknowledge her gifts.

"How shall I name my rescuer, Lady?"

And so I met Meive of Landale, which men oft named Honeycoombe. I would have given back the sword but she bade me keep it. To my astonishment great bees, the like of which I have never seen, came to settle upon her shoulders. One larger one seemed to whisper in her ear. I hailed her as Mistress of Power and she smiled, her face lighting so that I saw beauty.

"You lied to them?" Her hand gestured towards those who had not escaped.

"I lied," I admitted. I spoke briefly of Erondale and how it had died. Of how Paltendale had taken Berond and me within its walls and died in turn. "Yet I could not tell them so. The ransom they expected was my only hope." She nodded, understanding. "And you, Meive. What of your dale?"

Honeycoombe lay dead, she told me. I questioned the name. Had she not called her home Landale? It was then she spoke of her bees, and how her home had come to be named. She asked of my own plans. I had thought of that as I wandered. Now I spoke, thinking as my words came slowly.

"There are dales left without a lord. Some are dead, others have a few people seeking to survive, but without leadership. I thought perhaps to find one such and build a keep there. I could find some girl, sensible and of courage to aid me as keep's lady in that."

"And now?"

I spoke without thinking but my words were right to me. "Now? I took my life from you. When I took sword from your hand I became leige-man. The path you would choose shall be mine also. What would you wish us to do? Although," I gazed about, "there are good horses and gear here yet. And in other places we could find good men to use them. Women and children who would accept any honest refuge."

She smiled at me. "Then let us find what those wolfsheads may have left and plunder them. After that," her smile widened, "I have a dale you might consider."

I bowed over her hand. "Lead on, Meive. I think I shall be happy to follow you. So long as," I looked up at the circling bees, "so long as your friends have no objection."

She laughed and I laughed with her. The future looked to be interesting and Ayneta's prophesy came to my mind. I would wander, she had said, before I found treasure unlooked for. I knew not if this dale was the treasure. But of a certainty I had not looked for it.

I followed Meive as she moved through the undergrowth. One by one we found those who had fled. It puzzled me that each was dead and Meive found them without appearing to search, though she seemed distressed by the sight. At length, as we despoiled each outlaw, I spoke of it. Meive glanced up from where she wrestled loose a sword-belt, her hands determined despite the sickened look on her face.

"My wing-friends tell me. Who else should know where bandits fell save those who slew them. I told them not to kill once the bandits fled, but the queens overruled me."

I gazed with still more respect at her bees. "They are larger than I have ever seen. And darker in color. Whence came they?"

Her answer left me deeper in awe. "From a shrine of the Old Ones. They were a gift of she who dwells there. They came of their own will: they stay because they wish, and they are my friends." She must have seen my nervousness.

"Do not fear. They would never harm one who does not wish ill to me. They are friends, guards at need, watchers and protectors. Now, let us seek out where these men grazed their horses. I would know what number of beasts we have to deal with."

I caught up a chunk of stale bread as I passed the campfire. Then I led the way. When I whistled, Tas came nickering to me on over-tight hobbles. I fed him the bread, stroking his neck and muzzle as he munched. Meive looked him over.

"A good beast. But it looks as if he has not eaten well of late." I had seen that myself. I suspected that the man Tas had kicked when I was taken had revenged himself by starving my poor beast with hobbles so tight the poor animal was hard put to it to walk.

"That can be remedied." I freed Tas from his hobbles and let him move freely. He finished his bread and at once went to a place in the tiny valley where the grass grew lushly. His head went down eagerly as his teeth tore at the grass. Meive was counting the beasts that grazed with him.

"Counting those we have secured at the camp, there are sixteen. I would say none are of great quality, but all appear healthy enough." I nodded as she continued. "In my dale there are other bandit mounts and a full team of workhorses. The bandits who came there brought them. Later, when the outlaws lay dead, I returned to secure the team."

"Will not they have escaped?" She had said it was several years since she had been back to her dale. Horses wandered. Meive shook her head.

"No, I think they will not. At the far end of the dale there is another. Only a small valley, perhaps fifty acres, no more. The path lies around a great rock so that the bandits did not notice it." She sighed. "If my people had seen death coming they might have escaped to hide there. I know not how they were taken by surprise. But afterwards I took the horses there. The cattle belonging to my family, and the

goats belonging to Granny Warsten were already there. I
blocked the trail out and, save for some mischance, all are
like to be there yet."

I was surprised. "Cows? How many? That is . . ." I shut
my mouth hastily. I was about to say for a small dale to
have cows was riches. Usually the smaller dales had only
goats. Meive had an odd look on her face and I feared I had
offended.

"We had one cow for milk. And we had kept her bullcalf
since he was not yet old enough to sell or exchange with
another dale. She is a good cow and only six summers in
age. Long ago my family was given blood-price. It paid for
a cow and we have kept a cow ever since."

"A bullcalf?" My mind had gone in a different direction.
I grinned at her. "I think it likely your hidden vale holds
more than one cow and her calf by now. You have been
gone three years." I was working out the times. If the calf
had been too young to sell he must have been still sucking,
perhaps two or three months old. He would have been old
enough to breed at ten months. So it was possible by now
the vale held his mother, the bullcalf and two other calves.
Riches indeed to those who would rebuild a dale and feed
the people.

"I must go to the shrine," Meive said abruptly. "I am
called."

"Does your lady wish me to come, or should remain
here?" I was agreeable to either, although I would wish to
see the shrine—from a safe distance at least. I had always
loved the tales of the Old Ones.

"Come with me. If my lady doesn't want you to enter
I'm sure she'll make that known."

I was sure, too. That was what bothered me. Yet I followed Meive. I had named myself leige-man and it was my
duty. We entered the valley, and once I came in sight of the
place I halted to stare. It was beautiful, yet it was not the
beauty which called to me, but the peace. The sense that

here was sanctuary. I walked forward, leaving Meive behind on the edge of the pavement. I paced slowly through the door and entered a room. I cannot say all that I saw or what was said. I moved in a dream and all around me was the scent of flowers.

I only know questions were asked of me and I made answer. And in the end I bowed low over a hand out-stretched in acceptance. I left with the taste of heather-honey in my mouth and such serenity in my heart it was as if I had come home. Meive smiled at me as I returned to her side.

"The winged-ones accept," she said softly. "Come to Honeycoombe and be welcome there."

We returned to make camp where the horses grazed. I slept quietly that night. My pains from the rough treatment Devol and his men had given me were eased, my nightmares banished. I woke calmly to work beside Meive. I knew that other things would intrude, I could be injured, or ill, we could be attacked by other outlaws. But for a brief time the peace of the shrine would hold. It was a healing time and freely given.

We two worked hard the next five days. I found the bodies of the bandits who had attempted to flee; not one had succeeded. Meive found it a sorrowful sight, so that I alone disposed of the bandits, thinking no less of her. She had been strong when strength was required of her, now she had me and could take time to grieve at what had had to be done.

It was not as if there was no work for her. As well as my disposal of the bodies, the beasts all had to be cared for and Meive's hives readied for departure to Honeycoombe once more. We set out at last, the wooden sledges sliding smoothly, bearing their loads of humming hives. We reached Meive's cave and I asked her to remain.

"Whyfor? Honeycoombe is my home, too. Do you not think I would fight for it as well?"

Of course I did. I'd seen her mettle already. "I spoke wrongly. Come then. But let us not walk together. Thus, if we are attacked, the enemy will find us harder to strike down." We set out, I riding Tas and Meive astride Drustan. Ahorse it took only a few hours to reach her dale, but once we were near I dismounted us, tethering the beasts and approaching on foot.

"Circle to the right. I will go to the left as far as I can travel. If we find nothing amiss we can perhaps descend, though I would rather we waited the night to be sure." Meive nodded, seeing the sense in that, and moved away without speaking. Her bees paused, then divided, one half remaining with the girl and the others rising to circle above me. I was unsure, but the Lady of the Shrine had spoken me fair and Meive had named me acceptable to her wingfriends. I looked up at them.

"Of your courtesy-guard I thank you, winged-ones." The soft humming seemed to deepen. I made myself take care as I circled, though in truth I felt alive and joyful as I had not for many weeks. Best not to be so joyous over recent events that I was fallen on by outlaws again. Once had been enough. But there were none, and after a night sleeping Meive and I rode down into what had once been a small fair dale.

VIII

My gaze darted everywhere as we rode down the steep narrow trail. It was a hidden dale. I knew, had I been alone, I would have found it only by accident. That was well. It made more likely our chances of staying safe and perhaps rebuilding what had been here before Neeco's treachery showed bandits a way into Landale, where they destroyed all that Meive had held dear. Once the valley widened and the trail leveled I could see the buildings more clearly. They had been sturdily built, most of mortared stone and still standing, though the past three years had done some damage. But so isolated had the valley been that none had found them to plunder. All were still shut tight as Meive had left them.

"Meive, when you left, were the belongings of each family still within?"

"They were." In her eyes was the pain of remembrance. "Each home within is just as it was the day the bandits came. Where they looted, things lie tumbled. Where they slept the bed will still bear the mark of their filthy bodies."

I could see her sorrow that she had not tidied such imprints of the bandit's passage, but she had been thirteen. There was only so much she could have done. I said so;

some of the sorrow eased in her face. I sought for something to distract her from the work we would begin and found it in a memory which alarmed me even as it occurred to me. I had been a fool, how could I have forgotten? I must not let the serenity of the shrine allow me to become careless.

"There is a danger to us," I said abruptly. Meive turned to look at me sharply. Her gaze flashed about the dale.

"A danger?"

"Aye. I had forgot in all the excitement of your rescue and our coming here. Listen," I recounted more fully the tale of Devol's plans. How I had been taken for ransom. When I finished Meive was quick to see the same danger.

"The men, Todon and Belo. They have not returned."

"Even so. Devol thought it may have been some treachery on my part. Or perhaps they had been slain on the trail. Either way, had they not returned the day you rescued me, he planned to move camp a good distance, then—" I hesitated and temporized my words. "Well, then they would have dealt ill with me." Her glance said that she understood how ill that would have been. I did not doubt she knew. If she had not been here when her own dale died, at least she had come later. She would have seen the bodies as she laid them to rest.

"So there is no proof the men are not on their way back again. Paltendale may not have held them. They may well have been delayed some other way. But, Lorcan, would they be so eager to return to Devol?"

"Not eager, perhaps. But where else would men like those go? They had probably been bandits for several years, as I judged from their talk around me. As for all outlaws, there were times of want and times of plenty. But it is the fat times they remember. The joy of drinking, eating, and well, you can guess. They obey no laws, they have no lord. To them it is a life oft to be preferred despite the times of hardship. And the most effective bandits are those with numbers and some sort of leadership. That they had here."

"So you believe if they live they will return?"

I nodded. "I do think so, and I fear it. They will return raging. Having found if they found aught, that I lied and there is no gold, no ransom. It may be worse. If they have found friends along the way they may return in strength. Then are we in great danger." I had not been mistaken. There was steel in the core of my lady. She did not flinch from my words but looked thoughtful for some time. Then she spoke.

"At this time of the year the bees might be safely left many months. It moves to Summer, and if we placed the hives in the high pastures they would have nectar enough to gather until near fall. Thus we could take horse and ride."

"Where?" I thought I knew, but this was her dale. To her the decision.

"To find those who would join us."

I let out my breath. "I, too, would have chosen so. It is well. If that pair lead men here, we are not to be found. If they go to the camp, none are there."

Meive chuckled. "They might flounder about these hills for a long time trying to find this dale, also. It was slain by the treachery of one who knew the paths. And there are ways to camouflage those, though of late they are so overgrown I think they need none. Let us set what we can in order here, then ride."

"That is well. Now, where do you lead us?"

We had come towards the far end of the dale and Meive was walking the pony along a faint trail beaten into the grass. It appeared to stop at a stone outcropping where a small stream meandered past. Without speaking, Meive walked the pony into the shallow water and splashed upstream around the rim of the rock. Past that she turned her mount sharply and thrust him through a clump of brush growing between two boulders which pushed from a cliff-side.

I followed, wondering where we went until memory reminded me. The place where she had hidden the dale's beasts. This must be it. Indeed, she had spoken only the truth.

It was well hidden nor did I think any who looked about casually would easily find it. I smiled. Likely it had first been found by a child, for children wander into odd places. Ahead of me Meive broke through into a small lush valley. I halted Tas at the entrance and scanned what I could see.

As she had said the area would have been some fifty acres. The sides sloped up abruptly, and while goats would have climbed them it was in my mind that goats, not being stupid, would stay within where there was good feed. Then, too, the steep sides had little grass growing and here and there I could see where small slides had been. The rock was unstable. No horse nor cow would even attempt them.

As for those animals, I saw then the team of which Meive had spoken and sucked in a breath of admiration. They had been stolen for certain. No bandit could have afforded to pay for such. There were six of them, large glossy-coated beasts wandering in their herd together. They were the rich chestnut of the Taradale strain, good and willing workers, sensible and with hard hooves that rarely gave way to hoof troubles. They were worth a daleslord's ransom and somewhere some owner must have been lamenting greatly.

Beyond them, in their own larger group, grazed a number of riding mounts. None looked to be of wonderful quality, but all were healthy enough, fat and glossy-coated from the past three years of good food and no work. They would need to be moved once we returned. At least their numbers had not increased. If any were mares it had not mattered: the others were all geldings. I would look them over later. If any were mares and we could buy a good stallion, we could breed better foals. I would have to speak of that to Meive.

Meive had come riding back. "You were right. I found Cream, and she had a bull with her. She has also a yearling heifer and another calf at foot." I laughed at the name. No doubt they had named the beast after the dales saying, that a life of cream and honey palled after a time. Meive laughed with me. It was good to see her face light up. I resolved that she should laugh more often.

I rode with her about the valley and studied the animals that lived here. The team we should keep, at least for a time. Later, perhaps, we could find whence they had been stolen and return them. If there were owners still living. If not, they should remain here. The cows we should keep also. There was enough pasture to let us graze the four, though further increase should be sold or traded.

The goat herd would have to be thinned. They are destructive creatures, and unless we reduced their numbers they would have their pasture here eaten bare in another year or two. From Meive I knew there had been only a half-a-dozen when she left them. Now, I counted the moving forms. There were over thirty. At the very least they needed to be removed from here.

Meive, too, was counting. "Thirty-six. Lorcan, they'll have the valley bare shortly." I could see her calculating. "It must have been this last kidding. The kids from the first year I was gone have themselves become old enough to breed. This year's crop was twice as large. They'll ruin the pastures and if we are late returning we'll find Cream and her calves and the horses with nothing left to eat here."

"Then we move goats," I said. "Let them roam about the main dale. If anyone finds it they'll likely kill or steal a few of the goats. Better that than the cows or horses starve. Let us move the goats tomorrow. Tonight we find a place to sleep and make our plans."

It was late that night before we slept. Long after dusk we sat watching the flames and talking of how we should accomplish our plans. In some things we disagreed, but never harshly. Meive might be no fine dales lady but she was quick, clever, and not unlearned. I was surprised at that.

"You read and figure? How so? It is an unusual skill for—" I broke off lest I offend her.

She smiled at me. "That I know. But our wise woman Ithia was learned as well as wise. All of Landale knew how to count, how to read and write numbers. Ithia taught me to read. She said it was important a wise woman know how to read recipes and write them down. Our lord agreed. It pleased him that we could be less easily cheated if we traveled to any market."

"A wise lord," I said approvingly. After that the talk turned to other concerns and at last we slept.

It took several days, but with hard work we had all of the goats moved into the main dale. At the mouth of the entrance to the inner valley I built the appearance of another landslide. It was not high. Just a mixture of tumbled rocks and a scattering of earth all laid cunningly over a frame of branches tied together. It would keep in any of the cattle or horses that might have wished to leave and it would further hide them and the inner valley. I transplanted shallow-rooted grasses to the earth covering. Within a few weeks they would settle, continuing to grow.

After that, we turned our attention to the houses. There was work aplenty to do there. Most had survived well their time abandoned, but Meive had not searched them before she left. In one I found a small store of coins the bandits had missed. They would go to help the dale and I believed the owner would not have protested that use. Meive came riding back after a day with her bees.

"We need to move the hives. Where we left them was temporary. The hives must be better placed and in a higher pasture. But they do well and are happy. I have bespoken the queens. Should we be still away when the chill comes they will lead the swarms to the shrine."

"The hives are straw," I said doubtfully. "Will they be undamaged after a Winter here?"

"They are strongly made. They will last." Meive was certain.

We rode out the next day, and under Meive's instructions

I learned much of how to correctly place hives. The winged-ones hummed approval at last and one of the warriors settled on my shoulder. His wings brushed my cheek so that I was emboldened to reach up with a finger. I stroked his fur and marveled at the softness. His hum softened until it seemed as if he drowsed under my touch. Meive turned and laughed, but her gaze was warm on us.

"Beware, Lorcan. They will have you do nothing else an you please them so well."

"I think it a small return." I was serious. "They helped in my rescue, they give us food, they aid and guard. And," I looked sideways at the warrior, seeing the faceted eyes, the short plush fur in glossy black, "they are beautiful."

I think she communicated my words to the winged-ones. As I spoke, others came to touch me with their wings. It was as if they caressed me in affection. I had never found bees frightening, and I knew these, though huge for their species, still meant me no harm. So I flinched not but reached out my hand, allowing them to settle in turn and be stroked. How long we shared friendship I do not know, but again I felt peace enter my heart. I marveled that they were so different, yet we could stand one with the other. It was a lesson I must remember.

At last we had the hives where the queens wished. We rode home slowly, the warriors of the winged-ones circling high about our heads.

"What of them when we ride away?"

"They come." Her tone was serene.

"If they are seen they may bring us attention we do not wish."

"They know. They will not let themselves be seen unless we are alone."

I said no more. In truth, I did not mislike it that we would have such help. The bees could see where we could not. They could cover much ground and warn us of any who approached. At great need they could kill, as they had done to rescue me from Devol. I would feel happier that Meive traveled with me when she rode with such guardians as her wing-friends.

We set out ten days later. I had given thought to our journey. I did not wish us to look so rich we should be a target, nor unarmed that we might be fair prey. Yet supplies we must have. Nor did I wish to be recognized by any who might have known me as Lorcan of Erondale. Before we rode out I again rinsed my hair with a wash of herbs Meive assured me would do as well as the market dyes. I had hair now of a darkish brown, and I had cut it in a plain sloping cut which ended square at the nape of my neck.

So we rode steadily to the North and a little West. That first night as we camped Meive questioned me.

"Where do we seek?"

"I think it best we go far North. At least as far as Jurby before we turn for home again. See here," I sketched with my finger in the dirt. "Here are the dales and the coast. Here the invaders landed and all through this portion of the land they laid waste to anything they found. It is here the people who survived may be most desperate. In some places the machines the invader used destroyed the very land. Fouling and burning. Erondale was one such dale so I know how little is left. We ride as far North as possible, then once we turn, we begin to seek out those who will risk a new dale. A new lord and lady."

I saw her look quickly at me, then aside. I said nothing. I had known her for my heart's lady when first she stood before me, but I knew, too, that what one feels is not always felt by the other. I would show her I was not of the kind of some lords who deemed any woman not of noble blood to be fair game. I would woo her slowly. There was time. We were like to be gone from Honeycoombe many months. Mayhap even a year. Surely over so long I could incline her heart to mine.

"I would go first to Tildale," I continued. "My friend

Aran lives there. If he will join us then we shall have a good sword and a valiant friend. He will know the dales about him and may be able to advise us whom else to speak to who may be interested."

I looked across the fire into her eyes. "There is something else. I am Lorcan of Erondale and my dale is no more. But within it still lies wealth." Her eyes widened.

"Aye, indeed. Long ago the Lord of Erondale did a service. For that he was given treasure by one of the Old Ones. Erondale's lords since then have kept it hid, used it little and wisely. When Erondale fell that treasure was unfound. I was a child and knew not, but Berond, our master-at-arms who escaped with me, knew the secret and revealed it to me before he died. When the war was ended I rode to Erondale to see. The treasure lies there still, unless some other has come since last I rode by. I think it unlikely. The coin is well hid and secured. It is in silver coin mostly, with some copper and a little gold, a few gems." I reached out my charm bag and spilled the contents into my palm.

"See you. Here is what I carried against great need." Among the pinches of dried herbs the gems and small gold coins glinted in the firelight. "Listen, Meive. If aught happens to me, let you take this and return to Honeycoombe with any who would come whom you trust. There is still wealth enough to aid in the rebuilding." She nodded silently.

"Good. As for Erondale we will pass by when we return." I grinned darkly. "I have a plan whereby we may take much of the hidden coin with us then. None shall know what we have. I will buy supplies, none anywhere so much it arouses suspicion. Once we get them safely back to Honeycoombe, we can begin to rebuild. The people can live on what is purchased." I remembered the many goats, smiled, and added, "And on goat stew," while Meive chuckled. "Once we have the keep repaired and a guardhouse built at the edge of the dale, we can put in crops. I would see that inner valley of yours fortified also. What do you think, my Lady?"

"I think it is well. I have wished many times that we had kept a better guard. Then when Neeco came sliding like a snake in the heather we would have had warning. Perhaps some of the men could have held him and his back until others got to safety."

I could make no true reply to that. It seemed from what Meive had said of events, that the Lord of Landale had never thought of treachery. He may have believed that isolated and hard to find as the dale was he had little to fear. Even when the larger dale nearby was ravaged he took few precautions. He had paid high. Let the Gods judge his folly, it was the innocents I regretted, though I said none of that to Meive.

"Meive?" She could write. "Once we turn back, let us buy writing materials. I think it would be well if both of us wrote the stories of how our dales fell. Let those who rule after us remember our stories as a warning. Let them know they must ever guard and not forget that, no matter how long it be, evil may still come creeping. They must be always vigilant."

"That sounds well." She turned to another subject. "Lorcan, do you mean to expand the keep? And where shall we obtain the stone?" We began discussion on that and I said no more on the death of Landale.

The land seemed empty as we rode, yet it was not. The winged-warriors told of those who saw us and hid. Twice they warned of larger groups so that it was we who turned aside. I had taken the less-used trail through the hills close to the fringes of the great Waste. We had supplies enough, and on this path fewer would mark our going. With the winged-ones we feared no ambush, and I believed that no handful of outlaws would attack two well-armed mounted fighters unless there were a number of such bandits to make the attack.

There will always be outlaws so long as men wish to

gain without work. But now the war was done, lords would begin to move against those who despoiled the land. Some might do so because the lord preferred no competition. But most had a real concern for those of their dale. Meive and I knew we must be cautious. Some daleslords would not appreciate our luring away of their people. We would approach only those who no longer had a place in which to live, those who were lordless and landless.

I wanted families, but I would look also for a handful of fighters, men who would act as guards for Merrowdale, the dale nearby of which Meive had spoken. That, too, had been ravaged and brought down. It was possible we could take both dales and hold them. Binding each dale one to the other by a regular exchange of those people whose occupations would allow it. I would think further on that.

We must also be alert as time passed. Once the lords began to reorder the dales further north those outlaws who would not change their ways would have to move. They would seep South towards Merrowdale and then to Honeycoombe. At first it was likely we would see few, but they would be more numerous as the northern dales became more vigorous in defending against them.

I resolved to teach Meive all I could of weapons-work. She had told me she was fair enough with a sling. She already knew the rudiments of handling a light bow and I could teach her further. Sword-drill she had taken to as a fish takes to water, since she was lithe, with quick reactions, and her life had left her with good arm muscles. Besides all this I would add to her lessons the tricks Faslane had taught to me: city street-fighter tricks, most of them, and none the worse for that. Not when one fighter was a light-boned girl who needed any advantage I could contrive.

The journey was peaceful as we traveled. We talked much, so that I came to know Meive as a friend. I learned she had a ready wit, and while she mourned the death of her people, she was slowly beginning to come to terms with her grief and her bitterness at Neeco's betrayal of

them. Once I spoke of Erondale. The discussion led further
as I talked of my family.

"I loved my brothers, but Merrion was not close to me."

"How so?"

"He was seven years older. When Erondale was attacked
he had only been back a few months. Before that he was
visiting friends in other dales for half a year, and two years
at Paltendale learning to be a warrior and to rule a keep as
a lord should. I was closest to Anla. He was only three
years older and should have gone to Paltendale earlier than
he did. He was home again when the invaders struck at
Erondale." I remembered Anla, his laughter, his affection
for the small brother I had been to him.

"I miss them all. Paltendale, too, is not as it was: there
was only Hogar and his three sons in direct line."

Meive's head came up. "Lorcan? Didn't you say one of
the sons survived the war? Why do you speak as though all
the line is ended?"

I looked out into the dark beyond the fire.

"Because there is more to that." I told her the story. Of
how Faslane had believed Hogeth had slain his brother to
inherit Paltendale. Of how, when I found the pass where
the men of Paltendale had stood firm, only the dead
remained—Faslane with a deep dagger-thrust to his
back—and the hoofprints of a single horse which led away.

"You cannot swear," Meive said consideringly. "But like
Faslane you believe. You think Hogeth slew his brother,
slew Faslane perhaps because he saw Faslane suspected.
You think he fled the battle and escaped. Mayhap while his
father and the guard still fought. Has this Hogeth anything
against you, Lorcan?" So I told her, too, of Hogar's chiding
of his son over Hogeth's words concerning me when I was
still a boy.

"He made an enemy for you there. If Hogeth is one such
as you say he would not take well to being criticized before
others. Nor would he blame his own words, but the one
who had brought them forth." With that I could only agree

and be thankful Meive was one with sense. "Tell me of Hogeth?" she continued. "What does he look like, of what manner is his speech? Should I meet him it were well I could recognize him though he will not know me."

I described Hogar's son carefully. Now and again she nodded until at length she seemed to have him firmly fixed in her mind's eye.

"I think I shall know him if I meet him. Thank you, Lorcan."

I turned away to mend the fire. The Gods forfend she must ever meet the man. Hogeth was another such as Pletten the Wicked. There'd been tales at Paltendale within the keep. Soldiers and guards will talk no matter what a lord says about gossip. Once I had overhead something else. Not to speak of that to Meive was to disarm her against danger. I summoned up my courage and cleared my throat. She waited to hear what I would say next.

"It is shame to my House that I should say this. But I owe you sword-debt and you should know. My father said once that there was a curse on the blood of Pasren who founded Paltendale. I know such a man was rare in the dales, where men rarely ill-treated women until the war came to make some men mad. Yet it is rumored that in every fourth generation of the Paltendale line one man will appear who is evil, desiring women and caring not if they say him nay. Four generations back it was a son of the then Lord of Paltendale. This time it is Hogeth." I found myself reddening as I made the tale clear.

"I would not have believed mere gossip but I know that it is the truth," I said briefly. "On one occasion I was in an alcove behind hangings against a window. None knew I was there. I heard Hogar speak to his son about a complaint made by one of the dalesfolk. I heard enough to know Hogeth had done as was claimed and did not repent his deed." I stirred the fire while I waited for her to absorb that. "Meive, he thinks any woman not of noble blood is his by right. It may be that we will meet up with him on this journey. If so I beg you, trust not his words nor ever be alone with him unless it be in a place where your warriors can come to you. For your own safety I ask this."

She flushed slightly but her eyes held mine. "It shall be as you ask. I will be well aware of this man and take no chances."

I was growing to know her now. I saw she spoke truth, and I was content.

IX

I said no more on the subject. I would have said less but for an uneasy feeling. Something warned me that while I wished never again to see Hogeth the same thought was not in his mind. I put foreboding from me, I was no wise woman. What would be would be and worry only weakens. Berond had taught me a warrior must take all precautions, then relax, waiting tranquilly for the time to come when he may act.

Our journey towards Tildale was taking time, yet it was very pleasant. The more I knew of Meive the more I delighted in her. I no longer thought, perhaps a little smugly, a little patronizingly, that she might be a fit lady for my keep that would be. Now I watched humbly and knew if she would be my lady in truth as I oft spoke of her, then would I be more fortunate than most who wed for estate. But of my feelings I did not speak while she traveled with me. It would be wrong to do so and besides, I who had thought my blood and line of the highest, was now afraid to bespeak a dalesgirl lest I be rejected.

Meive was not to be swayed by recitation of long heritage or high estate. She would love one she found who merited that. I was unsure I was that one. Instead I worked to teach her weapons-skill. I praised her when she did well, but I spoke as an instructor or friend and let nothing show of my true feelings.

"Could we purchase a bow for me?" Meive sat cross-legged in camp during the third week of our travel, wiping the bow-string dry on my own bow as she questioned. "This one requires too much strength. If I had one of my own I could learn as I learn the sword."

"I know the land hereabouts," I said absently. "There used to be an inn and a permanent market on the cross-roads of the main road. If it was not destroyed, or if they have set it up again, we could take the over-hills trail. We might find a bow in the market there." I turned to see her eyes widen in pleasure. "We must be careful," I warned.

"Whyfor? Is there likely to be danger at this market?"

I nodded. "It is not unknown for bandits to send one of their number into markets to note any who might be good targets. If we are seen as armed fighters they will be less eager to engage us. Keep your helm on, let me speak. If you need query me draw me aside so none hear your voice. If I must give a name I shall call myself—" My mind went back to the name I had used while I rode with Lord Salden. "Farris of Eldale. You shall be my younger brother, Faldo."

"There's more to this, is there not?"

"Somewhat. I left Paltendale retinue and the Lord Hogar was unpleased I did so. To save trouble when I joined Lord Salden I took to me another name. We go to Tildale where they know me by that name."

"But if the Lord of Tildale was slain at Hagar Pass who will make you free of their House there?"

"His father, Salas."

"How was it his father did not lead?"

"His father was old then, and older now. Aran told me that once Salas's lady died Salas had no more desire to rule. So he gave the rule into his son's hands. Lord Salas lives yet, unless he has died this past year or two. He met me often enough and will open his gates to us both." I leaned back to toss wood on the fire. "Besides, Hogeth would know my true name if it came to his ears through any at Tildale. Belo and Todon, if they live and hear it, would know also who I am. And if I am Farris, best you are my younger brother lest men talk for other reasons. However, I will tell Salas the truth. He is an honorable man." The talk went then to what else we might wish to buy if we found the market.

We took the side-trail next morning. By mid-day we were near enough to see that the inn and the cross-roads market yet stood. Either the invaders had never reached the place or they had bypassed it on another road. I could tell from the wood of the buildings that they were very far from new, so they had not been rebuilt after destruction. I led the way downhill, seeking stables first for the beasts. With them safe, Meive and I plunged eagerly into the mass of people. I had warned her to keep her belt-pouch within her jerkin at the market. There were cut-purses in any market and with lean times after the war, there were more thieves than ever and some were desperate.

I would have turned to the left in the main avenue between the stalls but for her touch on my arm. She said nothing, but signaled my attention with a jerk of her chin towards one stall. I looked. A weapons-seller with good bows for sale. I strolled towards the stall. Once there I took up the bows casually, checking staves and pull. There was one there, a bow made for a woman or boy, which would be suitable. The grip was well-worn but it was in good condition. I settled to bargain. In the end I paid well enough, but for my price I received bow, quiver, spare strings, and a flight of ten good hunting arrows. I waited until we were away before handing the bow and quiver of arrows to Meive.

"I think this will suit you very well. Do you wish to return to leave it with the horses?" She shook her head in silence. Accepting the weapon she hitched it to her back as she had seen me do with my own bow. We began to stroll along the stalls again. I bought journey-bread and cheese, ale in an ale-sack, wound salve, a spare whetstone, and other small purchases. Then I returned to the stables. Once there I looked cautiously about me. None were close.

"Meive? There's a risk, but a small one. We could stay tonight at the inn here. The Inn of the Cross-Roads had a good name in the old days. Two rooms—I shall claim that I have a cold and you are prone to the lung-fever, that way I can ask for two rooms without it appearing strange. Two rooms and a bath. A few good meals we do not have to cook for ourselves."

"A bath?" Her tone was like one who spoke incredulously of treasure. I could understood that. It had been months since I could bathe with soap in heated water. I swore by Cup and Flame I would have a fine bathing-room in our keep. During an errand for Lord Hogar to another keep I had once seen a bathing-room in which the fires to heat the water were above the room so that the heated water flowed down in pipes. I grinned at Meive.

"A bath, yes."

She became practical. "You said there was some risk?"

I shrugged. "To any action there is risk. But I think it is not great. Make certain your door is barred while you bathe, and later when you sleep. Beware of quarrelsome men in the common room."

"We could eat together in your room."

"That is sense."

"Then we stay the night here?"

I smiled. "It seems we do. Now, is there anything else you can bring to mind which we might need at the market? If not we can go to the inn and bespeak what we wish."

Meive's voice rose a little. "Oh, yes. Let us go now."

I saw a stablelad's head turn, but it seemed he merely pointed out one of the horses to his client. The inn found us two rooms. They lay together in one corner of the upper floor and had a door between. The innkeeper took us up and bowed to me as he opened the doors.

"I am Keris, owner of this inn. These are good rooms, Sir. I keep them for those who are kin. If the inner door is opened there is more room for both. And you wish baths? To eat here? That can all be provided."

I haggled. Just hard enough to convince him I was not one with over-filled pouch. Yet I halted soon enough that he should know, too, that I was not so niggardly that good food and service would not receive its due. I also made sure to cough rackingly four or five times, and allowed myself to be overheard warning my brother to be sure he wore his warmest shirt once he was out of the bath.

We bathed, and I can only say that for me, who had not lain in hot water for many months, it was almost a religious experience. Meive emerged pink-faced and smiling, wrapped in her clean cloak. The food appeared on trays and we set to until at last there was only the wreckage of empty greasy plates. I leaned out to glance at the sky before looking at Meive.

"It is not late, but if we sleep now we can rise to eat early in the morning and be gone."

"It sounds well. Let whoever wakes first, wake the other. Should we go to check the horses before we sleep?"

"I will do that, and take back the trays. You seek your bed, and Meive, be very sure your outer door is barred. I think our host is honest, but he has others within his walls."

She retired and I hurried down to see to our mounts' welfare. They were happy, knee-deep in clean straw with filled mangers and water buckets also. They had been well groomed and stood sighing in contentment. I tossed a generous number of coppers to the lad and smiled at him.

"They have well been cared for, thank you. We ride early. See to it that the beasts are fed and watered again at first-light." He caught the coppers neatly and bowed.

"Yes, Lord." He hesitated as if he would speak then, and I waited. His words came slowly, the way a man might speak to himself. "Two horses, none so bad, and the pony with a pack. Some might be interested. Men like one who was here earlier looking about him. He marked you both well. He has no great reputation, so they say."

I matched his tone. "Such a one might ride in company?"

"Aye. So I have heard. Two more of them and each as bad as the other." He rattled a bucket as he filled it. Tossed hay to a nickering horse then spoke as he turned to go. "They bide here tonight." As he went bearing saddlery to clean, I looked after him, my eyes slitted in thought. Surely I had been warned. The lad could be in league with those of whom he warned me, but where was the profit in the warning if so?

I returned to my room and tried the door between Meive and me very quietly. It was unbarred. I listened to her breathing and lifted a candle. All was well. The outer door was barred as I had told her to do. In the candle-light I saw that her window was ajar, and above her the light glinted on her sleeping warriors clinging to a beam. On the sill stood a small flat plate. She would have fed them the honey-water they loved before they slept. Had we been attacked in the open I would have called upon her warriors willingly. But within walls I thought it best none should know of them unless my case be desperate.

From my pack I fetched two wedges and thrust them under her outer door. Each had two spikes at one end, one at each side and at right-angles, which could be trod into the floor. I had learned the carrying of them from Faslane and now in my heart I thanked he who had been a friend. I made sure to bar my own door and retired to the bed. It was soft, and still warm from the warming pan, and I fell into its embrace as a lover.

Still, I had soldiered and scouted. Even in my deepest sleep something in me remained alert. I woke somewhere in the early morning hour to faint sounds outside my room. I judged it perhaps two hours short of dawn, a suitable hour for rogues to be abroad. I moved in the direction of the noises to touch the door. It was from that the sounds came. I smiled, moved through to Meive's room and laid my hand across her mouth.

"Meive, it is Lorcan." I felt her stir and spoke my name again until I felt her nod. "Speak soft. There are thieves or worse at my door. I have wedged your door so they can enter in one place only."

"Why let them enter at all?"

"I think if they cannot come at us this night they will follow. Better to stop them now where we may have aid within call." With two wedges thrust home they would have to smash down her door to enter and that they would not risk. "Let you stay within your room, bar the inner door, and wait. Keep the bees with you. I will call if I am in great need or once it is safe." I thought she might protest that. I had no doubt of her courage, but in such a fight she would be more liability than aid.

"Better you fight alone, knowing each you strike is an enemy," she said at last. I let out a breath.

"That is truth. Yours is the harder thing to do, I know."

"Then go to do your share that I may not wait so long on your call." I reached out to grip her shoulder once in reassurance then sped hastily to my room again to don my mail.

The scratching at my door was a dagger whittling at the door's edge. With a thin blade and a strong wrist, once the gap was made a thief could raise the bar from outside. If they planned only to steal they would first enter a loop of wire to hold the bar from falling. Faslane had shown me the trick once. It was easy enough to intrude the wire above the bar, then retrieve it with another piece of hooked wire from below the bar again. With the bar secured the door could be opened silently, the sleeper within plundered, the thieves long gone before he woke. That was if they wished to steal only.

Otherwise, when the bar fell they must burst in swiftly to take me before I woke to the sound of its fall. If I was fortunate they only planned to knock me on my head and steal. But many a traveler had been found dead in his blood before now. I dare not hold back my blows, the more so as I could feel no wire and there had been the same scratching at Meive's door. I waited, letting my hand touch the bar lightly now and again until I judged it ready to leave the iron hooks on which it lay.

It would open inward. I moved to stand to the side, drew sword and dagger. I poised ready as the bar fell. The thud of its landing was not great, yet they, too, must have been ready. The door was flung open and a man burst through. I allowed him to pass me then struck him down just as his comrade entered. My blow had been true so that the thief died without cry. I think the one who followed believed the small sound of a blade cleaving flesh was made by his friend as he slew me.

He grunted approval, then spoke low-voiced. "Is he dead?"

I closed with him, my dagger went home even as my other hand choked back any cry in his throat. His own dagger snapped on my mail. He thrashed somewhat after that as he died. The third of them must have been bewildered by the dark. He blundered into me, seized my arm, and muttered angrily.

"You make too much noise about it, you fool. You'll have the innkeeper up here."

"A good thought," I agreed. I lifted my dagger, striking him hard across the side of the head with the pommel before he understood my words. He staggered and half-fell. I caught him as he sagged, flinging him to the corner behind the door. Then I lifted my voice in a bellow. "Ho, innkeeper, aid here! Aid to your guests beset by thieves."

I heard the bar on Meive's side of the inner door fall

free. She sprang into the room sword in hand, mail and helm in place, her bee warriors at the ready above her, even as I lit a candle. At a glance she saw I was unharmed. Her eyes questioned me. I waved her and her company to retire and moved to shut the door again behind her. She obeyed hastily, just as the innkeeper arrived, still in his nightshirt but with a businesslike sword clenched in one meaty hand.

"Thieves? Where?" I stepped aside from the door. "Ah." He turned the nearest body over with one foot. "Melcan and," he thrust over the other body. "His comrade, Deggs. A good nights work on your part, young Sir." Behind us, sprawled in the corner where I had flung him, the third thief groaned. The innkeeper turned like a cat. His voice carried vast satisfaction as he raised the lantern his scullery boy had brought.

"Marteyn Crowsbait—and alive! Long have I waited for justice on this one." He raised his voice to his staff as they gathered behind him. "Bind him, lads. Bind him very secure and call the market guards."

I went to sit upon my bed while men tramped in and out, guards were called, and the bodies of those I had slain were removed. I told my story several times, each time to louder approval, making sure I coughed rackingly now and again and sniffed hard after each coughing spell. Once all was cleared Keris the innkeeper remained. He shut the door and turned to me.

"You were waiting for them. Nay, do not tell me I am wrong. I was a soldier before I took up this trade." That I had guessed. He moved still like a man who was sword-trained. "I ask no questions. I am only glad to know that Marteyn will bother us no more."

"There was a grudge between you?"

"A grudge indeed. Two years gone at war's end I hosted a young couple. Recently wed when it appeared the war would be soon over. They were no lord's kin. Merely two dalesfolk who wished to be happy."

"What happened?"

"They were found dead in their room. The boy had been daggered, despoiled of belt-pouch and weapons, but the girl . . ." His voice trailed off, so I guessed what he would not say.

"Marteyn and his fellows?"

"So I have always thought. They guested that night here. They had not the name for such doings then, but later I heard it, so came to think it had been their work. Since then I have watched them close should they take beds here." He looked at me. "I thought not that you and your brother would be in danger. Marteyn was not one to risk his hide 'gainst two men to his three, and those two armsmen by appearance. I was wrong and I beg pardon of you. I should perhaps have spoken to the market guards."

"It's their job to know. Would they stand guard outside the doors of all who might be at risk? If they could find no proof what could you have said since you also had none?" I consoled him. "I and my brother are unharmed. We have lost nothing. Let it be."

Keris looked me in the eye. "Still, I should have denied them a room. Accept your own fees paid. I take nothing from you and would that you remained another day so I may repay the debt I feel."

I stood in thought a moment. Meive would delight in another bath and a second night in a real bed. And I could talk privately with Keris on the morrow. He would know of all the dales around and of how they had survived the invader. He could maybe name some who might be eager for land and their own homes again. I need not seek them out until we returned, but to know of them now would save time then.

"We will stay the second night. I thank you, Keris." I spoke to him not as customer bespeaks an innkeeper but as a soldier answers a comrade. His spine straightened further as a glow of pride lit his eyes. He departed and I went to the inner door to tell Meive of events. I found it ajar and knew she had heard.

"If you object, we shall leave," I offered.

"What, deny another bath and a real bed? I'm not such a fool." Nor had I thought that of her.

We spent the day pleasantly in the market. There was a commotion at sunhigh when Marteyn Crowsbait was aided to live up to his name. Most of those about in the market went to watch, though neither Meive nor I wished to see. It was justice, but we had seen too many dead men already. That night we bathed in our rooms before being treated to a feast fit for any lord of the dales.

During the next day I sought out Keris—making sure to continue my coughing, though by now I was heartily sick of the ruse and wished I had thought of some other reason why Meive and I should have separate rooms. However, Keris was able to tell me much about those dales which had not survived. I made notes in my mind. There were both landless families and lone fighters about in the area. I would recall the names he had given me. When we returned I could seek some of them out.

After that I found the stable-lad who had warned me. He did not wish it to be known, he said. I swore I would keep silent to Keris. I wondered if the boy had known one of the thieves but still warned me. I thought him not involved in what they had planned. I thanked him.

"We think to return this way in some weeks. If you would have a place in a dale, work you may prefer to this, there would be a place for you. Think on it until we return. If you decide to remain here, well, this will smooth your path." I gave him coin and saw him flush as he counted.

"I was glad enough to do it."

"As I am glad to be alive, I and my brother." I saw his eyes slide away at that and suddenly knew. It must have been when Meive raised her voice in this stable. I had seen the boy turn his head. He had guessed Meive to be a woman in disguise, and I thought it was for that he had warned us. I had best be grateful the boy was perceptive, else likely he'd have said nothing and we two could now lie dead. "There'd be a place for you," I said again, and left him.

We departed the next day after breaking our fast with a large platter of bread and cheese. I pushed the pace as we dropped back over the hills and followed the road along the Waste fringe once more. Above us Meive's wing-friends hummed happily. They had not much liked our nights under a roof at the inn. It took another ten-day, but at length I saw a trail back across the mountains.

"This should lead us direct to Tildale. It will be pleasant to see Aran again."

Meive studied me critically. "The dye fades from your hair," she told me. "Do you wish to renew that before we meet your friend?"

I did. It took the remainder of that day for my hair to be rinsed in the powdered herb and dried. But once that was done we had a merry camp. After we retired I lay looking at the stars. It had been late Spring when I met my lady. Now it was Summer. There would be no need to worry about shelter once we were back in Honeycoombe. A few weeks work and the village houses would be weather-tight. It was the keep which would require time and labor.

If none had survived to return to the neighboring Merrowdale we could plunder the stones from their keep. Or perhaps they had built some cot or barn in stone, that we could take without further damage to their hold. I had not seen Merrowdale, the trail we had taken led us another way, but Meive said it had once been a prosperous enough place. There might even be livestock there gone wild which we could take for ourselves.

In the morning I found I had slept well. Berond oft said that a busy day makes for a sound sleep. By mid-morning we found the side track into Tildale. I led the way; Meive, mailed and helmed, riding behind me; Drustan trotting after us. I sucked in a breath and Meive glanced at me. Her voice came thoughtfully as she looked at the land.

"Hard land, small acreage. They do not do well here. I see few men and most of those too old, too young, or crippled. The crops are scant, the animals thin. Last Winter was hard, but I think it was far harder here, though it is so much further to the North."

"It looks to be so."

"How many rode from here to fight beside Imgry?"

"Aran said they stripped the dale. Even Lord Salden's father, Salas, rode with us a while, and Salden was of middle-age."

"And of those who rode only Aran, Lord Salas, and two others lived? What of the lord's family? Were there other sons?"

"Aran told me there were none. Salden was the son still living. Of daughters there were two, both long-since wed. But both lived in dales which were laid waste by the invader. It was for their deaths that Salden and his father chose to ride with Imgry."

Beyond us the folk drew together, women holding pitchforks in a way which said they would fight at need. I saw a boy running towards the keep. I halted, dismounting in courtesy to wait. Meive stayed on her horse, ready to flee. The workers moved in until they stood some short arrow-flight away in a half-circle. I had tossed back the chain coif so my face might be seen, which was as well. Lord Salden's father came riding quickly, but as he recognized me he slowed his mount.

"Farris of Eldale, well met man. Do you come to take up the service I once offered or to visit friends?"

As he spoke he was dismounting and advancing to hold out his hand. His hard palm met mine in a strong grip which I returned happily. I had always liked the old man.

He had ridden to war, even as his son, but had been too old to match the hard riding of our band. Still, his desire for vengeance had been greater than lordly pride. He had remained acting as clerk and sutler for his son, and a very fair job of it he had made. I had a goodly amount to do with him over the time I rode with his son, and when I returned after the battle at Hagar Pass the old man had offered me a place in Tildale.

"No, Lord. I come as a friend to see friends. Is Aran here?"

His face clouded as he shook his head. "No, and there is a sad tale to tell you there, Farris. Would I did not have it to tell. But let that bide. You must be weary, you and your comrade. Come to the keep, wash, share food, fire, and wine. We'll trade stories of what has happened since I saw you last."

"May I speak privately with you, Lord?" I knew Salas well. Lay oath on him and he would see everyone he knew dead at his feet and himself added before he opened his lips. He waved back his people and they obeyed. I nodded thanks.

"Lord Salas, I present my lady." I gave that the twist in tone which meant leige. "Meive, Wise Woman of Landale, to whom I owe sword-debt." I signaled to her so that with her back to those others, she raised her helm's visor to smile on the old man. "Who we truly are must be secret. I ask only your word on it."

His back stiffened. "My word is as good as my oath, Farris. That you know. Yet you shall have both. None shall know your secrets from me. But you say who the both of you are in truth? Therefore I must guess that you, too, are not as you seem."

"No harm to you or yours from me or mine," I said quickly. "With your House I have neither feud nor grudge. But I have enemies. I would they did not hear of me or my lady until I can coax them from hiding or get word of their deaths." In which things I was hardly alone in the dales. Salas smiled.

"Be welcome under my roof, the two of you. Guest-rights I offer."

"Guest-rights we accept," I said for us both.

So we entered the keep of Tildale, and that night as we three sat alone to eat and drink I heard of my friend Aran. And it was a grim tale I heard.

Meive

X

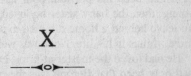

I had listened carefully to Lorcan's initial plans for my dale. They were of good common sense and that was no mean thing. For what they call "common" sense is none too common. I lay in my bedding and smiled upwards to the dark. I knew above me my warriors had swarmed and now hung from a branch of the tree underneath which we lay. This they had done any night there was a suitable campsite. At other times they found a rock crevice or some such place. They had been valiant scouts during our journey. I opened my mind and basked in dim, sleepy thoughts of nectar and queens.

I enjoyed our ride down into the market. My wing-friends took to the air and left. They would return when I called to them, which I would not do until we had a safe place to lie for the night. In a market stall Lorcan found for me a good bow which I liked. There were blue and green beads on the grip and the black wood tapered smoothly. I thought it foreign work perhaps, but none the less good for that.

"Will you risk the inn, Meive? We could have hot baths and eat well, we could sleep soft for once if you wished?"

A foolish question and I was no fool. I yearned for a hot bath and soap as a lost lamb yearns for the ewe. I told him so and watched as he laughed, the amusement on his face making him look no more than the boy he yet was. It pleased me that I could bring him laughter. Little enough of it had been his portion, poor lad. To lose his mother young, then the baby sister he loved, his father, brothers. To leave behind a home tumbled to ruin, losing all the familiar things in his life. None was well for a child.

He had loved the master-at-arms, I thought, or perhaps it had only been that Berond was the one thing left to him. Faslane had been a friend but he, too, lay dead. It must seem to Lorcan as if anything for which he came to care was taken by death. Well, I did not plan to die just yet. Let him care for me. I stole a look at his face as we walked the market. He had not the arrogance which I had heard of some daleslords. Best he did not show it to me were it there. A wise woman is equal in status to a lord if she has true power.

"Meive?" Lorcan's low voice recalled my attention to him as we finished eating. "Is there anything here you wish to purchase?"

We had been strolling as we ate lightly. I took the lead searching the stalls with hand and glance. I added needles and thread to my pouch, then dried herbs. Lorcan dyed his hair the better not to be known if seen by his enemies. I made sure we had packets of the dye before we turned back to the inn.

We talked as we ate the good food our innkeeper brought us. The ale was a fair new brew which both of us relished, though we drank only a small amount. At last we were done with talk and food. Outside it darkened though it was not yet late. I peered from the window to see clouds covering the sky. I hoped that it would not rain. With all my heart I dislike riding wet.

"Best we sleep now," Lorcan told me. "Early to bed and we wake early." I agreed. It was pleasant riding in the clean quiet time when none save we two were awake and small birds sang. I retired, stripped to my under-garments, and opened the window silently. A flat plate I laid on the sill contained honey-water. I called. The winged-ones hummed in to join me. They drank, then found the warmth of our rooms pleasing, choosing to sleep on a ceiling beam above me so that I laid down in good company. I slept, knowing I was twice safe.

I woke to a hand over my mouth and Lorcan's voice whispering my name. I nodded to let him know I was awake, then listened. It was not well but could be worse. Let Lorcan fight: he was a warrior trained. But I, I was Meive of Honeycoombe and I, too, could fight. I heard Lorcan's outer door flung open. Heard the struggle as I armed myself and warned my warriors. Then I flung open my own door at Lorcan's shout.

I saw all in one swift look. Two men down, dead or dying, another half-stunned, sprawled in a corner. And pounding footsteps approaching up the stairs. I spared Lorcan a glance. He needed no aid, being unhurt, and best the innkeeper saw me not. Let him think me a slugabed who slept through any sound. I retired again hastily, sending reassurance to my bees, to come forth later once all the inn staff and others were gone again. And Gods know that took time enough, for those who came would have the story again and again. I held the door somewhat ajar and listened to all that was spoken. At last I was able to rejoin Lorcan.

"So, we stay another day and night?"

"I thought you would wish it." He looked a little anxious. "It would mean another hot bath and a soft bed. I believed you would like that?"

He meant he, too, would find pleasure as well as I, in which he was very right. I said so, watching his gaze lighten. The next day was like a fair day. We walked the markets, buying small items and watching the sights. At midday there was a commotion as people pushed away to the gallows-ground to watch the man Lorcan had taken be hanged. I did not wish to see and was pleased to find Lorcan also had no desire to watch the man die.

On the morrow we rode out. We followed a rough trail until we could swing back to the dales again from the fringes of the great Waste. But at last we came to Tildale where I looked for a welcome from Lorcan's friends. My first sight of the dale was not encouraging. It was poorly farmed, the soil stony and thin. The beasts looked hungry and the people gaunt. Since it was Summer, and they should have had Spring to recover from a hard Winter, it suggested all was not well. I said something of this to Lorcan, who agreed.

Most of those in the fields appeared to be women and children, so that I wondered, where were the men who should have been there to aid? A question or two and I understood. Lord Salden had taken most to Imgry's army. Very few had returned. This was a dale of old men or cripples, women and children, until the children should grow. Tildale was an old dale, the fertility of the soil almost worked out. It seemed as if it had never been a large or rich dale. A thought came to my mind then, though I said nothing. The idea might be good, it might not. Let it wait until I saw what manner of lord ruled here, what manner of people he ruled.

That I saw. Once Lord Salas arrived it was clear he both held Lorcan in high regard and was in turn honored and respected. We bathed again, drank light and ate full before Lord Salas turned to speak of Lorcan's friend, Aran of Tildale. I had heard much of that rogue. Lorcan had ridden with him more than a year, and they had been good friends, in the manner of men, which is different from that of women.

Back to back they had stood against the invaders before Aran returned to Tildale. His friend had planned to settle and wed, Lorcan had told me. But it was not to be. Instead Aran had been slain, by men it appeared, in a manner most foul and without cause so far as any knew. The dalesfolk had hunted, Lord Salas told us. Hunted out from Tildale seeking any who might be responsible, but they found no one and nothing.

"It was a poor death, lad." Salas bowed his head. "They tortured him; we found him half-naked, dying, the marks of whip and fire upon him. What could Aran have done or known worthy of that?"

"I cannot think. True, he was not always honest, but he did nothing which would draw such a death." Lorcan, too, was grieved. "He fought well. No battle-comrade could say Aran did not do his share when the fighting was hard. You say he was dying when you found him, did he say nothing?"

Lord Salas shook his head. "He raved. Speaking of a man with an eagle's eyes and antlers. He died before we could bring him home." I saw this meant something to Lorcan. He said nothing of what that might be but asked another question.

"How long after you returned to Tildale did this occur?"

"It was late Summer when we returned." Salas was reckoning it up. "We worked hard until Winter, digging over and weeding much of the land, which had lain fallow while we were at war, then it was the Spring sowing, and Summer harvest again. Aye. It was on the edge of the next Winter. Somewhat over a year. Does that have meaning to you?"

"Only this," Lorcan said thoughtfully. "It is such a time as it might take a man to find another if he knew only a little of where to search."

"You think then that those who killed Aran hunted him?"

"It is possible." I knew he did not tell all he thought—or knew. We drank little more before retiring, but once Lord Salas was away to his bed I sought out Lorcan's chamber.

"You should not be here."

I eyed him stubbornly. "I am no lord's daughter to care. Tell me, Lorcan. When Salas spoke how Aran babbled of

eagle's eyes and antlers you guessed who might have slain
Aran, did you not? Will you withhold that from me? What
if this man seeks me also and I am taken unawares?" I
watched as Lórcan thought that over. I could see his decision when he turned to me, waving that I should sit. His
voice was grim.

"If it is the one I fear then you know him. I have described him well to you before-times."

My mind flew to that time we camped and he spoke of an
enemy. I gasped. "Hogeth. You believe it was Hogeth. Why?"

"Why he should do this thing, I know not. But whyfor I
believe it to have been him? His eyes, Meive. Of what
color are mine; what hue are your own eyes?"

"Your eyes are hazel," I said slowly. "Mine are more
green, though I am told they, too, are hazel in some light.
What of Hogeth then?"

"Yellow. Like an eagle or hawk. Wicked and without
mercy, as I guess Aran to have seen them. As for the
antlers, what of Paltendale's House badge? What is that but
a deer with one antler broken? Hogeth is Lord of Paltendale, he would not lightly discard his House badge and
name. I think he came seeking me here, perhaps without
knowing I went under another name. Aran might not have
recognized a description given and denied my own name.
Therefore Hogeth questioned him more stringently.
Though why he should be so insistent, I know not." He
shook his head sadly but I, too, was thinking hard.

"What does this Hogeth care about? Women, wealth, his
own dale?"

"As to such things, aye. Women he likes well enough,
though he considers them there to be used at his whim.
Wealth I think he would like. More to make a show before
others than because he would gloat over the coin itself. But
Paltendale, yes. There he does care. Faslane believed
Hogeth cared enough for Paltendale that he slew his elder
brother to inherit dale and heir-right."

"Paltendale fell. Could he return?"

Lorcan shrugged as he looked at me. "He could return. Now that the invader is driven out nothing bars him from the high seat of Paltendale. His father and brothers are dead . . ." He paused and I knew he remembered his own family. "Faslane, who might have spoken, is dead along with all who rode out with Hogar. With all others of his line dead, Hogeth could return unopposed to rule. But the keep wall, the great door, both were broken in. The dale was ridden with fire and sword so that many cots burned. Those scavengers who came later would have swept up straying beasts. It would need hard coin and a goodly amount to bring the land back, to restock it and to repair the keep."

"Even so," I said quietly, looking at him with meaning. His face changed as he saw it then.

"Coin I have knowledge of. But how—" He swore savagely, bitterly. "I killed Aran. I with my folly. Well did Faslane chide me after I renounced service to Hogar. Did Berond not teach you to keep tight purse-strings and tighter lips? he said. But in my pride I fumbled what I did and flung gold instead of silver at my lord to pay the price he demanded for the clothing he had given me over the years. And what occurred about his father that Hogeth did not come to know? Or mayhap the old man told him in anger. So now when Hogeth must have coin to rebuild his dale he remembers that gold coin and comes seeking me." He bowed his head on crossed arms. "Hogeth was my enemy, I knew that. I never thought to warn Tildale or my friend. Now Aran lies dead, tortured to buy Paltendale's rebuilding."

I grieved for his sorrow and the guilt I knew he suffered. But now was not the time to weep. Better to take up sword that others weep. I said so and saw him lift his head to stare at me. His eyes glinted fire through the tears.

"Well said, my leige-lady. I knew Aran. I would guess at first he knew not for whom they asked. Once he understood—if so be it he ever did—he would set fast his mouth. He was no hero but he could be very stubborn. He would know they could not leave him alive to talk. It would please him to know he died and they got nothing from him."

"What could he have said?"

"Very little, in truth. I had no plans when we parted. I rode a time with those who patrolled seeking out invaders who might be in hiding. It was after that I chose to ride South. I think I had said to him, once, that was in my mind. But 'South' is a great area. What does Hogeth know, after all? That I once had one gold coin. That my own dale is so ruined I can never rebuild my estate there again and hope to prosper."

"Maybe so. But what does he wish to believe?" I queried. "Will he not wish that where there is one coin there may be many more? That if you have no dale you will go seeking another to take, as would he? He will return to your dale to see if anyone had camped there. Then he will seek out those with whom you rode to ask questions. Are not many of the dales, much of the lands in the South and East, unharmed? Where else should a lord seek a place to raise his house and his bloodline again?"

I had not learned from Ithia for nothing. She had taught me to lay one fact upon another and learn a direction. In her own young days, after a great loss, she had wandered far, learning from the good Dames and from others in far stranger places, before she came home to Honeycoombe to build hives and tend her bees. She had taught me of the world beyond Honeycoombe and of the hearts and desires of dalesfolk. It made sense to me that Hogeth would hunt a man who might have gold. Where else would he find the price to rebuild? No lord could spare it. The dales lay poverty-stricken after the war and lords hoarded every coin to themselves, spending only upon their family and essential supplies or repairs.

Hogeth would get no coin from them who were not kin

or clan to him. So he must find any coin he needed else-where, and where else but from a man who had once shown he had coin? Gold which would be the sweeter if taken from one Hogeth disliked. So he would hunt a trail. What of the ruined dale, what of those with whom Lorcan had last ridden? I asked.

"Aye," he answered me slowly. "I rode home. If he found my camp site he would know at least one rider had been there of recent times, though our treasure is so hid he would find nothing even if he brought a dozen men and hunted all year. No, if he believes there is more gold where that coin came from, then he knows he has to find me. As for the men with whom I rode, I said nothing worth hear-ing to them, since I had no plans. But I did say as I left them that I would ride South. That much they would know and could tell. But that was all Aran could tell." He nodded to himself.

"But Hogeth would not know that unless he asked. So ask he did, and Aran died of that asking. I owe Hogeth a debt for that which I shall repay if ever I meet him again."

"Do you think Hogeth is seeking you while leaving Pal-tendale to stand alone without a lord?"

"I think not. He would rebuild as best he can without coin. Work hard those who returned, in plowing fields and sowing crops, to rebuild cot and barn. He will hunt out nearby dales where a lord is dead and take from them any beasts left alive, taking any property or gear he can terror-ize the people into allowing him. He will cozen their peo-ple to join Paltendale, and once they are there he will see they remain to work. But between times I think he will ride out to find those who may tell him of me. It would take time to find men who could say one of my description had ridden with Tildale. That may be why it has taken him so long to find the trail."

"Then I have a plan," I said. "You know whence he can obtain news of you. First we do as we had planned for Honeycoombe. We return before Winter with those who will come. We repair the keep, the cottages, and barns. I shall care for my bees when Winter strikes. But once Spring sowing is done we shall ride again. Let us seek out those who have known you and ask of them if Hogeth has been there. Thus we shall find him before he and his find us. Then let you deal with him as you desire."

I think my look may have been most unmaidenly fierce as I said that last. I did not care. I had talked to one in the keep who had been a friend to this Aran. She had been there when they washed the body, preparing it for burial. From her I had learned how hard my lord's friend had died. If Lorcan found the man who had done that and slew him, it was no more than justice. Nor would I speak one word against it.

In the end we stayed ten days at Tildale. We talked often to Lord Salas of the better dale to be found near my own home. In the end, he was swayed by his own kin. We had heard from some in the keep that his daughters and their lords had died. One girl, however, had borne children before the invaders came. When she began to fear for her dale, she made arrangements in secret, her own lord being a pompous and obstinate man. Salas told us of this.

"The children had a nurse." He smiled sadly. "A daleswoman in body and spirit. Sturdy of body, stout of heart, and loving to children that were not hers. When the invaders drew onto the borders of my daughter's home, she sent the woman away alone with none but the children and the woman's son. They came to safety before their dale fell."

"Why then did the woman not tell you she had your grandchildren safe, Lord?" Lorcan queried.

"She could neither read nor write and the war had raged through the dales between us. It was more than a year before she could get word to me. By then it was the edge of Winter. I looked for them in Spring but the girl took a cough and had to stay abed." He sighed. "I received a letter from the Dames at Norstead saying the boy had taken the cough from his sister and that they feared for him. Best he and his sister remain yet. I agreed. Thus is it that my heart leapt when the boy here ran to say riders approached."

I understood first. "Then they are due at the gates of Tildale?"

"Indeed, and long awaited."

So that was why we stayed longer than the day or two planned. The small weary group arrived three days after our own arrival. The old woman, nurse to Salas's daughter's lord once, was now nurse to Merria and Malco. I judged the older child, Merria, to be around seven. The boy was barely three. He can only have been a babe when he fled his home. But both appeared lively, sensible, healthy children so I thought Salas was fortunate.

But it made up his mind. Over the next five days I saw him riding or walking the fields often, stooping to study the meager crops or take up a handful of the thin soil and let it trickle through his fingers. One's home is one's heart, no matter how poor it may be. To leave one's home behind, and more, to uproot others to follow you, is no light or easy decision. But he was a knowing man, the Lord Salas. Tildale had never been rich. It was one of the earlier dales settled and the soil was worked out. Let it lie fallow some generations and it might recover.

As it was, each Spring the land was less fertile, the people more hungry, the keep poorer. Better Salas took our suggestion, rode South with us and settled a dale both larger and richer. And before others came riding with the same thought in mind. I talked of it with him.

"Merrowdale is a fair dale. They bred sheep, the Mountain strain with fine wool. We saw some running wild when we rode out past the dale. They had a good keep and were taken only as we were, by treachery."

"How many families did it support?"

I shook my head. "That I cannot say for certain. I know it to be larger than Honeycoombe. My dale had almost one hundred and twenty folk. I think Merrowdale sheltered half again, at least. Neither dale was feeding as many as it could have done." Lord Salas stared at me. I could understand his surprise. In my wanderings over Tildale I had seen it held some sixty folk in want. A dale which would hold thrice that number in well-fed and spacious comfort was a prize worth the taking.

Five days after the children had arrived I met Merria riding a small fat pony. She halted to greet me. Since I had ridden to the dale entrance and away from the folk, my warriors had taken to the air as guard. Now one winged down towards the child. I looked for a cry of fear but she held out her hand. My warrior settled upon the flattened palm, fanning his wings and looking back at Merria through black faceted eyes.

She beamed down. "He's beautiful. Would he mind if I touched him?"

"Very gently. He enjoys having his fur stroked with a fingertip." Others of the winged-ones were descending to land upon me. I heard then the sound in my mind which must have alerted Ithia seven years gone. A honey-sweet humming. Approval and choice. This girl was acceptable to them. In the last few years I had sometimes wondered who would follow me. Now my wing-friends chose. I rode back with Merria, telling her about them, seeing her interest in all I could say. Then I sought out Lord Salas.

"She has the gift," I summed up. He sat saying nothing for a long space of time until finally he spoke.

"Will you wed Lorcan?"

I would have answered tartly that it was no business of his, but then I saw the fear behind his question. He meant not, would I wed, but would Merria be able to wed if she took my road? All know that across the sea the Witches of Estcarp cannot lie with a man and keep their powers. That did not apply to those chosen by the winged-ones. That difference I had been careful to mention, as if casually, to Lorcan.

"I do not know if I will choose to wed," I said now. "But it would be no loss to me if I did so." Lord Salas leaned forward awaiting my words. "The gifts I have are not changed by wedding and bedding. Ithia before me was wed, she walked alone many years because her man died in a hill storm, and she had borne him no children. Once she returned to our dale she lived alone by choice, taking an apprentice when one was shown her by the bees. I was that one. I may well wed in my turn. If so, the home that was Ithia's and is now mine, will be inherited by my apprentice on my departure so that she may always have a roof over her head."

"That is well. What of your own children, if you have them?"

"If I bear children they may carry no gifts. Often it misses a generation. If I take Merria as apprentice it may be a granddaughter of mine who is next apprentice in turn."

"What if I deny her apprenticeship with you?"

"Shall Lorcan and I steal her away? The gift's seed she has, yes. But if she does not use it, nor is trained in the use of it, then it shall wither. That choice, too, is part of this gift. Yet," I looked at him strongly, "Ithia made our dale very good coin with her knowledge. The cordial she could make saved many lives. Nor do the Gods approve one who denies the gifts they give." I said no more. Let him consider my words and his granddaughter's future without feeling I pressed him for my own ends.

Aye, he was a good and knowing man, old Lord Salas. He considered to some purpose. When we rode out of Tildale it was with his agreement pledged on two counts. With the next Spring crops gathered in, with Summer he and his should ride to take over Merrowdale as our neighbors. Leaving, he said, some few of his people to hold Tildale until his ownership of Merrowdale was assured. He was not one to let loose reality to grasp a dream and lose both.

He would come in a year and with him would ride Merria, to be my apprentice once her years were enough. Lorcan and I rode South, and if we smiled often and, laughing, sang songs of the dales, who would deny us our happiness?

XI

——◦——

As we rode down the track, almost a week after leaving
Tildale, clouds were beginning to loom over us and
darken. I looked up at the sky, Lorcan's gaze met mine, and
in wordless agreement we hurried the horses. The weather,
which had held off some time now, would soon be upon us.
It would rain before dawn and that rain would not be light.
One of the dales storms was on the way and they could be
ferocious at this time of year. Best we find good shelter so
we and the beasts would sleep dry.

"Do you know the land hereabouts?"

Lorcan glanced around. "Not well. I rode through a few
times taking messages and later in pursuit of stragglers
from the invaders. But it was some time ago and I was always in haste. I recall little, save," he paused to cudgel his
memory, "I do recall a shelter in the hills. The man with
whom I rode knew of it. We stayed the night there when we
met such a storm as we shall see here soon. I think the
track to the shelter goes into the hills from the road no
great distance from here."

"How deep in the hills?"

"Deep enough. An hour's hard riding at least. But I think
this storm will last the night and maybe the following day.

Better we go a distance and have good shelter than we stay on the road and hope for it but find nothing."

With that I could only agree. We rode hard then, pushing our mounts, Drustan running behind them. The track Lorcan recalled appeared to the right and we swung our mounts onto it. The faint narrow path led steeply uphill so that we and the horses had to lean into the climb. I thought as we rode that most likely it had been made by feet rather than hooves. Who would place some building here? Perhaps it had been a shelter for beasts and their herders once.

Thrice as we rode I had a strange feeling, as if one watched to see us pass. I saw nothing but rocks here and there. Three such stood tall like fingers raised to the sky. They appeared featureless and I did but glance as we hurried past. Yet chilly fingers walked my spine at the look of them. The track was trod deep and baked hard by Summer sun. If any had come this way recently there were no signs. If the shelter was known I thought it not unlikely someone had found it. Those who lived thereabouts would know of it.

Many of the dales in this area were ruined, some so devastated by the strange weapons the invader brought first, that it might be many years or even generations before the dale returned to life. So it had been with Lorcan's home. It was for that reason he had to seek a new place. I allowed my gaze to touch his face as we moved on. I had come to care deeply for him over the months as we rode together.

At first I had bid my warriors be vigilant. Lorcan was of that House I knew to be, at the least, untrustworthy with women: Paltendale, whose son had ravaged my great-grandmother thinking her honor valueless since she was not of noble birth. I smiled to myself. Lorcan sorrowed that of all his blood only Hogeth, his enemy, remained along with Lorcan himself. He said little but I knew he grieved. How wrong he was. I who rode beside him was of that House, and his own line.

I claimed it not, what honor was there in claiming blood begotten thusly? But that blood was yet mine. It seemed also that there were gifts in the line. Had not one of the strange ones appeared to the Lord of Lorcan's dale once and given treasure? True, they owed a debt, but they had spoken face to face. A rare and wondrous thing. I did not think then of the Lady of the Bees. That was more natural to me. I was her daughter in gift. Why should I not see her and hold speech?

Lorcan reached over to touch my arm. "I think we are close."

"Well enough. I'm tired and the horses are no better."

We rounded the corner of a hill. In my mind I heard a shrilling hum of alarm. Of our warriors, several flew always well ahead of us as scouts. Now they cried out to me, warning us back. The winged-ones rose up, wings glittering in the last rays of sun before the storm-clouds. They hung before me, a shimmering curtain of anxiety. I pulled my mount to a halt, hand lashing out to catch at Lorcan's reins.

"Danger, Lorcan, there's trouble ahead. Hold back." Thanks be he knew to listen.

"What danger?"

"I know not, but the winged-ones are certain. Let them go ahead to see for us. I think the shelter is close by." He glanced up at the sky. The storm was gathering slowly, it would be the more powerful for that. Fast gather—fast fade; slow start—slow end, is the dales saying on our storms—and it is very true.

"Tell them to go swiftly. Or the choice may be between whatever is the danger they see, and our pneumonia."

"The latter may be treated," I retorted, before I slipped into the hive mind.

My warriors darted ahead and I saw Lorcan had been right. We were barely a half mile from the shelter. But about that shelter horses were tethered. They were good beasts but hard-used, and with them were a couple of the hill ponies bearing packs. I studied the shelter through many eyes. This may have once been something else, but it had long since been converted to use as a herd shelter. I could see where the stones had been replaced, the wood of the watering troughs repaired. Even those repairs were old. Whatever had once resided here should be long gone.

I knew that very long ago it had been a building of a different sort. The bees could read that and I through them. The winged-ones floated in the air, allowing me to see all clearly before they drifted high to pass through the open door barely below the lintel. I was speaking, relaying what I saw to Lorcan. And what I saw was an ill thing to see.

"How many men?"

"We see seven. I think they are of the kind which slew my dale. Men gone outlaw."

They could be men who had run mad from grief at some great loss the war had brought. Yet I knew that their loss excused nothing of what that kind did, in Landale or in other places. I, too, had lost my home, my family, and Ithia my teacher. I had not run crazed, slaying all I met as if their deaths would somehow ease my sorrow. Or had I? I had killed, I and my warriors, without mercy. Maybe that had been my own easing. I would think on that later. Lorcan was muttering at me. I obeyed his demand, sending a warrior outside to count.

"There are seven horses."

"Then that may be the complete tally of the men. The hill ponies you see may belong to those others."

Those others, yes. I judged them a family. Like many of the dalesfolk they clung to kin. I could see an elderly woman, two women of middle-age. A man held by one of the women lay flat, blood about his head and face. His arm seemed crooked, so that I suspected it to be broken previously. Three young women and an older boy; he, too, was injured. And several children. They huddled together and I could see the fear on the faces upturned to await their fate.

Only the old woman's face showed no fear, only determination and a kind of waiting. In a corner stood several goats, two with kids.

"Likely they are refugees from one of the coastal dales," Lorcan commented, as I relayed what I saw, "come upon this place by accident. Any dales-bred seeing this side path would guess there was some sort of shelter at the end of it. But the men, what like are they?" I knew him to mean those who had come raiding, so I turned the gaze of my warriors upon the seven men.

"They have two small barrels which one man seems to guard. They are well armed," I reported. One turned as I spoke. I could see now what lay upon one hip. I sucked in my breath. "One I would judge to be leader wears a dart gun!"

"A dart-gun?" Lorcan echoed my words. "Only Alizon had those. We use them not in the dales. They are man-slayers and useless for much else. One pays for them in gold and the darts cost high. Better a bow. They are little better than one and a bow can be more cheaply had." His voice dropped to a snarl. "It was said in Imgry's camp that a few of our kind who rode renegade with Alizon were given dart-guns in token. When we flung back the invaders, breaking their army and camps, I heard such renegades ran back to the dales. They are of us, therefore they could disappear more easily. Look closer at these men and tell me more."

I obeyed. "The leader is tall, he wears leather clothing. He looks like a dalesman, not of noble blood. More like one who has been well-fed but hard-worked. He is strong and quick. I can see it in the way he moves. He has the dart-gun upon his left hip, on his right he wears a good sword. A lord's weapon, with a hilt of gold and gems. His dagger is the same."

"Loot?" I heard Lorcan mutter to himself.

"The man who stands by the door is another of that kind. He wears a tabard beneath a cloak. I cannot see all the device, but what I can see appears like a pard's mask. He wears jewels about his neck and on one wrist. The man beyond him looks very like him in features. I would think them kin. He, too, wears a tabard. I can see the corner of it when he turns. Lorcan, all have gems of some sort. Whatever else they may be or have, they have wealth, but I don't think it honestly gained."

As I spoke we both glanced skyward. The storm was holding off from us, but not for more than a few hours more, I believed.

"I would judge that the riders came only recently upon this place," I said. "I think the ponies to be theirs. The outlaws guard barrels the beasts may have borne atop their packs. They seem to be awaiting a decision from their leader."

"And not like to be a pleasant one for those they found before them," Lorcan added. "I would not stand by. Yet we are two. They are seven and well-armed almost certainly trained for war. What use are old women and children on our side? Even if they understand their danger and that we fight for them?" I nodded grimly. It was a hard thing to say and harder to accept, but better Lorcan and I lived, better we saved most of the innocent lives, than we rushed in to die with them.

"We have more than us two. With us are warriors who will fight. But it is as it was when I slew Devol and you lived. Let us lie back and wait. The storm may pass by. It may hold off longer. We must chance that and wait outside until those within make up their minds. Let them lay hands on the dalesfolk and their victims may count us for friends when we attack. At the least they will think we could not be worse and will side with us in the battle."

"I do not like it."

My temper flared abruptly. "Think you I do? To stand by while women are abused in such ways as those men will choose? But at least they will live and, the Gods willing, we will bring them out alive. Can we not then offer them a place in Landale if they come with us? Of what use would we be to them if we attack openly and are slain? Then will they be still abused with no aid and no hope of another home."

Lorcan bowed his head to my anger. I saw that he agreed, yet it wore hard on him as it did on me. I hid my own horror of what I could soon see. I remembered too well what Neeco and his friends had planned for me. It had been only by the aid of my wing-friends that I had escaped that. I felt tears gather in my eyes. My dales, my home. All our land. When would it recover, when would the dalesfolk be safe again and brutes like these dead? Lorcan's arm slid about my shoulders as he pressed his mount closer.

"Meive, I'm sorry. I spoke in anger and I was wrong. Please. Do not cry. It hurts me to see your tears." I lifted my face and found a watery smile as he dabbed at my cheeks with gentle fingers. "Don't cry, Meive." His voice faltered. "I hate to ask it of you but you must watch what happens for me. I cannot see as you can."

"I know." I sniffed inelegantly. "I will watch. Should we let the horses graze and rest?"

We dismounted, slackening the girths and freeing the animals of their bits so they could graze. Beside a hollow in the rock which held water from the last storm I saw another of the tall rocks. It stretched up like a warning finger pointed to the sky. Some of my wing-friends alighted upon the surface; I felt what they felt then and bit back a cry. There was power yet in this one. Called by the winged-ones it now called to me. I glanced about, but Lorcan was out of sight watching the shelter. I advanced to lay my hand very softly against the warm stone.

It turned chill. That was not what was wanted of me. I slid into hive-mind. It appeared as if the bees could speak more clearly to that which lay in the stone. What then was asked of me? I queried. Dimly came the answer. The place ahead had once been shelter of another kind. Now human beasts laired within. Let me lay against the stone my sword and see what would be. I obeyed in silence, watching as a faint glimmering of light glowed within the stone. It ran like water onto my blade and vanished. The feeling of presence faded and as it did so I believed it had been female. Not of my kind, but female and sister in power none the less.

I sheathed my sword and rejoined my comrade, saying nothing of events. Lorcan took up a position watching along the section of path before the final bend. Between us we should be alert to the outlaws' departure if such should occur. I wished it would. If they left, then those others within the shelter might be safe. But I had lived through the deaths others of the bandit kind had brought. They would not leave while there was prey.

So it was. The outlaws had built high the fire so that the shelter was warm. For that reason my warriors could lurk in the heat above the beams and watch even though night fell and it was chill outside. I spoke of what I saw as tears ran down my face and Lorcan turned away from my distress. The outlaws broached the first of the two barrels, drank deep of some drink I could see intoxicated them. Once mad with the drink they turned upon the women. I think the oldest of the women must have counseled obedience. None fought, but went meekly to their temporary masters.

I saw as little as I might and yet know what occurred in case we must act. When at last the outlaws left a man on guard while the others lay down across the door and slept, I could cease to see. Then I laid my face in my hands and wept while Lorcan strove to hold and comfort me.

"Meive, Meive. None have died?"

"None, but, Lorcan, what I have seen . . ." I turned on him then, my outrage and the grief I still felt at the loss of my home and family finding a target. "What beasts are men. I swear if ever you think to use me so I will slay you." He released me and gave back, his face twisting in horror.

"Meive? What are you saying? You are my leige-lady. I am sword-sworn. Rather would I fall upon my own blade than harm you."

So great was the pain in his voice that I believed him immediately. Son of a tainted line he might be, but my Lady of the Bees had sent me to aid him. I did not think she would have done so if she thought him evil. And I, had I not ridden many months beside him? Lain down at nights beside him as a comrade in safety? I was wrong to accuse him. I said so and wept again while he held me gently.

"Forgive me, Lorcan." His hand lifted my chin so that I must meet his eyes.

"It is forgiven. Listen to me, my leige-lady. I know with Neeco and his friends, what you would have suffered if you had failed to kill them. And here, I am aware of what you have been forced to see. Think you I, too, have not called such men brute-beasts? Nay, worse, for beasts do not so abuse their own females. I understand your distress at what you have watched." He sighed very quietly.

"I, too, have cried out in anger at the nearest one when I saw evil. It is forgiven and forgotten. Now let us make plans that we may save what we can from bandits who are neither decent men nor innocent animals."

So we plotted. Their guard drowsed and while he did so Lorcan slid through the night to steal away the mounts and pack-ponies. We hobbled these behind us in a curve of the hills and took from them their gear. Should any outlaws escape us it would take time to find their mounts and ready them to ride. My warriors watched the outlaw guard but he did not hear the faint sounds as Lorcan led away their horses. Had the man moved to raise the alarm he would have died, the words stopped in his mouth. With the horses safe we waited, my winged-ones intent on those below them in the firelight.

The guard slept openly now, while in the far side of the shelter the old woman opened her eyes. She reached out, waking those who slept about her. Silently they began to seek for weapons. I hissed. Lorcan returned as I spoke swiftly.

"I think they will fall on the outlaws while they sleep."

"They'll die," Lorcan assured me grim-faced. "Those men are wolves. They sleep light. The first raised weapon and they'll rise ready to slay. The people there have no weapons of their own." He looked at me. "If we give aid at the right moment things could be different."

"I know. I have told my warriors to creep down." They would do as they had done once before. Crawl upon the clothing of the enemy until they reached the throat, or some other deadly target. When I called them they would strike, injecting poison into the bloodstream of those they fought. The outlaws were well clothed and most had donned their mail again after their sport. But the warriors, though large for their kind, were yet small enough to reach uncovered skin with their darts.

Within the shelter the dalesfolk were moving with caution. One held a sickle, another a hammer. Two had eating knives, while one of the girls had wound a length of thin rope about each hand as a strangling cord. Their faces were hard with outrage and hatred as they closed slowly. I thought it likely even if we did not aid they would give a fair account of themselves.

Lorcan and I caught up our mounts again, tightening their girths and bitting them ready before mounting. I watched through the winged-ones eyes as we sent the horses walking slowly along the track. In the shelter the old woman lifted her sickle and advanced. Our mounts rounded the bend so that ahead of us lay the shelter. We reached the door, dismounting to stand, as I held Lorcan back, awaiting the right moment.

Within the shelter the sickle flashed down. Lorcan had been right about the outlaws. Even as the sickle blade curved through the air the outlaw leader rolled aside. His

hand seized his sword hilt, his face feral with the killing
hunger. But fortune had granted us time. Many of the
winged-ones had found unclad skin and clung ready.

As the outlaws roused to attack I called my warriors.
They struck even as the dalesfolk closed in to kill or die.
Had it been the dalesfolk alone they would have fallen
quickly before the outlaws. But it was not. Even as I bespoke my wing-friends Lorcan tore open the door and
struck from behind. An outlaw fell with a groan. I set my
back against the door and guarded Lorcan, mine not to attack but to shield.

Within the shelter all was bloody confusion. One of the
women was down, dead from a single blow. Two women I
thought to be her kin attacked the killer. They could not
drag him down with farmers' tools but they kept him too
occupied to break away. With their attack made I had
called back my warriors. Most of the outlaws carried at
least one sting. That would not slay them at once but it
slowed their strokes.

Three of them were dying, however. Even as the dalesfolk reached them the outlaws gasped for breath, choked,
and fell. Seeing himself trapped and his men dying for no
apparent cause, the leader gave a great shout of fury. Before we could prevent it he had flung himself forward,
sword-blade licking out. A girl and the lad died before any
could save them.

But we had the renegades well snared. They could neither
pass us at the narrow door, nor escape the fury of those they
had outraged. They died one by one, until two remained: the
leader and another. That second man came at me, teeth
bared, seeing only a slight lad to bar the door, Lorcan having
stepped a little aside to engage the outlaw leader. My sword
crossed blade and in that moment I felt a flow of strength
pour into me. I found my own lips curling back as I struck.

Light flared weakly about my blade. In the shadows the
people we would save gaped and whispered. I snarled, a

low growl of hate. I remembered those I had buried, the faces of my kin, my friends. Light flamed higher as I struck. It could not be. I was a girl against a full-grown trained soldier, yet I held him back. He fought in growing desperation—and could not pass. Something took my arm, twisting it cunningly. I obeyed and my enemy's sword spun from his hand. He lunged to seize it and I ran him through.

I backed, and moved to join Lorcan, who battled the last man, leader of the evil ones. We would have taken the man alive: there were questions Lorcan at least would have wished him to answer. But the man was a rabid beast and fought until we had no choice. When all were down, the dalesfolk turned to stare at Lorcan and I. The old woman gave him an approving nod, then a polite bow.

"For your aid I thank you on behalf of all who are left of our dale. Of your courtesy now I must tend the injured."

Without further ado she dropped to her knees, her grip slowing the bleeding of a girl whose shoulder had met with an outlaw dagger. I moved to those who lay still. The man had been dead perhaps an hour. From his injuries I thought he had suffered a fall in the hills. The two the outlaw leader had slain lay side by side while the older woman, too, was dead. Alive still were the old woman, a woman of perhaps forty Winters, two women a few years older than me, and four children.

I grieved for those we could not save, but the outlaws would have slain them all before they moved on. Dales courage, a gift of power, and our swords, with the aid of my wing-friends, had given back eight lives. Lorcan had gone outside. He returned some time later, led out the goats, and returned again.

"There's a second shelter which backs this one. I've placed the horses in that." He hefted one of the outlaw packs. "Let's see what's within these. We need food and drink, more than we have to share with these people ourselves." He looked at the children. "Help me see what treasure is within, if there are sweets then you shall share them amongst you."

In a very short time all four children were helping him plunder the packs, laying out what they found in the light of two lanterns found hidden at the back of the shelter. There were sweets, though, looking at them, I knew they had not come from the outlaws. Lorcan himself had a sweet tooth and had bargained at our last village halt for sugared stalks of angelica. It was near moonhigh when we were done and the storm broke over us in a torrent of wind and rain.

The dead lay quiet in the other barn. In the morning we would bury them. The outlaw bodies had been removed and dumped some distance away in the hills. Before Lorcan and I left them we had stripped their miserable carcasses of all that might be useful. Let the wolves eat their meat undressed. The old woman stood looking about her. Then, slowly, as if her very bones ached, she turned towards us.

"I am Elesha of Drosdale. These with me are all who are left alive from that dale. Our good Lord Drosan fought when the call came. One man came back from that slaughter to say Lord Drosan and all others with him had died. Then, despite those who died to hold them back, the invaders came to Drosdale and we fled. Later we returned to what they had left us, though much of the land was poisoned and the beasts mostly dead. It was the only home we knew. But there was no longer a hold, the crops were gone, and sickness fell upon us. Our people died until there were few of us remaining.

"When we heard the war was over, we rejoiced, believing all would be well again in time. It was not. Bandits came seeking food. If we gave nothing they killed us. If we gave they used the women and left us new mouths to feed if the woman did not slay herself and the child. Last Winter was bitter: When it was Spring only twenty of us were left alive. We talked together and took up what we had to find a new home. Since then we have wandered. More of us died until we are as you see us now."

Her voice rose up in anger. "We won the war forced on us. Why now does it not cease? Why have we no home, no place? Must we be wanderers forever without shelter? Must we live in the hills, die like the deer until the last of Drosdale is gone?" Tears streamed down wrinkled cheeks so that I could not be silent.

"No," I said, reaching for her hands. "Elesha, there is a place for all of you. I go now with my liege-man to reclaim it. I offer you a choice. If you would accept Lorcan as your war-leader, then you may travel with us. Take time to decide. If you see us as two you can trust and the reverse seems so to us, then you shall have a home."

"At what cost?"

"At none save your hard work, your honesty with us always." I smiled into faded eyes. "Oh, yes, one thing. The goats."

"I'll not leave them behind," Elesha warned.

"I do not ask that. But we would travel too slowly with them afoot. They must be placed on the ponies. The kids must be taken up before those who ride. The outlaw packs shall be shared among you and each shall carry their own. If this is done then we shall each have a beast to ride and a second pack-pony to carry the goats."

I could see she was thinking hard. "If we place the children two to a mount then we have three pack-animals. That would be easier." It was good sense so I agreed. Elesha eyed me. "And you, Lady, who or what are you?" Her gaze touched my sheathed sword, moved up to where my warriors clung to beams. "To whom do we swear allegiance?" I was uncertain what answer to make and it was Lorcan who moved to front Elesha and her kin.

"I am Lorcan, once of a dale which is no more. There, too, the invaders came. Dale and house I have renounced, being liege-man now to my lady. She is Meive of Landale, wise woman of some power. Accepted is she within a shrine of the Old Ones, named daughter to she who dwells within. About her fly wing-friends who are also warriors." His voice was strange, as if he prophesied, so that I saw Elesha was impressed, yet she strove to keep her head.

"There are old ones and Old Ones." Her meaning was clear: acceptance within such a shrine was no guarantee of my goodness.

"Let you travel with us and judge," was Lorcan's reply.

Her head bowed in agreement. "It shall be so. We have eaten, let us sleep. In the morning we take the road with you. After that, what shall be we shall see."

We laid up in the shelter for two days. The storm came late that night and the following day it continued until darkness. It was too cold and wet to travel with people who were long underfed and who had little resistance to chills. Also, one of the women was ill from the rough handling received from the bandits. At length Elesha came to me, stretching out a hand towards my sword.

"Lady. This is a thing of power, can it be it could aid poor Vari?"

"I do not know." Yet I considered carefully. I believed it would at least do no harm. So I walked to the woman as she tossed on her bedding. "Vari. Do what you feel right."

To my horror she closed her hand about the blade edge as I offered it. I had meant her to touch the flat only. But she showed no sign of pain. A few drops of blood trickled down the blade. Light pulsed from the blade, soaking into her skin. The cut was gone, and along with it her fever. The light dimmed, faded, and it, too, was gone. But as it vanished I felt again that dim quiet regard. Whatever had given the gift, now expended, was well pleased with me.

XII

——◆——

*B*efore we left, two days later, I went alone to the nearest tall-standing stone. Upon that I laid both my palm and my naked sword blade. Shutting my eyes, I sought the hive-mind and through it gave thanks. The response was a gentle amusement. The one who had dwelled here long ago was gone. What remained was only a shadow of power, yet that one had been female and kin in some sort to my lady. The fear and need of Elesha's people so close to what had once been a shrine had awakened power, and to my gift it had answered. I had done well, it said, and now would let me depart in peace. I had the sense that it was gone after that, so I did likewise.

Travel was slower now. Often I thought that Lorcan must be weary of so many women about him, for we were now five to his one. The children were two boys and two girls, one of each being Elesha's great-grandchildren, and the other two being orphans from Drosdale. It had been their older siblings the outlaw leader had slain. They, like most in a small dale, had been distantly related to Elesha so that she counted them kin. We were ten, but only two of us well-armed, and all ahorse, but thus were we the more tempting to any outlaws who might see us. We needed fighters; luckily Lorcan believed he could find those to join us.

"There are bandits, yes. But there are some who were decent men, who turned bandit to survive being without lord, or dale, or land after the war. Give them coin and one to follow and they will return to what they were. Blank-shields, too, there are, who need employment and will be faithful."

"How do we know which they are?" I asked dubiously.

Lorcan grinned. "Why, our wise woman of the bees shall try them. Soon there will be another inn on the road. We shall leave our folk to lie up there while we bespeak the innkeeper. He will assuredly know where blank-shields ride, men who seek a permanent home where they can take a wife, raise crops and family. Or serve the keep as guards for their family's bread."

"It is a good thought, but how am I to test them, Lorcan? That is not something I have ever done."

Lorcan smiled at me. "Such men are oft superstitious, fearing anything they do not understand."

I pondered his hint, so that when we found our inn two nights later I was ready. The host knew of men who sought work. At our bidding he sent a messenger to them so that they attended us the next day. I paced outside to meet them, my winged-ones flying about me. On the wisdom of my choosing might lie the lives of us all. Let me choose aright.

In a line by Lorcan stood three men. Five more waited in a small knot to one side. They muttered together, so I thought them yet deciding if they should step forward. I noticed the leader of the five was eyeing me dubiously, then seeming to study the three men without appearing to look at them directly. Lorcan came to meet me, his voice a quick whisper as I joined him.

"Let me do the talking. You be remote, as if you were calling up powers. I have my doubts about the three here."

I swept past him in silence, my eyes blank. I did not think seeing my wing-friends would panic those before us. There had been powers and shrines in this land before the dalesfolk ever arrived, and when they came they met such powers often enough to be wary but not panic-stricken.

In my mind I was reaching out for my warriors. Bees have an ability to tell lies from truth—to some extent at least. Deceit has a scent bees can catch; I knew this from the time I had spent sharing hive-mind with the queens. Linked to my warriors, I believed I could learn the truth of those who offered themselves to us for hire. I moved to front the three men. Then I called for all to hear, a soft rising hum which strengthened until my bones vibrated with it. I felt the bees respond to the hive-call. Lorcan spoke in a slow, almost casual voice, without emphasis. It was oddly impressive.

"We see truth and honor. Those who come to my lady's call will know and judge. Let men who would join us stand forward. Her warriors will see their hearts." He left it at that, knowing long speeches often betray the man who seeks to impress with no more than wind and empty words.

The first man stepped forward, saying his name. I lifted my hand. In a glittering cloud my wing-friends descended to hover about him as he stepped back, a worried scowl on his face. I was linked, feeling his tiny movements, scenting his sweat through my warriors. He was afraid, that was natural. But there was something about him they did not like. I shook my head looking at Lorcan who addressed the man.

"We have no place for you." He received in turn a glare which, had it been fire, would have sent him as a cinder to the ground. The man slouched away and from the corner of one eye I saw the leader of those to one side nod very slightly, an approving expression curving his lips.

The second man was judged more swiftly. The warriors rose in a humming cloud to draw away from him so that Lorcan spoke even before I indicated. "Go, we have no place for you." He went and, before we could judge again, his friend went with him.

The leader of the five blank-shields who had waited walked towards Lorcan then. I could see that our method of

hiring might seem strange to him, but he had agreed with
our decisions. After all, in the dales where Old Ones still
walk now and again, where their shrines still hold power,
my method of testing was not unbelievable. I thought he
would accept it provisionally and await the outcome. His
voice when he spoke was that of a man of some breeding.

"I am Levas. Once I was a fighter against the invaders, a
blank-shield captain with my own troop. These four are all
that is left of us. We are good fighters, experienced. But
none of us grow younger. We seek a place where we might
live out our days as guards. We offer standard contract with
further terms to be agreed."

I considered him. To the eye he and his men were all
competent. I saw no rust on their chain. Their clothing was
clean; their cloaks, though threadbare in places, had been
neatly mended. They looked hard-faced, yet I saw no signs
of evil. Only a weariness, as if they had fought too long
without rest or safety, as well they might have, for none
would be less than late thirties and most in their early for-
ties. I signaled the bees, who rose to surround the five men.
None of them flinched, standing steady as my warriors
hovered about them tasting the air they breathed out.

Slowly the bees judged. Here was no hint of deceit, no
feeling of evil. They could be wrong, they were not perfect,
but they could judge evil and that did not stand before me.
They could feel, too, where deceit or betrayal was being
contemplated. Whatever these blank-shields might have
done in battle-heat, they carried no taint of true evil, nor
did they plot deliberately to betray us. I nodded to Lorcan
as the bees rose up and away.

"Levas, will you take service with the lady and me?"

"What terms?"

Lorcan was not to be caught so easily in any trade. "Let
you state them. We will consider." The blank-shield looked
at us. A faint smile glimmered in his eyes. That was good,
let him see that we might be young but we were not fools.

"Very well then, Lord. If we take service we ask these

things. First, horses for each of us and one pack-beast."
Lorcan nodded, that was fair. It was to our own benefit as
well; afoot they could not keep up with us even with our
slow group of women and children. If they chose to remain
with us the beasts could be theirs. If not, then we could
match those purchased against the ones held in Honeycoombe's inner valley. Those of lesser quality could be
sold again.

"Second, let you pay us one silver a ten-day in the hand
and all found. One half of the first silver in advance."

That, too, was fair. It was less than most blank-shields
had used to be paid but after the war there were many who
had been fighters who now had no place. The "found" he
asked would see he and his did not starve or go cold without bed or roof. Levas was naming a price we could not call
too high. Nor was he rating himself and his men too low.
As for the advance, I suspected there were small things
they required and had not the money to purchase. They
could take the money and leave, but by and large blank-
shields were honorable. Lorcan spoke after he had seen my
agreement.

"That we agree. What else?"

I could not swear to it, but the man seemed embarrassed.
Yet, what would embarrass a blank-shield who had seen
everything and done much of it himself? Twice he seemed
about to speak and shut his mouth again. I could see a red
flush spreading over his cheekbones as he looked back towards the nearby stables. What was this? Did he have some
woman he wished to bring? Some girl they had been sharing who otherwise would be left penniless to starve?

I spoke carefully. "Levas, if there is one you would bring
let you call her to you. If the bees judge her as well as they
have judged you and your men then she, too, has a place
with us."

I knew in the last few years I had been fortunate beyond
my own deserving. It was through no great virtue of my
own I stood a maid still. Neeco's band would have left me

ravaged and dead but for my warriors and the advice of the
queens. I would lay no harsh names on another who had
done whatever she must to survive.

Levas's face lit in relief. "I thank you, Lady." He half-
turned, pursing his lips in a low whistle. A small furry form
ran to him, climbing his leather trews and nestling into his
arms. From there it eyed me doubtfully. My gaze met that
of Lorcan, both of us muffling our mirth. I could see that
he, too, had leaped to my conclusion. Levas fronted us.

"We found her in a keep which had been raided. She was
so tiny then, but fierce. The raiders had slain all her family
disliking her kind as they do, yet she stood against us wailing in defiance. We buried her kin and took her up. She is a
fine hunter, Lady. She has brought us luck since the day
she came to us."

I found my face had creased into a wide smile, so wide
my very cheeks ached. The five men clustered about her as
she looked up into their faces in turn. Something inside me
suddenly wished to weep at the sight, that in the midst of
war and death such men as these should take up a kitten
and love it.

I eyed the small beast. She eyed me back. I know well
what she saw; I saw a half-grown cat, perhaps six months
in age, her fur a soft gold, darker gold spots against the
lighter fur. Her face and body were broad but lithe. Her
paws were larger than I had ever seen on a cat her size before. She was small, but I believed with ample food she
would grow considerably as yet. I should judge her, too. It
would not be well if she attempted to make prey of my warriors.

"Place her upon the ground again."

Levas obeyed. My wing-friends came, their leader and
the largest of them floating down to hover by her face. Bee
and cat eyed each other for long moments. Then the cat
turned away to wash. From the bees I felt a humming in my
head. They approved her. She was wise and sensible. She

knew them and she would not foolishly harass the hive.

"The winged-ones have judged," I said, as Levas and his men waited. "For her, too, there is a place. Hearth and home. Let her ride with us, one welcome holds for you all." Lorcan grinned.

"It seems I bargain better than I know. I hire five and gain six, and the sixth asks no horse and no silver." Levas began to chuckle; his men joined in, and as Lorcan and I laughed with them what had begun as amusement became gales of laughter which left us with tears on our cheeks. Oh, it was good to laugh in such a way. I had not laughed so since I had dwelled in Honeycoombe with Ithia and my family. I moved to stroke the cat's soft fur. She looked up at me and mewed, then purred.

"Levas? I am Meive of Landale."

Lorcan cut in, "Wise woman, wing-friend, accepted by a shrine of the Old Ones and given gifts of them. I am Lorcan, once of the line of Paltendale, now liege-man to the lady. Let you name your men and this small comrade." I saw their eyes react at the name of Paltendale. It had been a name known. But Lorcan had not said he was of the House, only the line. By that they would know he came from a cadet branch and made no claim upon Paltendale itself. Levas named his men, then nodded to the purring cat.

"We named her Gathea." Both Lorcan and I recognized the name. It was that of a legendary wise woman who had been with our people when first we came into the dales.

"Well named," Lorcan said. "Another Gathea shall lead you home."

It took time after that. We had to bargain for five mounts and a pack-pony. We could not find the latter but found instead a mule, a jack, middle-aged, sure-footed and steady. With him was a second, a jenny. They stood together, obvious trail-mates, and I begged Lorcan to take both.

"Drustan is old. Once we reach Honeycoombe he should

be turned to light work. Let the children ride him for pleasure. But the mules have worked as a team and that will be
useful."

"Then, too," Lorcan said dryly, "you do not wish to separate them."

"They will be useful," I said again. Both comments
were true but I did not wish to appear foolish in his eyes.
Lorcan looked thoughtful, then he bargained with the owner, buying both beasts. We purchased other items, amongst
them bags of grain. He loaded those onto the mules, smiling at me.

"You were right. This pair will indeed be useful." He
said no more. With loaded mules, replenished supplies,
and our caravan now numbering thirteen—fourteen if one
counted Gathea—we moved onto narrower roads. The
beasts ate the grain Lorcan had purchased, but I noticed
each night he added kindling wood bound with dry grass
within the sacks so they appeared no thinner and still as
heavy. I kept silence, as did Levas, though I saw that he,
too, took note of this.

As we entered the area closer to the coast, Lorcan swung
us towards the South-east. I knew it was hereabouts his
own dale had lain and believed that we were to go there.
That night, as we made camp and I moved to stand my turn
at guard, Lorcan took me aside.

"Meive, how do you judge Levas and his men?" I had
watched them as we traveled. Old Elesha's daughter Vari
had lost her man several years earlier. The eyes of our
blank-shield leader had been drawn to Vari from the beginning. I believed them of similar age and she would bring
children to his roof. A ready-made family. Indeed, already
there was a faint air of paternalism about him when he
spoke to the small ones.

"I judge Levas a man who needs hearth and family. His
men are the same, Lorcan. They are not wild lads, nor even
young men who must prove themselves. They have fought

their wars, taken their wounds. Now they seek a home, a place they may defend because it is in their hearts, and not for coin. I believe we can trust Levas."

He sighed. "So do I. But before I tell him anything I must tell you more than I have said before." Then he spoke of Erondale's treasure again. "It should be here still, Meive. There is little gold. Mostly it was changed to silver generations ago. But of silver there is, well," he paused. "There is enough to rebuild Honeycoombe. To enlarge the keep, to build guardhouses upon the track into the dale. To make of it a place of comfort and security.

"I plan to take part of it now. The grain sacks the mules carry are all but empty. Yet they still appear full from the wood I have placed within. For the remainder of the night that shall fuel our fires, leaving small trace of what we carried. I will go down alone and place within the remaining grain small sacks of silver. Enough that if any study the pack-beasts tracks they will but think them to be carrying an ordinary load. Keep all of our people here, watch that none follow me."

"And Levas?"

"Stand guard with him alone after I am gone. Once you are alone tell him as I have told you." I saw the wisdom in that. Levas would know we trusted him, though he would not know where the treasure lay nor how to find the rest of it. I said so.

"As you say. I will tell you how to find the remainder once I return." His gaze seemed to fasten upon mine. "If I am slain it would please me to know you need never be in want; that Honeycoombe may still prosper." His voice became a whisper so light upon the air I could not be sure of the words.

"I would never wish anything but good for you . . ." Were those last words "my love?" I could not be sure, nor dared I ask lest I was wrong. But my pulse raced. I found myself swaying towards him. Then I caught at my scattered senses. Was this a time to stand in the dark desiring kisses? With all others of my dale dead, I was Landale's lady. My behavior must be an example. Let Lorcan ride while I guarded. If he truly cared for me as I knew now I cared, then there would be time. Once we were safe in Honeycoombe I might have all the time we wished.

"Ride safe. Return soon," I bade him.

"Guard well, be safe until I do." Before I could reply he was gone into the dark leading Rez and Reza down the narrow path into his once home. I had no great fear for him. The mules were sure-footed and like most of their kind could see well in the moonlight. His mount, Tas, was neither sweet-tempered nor beautiful but he, too, was steady and walked as with eyes in his hooves. I had seen him canter down trails that I would only risk at a walk. Once all but us two were asleep in the camp I talked to Levas, who asked questions, listened carefully to my replies, then spoke slowly.

"Lorcan is wise, Lady. If any have seen us pass it will appear that we carry grain to our dale. Why should they think it to have changed to silver overnight? Do not tell the women. I do not think they would betray us, but they may speak of it amongst themselves. Children overhear such things."

"And may without wishing to bring danger, speak of it to another child or talk about it while we are at a market?" I saw the sense in what he said. "Yes. You are right, Levas. Let you not discuss this with your men either. I trust them but the fewer who know, the better a secret is kept."

He glanced upwards. "The night wears on, let you sleep since your watch is done. I will wake you once the Lord Lorcan is returned." I went to my bedroll as he had said. I thought to lie awake awhile waiting for Lorcan's return, but I was tired enough to sleep quickly. It was some hours later that I was shaken by the shoulder. I came awake and started up.

"Be at ease, Lady. Lorcan returns."

We met, the three of us outside the camp. The two men unloaded the mules in silence while I brought food and drink. Lorcan ate and drank eagerly.

"I have the silver. Enough to begin what we would do. While I worked I thought. Levas, look about you while we travel. I would take more folk, perhaps steady men with families. Then once we are home and work has begun, I can ride with them and with you as master-at-arms, to bring back more silver. It will appear as if we go to trade. Once back here we gather the silver left and return, trading as we go."

"A good plan. Men with families are best." He smiled gently. "I shall seek men who love their kin and would not betray us since that would betray them also." They finished stacking the grain sacks and freed the hobbled mules to eat. We slept late that morning and were not upon the road until near noon. It was good for the children to have rest from the riding and they took full advantage of it, making up some children's game which involved much running about and yelling.

We rode steadily another ten-day until we were near to the edge of Merrowdale. Leaving the women and children to wait with Levas's men, we three rode on down the shallow road to the dale. I had not seen it since a visit with Ithia the year before she was slain. But we had stayed some weeks so I remembered it well enough. What a change was there. The dale, once beautiful and well farmed, was desolate. Fields were overgrown, the remnants of crops straggled up again in places. Some of the cottages had burned. The main door to the keep was broken and hung askew.

Neeco and his friends had never returned. I had seen to that. Those from Merrowdale who fled to join us had not returned home before the bandits came also to Landale. Perhaps they feared to leave, or perchance our lord had bidden them stay lest coming and going from our home they were followed back. If so, then he might as well have saved his breath. With Neeco's aid we had been found anyway. I had stood only moments alone thinking thus before I opened a door. I stepped back at once with a small cry of disgust and horror. Lorcan was at my side even as I cried out.

"What . . . oh!" He signaled Levas to join him. "I think we have work to do before we consider anything else."

Lorcan called some others of our men to join us, and gave orders. They were busy for some hours as they went from house to house and through the keep. I went elsewhere. I did not wish to see the poor bundles of rag and bone which had been those inhabitants of Merrowdale who had remained forever, as they were carried out, wrapped in linen from their homes, to be laid in the earth.

The work went swiftly though, and when at last I returned to see what Lorcan and our men did, I found Lorcan to have discovered a deep crack in the earth against a side of the surrounding cliff. There he had dropped in fresh branches and grass. Those who had once lived here would lie decently enough. Without the need to dig trenches but only to fill in the graves, the work was over quickly.

"If Lord Salas brings his people here they will bring their own possessions?" Levas, who had heard of our plan for Merrowdale, asked us. Lorcan looked at me. I nodded. "Then all here which we can salvage belongs to Landale?"

Neither of us had thought of that but it was the practical sense of a blank-shield and he was right.

"Not the sheep," I said. "I think we shall not require so many as are now about. Let us take a dozen of the ewes, the lambs they have at foot, and a young ram or two, but no more." I recalled something. "They had two flocks here. One, the greater number, were white, but they had some few that were black or brown. Let us take all of the smaller flock in those colors. Thus we can exchange fleeces with Merrowdale. And there will not be any question as to whose sheep they are if any stray."

Levas eyed me with approval. "That is good sense and

will help to bind the two dales closer with the exchanges of wool. Now, Lord. You have said you plan to extend your keep. To enlarge it and add guard houses. Here there is spare worked stone; we need not take stone from their keep here. The land is baked hard with summer. If you have beasts enough we can build stone-boats with which to drag the worked stones from this dale to your own. Moreover, once Winter is come, then Spring again, the weather will hide any marks we make in doing this."

As he spoke, his hand gestured towards the two cottages nearest the dale mouth. I believe they may have been the oldest buildings in Merrowdale, since both were of a considerable size, half cot, half barn. Both were built from roughly-squared blocks of stone. I suspected that originally they would have held those who came here until the proper keep, barns, and cots were built.

"The road out is steep, yet if we harness six of our strongest beasts they may pull a fair load." Levas looked a little doubtful as he studied the slope, shallow though it was from Merrowdale. I smiled.

"Once we reach my home we shall have a matched six-horse team. Heavy horses of size and power."

Levas gaped at me. "Lady, such are worth half a dale. From where got you those?"

"From bandits," I said wryly. "They were not willing but I insisted."

His gaze became respectful. "Lady, I believe you. Now, let us search each house. We need not take all we find at once, but let it be marked so we can return for it once we are settled."

Lorcan ran for paper, though it cost heavily. Several times as we halted at markets during our journey he had bought us some sheets. I had writ on many sheets, telling my own story as he had suggested. I knew he, too, had done this. But some unused sheets we had still.

From house to house we went, listing items we could return to take, calling each other to see what treasures we found. They were not such things as would appeal to bandits. What use would they have for dye cauldrons, for bolts of plain cloth put away in chests? But to us they were treasures. Before dusk Levas brought down the remainder of our party. Elesha saw to it that food was prepared and beds allocated.

With the dawn we rose to eat. Then we readied our mounts. I led. It would be a long ride but I was determined. This time we should not stop until we reached Honeycoombe. I had left the hives safe. The ponies, too, should still be grazing by my cave. Before Summer's end I must fetch them home and I would be glad to do so. I would bespeak my Lady of the Bees, once I had time to make the journey to her shrine, sharing with her all I had seen and done. I hoped she would feel I had been worthy of her. If Lord Salas's resolution did not fail him so that he came next Spring, then would I take Merria to the Shrine in another year or two. I dreamed away the journey home so it was a surprise to me when Lorcan called.

"Meive, are we not close?" I roused, seeing that it would soon be dusk. The land about me was familiar. The joy in my voice must have been clear when I replied.

"Very close. Half a candlemark to the entrance, no more. We shall go to the keep. It is large enough to house us all at first while we make plans."

I spoke the truth. In less than the half-candlemark we were entering the upper trail to Honeycoombe. A little longer and ahead in the gathering dusk we could see the dark bulk of the keep. I left Levas and his men to deal with the horses and our two mules. I took up a lantern, led Elesha within, then waved about us.

"Let your family sleep where you will tonight. In the morning we shall talk." She wasted no time but gave orders. Her daughter Vari swept the children upstairs in search of a bedroom. With them went their own packs. For some time all was abustle. I remained in the great kitchen to make suggestions from what I knew of the keep. One of Levas's men came in with firewood, lit the fire, then left again. I put on soup and a kettle filled with good clear water.

It all took time. In the end it was far into the night before I could seek my bedding. I lay awake a while remembering how Landale had been before Neeco came with his friends. It been my home and I had loved it. But the wheel turns. Those who had made Landale my home were gone. Now it was for Lorcan and me to build anew.

We would make a stronger, safer place with good people who would care for each other. But not so good they would not fight for their home. Nor so foolish they would assume all were as good as they. My grin was fierce in the dark.

I would finish writing the story of what had happened when Landale had been betrayed and attacked. Those who joined us should learn from the tale. Lorcan had talked of guards and secret places from which they could watch our road. I would see that he did not forget.

After that night it seemed as if time flew. Goats roamed all over my dale eating the outer land bare, too many of them, and several went into the stewpot over the next ten-day. The horse team were where we had left them, as were the cattle and other horses. We made stone-boats, and with those and the team, Levas and his men dismantled the two ancient barns in Merrowdale and dragged back all the stones we required to extend what had once been the lord's house, to make our larger and more fortified keep here.

That work they did first, saying that there was food enough to be found and it was too late to plant crops. Better they built a keep where we could be safe. At that task they worked mightily, they and those of us women who could do anything to help. But before we began the building Levas came with Vari to bespeak me.

"Lady," her eyes were shy. "Levas and I would wed?" Of course I was pleased. I hugged her several times and even kissed Levas's weathered cheek. Then I saw the deeper implications of such a request. In asking permission, both acknowledged me as Landale's Lady. I must behave aright else they would feel themselves lessened. I stepped back, making my face serious.

"For such a wedding all must be as it should be. Vari, I will give you cloth to make a dress. You shall chose one of the cottages in which to live. Levas, you shall choose two milk-goats for your house. There shall be a feast and you will stand before us all."

"Will you say the words of Cup and Flame, Lady?"

I promised and they went away happy. But after I had considered further I sought out Lorcan to talk to him apart from our friends. If I was accepted as lady to our folk then he was their lord. Yet we were neither wed nor kin. Before any visitors came here to look askance at us and gossip, we must decide how we wished to appear before them. Should we wed, or at least announce ourselves as officially betrothed? That decision I could hardly make on my own.

Lorcan

XIII

I lay in my bedding the night after we had saved Elesha and her kin. Sleep was far from me as I recalled Meive's tears. I had known many good men in my time. Yet I had to admit I had known many evil ones as well. In times of war it seemed as if all the wrong in a man leaped to the surface. Men who in their dale had been decent kindly husbands, loving fathers, became demons once they rode under the banners of war.

I grieved that my lady might be able to consider me one of these. And yet, how should she know I was not? I had known she watched me at first and that her small warriors had watched me as well. I had striven, with all I was, to show her she need never fear harm at my hands. She had begun to trust, then we had happened upon this and all my patience was gone for naught again. I sighed as I stared upwards at the unseen rooftree. I would remain patient. Eventually she would come to trust me fully. Then might I speak.

After that my days and nights were too busy for me to brood over what had been. We found good men to ride with us, blank-shields but with a leader who was not quite of the common sort. I'd wager his breeding was good, though from the left-hand side most likely. Many a bastard took up the blank-shield when there was no other place for him. They mostly did well, being often trained by a noble father's weapons-master. Once I had gained back some of my keep's silver and we were on the road towards Honeycoombe again I asked Levas about his House. We had ridden on, just we two, scouting forward on our road. It was then I questioned him, speaking casually. He answered in the same way.

"Aye. My father was keep-heir in a small dale far to the North of here. My mother was a lass from his dale. It was no shame to either that they loved, but they could not wed. He was betrothed as a child and unable to marry elsewhere. She wed later, with a dowry given by him, to a good man who laid no hands upon me unjustly. My father wed as well when the time came that his betrothed could travel to him. I'll say for him that he did do reasonably by me. I was trained by the keep's own weapons-master. When I left to be a blank-shield he gave me good chain and sword, a fair mount, and a belt pouch full of silver."

"What of your dale then?"

"I've never returned. I heard the invaders had struck hard. I know not who lived or died. Nor does it matter to me. I have no claim on the House and my mother died of the winter cough soon after I departed. She had no other children. Her man remarried. I had some word of the place from time to time until they fell."

"Are you sure you have no claim?" I asked shrewdly. "In this war many lords and heirs have fallen. Often enough the whole family has died out leaving none save those of the left-hand side. You have the blood of the lord of your dale, and that was known. You could return there, wed a girl of the house, and hold the dale."

It was a reasonable idea. Many of noble blood had fallen, but most had got away their women first to some sort of safety. There would be many dales now with only women of the house left alive to inherit, and many dales, too, which were ruined. There would be a great shaking-up of noble houses in the years to come. New blood would enter the lines of many houses, and I thought that to be no bad thing. Levas was shaking his head.

"There were sons of my father's begetting. They may have stayed to fight and die. But the eldest had also wed and his wife had a son and daughter of him. They'd have been very young, and noble children such as they would have been sent to safety, I'd have no doubt. They'll inherit, if there is anything left. Nay, there was nothing there for me. I've thought well on your offer. I'm willing to take it up so long as there be a home for us. My men and I will be guard to your dale if that pleases you and the lady?"

"She has told me it would please her well. She sees you as one who can be trusted, come sword come fire," I made reply. "As do I, Master-at-Arms to Landale." I saw his cheeks redden slightly.

"You do me honor to name me so to your dale."

I grinned at him. "Great boast, little roast. It's an honest title but will bring little but hard work and long hours to begin with. Yet if all goes well it may be a position of honor in years to come."

"I am content to wait."

"That's as well, since you'll have to. As for the cottage, she has said you should see the dale then choose for yourself. There are a number, though you must also have rooms in the keep." I turned to another thing which worried me.

"Levas, you've ridden not only in this war but as a fighter. Once we reach our dale look about you. I would value your opinion. Landale fell by treachery, but also it trusted too much in isolation. Their lord raised no guardhouses, manned no sentry-posts. I shall not make that mistake. Let you spy out the land and see where you would put such positions if you had the placing of them." He nodded and we fell to scanning about us as we rode.

We reached Merrowdale and a woeful sight it was to me.

There is nothing so sad as a place that has been abandoned by its inhabitants. At least, that was my belief, until Meive opened a door and cried out. I was at her side in an instant. I drew her away gently. After that Levas and I and his men worked hard to clear keep and cot. We laid the pitiful remnants of the people of Merrowdale to rest, and I spoke the words of Cup and Flame over them. The women cooked food for us so that we ate while Meive showed me lists. There was much here still which the bandits had not valued, but we should. Not the least of that would be the stones to rebuild and enlarge the keep at Landale.

"Do you think it right we despoil the dale when Salas may come?" Meive asked me.

I pursed my lips in thought. "Levas spoke of that and I think that what he said is right. Will Salas not bring all he and his can carry of their own possessions? Sheep he will find here, and a keep which stands strong apart from the door. Cottages and barns, all are here. Let him be content with the bounty he finds—and I think he will be. There is also this. Tildale, which he leaves to come here, was never taken by invaders or bandits. Those we find as new settlers and bring in to our dale will often have little of their own. They have need of anything we can provide them. Why spend our coin to do so when we can scavenge here?"

Meive nodded. "I have thought about Landale. Lorcan, I believe we should take for it another name. It was named Landale for he who first took it as his place, though few used the name. But his line is gone. You have said you will not be lord in Paltendale's name?"

"So I have said. What name do you think then to give it?"

"I have thought on that. It seems to me that since all knew it as Honeycoombe then that should be the name?"

Her tone questioned, so I considered that for a while. She was right, for I would never again name myself of Paltendale. Nor would I lay that house or name on my new home. Dales are usually named for the lord who takes up the land for his own, yet here that lord and all his line were gone. Meive was of his dale but clearly did not wish to use the name still. I nodded at last.

"Let it be Honeycoombe. Furthermore, let the arms of our home be thus: halved diagonal by a rope of braided straw, a sword held point down. A sign that we live in peace yet can we fight at need. And upon the other half . . ." I nodded to her, "a spiral of bees rising, queen in the lead. The background shall be green, the sword in silver and gray, the bees black and gold, the straw rope a pale yellow." I thought that well. Hives were made in our dales from straw rope, braided and coiled. The sword for me, the bees for Meive. I looked to see her smile and was well pleased when I saw she approved.

"It feels well to me. It is right, Lorcan. I shall tell Elesha that we will begin to embroider feast tabards once we have time and are settled."

"Then best we sleep so that the time shall come the swifter."

I watched as she went from me to her bed, wishing I had not the thoughts which burned in me. I hungered for her. But I loved her, too; I would not frighten her by moving too quickly. As it was, once we were in Honeycoombe our situation would be awkward. We were neither wed nor kin. I must give thought to what might be done about that.

In the event, I had no time to sit about considering my desires. We labored from dawn until dusk, the women to till the fields, the men to repair the keep. Once that was completed I walked with Levas and my lady to study the walls and what lay about them. There was a good spring within the inner wall. Doubtless it was why the keep had been placed in that spot. But Meive led us sideways about the keep. Then she pointed.

"See, there is the entrance to the inner vale. If we built out to encompass that from the keep we could have twice a keep, a second in the vale entrance, and we could retire from one to the other at need."

Levas and I considered that. In the steep cliff which

bounded Honeycoombe at this end of the dale the valley entrance was a crack, perhaps twenty feet wide at the bottom, narrowing towards the top. The keep had been sited close by, its back against the cliff also. But it would cost us greatly in stone to build several walls and enclosures out from the valley entrance to the keep. Yet I thought it no bad idea. How could we use keep and vale as retreat but still allow access to both while building walls?

Levas was walking about. He measured with string, then walked into the vale to stare at the inner cliff. He returned, measured again, then walked to one side of the keep wall and studied the distance. At length, while Meive and I watched hopefully, he came to us.

"The vale entrance is too far from the keep. It would cost dear in time and stone we do not wish to spend."

"What do you advise then?"

"That if the entrance is where we do not wish it, why, then we move it to where we do." I looked and saw at once what his plan might be.

"Yes! Indeed yes, Levas. If we blocked up the entrance to the inner valley, then we could—but surely it will cost more time to bore through the cliff?"

Meive interrupted then. "Perhaps not. You have not had time to look within the valley closely. Come." She led me through and to one side. "See, the cliff-face is cracked there. It could be that the crack leads deep within." All that was possible. Equally it might not be. I said so, to receive agreement from my lady and Levas.

"Let Levas spend some reasonable time to explore if it be so," Meive said. "If it is, then can we place a tunnel or gate of some sort." It was agreed and Levas went to work. To our annoyance, after much labor he found the idea impractical. Meive sighed to me once it was made known. "Life is not as the bards sing. If it was, that would have been a cavern within the cliff and required little work of us."

I laughed. "Aye. But if life were as the bards sing there

would never have been a war. Nor would death come for any of us." Her reply held a slight tartness.

"Oh, I think we would have death. How else would they have sad songs they might sing to wring hearts and thus coins?" I blinked at her. My gentle lady who, under her kindness, her gifts which were the stuff of bard songs, was yet also possessed of an almost brutal realism.

"Lady," I said then. "I shall work to see war and death are kept far from us. I may not succeed, yet all I have shall be bent to that end."

"I know." Her eyes on me were understanding. "But remember this, Lorcan. No man can hold back the tide. Nor can he prevent death when it is time. Yet," her voice became more cheerful, "I know if anyone can do these things it shall be you. Now, let us consider where we might place a guardhouse on the upper pastures by the road there."

So we turned to other work. Yet was my heart high as I did so. For it seemed as if she began to trust and to value me honestly. The keep was sound once more; at the entrance to our dale we had both a guardhouse with a tiny stable, and a secret hiding place nearby. By Levas's cunning we had placed a tumble of boulders between. Through them, out of sight from those who might approach, there was a thread of trail. Thus one could watch from the secret place for any who came, then run down the trail to the guard-post. The secret trail was direct. The road wound. One afoot could thus be well before even a swift rider—and we had seen to the road, no rider would ride down that too swiftly unless he wished for a horse without four good legs.

Levas explained. "We post two here. A child and a guard. The child, should he see anyone, runs to the guard. With the man warned the child takes to horse to warn the valley upon the guard's word. The guard remains to hold the entrance with bow and arrow." He showed us. "See, the field of fire covers any who would enter Honeycoombe. At night there are other ways." He showed us those so we saw that few could come unheralded.

The children took to this as a game in which Meive paid the winners in sweets, yet they watched well and saved us the loss of a second man's work in the fields. After some days they vied with each other as to who could make the best report. Thus we heard of sheep, of deer, of a wild pony which approached. They noted when the beelove bloomed, and when the pheasants or hares leaped up alarmed by a hill-cat. After some days I was confident no enemy would steal up upon my watchers.

Gathea, the blank-shields cat, was growing. There had been a great slaughter of mice on our arrival so that now, at the least, all of their tribe stayed out of the keep. She was a friend to all in Honeycoombe and honored was anyone on whose bed she would sleep the night. Meive and I had taken bedrooms within the keep and it was often on our beds, during the day at least, that she was to be found. We were very willing she should, since her rent was paid in dead mice and safer food supplies. We had been in the dale a month and a half when Meive came to me.

"In the morning I go to the shrine. I would bespeak my Lady of the Bees and return with the hives from the plateau where lies my cave."

"You do not go alone?" I said in alarm.

"I thought to take Vari and Levas. It would be a pleasant trip for them." I thought she was right. But if she had forgotten our enemies I had not, nor would I.

"Take another man, at least." My words were close to an order but she bowed her head.

"As you will."

I took her hand. "What am I to do while you are gone from me?" I made a moping face, yet were my words half serious and that she knew.

"Long ago, when I was a child, Ithia chose me. Soon after that time I was wandering to fetch in the cow from the inner vale. I lingered playing and there I found another place."

"Another place?" I echoed. Did she mean a cave, a second vale?

"Another small valley. It leads from the inner vale. The walls about it are higher and rougher still. Nor is the entrance easy to find." She paused. "Indeed I think it is hidden from most in some way. Ithia bade me say nothing of it nor enter once I told her. I listened yet never did I hear my family or friends speak of it. I think none knew."

"How large is it? Is there good grass, water?" I was eager.

"I think it twice the size of the inner vale. There is good grass but there are also many bushes. Like to beelove but with larger flowers. There is water. A stream, very small, which comes down the cliffs then vanishes into the ground. It may be from that our spring in the keep derives."

This was good. But had Honeycoombe been so rich they had no need of the land? I knew they had not. Ithia had bid Meive stay apart and speak not of this place. Well, whatever reason she might have had for that had died with her. Meive knew it not. I would wait until my lady was gone, then occupy my time in exploring this new dale. If the entrance was truly so hard to find it could be an additional refuge for us all in time of trouble.

I saw Meive off next morning. Then, taking up a carry-sack, I added a wineskin, bread and cheese, and a piece of honeycomb. I took my old Drustan. He would enjoy the quiet ride, and though he was now well on in years, being almost seventeen, he was still able to carry an unarmored man if there was no haste. The day was good, fine yet not too warm. I rode slowly, enjoying the clean air, the hum of bees, and the sight of a hawk high up over the hills.

Once I reached the far end of the inner vale I dismounted to search. Meive was right. The entrance was well enough hid yet not so greatly others should not have found it. I know what children are, being none so aged myself.

They run here and there, prying into holes and corners. Thus they find what many adults would pass by. I walked the pony past boulders, behind them I found an arch barely high or wide enough to pass a tall man afoot or a laden pack-pony.

The hole reminded me of a man knapping flint. He strikes off rounded flakes as he works. It seemed as if some giant had paused here, struck away a flake then moved on again. For that was the shape of the gap, and never did I change my mind. But as I stared through the opening I knew, too, that this was the place of which Meive had told me. I could see the stream, the beelove, and other bushes I could not identify. It was true the entrance was not so obvious yet I had found it with no great difficulty.

From where I stood in the archway I judged the valley to hold some hundred and a half acres in the shape of a long oval. It was sheltered so that once through the arch it was warmer. The winds soared above the high cliffs about it and did not descend to chill. Maybe that was the reason for the presence of the strange bushes. Perhaps only in such a sheltered spot could they live through Winter. I thought that in the very height of Summer it might not be so pleasant here. I had come in the early morning and Summer was waning. Yet by sunhigh it would be so hot here a man would feel as though he melted. I stared about and marveled no child before Meive should have found it. Leading Drustan, I walked boldly in.

It was as I entered that I felt it: a sort of questioning touch, as if something reached out to sort through my mind. The feeling changed then to a kind of recognition. Now it welcomed me. I shrugged such ideas away as I tramped on. Drustan followed but nervously, his eyes rolling as if he, too, felt that touch. I followed the thread of stream up the valley. It would be interesting to see where it led. I think it may have been in my mind that if the inner vale led from Honeycoombe, and this led from the inner vale. Then there might yet be further valleys.

I must admit that, at first, I had wondered if we should

not take Merrowdale to hold rather than Honeycoombe. Since I thought that if we chose the latter, although it was Meive's beloved home, it was also the lesser dale in size. But as I now knew, if we added the pasturage of both inner and outer vales, Honeycoombe was a prize. Easier to defend, easier to pasture stock which could not easily stray, and sheltered so that the grass would continue to grow well into the cold months.

Drustan hauled nickering at his reins as we passed some of the strange bushes. I saw then that they were laden with small fruit. Some sort of berry? I had remounted to ride up the stream. Now I stepped from the saddle again and approached the fruit. I studied it. The globes were full and firm, colored a rich orange-red. I would not risk eating any since unknown fruit can be poisonous. But I would bring some back with me.

Levas had found a wild sow and her piglets last week. After some trouble we had them penned by his cottage. I would feed a piglet the fruit and see. If all was well the fruit might be a fine addition to our own diet. Meive might know more if I brought some back to her. I would ride on, circle the valley, see what else there was to be seen, before picking a generous bag full of the fruit on my return circle.

I reached the end of the valley by late morning. The stream seemed to tumble down the cliffs at that point. It had worn a deep crevice in the cliff edge high above, and down the face. The edge of that was starred with tiny white flowers and green ferns. I dismounted, unsaddled, and hobbled Drustan, brought out my wineskin and the food, sharing a crust now and again with my pony. As I ate I whittled at a reed. There was a stand of them at a marshy corner of the stream edge once it reached the ground.

I thought that doubtless when the stream increased with the Winter rains it created a reed-fringed pool here. By the time I had finished my food I had made of the reed a fine whistle. Then I began to play. My brother Anla taught me first to make reed whistles thus and I always thought of him when I did so. I played first a marching tune from my days with Lord Salden. From that I found I was playing a ballad. A song born in my own dale which sang of how my ancestor had met a child of the Old Ones and saved her. From the crevice behind the water a voice spoke.

"Who are you to play that song?" So deep in memory had I been that I answered without thinking of the strangeness.

"I am Lorcan, only child left alive from the House of Erondale. Who else should play it?" I saw a stirring in the crevice. I could see no definite shape but the shadow was large enough to be a small woman, or an older child.

"Of that House? What do you here then, Lorcan of Erondale?" No, this was no child. The voice was that of a woman. Not young, but beyond that I could not tell.

"Speak! What do you here?" The voice became urgent. So I talked, still wrapped in memories. I think now that she held me in some small spell so I should talk freely without fear. But at the time it appeared natural, as if I conversed with a friend who would hear all which had happened to me after long apart. So I spoke of Erondale and how it had fallen, of the death of all my family and how Berond and I had come to Paltendale. Then I spoke of Meive and how she had saved me, of the shrine where she was claimed as daughter to the hive. At length I was done and my voice drifted into a long silence before that other spoke again.

"You came here then, fleeing the death which was laid upon your own dale. Sad am I that Erondale has fallen. Always I meant to return for one last time."

"You knew my home?" I asked.

"Long before you did." The voice was tart but amused.

I challenged that amusement. "How long before?"

It did not answer my question but spoke of Meive. Was it indeed true that she had dwelt a while in the shrine beyond the hills? Had I also seen that place, had I entered? So I talked of Meive. Of the Lady of the Bees who dwelled in the shrine, and the peace Meive and I had found there. Af-

ter that I spoke again of Meive herself. I think then I betrayed my love for her because the voice became gentle.

"The girl, Meive. What like is she?"

So I talked of my love. I found I was confessing that time
in the hills when we saved Elesha and her kin. How Meive
had hurt me, turning in anger against men who brutalized.
And yet, was she not right? It was men who brought war,
suffering, death. Men who . . . The voice cut in.

"Lorcan. Do you think women, too, cannot bring these
things? I have heard of women who rode to war. Of those
who killed and tortured. Each is accountable for her own
sins. Let you not take upon your own head those deeds you
have not committed." I found myself comforted by that
thought. I had been tempted during the war, yet never had I
laid hands on a woman unwilling. Nor had I harmed children. Those I fought and slew had been the enemy alone,
men trained and armed. As if the voice followed my
thoughts it spoke.

"Yes and yes. In war a man does right to protect his kin
and home. If he must kill to do so then that is no evil. The
evil is those who come seeking to take by force what is not
theirs to have. And if a man will not fight for what is right,
who shall? Yet the girl spoke to you out of her own fear I
think. For as she watched she saw what would have been
her earlier fate had she not been defended by her wing-
friends. Do not be angered by fear, Lorcan. It is fear that
often reminds one of what should be done."

At that I, too, was reminded. Of how I planned to set
guard-posts about Honeycoombe, and how I was enlarging
the keep. The voice seemed interested, asking questions,
encouraging me to talk of my plans, my hopes and dreams.
Much of what I said or saw in that day is lost to me. I do
not remember. Only that finally I was given leave to go. Yet
the feeling was laid on me I would be welcome to return. I
and Meive alone. That none other of our small company
should enter.

So I rode back to the outer dale and kept silent. Meive returned with the hives in six days and I was glad to see her again. I showed that pleasure openly and saw her smile. Nor was it the indulgent smile women are wont to show at such times as they think a man most like a happy child. No, her gaze met mine and clung. Then, after a time, she flushed, smiling more sweetly before she turned to oversee the hives as they were placed in the lower pastures of beelove. That night I took her aside and told of the valley.

"Did you see who spoke?"

"I am not certain yet I believe not. Some things are blurred in my memory. But we talked long and I felt no threat. Yet," I hesitated then finished. "Yet, I do think that one is such as could threaten very well if she wished. I felt power, old and very strong. And she knew my home, she knew Erondale. She said she sorrowed for its passing, that she had wished to look upon it one more time." At that Meive questioned me hard. I had only impressions, feelings about what the voice had said, but Meive's questioning brought me to know what I believed.

I spoke slowly when her questions ceased. "I think she was either the one whom my ancestor saved from an evil man or that she is kin to that one. That she has known my dale from that time—it is four generations, Meive. It was my great-grandfather who saved a girl-child of the Old Ones from the hands of Pletten."

"Pletten?" Her voice was without inflection as if she merely repeated the name. Yet I felt the query, so once again I found myself talking, telling old tales of rougher times in the early days of Erondale. I had mentioned a little of the story to her once but now I told it all to her, just as it had been told to me by Berond. I fell into the cadence and rhythm of the storyteller and saw with pleasure that Meive was entranced. She listened in silence, hanging on my every word. Never did a man have a more appreciative audience so that I spun it into a greater length, the more to enjoy my moment. Once I was done she stood.

"He was a man like those who held Elesha captive." Her tone was that of a lady who judges in a Dales Court. "Your great-grandfather did right." With that she left me abruptly so that I was sorry I had told her. Likely my foolish tale had brought back to her all her own dangers and fears.

XIV

—◦—

I might have warned our people to stay away from the valley but for Meive. She counseled I say nothing.

"Many went to the inner vale. None I ever knew save myself and perhaps Ithia found the strange place beyond. It may be that the archway is hidden to other eyes."

"I entered," I objected.

"Aye, and were welcomed. But we have pastured cows and horses in the inner vale. A few of the goats I could not chase out roamed there while I was gone and you know what they are. Did you see signs they had entered? Was the grass cropped?" I had to admit I had seen no signs. Meive nodded. "I think people and beasts both see no entrance. Let be, Lorcan. If we speak of it there will always be one who must seek it out and I do not think whoever abides there wishes other visitors."

Since such had been my own feeling I did as she said and kept silent. After all, there was no need to hunt out other work. The keep was completed, the cottages all put into good repair. Meive's bees worked long and hard gathering nectar, and one of Levas's men, Criten by name, was a fair hunter. He brought in game ranging from deer to the small fat hill-hens. These we ate, but much of the spare meat was also smoked or cured by the women. Vari had taken over the keep kitchen and most evenings we all ate there together, talking of the next day's work.

It was closing to Fall one evening when one of the children had news which startled us. It had been Meive's idea to use the children—even the little girls—as watchers and to my surprise it had worked well. Meive made sweets, candying stalks of angelica and rose petals, and these were given to any child on watch-duty who could bring us interesting news or information. It had become a source of pride to the children to do so—and the sweets had only added to that. There was little that did not happen now on which some pair of sharp eyes did not alight, and a small mouth announce it, in sometimes embarrassing detail, during a shared meal.

It had been Isa's turn to watch the road into Honeycoombe from the hiding place. She was about seven, a serious, responsible child who remembered the flight from her home and the bandits' actions at the shelter. Because of those memories she watched carefully, although she would accept the sweets as her due once she reported.

"I saw a man today."

Meive sat up. "A man? Where? What was he doing?"

"He was riding about like he was looking for something." None of us liked the sound of that. Further questioning revealed that the man had ridden leaning over his mount's shoulder, studying the ground as if he sought something lost. He rode a good mount, Isa was all admiration for it.

"A gelding, Lord Lorcan. The most beautiful horse I ever saw. All glossy black with one white hoof."

Meive looked hard at the child. "Isa, why didn't you tell the sentry when this happened?"

"The man never came near. Then he rode away, a long long way, until I couldn't see him any more."

I kept silent, but made resolve that the children must be told to report any man at once, no matter if he seemed harmless or departed again. Sensing she had mayhap done the wrong thing, Isa looked anxiously at Meive, who reassured her.

"You watched very well, Isa. Three stalks of angelica for you tonight. Tell us more about the man. What did you think when you saw him? Did you make up a story about what he was doing?" From the relieved child's prattle we gained much more. Meive and I gathered Levas with a glance and the three of us drew aside to talk in lowered voices. I had information to impart first.

"I know who that likely was."

Meive was swift. "One of Devol's men, one of the two who went to find a ransom."

"So I think. Belo had a horse like that. He was a man who counted a good horse above most else. He boasted he'd had the beast from an old man and paid him with steel coin. He said the horse was too good to waste on some old fool. Belo and the horse Isa saw would fit what description she could give."

"If he's a good hunter he'd find the path to Honeycoombe," Levas commented.

"I think he had been a farmer, yet he was good enough at tracking. Nor would he be out here studying the land for no reason. Perhaps he seeks for Devol and his comrades?"

Meive nodded thoughtfully. "He is one man. Yet bandits are like rats. Where you see one there is like to be another ten you have not seen."

I stood. "I had not thought to leave for another week, but if one scouts, better I be swift gone, swift to return. When we passed the cross-roads on the way here I bespoke Keris Innkeeper. He was to sound out those who might be willing to come here. He has had time to find some few and we have need of them. Levas, let me take Criten and another. We shall take two horses apiece. If we waste no time and those who would come can also ride hard, we could be back here in a ten-day."

Meive looked up. "Nay, Lorcan. If they bring livestock and families they will not be able to ride hard, nor wish to. Better I go with Levas and Criten. My warriors will fly guard and scout for me. Nor will they slow our journey. We can make good time to the cross-roads with two mounts apiece. After that, if we must be slower, then at least you shall be here to defend Honeycoombe knowing we bring reinforcements."

I did not like it but she was right. Keris knew her as my younger brother, yet, if she must reveal herself as she was, then a woman and moreover one clearly of some power would reassure those planning to join us, and, though I said it not, I would she was out of the dale if bandits attacked. So I agreed. Early the next morning she rode out with Levas and Criten. With them went three spare mounts. It would take five days riding to make the inn. Their return must needs be slower as Meive had argued. I watched her depart. For such time as it took to see her again I would be anxious.

With the three gone I gathered our people. I explained where my lady went and why. Then I called Isa to tell them of the man she had seen. She told her story proudly, speaking well and remembering small details new to us. I told them who I believed that man to be and why we should be very wary now. The children who watched must report anything at all which might be a man, even a great distance from us, or if they thought they saw danger of any kind. Better to have reported and be wrong, than be right and to have failed to warn us. The sentry must be alert always.

As for myself and our guards, three remained. The four of us would patrol the hills, coming together at arranged intervals to discuss anything we had seen. As Meive had said, bandits were like rats. Where you spy one there could be many. I thought one other at least might lurk somewhere about nearby, Todon had been with Belo when they rode away. If one lived and was in the area, the other might be. I thought they hunted for Devol despite the time they had been gone.

Though that time puzzled me. It had been early Spring when Devol laid hands on me, almost Summer when Meive freed me. We had not set out at once. Then, since we were moving North, the weather had been less harsh. We had not been in great haste. I wished to take time, to allow Meive time to trust me. Thus we had ridden the length of the dales over many weeks. It had been Spring again when we reached Tildale. Now it was almost Fall. Belo and his comrade had set out seeking one to pay my ransom nigh on eighteen months gone.

I had thought nothing that they were gone until late Summer. Likely they had ridden first to my own dale to check what I said, that the invaders had destroyed all. After that, as Devol had ordered, they would have sought out Paltendale. They'd have got nothing from there . . . My thoughts crashed to a halt. No! They'd have got no ransom. But what if they met Hogeth? What if they told or he wrung from them all they knew—together with my name. Might he not then have taken them into his own service until such time as they could be sent here seeking me?

We had believed Hogeth still to have no knowledge of me save that I had ridden South. But if Devol's men had talked with my enemy, if they had been able to tell him only that a year gone I had been prisoner in their hands, then where else would he seek me and my captors but hereabouts? I had none to counsel me. But perhaps if I did as Belo had done, if I rode as he had ridden . . . I called Isa and placed her in the hiding place to watch me closely.

Then, with Vari as a link between us, I rode Tas about the hill. Leaning over Tas's shoulder I peered at the ground as Belo had done. Isa, young though she was, had watched well. Vari called the child's instructions at intervals as I moved about the hill. It was a tiring morning, yet at length I thought I knew what the man had sought—and found.

"Isa says to go further West."

I obeyed. Tas snorted irritably. He disliked all this confusion, I should make up my mind.

"Isa says a little more to the South now."

I reined Tas that way slowly, moving a few feet at a time, and there was a sudden shriek from Vari.

"Isa says that was just where the man stopped and was leaning over."

"What did he do then?" I shouted back.

"She says he stepped down, touching the ground, then he sort of nodded before he mounted and just rode away. To the North. He didn't stop. She could see him out of sight."

I stared down. I'd wager he had. He'd found what he was looking for and unless I was a witless hill-hen, he was on the road back in haste to report. To whom I knew not for certain, though I believed I could guess and be right. What he would report, of that I was sure. At Tas's hooves lay a broad hardened track. Hidden in the heather but carven deep into the stony hillside was the track made, when with horse-team and stone-boat, we moved the squared building stones from Merrowdale to Honeycoombe. The track would be erased by the coming Winter, or disguised by water along the hills at thaw, but at the moment it was very evident.

Belo might not know who had made it but he would know such a deep mark bespoke a settlement of some kind at one end of the path or both. The question which disturbed me was, how far had the man to ride before he could make his report. If it was to Paltendale then we need not look for Hogeth or any attack until next Spring. It was several weeks riding straight to that dale, and a lone man had to ride carefully even now that the war was done. But if Hogeth was closer? I bethought me of a query that might tell us and called for Isa. She came with Vari.

"Isa. You watched the man ride out of sight. Was that far?"

She nodded seriously. "Yes, Lord. He was climbing towards the track along the upper hills. Once he was there he was high up an' I could see him for a long way."

"How did he ride? Was he in a hurry to reach the trail, did he ride faster or slower once he reached it?" I could see her thinking about it.

"He climbed up to the trail real slow. An' I don't think he rode faster when he got there. Maybe if you did it?"

I walked Tas up the hill to where the old high trail meandered along the upper slopes. It was one of the pack-pony trails traders had used before the war, though Meive said none had used it since she remembered and it was almost overgrown. It continued from the northern dales through Southern High Hallack past the Fen of Sorn and thence I knew not. Once Tas set foot upon it I rode North at a steady walk. I continued about a mile before I turned him to return. Back with Vari and the child, again, I saw Isa was clapping her hands.

"Lord, it was just like that."

Vari looked up at me. "You walked Tas?" I nodded agreement. "Then likely he'd some distance to ride."

I nodded. No bandit, no matter how proud of his horse, would walk the beast when he might run. Only a man who had a far distance to ride and but one mount. A man who'd had it impressed upon him he must take no risks. Or a man who thought better payment lay at the end of a slow-taken trail so he'd be fit to ride back with his comrades.

I returned in silence, Vari riding on ahead. Gods, what a careless fool I had been those years ago, to mistakenly fling gold instead of the intended silver coin in Hogar's face. Of course he would have spoken of it to his son, in outrage at what he would have seen as my ingratitude if for no other reason. Hogeth would care nothing for my reasons though. It would be the gold on which he fastened. He would remember the story in his own House, of how my great-grandfather had come riding to Paltendale, paid blood-price in gold for Pletten.

From there it was a small step in reasoning which was half hope. My dale had once paid a great blood-price. I had owned gold to fling in the face of one who angered me. Therefore the blood-price had not exhausted all my dale had. But my dale was ruined. I could not return to live there. If I had coin why should I not set forth to find another dale I could settle? And in the South where the war had mostly not come, or had come and gone quickly, was a good place to seek a dale of my own again. Thus would Hogeth reason and he was right.

In one way I was between the arrow and the sling. If I used my coin to hire more guards for Honeycoombe then I shouted to all I had coin to spare. If I hired no more men, then might Hogeth come in force with men from Paltendale. I mulled over the problem all the way home. Isa must have known I thought deeply and wished to do so undisturbed. She said nothing as we rode, but settled herself into the crook of my arm, leaned against my shoulder, and appeared to drowse. It was a pleasant feeling. A child's trust is a precious thing and mayhap it helped me think.

By the time I set her down at Elesha's cottage I had come to a decision. I should not hire more guards. But most dalesmen can fight, and many of the women are adept with light bows. I sat to write, then I sought for and found Dogas, one of Levas's men.

"You know the Inn at the Cross-Roads where go Levas and my lady?" He nodded. "Take two horses and ride there in haste. I would warn them." He was a steady man. I told him something of events that he might know where and of whom to be watchful. As he swung to the saddle he nodded again.

"I'll ride wary. If I look to be taken I'll destroy the message."

"Do so—in secret. Let them not know there is information to be had lest they attempt to wrest it from you." It was unnecessary to tell him that, yet I wished him to know I had a care for his life.

He should reach Meive almost as she arrived at the inn. I

had writ of all I knew and much I thought. She would understand the dangers. I could trust her to choose good people for Honeycoombe. There were almost thirty cottages here. Vari and Levas had their cottage but had also taken rooms within the keep, as had his four men. Elesha had taken a large cot, one which had belonged to the dale's baker. She and Vari's daughters Arla and Manan baked for us now. The four children dwelled with them.

Thus there was ample room for any new incomers, yet we must be cautious. If we took too large a group from any one place they could turn against us. There can only be one voice to command. Meive was lady here and I would see none deprive her of her rights. Yet Meive was no fool. She would have the same chance in mind and would choose carefully. Levas was a man well able to judge those who came seeking a new home. He would not wish the order overthrown we had established. I should put such things from my mind. There was other work to do.

Indeed there was. I drilled our people, walked the dale to see all was well-kept, listed who should be sentry and watcher, and oversaw all that was done within our lands. At night I fell into my bed and slept as though struck down. Twice I went with the horse-team and a stone-boat to plunder Merrowdale further. Elesha came with me both times, her knowledge and advice most valuable. We had fed the sheep from stored hay and grain so that now they came running when they saw us.

"Best we catch soon the ones you wish to have for ourselves," Elesha advised the second time. "We can pen them in the inner vale with the cattle. If none who spy on us can see them they may believe us poorer than we are. That is always safer." It was good advice and I took it. We made a day of the hunt, luring the beasts into Merrowdale with the grain then blocking the path by which they came and went.

We ended up with two rams, one older, one a yearling. Of the ewes we caught eleven, all of them black or brown and all I thought to be in lamb. With them we took a further half-dozen healthy yearling ewes, too young as yet to bear their own lambs but with good fleeces. After that I heeded Elesha and took a number of the yearling rams. Those could be kept apart and slain over Winter if necessary, whenever the hunting was poor and we were hungry for meat. We should also continue to eat the surplus goats, although some of those we had taken to Merrowdale and left to breed for the benefit of Salas and his people.

The inner vale of Honeycoombe was rich pasture since it was well irrigated by the water which streamed down the cliff sides when it rained. Yet with the horse-team, the sheep, Cream and her herd, and all the mounts Meive had taken from the bandits, the pasture there was becoming hard pressed. There were also our two mules, together with mounts and pack-ponies which belonged to none in particular but which had come with us. I left the mules and Elesha's goats to pasture openly within the dale. With them I allowed another eight horses, the poorest in appearance, to roam.

To any who spied it would look reasonable, as if the beasts were all we had. Tas and Drustan I kept in the keep stables. It was useful to have beasts that could be saddled swiftly in an emergency and needed not to be coaxed to hand. I left, too, the stone-boats, stacked under a pole roof behind one of the barns. Let any who came believe we had used our own beasts to drag them. The stone-boats, as the team hauled them up the trail from Merrowdale, would have torn out the hoof-prints so none should guess at our team.

"Lord, my Lord! Riders and walkers come, I think it is the lady who leads them." I ran, as eager as the child to see. It was as she had said, Meive led a small weary group of travelers towards Honeycoombe. She halted her mount when I came riding. I saw swift pleasure in her eyes as she saw me so that I forgot myself and swept her up in my arms. I hugged her hard. She freed herself gently, her cheeks pink, her eyes smiling.

"Such a welcome. I should leave more often." Her voice was teasing so that I knew she had taken no offense.

I spoke lower. "You need not leave for that."

She blushed. "I received your message. I purchased supplies here and there so none should remark. But I have five good bows and all the arrows I could buy. I have also three good swords. We should also send Levas out to buy elsewhere before Winter comes. It would be well for him to rid us of a string of our horses. There are too many for the land. Let you come now and meet those I chose for Honeycoombe. The winged-ones approve them all."

She turned to introduce me to those who came forward at her call. It was a mixed group. I could see that four there were of one family. A half-grown boy, his younger sister, a smaller boy, and with them a man. His right arm was injured so that he used only the left. His deftness one-handed spoke of long practice, so I judged it to be an old wound. Of the others I found we had a sister and brother, a middle-aged man who had to ride, since he was lame, and two women, also of middle age. I grinned wryly at Meive as I drew her apart.

"What of them? I know you chose not on strength of arm."

"That I did not and you should be glad of it. The man and his children came from a dale which the invaders found. His wife died as they fled. He was wounded and the injury healed awry since they had no healer. He cannot use his arm though he can grasp with the fingers. But he is a decent man, loves his children well, and moreover he is skilled."

"What skill?"

"He is a leather-worker. He can prepare hides or furs, and his children, too, begin to learn. Already the elder boy can mend footwear and cobble boots which are none so poor." I rejoiced in that. Such skills were useful in any dale.

"If you have done as well with the others then have you done very well." My tone was hopeful.

"I think we have done not so ill." Meive looked pleased. "The lame man is a potter. He can make dishes, cups, anything we require so long as we have clay. And that we have."

"I saw none?" I said in surprised question.

"Yet it is there. I can show him once he is settled in. The two who led the pony are sister and brother. They have no skill but are young and willing to work. Their mother is dead and their father died with their lord in the war. They did not like his heir, though I suspect it was more a case of his heir liking the girl too greatly. Therefore they took their pony and cart with their goods and set out to find another place. They are used to beasts and the work of the land. I thought to give them the sheep to tend. I think they will do well."

"And the last two? What are their skills?"

"They have abilities and knowledge we may use." There was something in her voice which said she felt here was a bargain. I waited. "Both spin finely. One weaves. See the cloak she wears." I had seen. It was very beautiful, of a soft green hue, the shade of beelove leaves in early Spring.

Meive was speaking again. "I have rarely seen so tight and neat a weave. The other sister is a dyer. The cloak's color is of her doing. But Lorcan, both can shear also. Are we not fortunate?"

I caught up her hand. "That was well done. We captured the sheep while you were gone. We have almost twenty to be our flock and yearlings to feed us during the Winter chill. So, we shall have plates from which to eat, mugs we may drink from. Leather and furs, woolen hangings and bedding, why, almost do we have all a dale requires."

"What else would you have then?"

I shrugged. "A horse-master, a weapons-master. A keep passage to the inner vale, Hogeth's being uninterested in us, the death of all bandits . . ." I went on, becoming more outrageous in my desires until I had her laughing. I thought how beautiful she was when her face and eyes lit with joy. Would that I might always bring her laughter. Would that she was mine. But of those wishes I did not speak.

The nine who were new to Honeycoombe settled in quickly. They rejoiced in cottages of their own, the sisters taking over what had been the weaver's cot and which still, in a room to one side, contained the large cloth-width loom. They had brought with them two smaller hand looms, dye-pots, dye-sticks, cakes of the dyes created, and other minor items. Within the week they had shorn the sheep we had and while one wove, the other was exchanging information on local herbs and dyes with Meive.

Meive set the sister and brother to tending the sheep. They would learn to shear from the older women and also save them the harder, rougher work of being out with the flock. They took a tiny cot, and settled in there with obvious content.

The leather-worker had received a vast stack of dried hides and furs gathered over the past months since we had arrived back in Honeycoombe with Levas and his men. I had seen to it nothing was wasted nor ill-done, so he was pleased with his raw materials. He took a larger cot so he and his three children would have room both to live and work. The elder boy was already taking boots from us to mend, replacing worn-through soles and nailing on new heels. The two younger children had joined Elesha's pack and added their sharp eyes to the sentry duties—something they enjoyed, since the other children at once explained the benefits. It was not long before the new children had earned their first sweets and loudly approved the system.

The potter took a greater time to be ready. Levas and I would have built him a kiln save that Meive knew of one in Merrowdale. To Merrowdale we went, returning in triumph with a kiln ready to use. It was then Meive revealed another secret I had not known.

"This way." We went where she led until she halted at a

distant corner of the inner vale. "Can you dismount and walk a few paces on foot, Master Elban?" The potter nodded, peering eagerly about him. We raised lanterns as Meive led the way. To my surprise she walked forward into a shallow depression in the cliff-face. At the back she turned sharply into shadows and vanished. I was close behind her, an arm ready in case our potter stumbled. Within the shadows lay a turn in the cave, behind which was a second wider cave, the back wall of which was of strange appearance. Our potter limped forward to scrape a handful of its substance into his hands.

"Clay, of fine quality. How does it come here? Is this some store?" I lifted a lantern to light the wall and could answer.

"I think it is natural. See, Elban. The wall here has fallen away and behind is clay. I think the lower under-side of the hill here is clay, and with a piece of the rock fallen the clay oozes through."

Meive was nodding. "We have known of this since first Honeycoombe was settled. Tomas, who had some small skill, made dishes for everyday use. Sometimes he took a pony-load of the clay to Merrowdale. They would exchange our clay for the right to fire in their kiln other work Tomas had done. The lord of our dale had finer things but they came from further North."

Elban smiled gently. "Your Tomas had only small skill, that is true. I have seen some of his work in the cot I was given. It holds the shape required without leaking and that is all one can say of it. But I trained under a master potter. I will make you such plates and dishes as will sell to traders. Better yet, when the land is more settled, let you take a load of my work, well packed in straw, and offer them to daleslords." As we talked we had moved back to stand outside the cave. I signaled Meive that she should leave us. When she was gone I turned to Elban.

"I believe you can. But why come here where you are far

from lords and markets? Why not remain in the North and reap the rewards of your skill?" I looked into his face and made my own stern. "You hide a secret. You are not the first to think our dale a refuge. So long as you have done no evil my lady and I would not drive you forth. Let you tell me why it is you chose Honeycoombe."

His look was bitter. "Because in the North, where the invaders came and stayed for whole seasons, too many know what I am. The son of the enemy. How think you I gained my lame foot? Was it my fault some sneaking spy of Alizon came into the North? Many years ago they looked first towards the dales. One came to my dale pretending to be an honest trader. He cozened my mother, who was barely a woman. She lay with him believing his lie of love, and I was born. I have never been of great size and strength, so once I was of age I was apprenticed to a potter.

"He was a good man and a fair master. He taught me well and I had a talent for the work, so what I did sold and I could keep my mother in comfort. Until Alizon came again. Then the men of my dale remembered; they saw my thin body, my fair hair, and they called me an enemy within their gates. One night they came hunting. Before dawn my mother was dead, slain by a blow gone awry as she tried to protect me. I was lamed. My lord said he would have no trouble-maker in his dale and sent me forth.

"By then the war raged and all hands were against a man who was of Alizon blood. I dyed my hair and kept a hooded cloak about me when I went abroad, but still some would always suspect and I must flee again. In the end I sought out the South where the hounds had never come or where they had been only briefly. I hoped here I might find a home again." The bitterness in his voice sharpened like a whetted knife. "Will *you* now drive me forth for the sin of being my mother's son and her a victim of Alizon herself?"

I reached for the mule's reins and turned him so Elban could mount more easily. Then I faced the potter. "There are none of us here who have not known fear or unjust grief. Shall we send them from us for that? Mount and ride to your home, Elban, Potter of Honeycoombe."

I said no more before turning to walk before the mule, but as I turned I stole a glance at him. The mule moved to follow. Aye, after me rode Elban with the first smile I had ever seen upon his face. I had never seen a brighter one.

XV

◄─◆─►

*I*n the last days of Fall, Levas rode out. With him went a
string of all the mounts we could spare. We had traded
away carefully those beasts which left with Meive for the
cross-roads. She had exchanged the six taken and Dogas's
two for three good young mares and supplies. Now Levas
sold our bandit's gleanings and returned with a fine colt of
a strain being bred by a lord in the North. There was Arvon
blood in the animal but also something of the Waste. The
colt had both strength and speed, and the endurance and
ability to survive on little water and less feed. His foals
should be an asset to Honeycoombe.

Within our dale the people had worked hard. I believed
with so many grazers gone we would have stored feed and
pasture enough for the snow months. Winter came after
Levas had returned, bringing with the first heavy snow a
great relief to me. Honeycoombe was well South so that
the snows came early. The dale had never been easy to find,
so said Meive. But with many of the passes closed and the
thin trail over the higher hills blocked we should not need
to fear Hogeth nor any outlaw band. None but the utterly
desperate moved in Winter. It was too easy to die without
adequate shelter. But we had wrought well. Within Honey-

coombe all was snug, each cot with its store of firewood, ample food, and a watertight roof. There were now twenty-four of us. I had talked in turn to each adult, explaining to them of Elban. Elesha set the tone for her tiny clan.

"The poor man cannot help it. And as for his mother, what? A young lass is cozened by a rogue. How is this a reason to murder his mother and drive him from his home? His lord should think shame." After that, for a few weeks she went out of her way to help him ready his cottage. El-ban accepted graciously, so they became friends. Our leather-worker was neither so kind nor so accepting, but, intimidated by Meive's glare, he shut his mouth after the first hasty words and said no more.

As for Levas, that experienced blank-shield warrior only grunted at the news.

"I guessed. What of it? Alizon fought well enough. If every fighter went around killing everyone whose parent-age he disapproved there'd be damn few left."

I had to grin at that. He was right enough. I used his words to the sisters, who agreed and swept into agreement also the two who had joined them. Our leather-worker and his family might have made trouble, still remembering the loss of a wife and mother, and the crippling of their father. But seeing how the rest of us thought, while they might never accept Elban, at least they continued silent. Thus it was as a fairly united group that we settled into the season of snows.

That first Winter was one I think I shall never forget. Most evenings we gathered to eat in the keep's great hall. After food we would take turns to tell old stories, sing songs, and several times the children had learned a small play to act for us. Small Isa was oft the lead in that activity.

Elban had spoken only the truth about his skills. In the short time before Winter he had fired several loads of plates, bowls and dishes, mugs and cups for us. They were of a quality I had only previously seen on a lord's high table. We praised them honestly so that Elban beamed, laying a part of the quality on the fineness of the clay. We had sited his kiln in a building separate from his cottage. Elban knew what he wanted for his workshop and thus we had taken apart one of the old cattle shelters, which was stone. It had been rebuilt by his home. Elban lined the small stone building with clay inside to fill every chink between the stones, so that even in the depths of Winter, as long as the kiln was hot, he was able to continue his work there without freezing. Nor, between the materials used and the care Elban took, was there danger of fire.

The sisters, Betha and Lirwas, had taken the weaver's cot, which was larger than usual, with more rooms. Thus they had ample room to set up their looms permanently and dye skeins of wool in their dye pots. They opened two of the rooms to the land, and once Winter came so did their sheep, huddling into the shelter provided and enjoying the warmth which came through the wall between them and the cottage.

Before the snows became too deep, Meive and I took the mules, more sure-footed in the treacherous footing, and went to the place beyond our inner valley. We dismounted and I spoke quietly.

"We come to tell you of what passes." There was a stirring within the crevice of the cliff-face. The reply was slow.

"Why?"

"Do not neighbors talk together?" Meive said quietly. "It is only courtesy that they should do so. It is also good sense. How should one neighbor know if what they do may not trespass on another if she does not speak of what she does and plans? And what if there is danger, or feud with another dale? Should you not know?"

The tone became more welcoming at that. "Speak then. I forget some of your customs, but, may I offer a guest cup?"

"Of your courtesy," Meive agreed.

We drank from strange guest cups then. A sort of spiced

warming wine in tall fluted containers made of a light
wrought metal. They were beautiful and the wine, though
unknown to us, tasted light and fruity with a clean after-
taste which cleansed the palate. We honestly praised both
wine and the beauty of the containers, our remarks bringing greater warmth to the voice as it addressed us.

"Be welcome to my home, be fortunate in your plans. I
listen, speak and be heard." So we talked. Now and again
the voice commented and always the words were sound.
Then it fell silent for some time before it spoke again. "I
am weary." Meive rose at once from where she was sat on
a small convenient flat-topped boulder.

"A good neighbor knows when it is time to leave. We
have not told our people of this place, nor shall we. Lorcan
believes you have safeguards which mean they see it not?"

"He is right. None may enter but you and he, since you
have gifts which permit it, to each his own." Meive turned
to stare at me, then at the direction from which came the
voice.

"Lorcan has some gift also, what is it?" There was no reply. She asked again. There was nothing: even the feeling
that said someone was there had vanished. She looked at
me. I handed her the reins of her mule.

"Let us go." So we did, cantering across the valley of the
voice into Honeycoombe's inner vale and thence to the
keep. But as we went Meive speculated. If it was true I was
permitted entrance to the voice's home because I, too, had
a gift, what could it be? I saw her remember, then.

"Lorcan, once you wondered if that one might not be in
some way related to her who was saved from Pletten.
Could that be your 'gift?' That you come of a line which
once aided one of her kin?"

She said what I had thought. "Berond said the girl's kin-
male told my great-grandfather that they were long-lived
and that they did not quickly forget a debt owed. It may be
the voice is kin also or knows them or the tale." I grinned

and shrugged. "How does one know about someone who is no more than a voice and a shadow?"

"She gave us guest cups."

"She did. But tell me, Meive. Did you see how the cups came or went?"

My lady stared at me then. "No. Lorcan. I do not even remember thinking it strange. I just turned and found the cup already in my hand. I put it down on my boulder between mouthfuls. When it was empty it was gone, yet that, too, aroused no wonder in me. We have been bespelled."

"No harm was done us. It was we who came uninvited so I daresay we have no cause to complain," was all I could think to say.

Meive was practical. "That is so, besides which, Winter closes in. There is no need to hunt stock in the voice's place. Let us stay away from it until Spring." So we agreed and still we spoke to none of our comrades about the hidden place. The voice agreed it was truly hidden. Both Meive and I, too, had long since learned that to allow a sleeping dog to slumber undisturbed is usually far wiser.

Winter passed quietly. We had our small joys, one when Manon came to Meive saying she wished her lady to approve a wedding between Manon and the new shepherd. That permission Meive granted most happily. Thus we had two weddings: one between Levas and Vari after the first snows, and the second towards Spring. Between them lay Mid-Winter's night and fair feasting as we celebrated the rise of the year towards Spring. I found then that roast goat-kid is very tasty when glazed with honey.

I did not know from Meive, but I had guessed at her fear she would not do well as daleslady. She was wrong. I think at first our people deferred to her because Honeycoombe had been her home and she knew her home well from cot to keep. Then, too, they respected her for her gifts and her warriors. But perhaps her gifts gave her more, a natural air of authority which guided without offense so that, over the

Winter, more and more those within our dale looked to her. I rejoiced to see it, and to see also how she met that expectation.

From the first I had respected her courage and good sense. I was uncertain when I had begun to truly love her, but I had long since known I wished her to be to me more than a liege-lady. It was heart's lady I would have her, but I was afraid to speak in case she saw it as a demand outside dales custom. I had no family to approach her, to ask her privately how she felt about me; I could not ask her that question myself, if she did not desire me how could she answer honestly and to my face?

It would not be quite dales etiquette for her to broach the subject to me, but less a breach of that than if I approached Meive myself. So I waited patiently; if she loved me, she would find a way to tell me her desires, if she did not—well, that was ill news I could wait forever to hear.

Sometimes in the southern dales Spring comes early—a false Spring, for after a week of thaw often the weather closes in again. Through Winter we had maintained guard. Not in the children's hiding place, but in the small sentry-post, which had a generous fireplace. The sentries stood their watches still in twos, however, a child and an adult to watch together and with both mules in the tiny stable under the same roof. It was well Meive and I had continued the guard for it was in that false Spring that we were called.

"Lord, come quick. There's a man on a horse."

Gera was tugging at my sleeve before I could rise. I had been mending a broken link on my chain hauberk when he burst in.

"Steady, lad. Calm down, take a mouthful of this."

I gave him a mug of the heated honey-sweetened tea we had always on the hob. "Take your time. If it's only one man he can wait while you catch your breath."

I was brushing snow from him as I spoke. In the warmth of the hall it would melt and wet him through. It was no longer snowing outside. This must be drifted snow kicked up as he rode. I waited until he was calmer, his breathing even, and half the contents of his mug were gone. Then I sat down opposite him.

"You say there was a man?"

"I was on watch with Criten," Gera began. I nodded, glancing up as Meive entered. She sat to listen in silence. "I saw something while he was tending the fire. It looked just like a black dot on the snow. Criten said to watch it so I did."

I could see if he continued this recitation Meive would die of frustration. I hurried the tale a little. "Yes, as it got closer you saw it was a man. What then?"

"He looked hurt. He was riding all to one side, kind'a hunched over. Criten thought he was heading South but when he got near us he fell off the horse. Criten saddled up one 'a the mules an' said I was to get on an' watch. If anything happened I was to ride for you and not waste any time." I jerked upright.

"Something did happen?"

"No." I bit back exasperation. Gera was a good child but painfully slow at explaining anything.

"Then what? Why are you here?" I asked

"Criten told me to come to the keep."

Meive took over the questioning, hastily, before my slipping temper resulted in a shout which would scare Gera into silence.

"Gera. Listen to me. You both saw a man on a horse riding by the trail." She held up a hand. "Don't interrupt me. The minor details aren't important just now. I don't care if he was on or just by the trail. Now! You saw this man. He was alone. There are no others following him?" Gera shook his head.

"Good. He seemed to be hurt in some way. He fell from his horse and Criten told you to be ready in case the man attacked him when Criten went out to see. But the man didn't. Criten told you to ride anyhow, to let us know. Is that right?" Gera nodded mutely.

"Does Criten want us to come and look at the man, is that it?"

"Yes, m' lady. Criten says he thinks the man's a bandit. Someone stabbed him an' Criten says he doesn't think the man's long to live."

"Good lad," Meive told him. "You've done well. I want you to stay here until you are warm again. Drink another mug of Tasflower tea. After that you can ride back to join us. Ride slowly, Rez did well, too, and it would be wrong to make him gallop all the way again." The boy nodded and we left hastily. Once out of the hall Meive turned to me.

"I do not like this, Lorcan. A lone bandit traveling in the false Spring. He must know the dangers."

"I know. It suggests an errand so urgent he would risk the weather closing in on him again." I looked at her as we saddled our mounts. "Bring your cordial. I would not waste it, only give the man a mouthful if you believe it should be used." In reply she touched a small padded pocket on the breast of her tunic. It fastened with an over-flap securely buttoned.

"I have a phial always."

We raced our horses for the trail out of Honeycoombe. Once we topped the entrance we swung left and North. There, in a clump of boulders, lay our sentry-post, the small thin column of smoke from its rearwards chimney masked from the trail by the clump of trees about it. We could see trampled snow but no sign of horse or rider. We paused cautiously. Criten popped out from where the door lay concealed. I held Meive back.

"Wait, be sure none force him to this." I waved the man to walk to one side. He grinned and obeyed, calling out as he moved.

"All is well, Lord. I put the horse in the mule's stable. Your own beasts will be well enough outside if we use my blankets. But the man has come seeking you and says you know him. If you would speak be swift. He is sore injured and I think he will not live another hour."

I left Meive to see to the horses while I hastily tramped inside. I looked down at the man. It was truth he'd spoken. I knew him. Todon, follower of Devol, one of the two sent to seek my ransom. If he was here would Belo be far behind? Yet Gera had said no other man was seen here and now, and Criten had ridden as a blank-shield more than half his life. If he said the man was dying then dying he was. Where was Belo and why had Todon come seeking me through a false Spring? The weather was closing in again. By tonight Winter would have returned and none could ride.

I studied the sunken face. Todon, what did I know of him? For one thing, I recalled I had thought him ill-suited to bandit life. He had none of the evil in him that possessed Belo and some others of Devol's band. Todon had cared well and kindly for the horses, including my old Drustan. He and a couple of the others had never practiced cruelties against me while I lay captive and before Todon departed with Belo to seek my ransom. Yet none of that explained—His eyes opened. At first he stared bleary-eyed, then his gaze sharpened and I knew he recognized me.

"Lord? I found you?" His voice was weak.

"You found me," I agreed. "Now tell me why you sought?" His eyes closed again. Meive drew me aside.

"Criten was right. The man's dying. Do you think he has anything to tell you?"

I kept my voice low. "That's Todon." I saw her remembering the name. "Aye, the bandit who rode out with Belo to seek my ransom. Now he's here looking for me, and with a wound which shouts he was stabbed by someone he knew." Her eyes went to the torn clothing and she nodded. "I think whatever he would say, it may be important. Can you revive him?"

Her gaze was steady upon mine. "I can, but for a short time only. And to do so takes his remaining strength. He will die the faster."

"He dies anyhow, let him at least deliver what words he

risked this ride to say." She stepped to Todon's side. The small carven bone phial was stoppered firmly so she must tug hard to open it. But once the stopper was freed we all smelled the scent of the cordial, a combination of honey and wildflowers, which was healing in itself. She allowed a drop to fall onto Todon's lips, then another and a third. She stepped back, stoppering the phial again as he licked his lips. After several minutes Todon opened his eyes, his gaze clearer, and his voice strengthening as he spoke.

At first I believed he rambled, but when I would have slowed him with questions, Meive again prevented me. I looked closer and saw then that Todon spoke, not to me as I stood, but perhaps to the other me, the young man who had lain captive in his camp nigh on two years gone.

"I liked it not, lad. Never meant to turn bandit but after my dale fell there wasn't nothing else to do. My wife died soon after we fled and the babe she carried died with her. After that nothing mattered greatly. I had no kin to open doors for me. I'd 'a starved. So I joined Devol. I hated some 'a the things we did but I daren't speak against them. Another man did once and Devol killed him like he'd 'a killed a fly.

"Two years I rode with Devol. Then we took you an' he laughed. Said he'd twist a huge ransom out 'a your kin then kill you anyhow. Some old grudge he said he had against your father. Devol chose me to go with Belo, said he could trust me better 'n most. I went gladly. If I could get ransom for you I could mebbe warn your kin to watch for treachery. Your dale was gone. We found it all black, grass gone, keep in ruins. Belo said we had to ride on. Said Devol had told him where else to try.

"But then Winter came on an' we had to lie up. Belo wasn't certain sure where this place was. Only the name. An' some of the people we asked didn't know at all. Other's said one way, some another way. It wasn't until Spring we could go hunting it again. We found the place in the end an' the Lord there spoke pleasant at first. He talked often to Belo. Just the two 'a them. I thought since he was kin he'd ride out quick with the coin to buy you free. But he never. He said at first that he was too busy, then that the weather was turning bad an' he wouldn't take the risk.

"I didn't like nor trust the man, lord or no lord, an' that's a fact. I tell you, lad, he's a bad one even if he is kin to you like he claimed. He held us there a long while. Don't remember how long right now. Belo went off for three, four weeks. He came back saying that Devol and the others was gone. Dead most likely and you escaped. I dunno how he knew, who he got it from. But the lord was pleased. I think he had a couple 'a other men out asking questions around the Southern roads after that." His voice faltered. Meive slipped past me to administer another drop of the cordial. Todon licked it up and his mouth curved into a painful smile.

"Thank you, Lady." His eyes turned to look at me. "I think the lord had men out asking once he knew you were alive. Belo was one, he told me things an' I talked him into lying some. Then he vanished an' never came back, but that horse he was so proud of, that were still in the lord's stable. Word came you was with some girl in a Southern dale. I was wondering, by then, why the lord wanted you, why he was looking, and why if'n he was so keen to find you he hadn't just ridden with your ransom."

Meive spoke very quietly. It may have been that the very quietness of her voice broke through his memories to bring answer. "What was the lord's name, Todon?"

"Hogeth. Hogeth of Paltendale. A bad man. Not a good lord to his people nor to his dale." His voice rambled. "The people say his lady would do better. Hogeth wed a girl from a ruined dale. She came with nothing so he reckons he can do what he will to her, the lass having neither kin nor dowry. His people are shamed at how he treats her. But she's borne him a son. There's an heir. Reckon the folk of his dale would

like Hogeth to disappear or die now an' give them a chance."
He fell silent a moment before he took up the tale again.

"I stayed. Reckon I was a fool but it didn't seem as if
there was any place else to go. Then one a' the dalesfolk
talked to me. Said as how their lord was gathering men to
go an' fight somewheres. I didn't know if it was truth but
we rode out. Thirty of us, few soldiers, most are just dalesmen obeying their lord, farmers an' such. Once we got further South he sent for me. Said I was the only one left who
knew the area hereabouts. They knew more or less where
you was an' they was going to shake you out of the place.
Get gold from you and make all their fortunes." Todon
stared up, his eyes seeing that moment.

"I told him I'd seen enough dead people an' ruined
dales. I wasn't going to be a part of another one. We argued. He isn't one to deal well with a man as says no to
him. He lost his temper in the end and stabbed me. Said I'd
be tied to a horse in the morning, happen I lived. Then I'd
show him where you were likely to be or he'd make it real
hard on me." His eyes went vague.

"Melis? I wouldn't let them hurt you." Meive took his
hand, holding it gently. "Melis." The name carried love and
a sort of satisfaction. As if he'd found someone long lost to
him. "Melis, lass. Bide with me."

"I will," Meive said softly. "Tell me about the wicked
man who comes to hurt me, Todon?"

"I took my horse and ran. Wasn't going to let him find
you. Not again. Wasn't going to see dead people everywhere, keep ruined and women weeping. Wasn't gonna,
Melis. I ran. Kept in the saddle. Knew you were somewhere near. Just kept going hoping you'd find me." I saw
her fingers tighten on his.

"I found you, Todon. How far away is he?"

"Three days mebbe. He isn't sure just where to look. I
got Belo to lie a little 'bout your dale entrance. Said it
would be good if'n the lord needed us to find it. Melis? You

still there?" Todon half-sat in a burst of strength. "Melis, I've done terrible things. Forgive me. I wouldn't never have hurt you or the babe."

"I know," Meive soothed. "I forgive you, Todon. Lie still now. It's time to sleep. Let me sing to you. What song would you hear?"

"Sing me 'Silver May Tarnish,' Melis. I always loved to hear you sing that." Meive held his hand as softly she began the ballad version of the old dales song.

> Silver may tarnish, gold may be stolen,
> Years may flow by like—wind in the grass.
> Nothing else matters but you beside me.
> Never alone again, love of my heart.
>
> Morning awakes me, the night is behind me,
> Sweet is the daylight on this, my land.
> Beside me beloved, you still are sleeping;
> I kiss your eyelids, I touch your hand.
>
> Beyond expectation, into love's dawning,
> I found you waiting, heart of my heart.
> Once I walked lonely, no one beside me,
> Now I have found you, never to part.
>
> Silver may tarnish, gold may be stolen,
> Years may flow by like—wind in the grass.
> Nothing else matters but you beside me.
> Never alone again, love of my heart.

Her voice dropped to a whisper as she repeated the last verse. Todon smiled, a smile that showed me all at once the man he had been before war came to turn him onto the wrong path.

"Melis." His grip loosened and his hand fell away. His eyes stayed open, seeing no longer. Meive stood.

"He chose right in the end. Let him lie in Honeycoombe. I would that we knew where his Melis lies so he could sleep beside her, but our dale will have to do."

"Well enough for him," I said. "He's gone, the trouble behind him has not. If Hogeth was three days away he's not like to be that now. He'll have followed as soon as he knew Todon had escaped." Outside the wind blew harder, spattering sleet against the walls. Meive looked sideways at the sound, her eyes a little cruel.

"Aye. I daresay. But think you, Lorcan. The Winter closes in again. Todon outran the false Spring. Hogeth is now in Winter's arms and how will he fare, he who comes from the warmer North and knows not the false Spring's ways? Will he have cared enough for his beasts to have brought blankets for them at night, grain to give them energy? What of his men, will they have fur-lined cloaks, lined boots?" Her face hardened. "How will they do here in this land where Winter fights for us?" I stared, then before she realized I swept her to me in a hug, before turning her free apart from my arm about her shoulders.

"My clever Lady. That's what we'll do. We'll fight Hogeth with Winter if he comes. With tricks and traps and the cold. If we can find him first he may never reach our dale." I looked about me. I could ride double with Meive, Todon's body could be taken back across my mount. We'd lay it out decently in a shed. In this weather it would keep until someone had time to dig a grave.

Gera slipped into the guard-post to stare big-eyed at the dead man. I was holding Meive against me still, unresisting in the curve of my arm. She made no attempt to free herself. I was half-conscious of her warmth, but my mind was on what we must do. Thirty able-bodied men was strong odds to set against our twenty-four—and most of them women and children. Even some of our men were unfit to fight. I must have betrayed a part of my thinking for Meive took my arm, turning me to face her.

"I brought bows and arrows back with me from my trip to find more settlers. Since then all of us have worked hard. Many are competent archers. You have Levas and his four, yourself, the shepherd, and leather-worker. He may have one arm which works none so well, but it is not his sword-arm. And of able-bodied women who know this land, who can shoot well and will do so, we have myself and perhaps seven more. The children, too, will fight."

"Meive, no!"

"Yes, Lorcan. Honeycoombe is their home, too. They are children in years but who among them has not seen what happens when war comes?"

I did not like it but she was right. Women are ever quick to be practical. Long ago I had overheard my father speaking to my elder brother, Merrion. My brother was smitten with some girl and Father talked then of women and how they differed in their thoughts from men.

"Men find love through desire, women find desire through love. They talk of romance and admire a man who sings of such, but given their choice, they will wed a man who is fit father for the babes they will bear him. We think of women as soft and gentle. Yet better you face a man than a woman whose child or kin you have harmed. Men fight war to win, women fight to make the enemy suffer. They have not our strength therefore must they be cunning. They can bear pain as no man could endure. Think no woman weak. Their strength is of a different kind, but it is there. They may be romantic, yet when danger threatens what they love, they can be so practical as would terrify any experienced fighter." Merrion had laughed but I had heard my father's voice. He was serious.

Remembering, I understood now why my parents had been so happy. They had been two halves of a whole. One did not order and the other obey, instead they agreed together. Meive was right. The women and children of Honeycoombe would stand. Nor had I the right to refuse that. It was their dale as much as it belonged to any. My heart quailed at the thought of Meive fighting, injured, slain. But I would not make of her the soft-handed lady she was not. She was my lady but she was also our wise woman, and no lord dictates to one of them. I took a breath.

"My Lady. Let you ride now to tell our people all we know. I will follow as I can. After that, order them to the keep. We will talk of what can be done to defend us. Once all is in train we will seek out Hogeth and his men, you and I both." I cupped her shoulders in my hands. "We shall be warlords and spies together, my sweet. I pray the Gods that they keep you safe, but the Gods forfend I hold you back. You are wise as well as woman and it is your right to ride as you will."

Criten had stepped out with Gera to saddle our mounts again and lash Todon's body across the saddle. Perhaps he saw what was happening and wished to leave us free to speak. If so, then that was kind of him and I thanked him in my heart. Meive grasped my hand in hers. Her mouth turned up to mine and I drank such sweetness that my head reeled.

"My Lady," I said once I could speak. "I think it well we wed as soon as this small war of ours is done." She laid her hand in mine, eyes smiling up at me.

"As you will, My Lord."

"No, As *you* will. Meive. I love you. I think I have cared for you since I saw you come out of the dark to bring back life and honor to me. I knew I loved you when you railed at me over what was done to Elesha's kin and I felt so much pain that you would fear I should be one of their kind. I would have spoken before but I feared lest I offend you. I love you, my sweet, most valiant Lady of the Bees."

"Then best we win this war that we may grow old together," Meive said softly. I kissed her again before stepping back.

"You are right. I will tell our people of this. Let them have a wedding to look forward to once Hogeth is beaten."

At that she only nodded before we went out to ride home and do whatever what needed be done.

Honeycoombe rode to war. This time let the Gods be on our side. Let us win, let us live, I prayed. We rode on the one mount, Meive before me, my arms about her. I could have ridden that way forever.

Meive

XVI

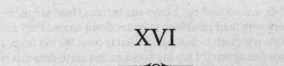

*I*n truth, it felt to me also as though our ride did last beyond its true time, as I said to Lorcan when he told me his thoughts. But all things, even such togetherness, must end. We reached the keep to find all waiting. Elesha had seen to it that a cauldron of stew and kettle of hot water steamed on the hearth. We ate, drank, and thawed before Lorcan stood to speak. He wasted no time in flourishes. All must know where we stood and what was required of them. Once he had told them of Todon's words, he spoke again.

"You have heard. You know who comes, and the danger. We have one decision to make first and above all. Do we flee? Do we give up our dale and all we have begun to build? Think well on this. We are twenty-four against thirty and they are all men. Perhaps half of them are trained fighters. They may not wish to be where they are but with Hogeth behind them they *will* fight, make no mistake about that. Nor can the one who leads them afford to leave any alive behind him here."

He sat down and listened to the swell of talk. Slowly one voice predominated, as I had guessed it would, saying some of the things I had expected to hear. It is a fact that men often discount the intelligence and courage of women, and never more than in times of disorder or war when men often seem to assume that it is they alone who can, or will, fight.

"No, and no, and no! I have run before. These are no invaders with their machines to batter down keeps. They are bandits who seek to take again what is ours. We ran once. I do not flee again. If I lay my bones in this earth then that is as the Gods desire. But I remain." Elesha did not shout, all but her first words were said in low clear tones but they were heard. In a knot behind her those who looked to her were nodding. Beside her, Vari spoke up.

"If my mother stays, I stay."

Levas clasped her hand before he looked at us. "I and my men swore an oath to you and the lady, Lorcan. Our sword-service for a home. Shall we now give it up to the first filth who seek a fight?" From the benches about the table his men grunted agreement.

Lorcan bowed his head in acknowledgment. "You do not fight leaderless. My lady and I remain."

"I and my sister and our shepherds stay." That was Betha, our weaver. I saw that her sister, and the brother and sister who cared for the sheep, were all with that decision.

My gaze swept around the room. Even the children had grim serious looks. It was as I had told Lorcan. They, like the adults, had seen the face of war. They would stand.

I felt then a rush of pride that all but choked me. Never did a lady have more valiant people. I reached out to clasp Lorcan's hand before them all. Still grasping it, he stood to speak.

"Hear me. We shall fight for our land, for our homes. Winter fights with us. We shall not face the enemy hand to hand. Instead we shall be cunning. Let them hunt us, wasting their energy on the empty air as we slip away. These are our hills and my lady knows something of them. I shall talk more on that later. But for now . . ." He held up my hand, linked with his, so all could see.

"My Lady has agreed to wed me in Spring once the enemy are routed. Lord Salas comes then with his people to take holding in Merrowdale. Together we shall celebrate joyous events. The end of Winter, the coming of friends, the departure of enemies, and greatest of all, love." I was blushing as he sat again, amid cheers from our people. We fell then to planning with care.

It would be a game of tag and run. Levas set out early next day with Dogas, and young Gera to act as their messenger. For Gera they took the mules, Rez and Reza, these mounts being more wise and surefooted in such weather. It took them time to find our enemies since, as we later found, Hogeth was well astray and had sought us further west. But Gera came riding in grinning, four days later, to report.

"Levas says they're fools and Hogeth the biggest fool of the lot. Like you thought, Lady, they ain't ready for Winter as we has it here. They may 'a started with thirty men, now they ain't got but twenty-seven. And one a' them's hurt. He can't hardly walk and has to ride even when the others get off to walk the beasts."

"What does Levas plan?"

"What you said for him to do, Lady. He reckons it won't be so hard. They ain't none 'a them real fighters, he says. Not even the lord." After that it was clear he spoke for himself. "My Lady, you ain't seen nothing like it. That lord's got a tent. Big fancy one an' a brazier to keep him warm. It takes one whole horse to carry them."

I listened, encouraging the boy to talk. Lorcan had spoken to me more than once of his kinsman. Now I began to gain the measure of his enemy: a man who had made a parade of riding out to battle—where the battle was close and against not too great odds; a man who might fight viciously but only to the last of his men, not to his own death. A lord who deemed it his right by noble blood not to risk discomfort if by the effort of others it could be avoided.

"Lorcan, he brings tent and brazier for his comfort. How

would it be if both were lost, if he must live as his men do, without shelter and warmth at night?" Our gaze met and I saw my lord was struggling to hold in mirth.

"He would not be pleased. But Meive—he would not turn back for that."

"No," I said, thinking as I spoke. "But he would be very angry. The more so if he thought it was the fault of his people. He would take that out upon them then. If we could drive a wedge between them . . ."

"Aye." I could tell Lorcan had taken the idea and was planning. "Gera, take Criten and ride for where you left Levas." He turned to an eager Criten. "Tell Levas that, if possible, he is to rid my kinsman of those impediments to swift progress, the tent and brazier. Let it be done in such a way that it appears to have been carelessness by one of their men. Tell Levas Meive and I ride to join him shortly." Criten half-bowed, then swept Gera off to talk. I heard hoofbeats early next morn and knew they rode to join Levas.

Over honeyed porridge, Lorcan and I made plans. Nothing set, better to know what twists and turns we could make as events altered. But we knew some things we could do, some we wished for. As yet, Hogeth was well astray from Honeycoombe. If Cup and Flame willed it, we could keep him far from our land while whittling down the number of those who followed him. We could lay ambushes, trips and traps, always things that appeared natural features of the hills.

"It was how we fought often against the invaders," Lorcan said thoughtfully. "Alizon had the machines and the fighters but the land was ours. We knew its heart and its ways. Often there were fewer of us against a greater number so we had to sell our lives dearly. Better to slay two and live to strike again, than to slay three or four and die." His fingers closed over mine in a grip that almost crushed them.

"Beloved. Swear you will take no chances you must not.

I would not wish to walk alone even if the battle is ours." I reassured him with a kiss, since we were alone. His lips clung to mine even as his hands held me tightly.

"I swear: let you swear also," I whispered. His oath was muffled by our joined lips again. At last we broke apart. "When do we ride?" I asked quietly. "I have a pack to make up."

"In two days, if Gera has not returned. At once if he does." He forestalled my question. "I know the area where Hogeth is. They have found their way further East and South now. I think before Belo vanished he must have told Hogeth of the places where Devol's bandits ranged. Their camps where shelter might be found. I know from talk in those camps, while I was held for ransom, that Devol's men had more than once fled this way. They would ravage dales, then flee once any great resistance was made or the dalesfolk showed signs of hunting them out. They shifted about the land, having many camps, I watched well, learning those camps they used while I was in their hands and also the trails which led to their hiding places."

I smiled, and if it was more of a wolf's snarl then was I not a hunter also? "I, too, know that area. While I dwelled in the shrine I still rode out often enough in good weather with my warriors once the ground was free of snow. I can follow or lead as you will, my love." I saw his brow furrow in thought.

"It might be well if we split apart at times. You lead one group and I the other. That way we can cover where they travel even if we know not their road." I rejoiced that he would leave me so free.

"That is sound sense," was all I said.

"Aye. Now, let us talk to Elesha and see what she has planned in case we must defend the keep. What will you do after that?"

"I plan to ride the land. I must be sure all beasts are cared for and our people snug."

"Go well, then." I went with him to bespeak Elesha, who had all safe in hand. After that I saddled one of the ponies. I planned to ride, but not where I had claimed. I set off towards the cots then circled to the inner vale. Once there I did not pause but pushed on as quickly as my mount might carry me. I rode to the arch, dismounted, and led the pony through before swinging into his saddle again. When I reached the crevice at the far side of the hidden place I bowed as a guest who approaches another's gate. I was answered, and for a long time I talked with she who abided there.

I gave her freely of my knowing and she spoke to me of events long past. I learned, and that was well. In the end she gave me a gift, and I rode back leaving behind one whose wisdom was greater than mine. Through sorrow, too, she had come to acceptance. Soon she would seek a longer-lasting peace, one of her own choosing. That was for her to decide. For myself, I rode home and said nothing to Lorcan. I, too, had decisions to make and would make them.

Near dusk I sought out my hives where they stood, safe within the bee-barn which had always housed them during the snowmonths. I sank my mind into the sweet dark and drowsed, dreaming of flowers and Springs to come. The queens half-woke to welcome me but they slept again quickly. After some time I left, calmer and more ready to face what must be. I would that I could have ridden out with my warriors. But in Winter bees do not fly. Even my warriors could not bear the chill of deep full Winter.

Over the next day, as we combed the hills, we sought for Levas and those with him. Two days later it was he who found us. We were camped when he came riding towards us, whistling very softly. I heard the sound on the wind before I caught Lorcan by his arm.

"I hear a tune whistled. Listen!"

"Levas." Lorcan slithered out of our brush camp to wave cautiously. Within moments Levas was with us again.

"What news of Hogeth and his men?" I must admit I was as eager to hear.

Levas smiled slowly. "Ah, well now. Seems they've had a misfortune." I could almost see events as he explained. "They kept a guard—if you could call it that—not that anyone in their right mind would. Man was half asleep and deaf to boot. I sent Dogas in to check the girths on that pack-horse carrying the brazier and tent. They were too solid to play games with, it would have been noticed, so he fixed the strap which held the load. He played it so's if the beast lurched hard or bucked the load should be thrown off." His grin broadened.

"And if any checked the strap later on, it would appear the loader had been a bit careless. After that we stalked them. They headed down the trail and part-way along there's a steep bit. Trail drops away there, 's a long way to the bottom. There's no track down and I think none of them will be too eager to try." His grin widened. "I put the lad on the hillside with his catapult."

"The boy's safe?" I queried sharply.

"Aye. He has the mules with him. No hunter's likely to catch him on a rough hillside with one of that pair. Boy's all right, though he was like to fall off the hill laughing. I'd given him stickers for his catapult." I smiled at that. Stickers come from a vine which grows in many areas of the southern hills. They're a seed pod, about the size of the end of my thumb with needle-sharp short straight thorns. These alternate about the seedcase with others which are small barbed hooks. They cling to whatever moves so the seeds may spread wide. They can be a trial at any time, at this time they could be rather more.

"He hit that pony square on the flank just as it was by the drop. Pony started bucking, man ahead grabbed the halter an' lost his balance. Boy stung the pony with another sticker. The pony went mad and the strap came loose. There went the load, tumbling off over the drop with the lord screaming for someone to stop it. None of his lot were that stupid and that didn't please him. Once he found who'd loaded the horse he belted him a good one. Aye, there's one man who won't put hisself out to stop his lord from a misstep in the future. That Hogeth slept mighty cold this past night and the only time I've heard such language was from an old soldier I served with as a lad."

Both Lorcan and I were holding our sides. I sobered first. "Where are they camped?"

"About two miles from here. I guessed you'd have made camp this direction. They were camping early when I left them. Hogeth's trying to make up for his lost gear with a good fire and hot food an' drink. Criten is on watch. Gera will ride this way after me if they move on early. Dogas is scouting ahead on their path. There may be another place where we can lay ambush."

"What had you in mind?" Lorcan asked. "When I soldiered it wasn't a bad idea to pick off stragglers."

"Aye. That was in my mind as well. Dogas is a good woodsman. If Hogeth's camp is quiet tomorrow night Dogas will see if he can sneak among the horses. 'Tis an easy thing then to lame a couple. Nothing permanent, just something to make them slower. If the riders fall behind we can see to it that they have accidents."

I remembered something. "What about the man who grabbed the pack-pony? Were he or the pony hurt?"

"Ah, well." I fixed him with a stare which said I wanted to know. Levas shrugged. "Can't have jugged hare without killing the hare, Lady. Pony was safe: the man as tried to catch it fell. Reckon he slept colder last night than even the lord." I was sorry for the man, some poor farmer who'd followed at his lord's command. When I said so, Levas shook his head.

"No, Lady. He was one of the fighters. We're better off without those. The more we can pick off, the better. Be sorry for him if you will, but not too sorry. He'd do that an' a lot worse did he lay hands on you."

Lorcan was counting. "So he started with thirty, or was that counting himself?"

"With him, Lord."

"Right. Then he lost three men floundering about these hills, another man over that cliff. There's now twenty-six of them. Is that it?"

"So far, Lord. And one lamed, one sulking. But they're doing something else daft." His explanation made me gape. I might never have ridden to war but even I knew better than what he described. One should never keep all the eggs in one basket. Not that I complained. Their folly could be our aid. We plotted quietly around the tiny fire. Then we slept, taking turns to stand watch. Nothing stirred throughout the night so we rose early and rode the trail quietly in search of our comrades.

Criten found us as Levas had done. We had talked of trails and meeting places, signs we could leave for each other. Once in the hills we had all done so. Criten came drifting up, Gera with him. He bowed, the quick half-nod of a soldier acknowledging his commanders.

"Two of their horses are lame. I sent Dogas to follow and listen when they halt. I know where they are. I'll circle, then pick up Dogas again if you wish?"

"Let be." I said. "He knows what he's to do. Why not seek out these stragglers?" I could see they agreed with that. Criten knew where Hogeth and his men rode and I knew the hills. I was able to bring us down from a higher trail to ride in cover behind them. Levas studied the tracks.

"They're slowing. I'd reckon them near a quarter-candlemark behind their friends. In an hour they'll be twice that. By then none will hear if there is a little noise so long as it's not *too* great." His lips curled in a look of satisfaction. "Dogas well chose the mounts he lamed. Both belong to fighters." I led us after that, for we were no great distance from the shrine. I took them by shortcuts to a place between the stragglers and those ahead of them.

We took the stragglers in silence, one with an arrow

through the throat from Lorcan's bow, the other with a stone from a sling I wielded. Gera had laid by under orders not to stir. Dogas had waited ahead, in case either soldier had lived and fled, so that he could lie for him in ambush. Once we had made our kills we gathered up the bodies, their mounts, and any gear dropped from the saddles as their beasts plunged in fear.

Levas nodded to his man. "Ride after them, Criten. Do not catch up with them but follow. Keep well back. We will signal with the mirrors at need." Criten rode away as Lorcan looked us over. "Best we get these bodies away some distance off the trail. Then we bury them deep."

"What about the horses, Lord?" Gera had rejoined us.

"We'll take those with us for now. We'll make sure to strip the men before we rid us of them."

That we did and gained well thereby. In their belt-pouches I found silver. There was a good dagger on each sword-belt and fair swords also.

As we had laid in ambush snow had begun to fall lightly. To the place where we had taken our prey I brought more snow in my cloak, flinging it into the hoof-prints behind me as I walked my mount away up the trail. In an hour or two there would be no sign anyone had ridden there. Levas judged our stragglers to have been almost an hour behind the main group when we took them.

"It's late. By the time they think it strange their friends have not caught up it will be growing dark. They'll make camp and hope the two come in on the fire. Once it is dark they'll not want to go seeking down that trail anyway. It's treacherous enough in daylight."

I nodded. "If they come back tomorrow they'll find nothing. It's ready to snow all night I think. There's a good place to camp in those trees, I used it twice when I lived in the shrine and I was out hunting overnight. If we set up there Dogas may find us. He knows where to look."

I was right. Dogas tramped wearily into camp some time after dark, leading his mount. He was tired, hungry, and the horse was shivering. I left Levas to rub down and blanket the animal while I fed Dogas and poured him a hot drink. After he ate he began to tell us what he had overheard.

"They will take the hill-path further South along the high hills."

"Did you hear anything they may plan?" Lorcan queried.

"Yes, Lord. They will circle, cutting down to the lower ground from the hills West. Then they go North again along the foothills. If they find nothing they cut over West again and return along the base of the lowest slopes."

"They'll find it's easier to say than ride," I commented.

Lorcan turned to me. "You know the trails hereabouts, my Lady. What can you tell us?"

I dropped to my knees near the fire to smooth a patch of snow. "Here, see." I marked in the line of hills, the trails I knew after three years living in the shrine and regularly hunting in the lands around it.

"Many of the trails will be impassable still. Others may appear passable, but because of the thaw and refreeze they will be so treacherous as to be deadly. At such times after the false Spring there begin to be great snow-slides." My tongue all but clove to the roof of my mouth as I looked at my companions. All understood.

"If they attempt the trails the lord said, where is the best place for us?" Levas looked eager. I smoothed my patch of snow again and talked. After that we slept the night away before mounting to ride. Criten would find us sooner or later, in that there was no haste. Just now we wished to find Hogeth and his men. Lorcan waited, until we were ahead on the trail they should take, before he summoned Gera.

"I have a message for Honeycoombe. Can you reach there before dark?" The boy nodded. "Good lad. Now, say to Elesha all you have seen and heard. Tell her this also, that we hunt Hogeth with fair results, but she is to ready the keep for siege in case. If any come demanding entry, let her deny them." Gera looked mutinous. He knew there would be danger the next day and he had no wish to ride home with nothing to show he'd taken part. I rose and took up the reins of the horses we had taken.

"Lead these back with you. Say one is for your family because of the part you have played. The other is to go to Isa's family because it was she who first saw Todon. You have done well." I clapped him gently on the shoulder. "Tell your father I said you are a good soldier who serves his dale well." Gera's face lit proudly. He drew himself up, gave the soldiers' bow, scrambled into the saddle, and rode away down the trail leading his prizes.

Lorcan touched my cheek. "You always say the right thing. Now the boy is proud to leave instead of thinking himself unjustly cast off." I took his hand in mine, holding it for a moment. Behind us Levas coughed.

"Where do we go now, Lady?"

I started my mount up-trail in answer. If we went this way then we would be cutting across the long shallow loop of paths Hogeth would take. He would not know that under the snowfield I crossed there was a thread of safe trail of which Ithia had told me. It could not be seen, but one who knew of it could ride from landmark to landmark in safety. It was long before I drew rein again. Then it was by a vast area of brush high into the foothills which marked the path for me. I turned direct downhill and pointed.

"Below us is the trail they would take if Dogas is right. Beyond here the track becomes more dangerous than they will wish to travel. But that they will not know until they ride on. Above us," I waved uphill, "the snow lies heavy on an area of unbroken and tilted rock face. It takes little to make it move. Dogas said they are loading two ponies with the blankets, both led by the one rider. If we are sure that, whatever else is in the snow's path, the blankets are lost, then we've done well."

And so we planned. Riders could outrun the slide. They had time to see and the path ahead of them was smooth enough. But if the led ponies were cast off by the one who led them, if the beasts panicked and were caught beneath the slide, taking with them all the blankets, that loss we would bless. In such night's chill as we suffered in these hills blankets were no luxury but an essential for those who traveled. Without blankets men slept poorly. They would wake shivering to lose strength and concentration both. Without a blanket across their backs at night horses would balk, unwilling to travel with morning light.

The horses would use up more of what they ate in keeping themselves warm. Thus they would travel more slowly and eat more heartily of the sacked grain. And of that there was less each night. Hogeth had not known how much he would require and had carried only a few sacks. In another two or three nights all would be eaten.

Levas was considering that. "Is he like to turn back?"

My lord shook his head. "Not Hogeth. He'll take the best of what they have for himself but he'll push on. Nor will he let his men leave the trail. He believes he must have what I own in order to keep his own lands. Paltendale suffered from the invaders. Hogeth would rebuild and become mighty among the northern lords. To do that he requires coin."

"Would there be enough?" I believed it an honest question and honestly Lorcan replied.

"No. I think he has persuaded himself there is more. I have sufficient to make Honeycoombe better. But our dale is small compared to Paltendale. Nor was our keep much damaged, the livestock neither stolen nor scattered so wide they were lost to us. The cots did not burn. In Paltendale all that happened. Hogeth has spent all he has, yet only a half of what was damaged has been repaired. The silver I own would not do more than repair perhaps a half of what is yet needed. Hogeth wishes to do far more than raise up what was. He would see a greater keep, a richer table spread for lords who call."

Levas looked dour. "Aye. I know the kind. They'd rather have silk on themselves even if it means rags on their folk. They'll eat until they can eat no more, then fling scraps to the dogs while their people hunger. A shipload of gold would not be enough. The more they have the more they seek. Such a man can not be reasoned with."

I looked at him. "You thought perchance if we offered him the silver we have he would ride away? My lord has said it. He is not of that kind."

"Ah, well. Then if there's no other way we'll have to kill him." He shrugged. "Sorry I am he's kin to you, Lord. But then, 'tis he who's come hunting this fight."

"I know. If you must kill, do so and owe me no debt. That's for any of you."

We understood, I, Levas, and Criten. I wondered if Hogeth had thought of that. One who rode in open warfare against another lord who was kin stepped outside Dales Law. Hogeth had not gone before a Dales Court to speak his grievances. He had brought none to mediate, no one to stand as peacemaker. Imgry or someone of his clan might have agreed. They had not been asked. Nor had Hogeth any honest grudge he could claim. Since this was so, his death could not be demanded as blood-debt even if it be proved against us. Lorcan was right. He could absolve any of Hogeth's fall if Lorcan willed it, since he was kin.

We laid up that night in a fireless camp, lest any of Hogeth's scouts see the firelight. With daylight I led my small group on foot to where boulders lay, far above the slope. If only two or three were sent rolling they should bring down the whole snow slope upon the trail below. Most of the trails Hogeth was following were deer trails. But if we dropped branches, sprinkled snow again in the right place, he would not see where the deer turned off. He would follow instead what appeared to be the easier path.

With morning we prepared. The snow was flung with care to hide the safer track. Above us Levas and Criten worked, easing the rocks from their beds, poising them on wooden wedges so unseating them needed but a quick powerful thrust. It took time and hard work and there was no sign as yet of Hogeth and his men. I was sent along the

trail with my small steel mirror. If Dogas followed our enemy I had to warn him to hold back.

I waited, the cold eating further into my bones. At last
along the trail I saw men come riding. As high as I was I
could see that Dogas trailed them perhaps two miles behind. That was well. I turned in my brush cover to wink the
mirror. Lorcan would read my sign and know to be ready.
The men drew closer, Hogeth riding perhaps a third of the
way from the front of the lagging column. I poised ready.
They reached the place I had marked with a fallen branch.

I signaled. High above and ahead of me, two great rocks
trembled. Then, very slowly, they began to roll down the
slope. They bounced high, struck, and bounced again, the
second time upon the snow slope. I saw a crack in the snow
flash into being, swerving jaggedly across the slope. Then
with a rush the whole slope was in downward motion. Below, faint screams echoed. I saw men point at their coming
doom, crying out in terror as they attempted to flee.

XVII

——◦——

*T*he rumble of the snow seemed to vibrate in the pit of my stomach. It was a sound felt rather than heard. I strained, trying to see what occurred below. Would our enemies fall or would some escape the traps we had set? I knew that with the slide would come all the debris on the slope below the snow. In the flying snowdrift, which rose above the slope as it rushed down, I could see nothing. Then the air before it cleared. I saw Hogeth first. Without regard for his men he was forcing his horse forward along the steep narrow trail. I moved, racing along the deer track which ran along the top of my slope. From the bend at the edge I could see further down the lower trail. Hogeth came into view.

I was safe where I stood, and in any event he was too much occupied with survival to stare about him. When the boulders fell he had been about one third of the way back from those who led his group. They had looked up, seen what would befall them, and run their mounts in terror. But Hogeth, more reckless, more selfish in his determination to escape, had overtaken most. Those who still led saw the flatter part of the apparent trail and took it. Hogeth, some yards behind, was slowing as if beastlike he somehow sensed a trap lay in that innocent appearance. I admit before the Gods that I cursed him for it.

Long ago a log had fallen slantwise across a rough broken area a fraction lower than the outer edge of the trail. That had produced a small dam. Rain falling over the early part of Winter filled it then froze. So where there had been a long piece of broken land turning a corner of the hill, there now appeared a flat section which looked as if it was part of the old trail's continuation. At least it did once it was beneath snow. That we had seen to. But beneath the snow was a long strip of ice which sloped to the outer edge.

The hooves of the first rider's mount met the ice beneath the snow just as the second rider thrust his mount alongside. The horses staggered, fought for footing, and fell. One rider was thrown, to fall twisting and screaming over the edge of the cliff and down a sheer drop of many hundreds of feet. The other was under his mount as the beast landed, sliding on the ice. He screamed once, then lay motionless as his mount struggled to its feet again before walking cautiously away up the slope. The other horse followed, head down, as it limped after.

Hogeth had been just far enough away, when he slowed, to take warning from their destruction. From where I stood in cover I could see how he wrenched his mount to a halt, thrusting it uphill. Another rider hard on his heels was less lucky or sensible. He passed Hogeth on the outer edge of the trail and suffered the fate of the other two men. Then all I could see below was blotted out as the snow roared high, like a giant wave, cresting onto the scene.

"Meive? What happened, did we succeed?" Lorcan and Levas had reached me with Criten not far behind.

"At least somewhat," I told them. "Of four in the lead two went over the cliff, a third was beneath when his mount fell. I think he will not rise. Hogeth avoided our trap but I think the snow slide has taken many others of his men. But of how many it will rid us we must wait to see."

"I felt it fall in my very bones," Levas commented.

"And I," Lorcan agreed. "I know not what snow weighs but that must have been great. I think those who were beneath are unlikely to be shaking off snow before rising to the attack bright-eyed and bushy-tailed."

Honeycoombe had been my home all my life. I knew about snowslides. If a man taken by a snowslide was not swiftly freed and warmed, he did not rise at all. The snow stole from him first warmth, then consciousness, and finally his life. In a candlemark an uninjured man beneath heavy snow was dead. And that was if he had air and was unhurt. In our dale the children learned what to do if a snowslide occurred. How to run downhill and to one side to escape. Slides happen in a limited area. If caught, we of Honeycoombe knew to swim with the snow and upwards, arms crooked before the face to make a space to breathe.

But what would these strangers from the warmer northern dales know? Besides which, they had been ahorse. While having the warmth of their mount to aid them longer, many would also have sustained injury if their mount fell on them when the slide struck. I thought it unlikely many beneath the full slide's weight would live. Beside me, Lorcan's thoughts followed mine. He took my hand.

"They came of their own will. They came to rob and slay those against whom they had no just grievance. If they lie dead it is their own doing."

"Their deaths under snow are easy," I said quietly, as Levas and Criten turned to listen. "A man trapped so dies without pain. He merely becomes colder, then all at once he feels warm again. He dreams and into his dreams death comes without his knowing. I have heard it said by those who were saved before death could take them."

"A better death than they'd have given any of us," Criten said sourly.

"That's so. But I'm satisfied if our enemies are dead." Lorcan was brisk. "Let us move on to where we may see if any survived and where they go now. What of Dogas, did any see him?"

I nodded. "I saw him before I signaled. He was some two miles behind those Hogeth led. He should have been safe." As we talked I saw a rider come into view, climbing his mount to the upper trail. Lorcan's gaze followed mine and he sighed in relief.

"You were right. Well met, Dogas," he hailed as our comrade reached the track to join us. "What can you say of those you trailed?"

"I caught another of them before I fell back. A lame man who'd halted to wrap his injured leg. I took him silently. I left his mount tethered on the lower path where we can find it again. Best we pick it up as soon as may be. There's no food or water there. But in case we cannot I did not tie the beast too tightly. It can free itself if it becomes desperate. The rider I stripped and left his gear with the horse. The body I dropped down a crack and scooped snow over it until it was well hid. I think none shall find it even if they bother to search."

"Well done," I said.

Lorcan grunted approvingly. "Aye, now the main query is of Hogeth. How many of his men survive?"

"Will he still think to attack Honeycoombe if there are few left to him?" Criten asked.

Lorcan's eyes met mine. "If Hogeth lives unhurt and has even one or two men with him, he'll try for us still," Lorcan told him briefly.

Criten's eyes widened. "Is the man a fool?"

"No, obsessed," I muttered. "He lived fat, from what my lord says. He plans to live that way again and rebuild his keep larger and more lavishly on Lorcan's coin. You could show him all we have and swear on Cup and Flame that there is no more. He would not believe. There must be all he requires because it is he who requires it. Only death will stop a man who thinks that way."

"Aye," Lorcan said quietly. "Kinsman he may be, but I am Lord of Honeycoombe. Against my dale, my lady, and my people, I would not count his blood as higher worth were Hogeth kin to Imgry and a hero of the war. And that he is not. Nor have I forgotten Faslane."

Long since had I told Levas of Hogeth's treachery against his own kin, and he had repeated it to his men. Now our men looked black. A blank-shield may be a fighter for hire, but they have their own strict code. A man who would stab another in the back in the midst of a fight against a common enemy is honor-broke. Were he one of their own they would put him to trial, then hang him. Hogeth was not one of them, but they despised him none the less. It would not make them careless. I had told them knowing that, to the contrary, it would make them more wary. Any trick might be expected of an honorless man.

We moved carefully along the upper track until below us we could see the trail as it wound past our snowslide. Very far below us lay dots which were dead men. Snow humped high over the trail before the slide. Looping around and past it we could see hoof-prints in the snow.

"How many, think you, Levas?" Wordlessly he dismounted, sliding downhill towards the marks. Being sure not to walk on the tracks but keeping to the trail-side he searched the ground, walked some way along the tracks, then returned laboriously uphill to where we waited anxiously.

"With the snow this deep I can't be sure between ridden and unridden mounts. There are tracks enough for eight beasts." He turned to me, "Did you not say you saw some horses escape the snow but still lose riders?"

"Aye. Those who lie below." I pointed. "Their mounts all escaped the fall, though one seemed to be lame. It might have been only a temporary strain. If there are the tracks of eight horses, then likely three are those beasts. Which means—"

Lorcan took up the count. "Hogeth escaped, that you saw. Three unridden animals of which we know, and perhaps four ridden. Five men left alive from thirty." He smiled at me before catching me to him in a hug. "You are my clever lady. You said Winter and the land should fight for us, and behold. They have."

I was pleased he acknowledged me before the guards, but there still remained five enemy or more. It was not yet time to celebrate. I said something of this and Levas nodded.

"Well said. We'll feast when all the enemy are fallen."

"So, now we seek out Hogeth, find where he goes and what he plans." It seemed logical to me as I said it. I saw that all agreed, so I mounted my horse and led the way. I knew this part of the hills and could guess which way our enemy had fled. I was right, but it was not long before fear came upon me.

"Lorcan, I like this not. They head for the road to Honeycoombe. I think it an accident that they have chosen this way, yet, accident or no, if they find the dale it may not be well."

Lorcan frowned. "Gera will have warned the folk. Elesha will have them watching. She will see that the gate is shut fast, not to be opened to strangers." He glanced at Levas. "Your two men will be in the guard-post on watch, I daresay."

"Best for them if they are, else I shall have something to say," Levas growled.

I felt a nervous fear overtake me. It was as if something warned I should not linger here. About my neck the gift the voice had given warmed my skin. I swung my mount into a trail barely seen.

"I am afraid the enemy may strike in the direction of our home. I ride for the dale by the quickest paths. Follow!"

With that I heeled my mount into a canter. It was madness on that path but I cared not. In my ear a whisper spoke of danger, death which came against all I had come again to love. I would not tarry to let my dale die in blood a second time. Once, I had buried everyone I knew. Better I die myself before I must do that a second time. In the end,

Gera had ridden back to the dale upon Reza. Lorcan had insisted I ride one of our mule pair. I was a light rider riding Rez. He and his mate Reza were big powerful mules and sure-footed as cats. On hills like ours in Winter they could keep their footing and move swiftly on trails where a horse might fall.

Then, too, I rode lighter than the men behind me. True, I was chain-clad even as they, but the chain being my size also weighed less. In a candlemark I drew ahead and ignored their shouts. I could feel the whisper strengthen. It spoke of death: it called and warned. I listened and heeled Rez for more speed. Snow was falling harder, not heavily as yet, but I thought that would come by nightfall.

Ahead the tracks turned toward Honeycoombe. I rounded the hillside at the path's entrance to my home and saw men lying sprawled upon the ground. Snow was already beginning to lie on their bodies and open eyes though the spilled blood still oozed. I slowed long enough to identify the dead faces: The two men we had left on guard. How they had been tolled from their safety, how they had even been known to be there, I knew not. But I knew who had done this.

I came down the last part of the hill trail into Honeycoombe like a storm. I had sword in hand before I saw the enemy, but I was prepared. I was in the midst of three men before I knew, but Lorcan had taught me a little of the sword. They saw a woman riding a mule. My chain coif was about my neck so that in the speed of my ride my hair, part undone from its plaits, blew free. Aye. They saw a weak helpless woman so they held their blows. I saw the enemy, those who would deprive me of all I had regained.

My sword swung, all the weight and strength of my shoulder behind the blow. I was riding hard so to my own strength was added the speed of Rez. The man fell and as I passed I saw my stroke had all but severed his neck. A lucky blow but I was no trained soldier. I had brought them to confusion, let me now be elsewhere and that swiftly.

From the corner of my eye I saw the small figures far back, which meant I had not completely lost my companions. They would see and be racing their horses. I spun Rez, dodged between the two riders, and lay over his neck as he pounded back up the trail. Lorcan was riding like a madman as Tas hurtled past me. With Levas and Criten flanking the attack he fell upon the two enemy remaining as though he were rabid-mad. There was a whirl, a clash of swords and both were down. Lorcan returned to me, hauling Tas back on his haunches as he leaped free. I was snatched from my saddle, kissed, hugged, then my ears boxed very soundly.

"You madwoman. What possessed you to fight three men?"

"I killed one," I protested, my ears still ringing.

Again I was swept into a savage embrace. "Aye, you did. Brave fool that you are. If you had been slain, I—I—I know not what I'd have done to you. Why did you leave us like that?" I remembered the warning.

"Something told me that our people were in danger. Lorcan, I'm still afraid. Where is Hogeth?" Levas rode up to touch Lorcan's arm.

"My Lord, she's right. There are tracks going on towards the keep. Here where the snow lies thinner we can see them better. I fear we could have been wrong. Hogeth rides, I know the tracks of his mount. But the other horses with him still number five though one is slightly lame. And Lord—all but the lame beast are ridden!"

I saw Lorcan's head seem to jolt upon his neck as he understood the words. Three enemies lay dead about us. But two of our own had died. Now we faced five men still, and some would doubtless be trained fighters. So long as Elesha had done my Lord's bidding and all our folk were within the keep it was none so bad. There were the five of us to stand against them. Nor would they know the three they had left on guard had been slain.

"Levas, your experience is greater, what do you advise?" Thus was my lord, ever quick to listen to the wisdom of others.

"Let us move in slowly, watching for them, Lord. The tracks run straight. I think they made for the keep, and once there they will hold parley believing that you are within. If we can come close to them unseen we may learn their intentions."

Lorcan glanced about. "Let us hide these bodies and the horses also. Let them think they still have three more men to call upon."

That we did quickly before mounting to follow Hogeth's tracks. As Levas said, they led straight for our keep. We came in sight of that and halted in cover of the weaver's cot. Within the sheepfold, under the edge of her roof, I could hear the sheep stir uneasily. The snow increased so that our tracks were filling. I welcomed that. We were close enough to hear some of what was shouted on either side.

Wise and cunning Elesha. She was pretending fear. We were abed, she said. Her lord and his woman. If she broke in upon us she would suffer for it. Hogeth did not pause to recall my lord was not that sort. Hogeth would have punished her for his waking even if the reason be of the best. Therefore her whining protest was believable to him.

"What do I care if you are beaten, woman. Tell Lorcan, that sniveling reject of my house, I would have speech with him." Elesha protested until Hogeth was red in the face with shouting and rage. Finally she agreed, departing long enough for her return to be acceptable.

"Well, what says he, woman?"

"That you should return in the Spring." And with that the small barred window above the main gate slammed shut. Nor would all Hogeth's shouts persuade it to reopen. It was strange, but in the midst of all my fear I struggled not to burst into laughter at her words and Hogeth's fury at them. Oh, it was well done. It never entered his mind that we were not within the keep. We withdrew a distance and watched. Hogeth led his men to one of the cottages. I saw them break in the door and soon after smoke began to rise. Levas snorted.

"They'll warm themselves and eat. It will be dusk shortly and the lord is not one to remain in the cold. The more since it is several nights since he slept warm."

"Is there some way we could attack them tonight while they sleep?" I asked thoughtfully. "They do not know we are out here. If they set a watch surely it will be towards the keep so those within may not attack."

"It is not impossible. Let us find a place in which to lie up ourselves. With food and drink we shall do better. Then we can plan."

It was true the day was almost gone: With snow-clouds so low, it was near dark already, and the falling snow made the landscape darker yet. I chose Betha's cottage and we huddled quietly within, the horses tucked into the sheep-fold with the indignant sheep. Once it was full dark we could light a fire and eat hot food. I made us a kettle of herb tea laced with a few drops of the honey cordial, and insisted all drink. It was a good preventative against Winter ills and the Gods knew that was something we might need. I added more plain honey so in the end all drank eagerly of the hot sweetness. We chose beds after that. Lorcan woke the men in turn, but me he allowed to sleep. I was angry but he was unrepentant.

"You were weary. Meive," he took my hand, turning my fingers over and caressing them. "Beloved. We need you more than any. If one of us is injured, you of all have the ability to heal." He smiled into my eyes. "There is another thing. Long ago my father told my brother never to dis-count the strengths of women. You showed that when you spoke of the snow-slide. None of us had brought that to mind. My sweet Lady, you have done more against the en-emy than any of us thus far. Let us now have our turn. But should you have any plan we have not, let you speak it and we shall listen."

So I was content I was not counted as less in their company. I would have said so but for a great commotion which arose outside in the direction of the keep. I sprang to the door and peered out. Levas, whose watch it had been, met me there, thrusting me backwards.

"They are searching the cottages, Lady. Let them not see you."

"What is that noise?"

"Gathea."

I stared at him. "Gathea?" Of a sudden I was angry. "They are not hurting her, surely?" Cats were valued amongst the dales both for their industry against vermin and their beauty. Yet Hogeth was a man who would care for none of that. If he had hurt Gathea . . . but there was a smile in Levas's eyes.

"Tis not he who has hurt her, Lady. But the opposite. I would imagine she has been mousing about the cot where Hogeth chose to camp the night. When the keep was shut she remained to sleep also. Once she woke she would search for food; Hogeth's men may have left scraps about. She made a sound. He believed it to be someone sneaking up upon him and flung open a door frightening or perhaps angering her. For which injury she well repaid him."

I moved to the window again and peered out past the hide which hung over it to keep in the warmth. Outside in the snow Hogeth waved his arms and cursed. I could see blood upon his face. Gathea it seemed had indeed resented his crude intrusion on her. I turned to look at Levas.

"Where did she flee?" He moved his arm so I could see the cat cradled in the crook.

"To me, Lady, when I whistled softly. She is unharmed." I let my breath out in a sigh.

"Thanks be. Now, do we attack Hogeth or wait and watch?"

Lorcan shook his head. "Let us lie up and watch with care. If we are patient it may be we shall have our chance at them with less risk to us." Levas agreed, so we settled to sleep, taking turns at guard. This time I, too, took my watch, Gathea choosing to keep me company. But nothing occurred all the long day until darkness fell again.

I wondered if Hogeth thought to starve us out? Or to threaten the cots and beasts, the possessions of those within the keep? Yet surely he could not think them such fools? Possessions can be bought again, and slain beasts replaced. Burned homes may be rebuilt. But the dead rebuild nothing and he must know we knew he would not leave any alive should he be let within.

As I stood my watch a thought came to me. Fire would not spread in the snow but if any cot caught fire it would work its will in that building. Once we ate together in morning light I should advance fire as a weapon. Perhaps we could trap Hogeth and his men. It would be a cruel death, and not to my liking, but better they died than we did. But, as events happen, all was decided for us by one we had not considered.

Isa had woken early on their first day shut within the keep. She sought for Gathea, who was her friend. Finding the cat nowhere, she believed her to be shut outside with the bad men. Sensible though she was, Isa was still only a child. Over the next days and nights she became consumed with fear the cat would starve or fall prey to the bad men who waited outside.

At last, as we waited in cover at Betha's, Gathea safely with us, Isa resolved to escape in search for the cat. With her she took a small parcel of cold meat scraps. The keep had a secret exit, a tunnel which, while supposed to be a secret, had not been so in my Honeycoombe. However, in the newly resettled dale, it was a secret from all but Lorcan and me. Isa knew it existed and had hunted hopefully. She had found nothing, so it was that she climbed down a rope hung from the back wall.

Once free of keep walls she moved like a tiny wild beast

in search of Gathea. Isa was cautious. She was aware that
the men outside wished only harm to Honeycoombe, but
she believed her own skills of crawling and hiding sufficient. That might have been so had the men remained together or in one area. They did not, so the first we knew of
events was a cry from near the leather-workers cot.

"Lord Hogeth? Something is out here?"

All of us turned to the direction of the call. Levas and
my Lord slipped out of Betha's cot to watch from beyond
the outer walls. Levas was standing in the shadow of a wall,
my lord flat-backed against another. I hissed at Lorcan
from a window.

"What can you see?"

"Nothing as yet, but they hunt something."

"What? Gathea is here with us, there is nothing else out
there to hunt which they would not find easily."

I had in mind one of the sheep perhaps. But Betha's sheep
were all tame by now. They would not flee from those who
walked quietly towards them. And—I scurried silently
across the room to peer into the sheepfold. I counted
quickly. It could not be a sheep. All were there: ewes, lambs,
and the solid wide-horned Master of the Flock we named
Bard, his apprentice son, and several other yearlings. The
horses and cattle were all safely penned within the inner
vale. Our own mounts were here under cover, I could see
them also. We had as yet no dogs for keep and guard. What
was it that Hogeth and his men hunted in and out of the two
close cots, laughing and hallooing after as it ran?

Something flashed across the space between cots. I
caught my breath. Then I flung myself towards the wall
outside where Lorcan stood. My voice was louder than
prudence demanded but those who hunted were too busy to
hear and I no longer cared if they did.

"Lorcan! They hunt Isa."

His reply was incredulous, horrified. "What!" Levas appeared around the corner vaulting through the window
opening.

"She is right. I, too, saw the child. They're playing a game with her. They have her cornered but they're letting her run."

"Can those in the keep see from where they are?"

"If they did not before they will now. The child tried to run clear but was turned back. They'll have a guard who will have seen that." Lorcan swept us all with his gaze.

"If we join battle with Hogeth and his men to rescue Isa I believe our people will come out to fight beside us. But I gamble. They cannot hit Hogeth's men with arrows from the keep. The distance is too great. They must leave the keep walls and come into the open, risking death. If they do not we are four against five. Also could we all be slain before any can aid in time." He would not allow me to fight, that I knew. Nor would I have been the equal of any of Hogeth's men. By now we had all had the chance to look at those. Levas had summed them up.

"Outlaws. But I'd wager most if not all have been taught to fight someplace. They move like trained men." I shivered now. Had they been blank-shields Isa might have been safe. Few mercenaries, save in the heat of battle, would deliberately injure or slay a small child. But outlaws would not care. Indeed it was more likely they would find amusement in the sport.

From outside there came a whoop of triumph. We all met in the shadow of the cot wall as we stared across at the scene. Either Hogeth had tired of the chase or Isa had at last run the wrong way. Hogeth held her. She dangled by the scruff of her neck from his hand, writhing and squirming. Her yelps of rage and fear were met by hearty laughter until Hogeth was incautious. He raised a hand to turn her and her sharp teeth snapped.

"Arhh! The little bitch has bitten me." His howl of pain was met with renewed laughter from his men.

"The puppy has sharp teeth, Lord. Best you collar her." Hogeth's face went red with anger.

"Collar her? By the Gods I'll leash her and teach her a

lesson." His hand came up and struck flat. Isa squealed as it met her buttocks. Hogeth struck again. As yet the punishment was no more than the child had suffered from Elesha for some foolish or dangerous prank. That could change, but for now the attention of Hogeth's men was on him and his victim. I seized Lorcan by the arm.

"Now, while they are all watching what he does. If we move in quietly behind the line of sight we can be on them before they know." I raised my bow. "I can take out at least one before they see us, perhaps two. That will even the odds. I shall ride Rez. If they attack on foot I can escape them. Will that satisfy you?"

"Get Rez. Hurry." I darted to the sheepfold, saddling my mount with flying hands. He smelled my excitement and was already dancing as I led him from the pen. I mounted and nudged Rez towards Lorcan. Together we five moved, being sure we remained hidden from Hogeth's sight in the lee of the nearest cottage. No alarm was raised from the keep. They had no need of that. But as I glanced towards the dark bulk I could see figures running along the parapet walkway against the walls.

From their higher vantage point they would be able to see both that Isa was in the hands of the enemy and that we moved to a rescue. We rounded the cottage corner and poised, waiting. Isa shrieked suddenly in pain. Whatever Hogeth had done it had moved beyond slaps. Lorcan's eyed blazed in fury. He lifted a hand and we tensed, ready. It fell and we moved to war.

XVIII

———◁◦▷———

I spun Rez from their way. Lorcan was leading as our guard ran forward. Isa was screaming. Rez danced beside Lorcan but far enough away that he was not impeded. I strung my bow, nocked a shaft, and laid the knotted reins across my mount's neck. As we came from the shadow of the cottage I drew and loosed. Then again, and again. Lorcan had fallen on Hogeth with a battle cry. Levas was fighting the largest of the enemy while Criten and Dogas were also engaged.

I saw with a savage pleasure that two of my shafts had gone home. One man had fallen, a large brute with a scarred face. Another had been struck in the left shoulder. He had snapped the shaft off and flung it from him. I thought it had not gone deep since he still fought ferociously. Yet, at least I had evened the numbers. I pulled Rez back from the battle. He fought me. Jack mules are fighters and Rez was no less so than most. The sounds of battle, the scent of blood, the fear and anger which flowed from his rider, all roused in him the desire to attack.

I held him back. Small use would it be if I should be taken hostage or injured. I nocked a shaft and waited. Criten was battling a fighter who was larger than our guard. The man wielded a good sword and as I watched, a clever blow loosed Criten's grip. He stumbled. The enemy sword struck, not edgewards but flat against his helm with a blow I could all but feel myself. Criten fell and the warrior turned. I saw Criten begin to crawl back to his feet. Nearby, Dogas battled. Before he could act he was struck from behind. He, too, had struck that fraction before the blow fell. His own enemy half-fell.

I shot, the shaft flying true. It would have taken the enemy in the forehead but for his move as I loosed. Instead the shaft struck beside his face against the chain coif. It was a hard blow but the arrowhead did not penetrate the chain. Yet he staggered and as he reeled Dogas ran him through. He straightened triumphantly even as I screamed a warning. Too late.

His first enemy had recovered. Dogas groaned and slumped against the man he had slain. My gaze swept across our tiny battleground. Of our side Dogas was down, dead or badly injured. Criten, too, was down again. I had not seen how he fell, but he breathed yet I believed, and his opponent had turned away to battle Lorcan. Only Levas and my Lord still fought against two men. I gasped. Two men and neither of them Hogeth. And Isa, where was Isa?

I turned about in the saddle, my gaze darting this way and that. Beyond our battlefield the keep doors were opening. From them issued a host of fighters. Two were mounted on the horses we always kept in stables. The others brandished bows and swords. Helmed, in trews and part-armor, they ran towards us. Elesha must have raided every piece of armor she could find to make it appear we had men-at-arms in plenty. Most of those who ran would be women, but in trews and with their hair covered Hogeth might not pause to look closer.

The battle had taken place to the far side of the cottage. The horses of Hogeth and his men all appeared to be there still. I turned Rez and from behind me there came a sudden blow against my neck. I reeled in the saddle, feeling myself falling. I rolled as I landed, still dizzy from the impact. Above me Rez reared, then leaped forward, Hogeth now in my mount's saddle, clutching Isa to him.

The child was limp, her small white face upturned as she lay across Hogeth's arm. From behind me I heard a wordless shout of rage. His men saw he would desert them and perhaps even for an outlaw that was the final betrayal. Hogeth would escape us, Isa hostage to his safe departure, and what else might he not demand for her return? I cried Rez's name again and then again as I scrambled after.

"Meive!"

Distracted by their lord's abandonment of them, his two men had fallen. Lorcan had seized one of their mounts from where they were tied. Now as he cantered by me, his feet firmly thrust into the leather stirrups, he slowed and leaned over, a crooked arm ready. I leaped, to be swung behind him. I had no time to think else I might not have done so. My weight would slow the beast, making it less likely that Lorcan could catch up with our enemy.

Then ahead I saw—and knew why I had been summoned. Perhaps Hogeth had feared we would indeed catch up with him. Or maybe he was used to his own mounts which must be coerced with whip and spur. For as he fled I had called Rez and the big animal had slowed. Hogeth had foolishly plied spurs, to the utter outrage of Rez, unused to such treatment and infuriated by the pain in his sides. Mules have a just name for obstinacy. Part of that is an expectancy that they be treated fairly and here Rez was being punished for obeying my call.

He had balked, great yellow teeth bared in rage. Hogeth had struck him savagely about the head with the ends of the reins, and Rez had gone in a flash from balk to bucking, shying sideways then spinning and dropping his shoulder as he did so. Hampered by Isa's small limp body, Hogeth had lost his grip on the saddle and fallen to the ground. Rez promptly cantered away, eluding attempts to seize his reins once more. Worse, he was showing signs that if Hogeth continued the pursuit he was likely to find a mule's teeth and hooves could be lethal. Lorcan was approaching like a thunderbolt as I clung behind him.

Hogeth must have seen that others would be up with us shortly. Already those from the keep reached the tethered horses and snatched at reins. Hogeth snarled despairingly and ran, Isa tossed over one shoulder. But it was where he ran which lighted my eyes. Into the long barn in which the bees wintered. They slept. With the departure of false Spring the deep chill had returned. They would be impossible to wake—unless . . . I dropped from Lorcan's mount and ran, my hand closing on that which hung about my throat. I heard Lorcan's frantic cry but heeded it not.

"Meive? Meive, wait!"

I ran for the bee-barn and as I ran I reached into my shirt and drew forth the gift I had been given. I spoke the word of invocation, feeling the beginning response. This was my time, my killing ground. It was for me to face our enemy. I reached the barn entrance, flinging myself through the door. A white-faced Hogeth turned, his blade at Isa's throat.

"Bring me a mount or the brat dies!"

I slipped through the door and to Lorcan's bewilderment I shut it in his face. This was his enemy, but at this hour, Hogeth was mine. I was Honeycoombe's lady. The last of those who had held here. I felt fury welling up within me yet I made my face timid, my eyes fearful.

"Do not harm the child."

"Then bring me a horse, nay, bring two. And set the others free. I ride on alone. Once I am clear I shall let the child down."

I knew he would not. Once he was away he would injure her at the least, thinking thus to slow us as we followed. I lowered my eyes so he should not see my knowledge in them.

"Please, good my Lord. Do not harm the child." Lorcan

would hear our words. He must be wondering what I did,
yet he trusted me. He had not attempted to storm the door.
More, he must be holding back Levas, and Criten, too, if
the guard had come up with him. I held out my hand towards Hogeth in supplication.

"I will beg them to give you the horses."

"Do so then, and remind them of what I can do."

I could feel within me what was moving, but with the
chill so great I feared it might not be in time. I clenched my
fist upon the tiny crystal, speaking under my breath the
word over and over. From my hand came a sudden warmth.
In my clenched fingers the hexagon broke, the shards of
crystal bit home, bringing blood. I was dimly conscious of
Lorcan as he lost patience, opening the door slightly to
slide within. He halted at the sight of Hogeth's blade
against that slim naked throat.

"Meive, what . . ."

And it was flashing sunlit Spring. From the shards,
primed perhaps by my own blood, burst sunlight. Warmth,
the scent of flowers, and the touch of soft breezes. The sunlight melted gold over the landscape outside. All the valley
seemed to be alight, warmth reaching to fill it as milk is
poured into a basin. I could feel the land as Spring swirled
about us, all the scents, the joy of an awakening after the
long Winter. Aye, the awakening. I reached out to merge
with the hives. They read what I knew, what I saw, my need
of them, and they arose, vengeance incarnate.

Hogeth had time for one terrible cry before they came
like a wave to cover him. I think he might have slain the
child but for my warriors, who chose their first target
wisely. His blade fell from his hand, the wrist paralyzed,
pierced and repierced by the venomed swords of my warriors. Isa scuttled to cower behind Lorcan as the bees
wrought vengeance, repayment for a brother, a master-at-
arms who had trusted, a kinsman hunted, and many others,
I thought, though I might never know who they were.

It took perhaps as long as a man might spend in taking two deep breaths. Hogeth staggered silently after that first cry, the breath choked in his swollen throat. Then he fell, quivered a little, and lay still. Dimly I heard the thudding of hooves. Through the door ajar I could see what passed. One of the outlaws had dragged himself to a mount and was fleeing. From the hives the queens read it. Let one man escape and he could return with friends.

"Lorcan, the door, open it quickly!"

Still he trusted me. He paused for no questions but stepped aside dragging it open. My warriors flooded out, a long shining black shaft. They swooped upwards, then the shaft drove home. In the distance a thickset figure crumpled from a horse, which halted, looked at the fallen rider, then turned to pawing the snow aside to see if there was palatable grass beneath.

My warriors returned, I could feel them singing as they covered me. I touched, caressed, melted in honey, sweet as the Spring my crystal had wrought. It slowly seeped away, Winter's chill returning. The bees murmured sleepily as they slipped back within their straw homes to sleep again and dream dreams of liquid gold. On the floor our enemy lay still. We were free of his greed and those he would have brought against us.

"Meive!" I was swept into Lorcan's arms. Levas was beaming, his honest face alight with pleasure as he scooped up Isa. Criten stood by the doorway, blood on his face, one arm limp, but he lived. I drew a last breath of Spring before the brightness faded. Yet it would return. That was life's promise. Always there is another Spring. In my hand the shards shivered, their substance fading into silver sand, then into mist and gone. The cuts on my hand were healed in that instant. I raised my mouth to Lorcan's kisses. This was our Spring. But one cannot live in Spring forever.

It took a day and a half after that to cleanse our dale, bury the dead, and care for the living. Gathea reacted in her own way. Three nights in a row I found a dead mouse laid

on my bed for me. I knew it for an honor but could hope
that after three nights she would feel I had been paid honor
enough. It must have been so, for after that she returned to
sleeping at the foot of Levas's bed and I received no more
gifts.

I might have buried Hogeth in the dale, but Lorcan
shook his head. "Nay, alive or dead I will not have his evil
on our land. Strip him of all he wears, that can be returned
so his lady knows he will not return alive to her. His body
shall lie in the hills in an unmarked grave. A fratricide de-
serves no more."

"You cannot be sure of that. Faslane himself would not
swear."

"I am sure," was all Lorcan would say, and in my heart I
believed him right so I protested no further.

Hogeth wore a lord's ring upon his hand. A fine pendant
upon his breast, his sword and mail were of the finest. All
was piled into his cloak. Lorcan lifted it, then signaled.
Levas brought a rabbit recently slain. The blood was
dripped and sopped across the tabard. I saw the sense in
that. To let Hogeth's kin know how the man had died might
bring them upon us in turn. Let them believe he died fighting. Lorcan looked at me.

"Once Spring is here, Levas shall take two mounts and
ride. This shall go to Paltendale."

"And what does he say?" I asked tartly. "My lord killed
your husband. Ask nothing of that or who or where we are
lest my lord be angry? What if she will have answers?"
Lorcan grinned at me. I caught my breath as I returned it.
Too long had it been since I had seen that smile.

"True. I will tell him that he is to send it on Hogeth's
horse a few miles short of Paltendale. The animal, when
loosed, will make for home. Once Levas lets the horse go
free he shall change his appearance and ride home swiftly
by a different route." That seemed safer to me, so I nodded.

After that things felt as if they moved more quickly.
Spring came, the real Spring which brought the beelove

blooming, turned the heather gold on the hills—and left us all wet-footed, awash in snow-melt. Nothing is ever perfection.

Levas rode with Hogeth's horse and gear as soon as the roads were opened. With him went my lord, flanked by the mules as pack beasts, Criten and another of our people as guards. They returned safely after many weeks. With them came the remainder of Lorcan's silver. That was hidden within a new secret place in our keep. After that Levas and Vari rode for the nearest market. There were things I would have before any wedding.

With early Summer came Lord Salas. I was startled when I saw his train. He appeared to have brought everything from Tildale which could be broken apart and carried. This was no tentative journey. Salas had made his choice. Lorcan and I rode out to meet him, having kept a watch on the road.

"Well met, and where from here is the dale of which you spoke?"

Lorcan gave him the bow between equals. "Only a short distance further, my Lord. Follow me." We rode with the old man, laughing, talking, while those of his retinue also seemed joyous. Yet if they had been hopeful while they traveled, the reality surpassed their dream. We halted them at the head of the dale where they might look downwards and see all they would own. I spoke.

"Once, before the bandits came, this was Merrowdale. Fair and fertile land. Their lord was kin to mine. Of both dales I alone still live. If I have any rights I renounce them now. All save one. That as the lord here was friend to Honeycoombe, let you now be friend."

"I hear your words." Lord Salas gave me the bow of equals. "Let it be so. Never shall this dale ride against your home. Rather, if enemies come, we ride against them beside you. Children shall be fostered between us, goods and gear exchanged. Friendship shall ever hold between dales,

on this I give my hand." He reached out to clasp my fingers
in his own large sword-roughened paw. I clasped back as
Lorcan joined his own hands to the grip. Then I reined Rez
backwards.

"Into your new lands let you go alone. Claim them as
you will." I turned my mount. Lorcan followed me as we
rode away, leaving Salas to ride on leading those he had
brought so far.

And so Lord Salas and his people took what had been
Merrowdale but which place they renamed Hopedale. Now
and again, as we could, we had rounded up sheep and returned them there. Tildale's old weaver was delighted by
the quality of beasts and wool. In little time the sheep had
a shepherd and care again. Looms began to clack busily.
That was as well. I had set my wedding date, but before I
wed I went again to the secret vale to talk with the voice. I
had labored in secret many days before I did so. I had visited the shrine of my Lady of the Bees once towards the
end of my toil. From her I had wisdom and aid.

Now Lorcan came with me to the secret vale deep within
Honeycoombe. With him alone I had shared the secret the
voice had told me. It was only right since it was his secret
before it was mine.

"Lady, we have come to speak with you. If that is intrusion and unwelcome, let you say?"

"Nay, Lorcan, son of the House of Erondale. You are
welcome."

"And my lady?"

"I welcome also Meive, wing-friend, daughter of——"
The name she spoke was the true name of my Lady of the
Bees. More a stirring in the air than a name one of our
kind could say. There was a pause, then the voice spoke
again.

"Lorcan, son of Erondale. Long and long ago a man of
your line took up sword in our name. My kinswoman was
in need and he did not count the cost. The power my people

can wield varies. Some have much, some little. In some it does not rise until they are of certain age. Thus it was with my kinswoman, who was a small child in our terms, so that she was unable to protect herself. Yet one came who stood as kin in our stead. We do not forget.

"I was ever solitary, yet once, long ago, I visited your lands and found them very fair. I sorrow with you that all is gone. Now I, too, go from this place, from the lands of your kind. A gate opens and it is my will to depart to be with my people again, even though my kin departed long ago as you would count the years."

"We do not drive you out?" It was both statement and question I made. We had no wish to do so and if she feared it then I would reassure.

"Not so. The time has come, that is all. But I heard talk of a wedding. To your lady, Lorcan, I gave a gift which she used well. To you also I would give a gift in friendship. Nay," as he drew in a breath, "no talk of debts between us. Nor of kin and blood. I give a wedding gift that the son of a house we knew shall prosper. And that this may be accomplished, let you send your people beyond your own lands on the morrow. Let them be gone by sun-high. Then shall I come out."

Lorcan and I stared. "Aye. I, who have not been seen by any of your kind yet living, shall come forth. The gift shall be yours, then must I depart and this my home, shall fall to you." She spoke further then. Instruction as to things we must bring her and do. We agreed. It never occurred to us to do otherwise.

With morning we cleared our people from the dale. Levas was with them to lead them in a variety of tasks out on the hillside, Vari at his side.

Then we returned. We walked: it seemed more fitting. At the entrance to the hidden place we were met by a pillar of mist from which spoke our voice. From that came a small hand which beckoned us. We obeyed. It moved out across the inner vale and past the keep. There it turned and I knew within it eyes studied keep and cliffs behind. The mist faded, thinning out enough so that we might see within it a slight form. The figure raised its arms.

Words came. It seemed as if they hurtled like great blue-green darts against the cliff. They struck at a point hard beside the keep wall. They clung, each seeming to cut deeper. Where they ate at the rock I could see a tunnel forming, the height of a mounted man, and the width of two ponies. The dart-words vanished from sight, but I could feel their sounds yet in the still air. At last they fell silent and I knew they had broken through to the inner vale.

The mist-lady raised her arms and spoke one short word as she turned. At the entrance to our inner vale the rock groaned. She pointed as if in command. It groaned again and fell. Not as a slide but as if the whole of the cliffs dropped that distance to settle again. Where there had once been a fault in the rock, an entrance, now there was nothing. Yet she was not done with her gift.

A third and final time she spoke, words which produced a great roaring in the air. I stepped back. Such power was fearful. I had no wish to stand too close lest I be consumed by it. As we watched, the rock flowed outward. It fell slowly, shaping itself as it fell. Great blocks of stone fell into place, timbers split and screamed. Dust billowed out to hide the scene. When it cleared we could only stare at what her power had wrought.

"This pleases you, Son of Erondale?"

Lorcan was gaping like a stranded fish. I understood that: I, too, felt as if there was not enough air to take in a breath. At last he bowed.

"Lady, I am greatly pleased. This is a wondrous gift. Not only as something I wished for but also refuge, safety, and life for our people in years to come."

"If it is as you wished, then that is well. I will depart. Once I am gone my lands shall be yours without let nor hindrance. Care for them, Son of Erondale. They have sheltered me so long."

"I shall care, Lady. Both for them and in your name." I saw the mist roil and before my courage was gone I ran lightly forward.

"Lady. Gifts you have given such as no great lady in all the dales could have brought us. But I, too, would give a gift. Let you remember us."

I reached out my hand, holding within it a small carved wooden box. It was good workmanship, nothing unusual but well made. A slender six-fingered hand showed clear for a moment as it accepted my offering, then opened the lid. It took out what was within it and as if even the land waited, the breeze fell silent, the birds did not call.

I had wrought well with the power My Lady of the Bees had granted me. The stones I had taken from the keep wall here, when I returned to find all dead and fled again, had contained few jewels of great value. Nay, they had been the semi-precious gems from hill and stream. Of them I had chosen one. From a large honey-colored agate I had chipped and smoothed out a bee. The gauzy wings were of silver spun fine as no smith of the dales could have done. Power alone, asked for and given to me freely, had made them.

Tiny black gems set in the head created eyes with which one might have sworn the creature saw. The body had been polished so that it seemed to glow with honey-fire. Loaned power had made it, yet it had been my vision and the desire to give a gift which had guided that power. I had not seen it for many days. Now, as our mist-lady opened the box, even I who had created the gift within was amazed anew by the beauty of that which I had wrought.

The figure took it up to admire. I felt a soft and gentle delight flow out to me. I smiled. If I had brought her joy in the gift then I was well pleased. Within the box, too, lay a long neck-chain made with gold and silver links. I had asked it of Lorcan, since that had come from the treasure given his House. He had given it and asked not why I requested it. Now he knew. The gift was from both of us. I looked sideways from a corner of my eyes, seeing his smile.

The figure took up the bee then, threading chain through the loop atop the glittering wing-friend. She lifted it over her head and laid the bee as a pendant upon her breast. Then she lifted her hands one last time, turning to look at us.

"I shall remember you always. Fare you well, Lorcan son of Erondale that was, Meive, wing-friend, daughter to the Hive and Honeycoombe." We spoke our farewells in turn as her hands lifted in supplication to the air. "Oh, let me now come home, my kin. Open the gates to me!"

Lightning cleaved the sky. She stood motionless, her hands upheld as the air split before her. Shimmering, outlined in silver fog, the air opened to her plea. Beyond we glimpsed a place I could never afterwards describe. Only that the beauty, the quiet peace, had been beyond any place I had ever known. She turned to pace forward through the gate, then, as she passed through, the mist fell from about her.

For seconds we saw with clear eyes—her shape, her inhumanly graceful loveliness. Not of humankind, no. Or not of any humankind we had ever known. But beautiful and a person, a great lady of her people. That we did know. The huge amethyst eyes turned to survey us and the triangular face moved in a smile. The white feathers which clad her form seemed to ripple in the breeze of her own lands. Her voice was clearer, a crystal ringing.

"Farewell, may you ever fare well." There was a flare as the sides of the silver fog closed together and she was gone. For a time we simply stood, hand in hand, letting the wonder of what we had seen slowly fade. It was Lorcan who moved, stirring as he looked at his gift.

"You told her what I wished, did you not?"

I nodded. "Was I wrong?"

"Never so. It is right. Most marvelously right. Look!" He pointed out the features to me, his voice rising in excitement. Indeed I could see why. I had not known how it should be done but the lady of our innermost valley had guessed—or known somehow.

The tunnel had been driven home from outer to inner valley through the cliff. Around it had risen a double wall, an extension of the walls about our Keep, although so close was the tunnel little additional length of the walls had been required. Set in them both were gates. Not one before the other, but stepped, so that should we be attacked the invaders could not fight forward in a straight line.

The gates themselves were a wonder. From where she had called them I could not guess. Perhaps from some long-abandoned keep of her own kin or kind. They were of bronze set so cunningly that they could be swung open or closed by even my own strength. And upon them lay signs. I could read several. They were runes of ward and guard. Lorcan, too, recognized them. He traced one with a finger.

"They are warm." He smoothed the sign again. "We shall carve these into all the gates of the Keep. Upon posts by our road and on the guardpost door also. No dark evil shall win past them. The inner valleys shall be a refuge for our people should war come again."

I smiled. "I shall move the hives to the lady's valley. I think they shall like it there."

So I did and so did they. The weeks flew past until it was high Summer. Levas went to the cross-roads again, bringing back another family of six who would join us. On the longest day of the year we were wed, Lorcan and I, before all our people in the great hall of our keep. My warriors attended with the queens of the hive, swarming to hang from the beams above us. Never was a dale's wedding so guarded. Lord Salas of Hopedale came with his grandchildren, among them, Merria, eager to become my apprentice as several of the queens dropped to consider and approve her.

Out of the dark of war and its aftermath, out of the death

of all I had, came love and happiness. This I said the next time I visited the shrine and to me there was made answer.

"To all things there is a season, daughter of the hive: Spring, when we rise to fly forth, when our daughters swarm seeking new pastures; Summer, when we gather nectar; Fall, when we prepare; and Winter, when we drowse away the dark days, the killing chill. Winter is done for you. Fly free, daughter. It is your Spring, may your land be filled with flowers."

She was right, my wise Lady of the Bees. It was my Spring and Lorcan was the honey I gathered. Yet always Winter returns. I shall pray only that it does not do so again in my lifetime. Yet if it should happen I shall know I do not stand alone. That is enough.

Lorcan

XIX

*M*ost holds and keeps have a muniments room. In such small rooms are kept safe all documents the lord and lady of the dale might require. All the latter half of that golden Summer Meive and I made time to sit, quills in hand, and write, finishing our tale. And when at last we were done the writings were laid in a wood-lined brass box. Above and through the sheets Meive strewed herbs to keep moth and insect from our records. Then we took aside Levas and Elesha and I spoke to them.

"In many dales none know the true tale of their founding. The man who took up the land is long since dead so there are only legends and songs. When first I met my lady it seemed right to me that this thing should change. Here we have written what happened. Of how my lady was bereft of all she loved. Of how the invaders slew my dale. And of how we two met and took Honeycoombe for our own. I have writ of the lady of the inner vale and her gift to us, of her appearance and words and the gift we gave her to take beyond in memory of Honeycoombe."

"And have you written of us?" That was Elesha.

"Of you, and Levas here, and Vari, Arla, Manon, Criten." I smiled. "I need not list everyone, but all have their place.

Each is within these records." I glanced at Levas from the corner of my eyes. "Even Gathea has her due."

"That is well. Else she might omit to chase mice should they seek out your papers."

"The Gods forbid." I turned to look from the high window. "The invaders are gone. The war is ended. But there were wars before-time. Mayhap their folk, too, said afterwards, 'the war is done. Forever now we live at peace.' Meive and I have written that we may all remember. Levas, what do you think?"

"That you speak true. Time passes, those who fought grow old and die. Those who come after forget."

"They shall not. For on the shortest days of each year, as we feast for mid-Winter, this shall be so. That one shall read what we have written and our words of warning. For evil does not die, it only steps back a while. It may come again and if that time shall be, then shall Honeycoombe remember and be ready." I placed the box upon a shelf, then Meive and I swept them out before us, closing the door as we departed. "But for now, I have work to do, as have you my friend."

Levas looked a question. "Aye, mouse disposal and a true soldier's clean-up detail. Gathea caught a plump prey last night and, being hungry, ate it. After which she was sick in my lady's slippers."

I drew down my brows in an effort not to smile but it was of no use. So, laughing, the four of us went on down the stairs, and indeed it was fitting that a tale which began in blood and fire should end in honest laughter. Might all our days so ever end, in joy, in mirth, and in the sweetness of Honeycoombe.

Meive

XX

My love does not know that two secrets remain to me. Nor shall he know one. Those who come after me need to be warned of that which is dark. Of the other I say this, that we shall be three and not two before next Summer lies on our land. I shall tell my lord the news tonight, watching his joy. The other secret bears upon this. For as is he, I, too, am of the line of Paltendale by the rape of my great-grandmother. And I have come to see that this is a thing upon which I should be silent.

Lorcan hated Hogeth, and also there is the tale of Pletten the Wicked. I think if I tell him of my blood he may see wickedness in those children who shall come after us. Every fourth generation, the story runs. I shall be silent on my bloodline, nor have I written of it in the pages I laid in the box of memories. Yet that part of my story and this page I shall leave to those who follow me. Let them know as my love shall not. Let them fear and beware as he need not. But let them also remember, from Lorcan's hive was the honey as sweet as my Lady of the Bees said. Thus is life. That there is always the good and the bad. One must take joy in the good and endure the bad, balancing one against the other. In the end I have deemed myself fortunate.

—Meive of Honeycoombe, Lady to Lorcan,
Daughter of the Hive.

APPENDIX

———◆———

The song "Silver May Tarnish" is a folk song of considerable antiquity. Legend says it came with the dalesfolk when they entered High Hallack. This is not impossible, since the first form of the work appears to have been a sword song. That is, a song which was chanted rather than sung, and to an accompaniment formed by the tapping of blades together, customarily the blade of an eating dagger against that of a bowed sword blade. The rhythmic metallic tapping formed the "music."

This type of song and accompaniment does date back many hundreds of years and may well predate the arrival of the dalesfolk to the land they now occupy. The possibility is strengthened by the fact that this form of the song extols the possession of land as something to be prized above all else. Some time later, after a gap of at least another two hundred years, the song altered, forming two variations. Both are quite different musically from the original, being in a format closer to the usual ballad. One variation is a love song, the other a lullaby.

The unusual thing is that each has retained the original name. This may be because in all forms of the work a number of the phrases, including the title, are used in common.

In order to differentiate between them, the person requesting the song tends to add a comment noting the preferred form. Alternately, the person singing uses a musical introduction that allows those listening to know which song is to be sung. The love song and lullaby have only three verses, and in each the first verse is repeated as a fourth verse. In the original song there are five verses and no exact repetition.

—LAUTRON OF ALSVALE, SONG-GATHERER TO LORMT.
YEAR OF THE PARD.

ABOUT THE AUTHORS

————◇————

ANDRE NORTON, named a Grand Master by the Science Fiction Writers of America and awarded a Life Achievement World Fantasy Award, was the author of more than one hundred novels of science fiction and fantasy adventure. Beloved by legions of readers the world over, she thrilled generations with such series as *The Beast Master, Time Traders, The Solar Queen, Witch World,* and others. Miss Norton died on March 17, 2005, and was laid to rest beside her mother in an Ohio cemetery; Andre Norton was 93. However, her spirit lives on in continuing reprints and foreign language editions of her works, and in the writing of her friends and collaborators. Visit her Web site at www.andre-norton.org.

LYN MCCONCHIE is the coauthor, with Andre Norton, of the Witch World novel *The Duke's Ballad,* as well as *Beast Master's Ark* and *Beast Master's Circus,* and other novels. She also writes her own fiction. A native of New Zealand, she has twice been awarded the Sir Julius Vogel Award for Best Science Fiction or Fantasy Novel by a New Zealander, in 2002 for *Beast Master's Ark* and in 2004 for *Beast Master's Circus.* A third Beast Master novel, *Beast Master's Quest,* will be published by Tor in 2006.

Look for

A TASTE OF MAGIC

by Andre Norton and Jean Rabe

(0-765-31527-0)

Available Now in Hardcover

Turn the Page for a Preview

*T*he tip of my tongue registered an unpalatable acridity, the distinctive taste of death and the lingering scents of fear and desperation.

There'd been a raid while I was hunting!

Our village is filled with farmers, hunters, and weavers, not warriors. Peaceful people! My heart seized with fear. I dropped the reins, knowing Dazon would follow me, and I rushed through a gap in the brush.

Who attacked us? And why?

I saw no one.

The gate to the courtyard swung in the wind.

Near Willum t'Jelth's house I spotted a snorter stretched on a frame over a now-smoldering fire, more than half of its carcass hacked away. I heard the bellow again, and I slipped along the hedge to the north, drawing upon all the stealthy skills Bastien had taught me and trying to force down the dread threatening to overwhelm me.

"Willum? Gerald?"

No answer.

I raised my voice. "Maergo? Lady Ewaren? Lady Ewaren!"

Now I could see a section of the yard beyond the gate, the

Great House and its various attendant buildings essentially forming the walls of the courtyard. Inside, a large cow tramped across the soft loam of a newly seeded herb garden and continued to bellow loudly, two smaller ones trailing behind it. Another cow leaned against the side of the Great House. The sun caught on shards of metal protruding from its black hide, as numerous as the pins in Lady Ewaren's sewing pillow. Blood dripped from its wounds. I vowed to end its suffering—after I saw to the village.

I looked elsewhere, cupping my hands over my eyes, shutting out the light and focusing on my wyse-sense and on my tongue and what the wind was telling me.

Death.

The wind spoke of death and suffering and confusion.

I thought I saw a foot and a torn piece of material just under the shadow of a jutting second story.

A foot . . .

"Willum! Maergo! Lady Ewaren!"

Loosening the web of my backpack, I sat it on the ground and placed my blowpipe and quiver of bolts next to it. I did not want to be encumbered when I faced the enemy, but I wanted to be prepared. I drew the longest of my knives and fought to keep my senses sharp. Fear and grief threatened to overwhelm me.

It was easy to suspicion all manner of horrid things, especially after seeing the throwstars in the cow's side and finding no one outside and no one to answer my call. I wanted more than suspicion to work with, and so struggling desperately to keep panic at bay, I again tasted the air, urging my tongue to find the scents.

Blood—blood is always strong enough to make itself known first. There was more blood than I had ever scented before. And I picked up a touch of sweat—of men and mounts—and the fire I smelled earlier, and ashes. Then I strained my senses to the limit, barely able to reach and identify emotions. I tasted terror, pain, and hate. And above all of that, I tasted my own horror, choking and dreadfully nauseating.

"Willum." My voice grew weak, a whisper. "Lady Ewaren."

Still, nothing stirred in the village.

The foot I spied in the distance did not move, and somehow I knew it belonged to a corpse. How many dead? I knew I would have to search the entire village to learn what had happened. My stomach churned with the grisly possibilities, and my heart hammered with each step I took. I was feeling faint from the scents and the notion that I wouldn't find a soul alive, that everyone I knew and loved had been brutally butchered.

But slain by whom? Slain why?

And why had I gone hunting so early this morning? Had I lingered, I could have defended this place.

"Willum!"

The coughing sickness had taken Bastien this past winter. The village had no guards, the elders thinking Bastien's presence enough protection. But after his death, the elders still took no steps for defense, thinking our world oh so peaceful and safe, and thinking that I could be sufficient defense, given the skills Bastien had taught me. Too, there had been no rumors of invasion from the Twisted Lands, and Lady Ewaren seemed held in favor with the neighboring countries to the west—even though it was said she was descended from the long-outlawed House of Alchura.

I sheathed my knife and tugged a long, thin chain free from my belt. I preferred it as a weapon because of its reach. Then I started down a gentle slope, making use of the shadows from buildings to provide me some cover. Within heartbeats I stood in the gate road. Once more I tongue-tested, finding more blood, ashes, terror, and hate. Oddly, hate was the strongest here, almost overwhelming. Darting around the corner of the gate, I came into the courtyard.

The foot . . .

The rags that had been her spring-green gown lay torn on the ground between myself and where the body lay. Her ripped undergarments were saturated with blood. Something stronger than anger welled from deep within me, and a horror I'd never felt overcame me. I grabbed on to a post to support myself.

I edged closer.

The foot . . . it belonged to Lady Ewaren, our House Lady. My breath caught and I went down on my knees beside her body, fighting for air.

"My lady!" The first words I'd spoken since entering the village were filled with grief. "By the Green Ones, my lady!"

Lady Ewaren had taken me in after the death of my mother ten years past. Hers was the only home I truly remembered. Her face . . . now a broken ruin. Sobbing, I tugged down from her curve cap a length of lace veil. It didn't hide all the blood, but it softened the worst of it around her face. Then I noticed her other injuries. Each and every one of her fingers—which she had used to weave such beauty that nearby lords and ladies begged for her work—every one had been broken. Deliberately, cruelly, I knew, broken while she'd lived.

Once more I heard the bellow of the cow. Though the mournful sound was muted now by the intervening buildings, it was nonetheless demanding. In the intervals between the bellows, I heard an incessant buzzing from the bees in the hive housed on a balcony above me. I noticed the sound of flies, too. They were drawn to Lady Ewaren's body.

Lady Ewaren, I should pray for her.

I hesitantly touched her broken fingers and under my breath, in the thinnest of voices, I uttered old, old words.

"Nesalah dorma calla—"

"Yaaaaaah!" The scream spun me around so quickly I nearly lost my balance. I saw a slip of a girl, just a heartbeat before her knifepoint flashed down and sliced my tunic at the shoulder. I moved fast enough that the blade only drew a thin line of blood. Without pause, I lashed out with my chain, whipping it around her arm.

She cried in surprise and pain, and dropped the blade as I dragged her close. But she didn't give in. Her wide golden eyes flashed with madness, and her teeth snapped at my throat. It was as if I held a night fiend instead of the slight girl that Lady Ewaren had taken as an apprentice almost a year ago. Lady Ewaren had hoped I'd be like a sister to this girl, but that hadn't happened. I didn't want to hurt the girl if I could help it—and it would be so easy for me to end this fight with a single blow. I was that much stronger, and she was half my age . . . at most ten years old.

"Demon!" she spat. "Thrice-damned demon may you be!"

I dropped my chain and grabbed both her wrists, shaking her roughly in an effort to bring her to her senses. She kicked at me now, her heavy boot landing a solid blow against my shin. I cringed and dragged her so close against me she had no room to kick again, while at the same time I twisted her arms behind her in a hold Bastien had taught me early on. I crushed the air out of her, and she swayed and gasped. I truly hadn't intended to hurt her, but she'd given me no choice.

I bent my head to her ear, as I stood several inches taller. "Alysen, what happened here?"

She went limp, and I held her up now.

"They came for you, Eri," she said after a moment.

"Who? Tell me, Alysen!"

She didn't answer this, saying instead, "They came for you because the Emperor's dead. And so is your father. You and your kin, the Empress has had you drummed!"

I loosed her then and she staggered back, stumbling toward one of the slender pillars that held up the outer edge of a narrow roof. Catching at the pillar with both hands to support herself, she faced me. Alysen's smooth face was a scarlet mask of hatred.

"They came for you!" Her voice was stronger now, spittle flecking at her lips. "You they wanted! And all this death, Eri, is because you weren't here! Everyone died because of you!"

Me? All this because of me? A wave of dizziness crashed against me.

"Everyone is dead, Eri!"